A Flame Run Wild

He did not wait to carry her to the bed, but covered her there with his body, arching over her as his lips found her throat. Quick with the impatience of growing desire, his hands slipped free the lacings of her tunic to bare her shoulders; then, as if realizing what treasure he had found, he cast aside his haste. With tantalizing languor, he began to cover her pale skin with slow kisses.

She had never dreamed of this sweet pleasure, this luring, erotic witchery.

"I am your prisoner," he whispered. "Free me to love you, and my body will be a slave to yours forever."

Other Avon Books by
Christine Monson

STORMFIRE
SURRENDER THE NIGHT

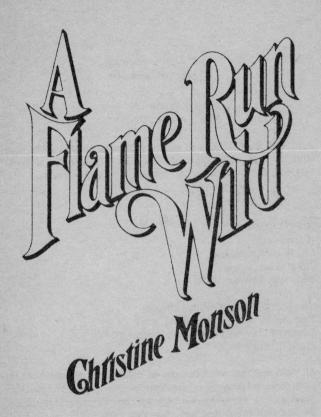

A Flame Run Wild

Christine Monson

AVON
PUBLISHERS OF BARD, CAMELOT, DISCUS AND FLARE BOOKS

A FLAME RUN WILD is an original publication of Avon Books. This work has never before appeared in book form. This work is a novel. Any similarity to actual persons or events is purely coincidental.

AVON BOOKS
A division of
The Hearst Corporation
105 Madison Avenue
New York, New York 10016

Copyright © 1988 by Christine Monson
Published by arrangement with the author
Library of Congress Catalog Card Number: 87-91700
ISBN: 0-380-89976-0

First Avon Books Printing: February 1988

AVON TRADEMARK REG. U.S. PAT. OFF. AND IN OTHER COUNTRIES, MARCA REGISTRADA, HECHO EN U.S.A.

Printed in the U.S.A.

K-R 10 9 8 7 6 5 4 3 2 1

*For Jenni
and all the adventuresses I have known;
also for Jon,
the sort of man who knows how to enjoy them.*

Prologue

The Startled Falcon

A coastal pine forest near Malaga, Spain
January 1189

The winter day was murky, sodden; the horses slid on rotted leaves as the hunting party skirted the marsh. The game birds were still, the falcons reluctant to fly, but Diego was undaunted by the morose weather. Liliane smiled as her husband, eager as a boy, rode ahead along the far end of the marsh, the sun breaking through gilt-edged clouds for him. In his last moments, he had the sun's hazy pearl gleaming directly into his faded, jubilant eyes. Suddenly, his destrier's squeal of fright shrilled across the long-dead grass. When the horse bolted, Diego's old body crashed into the brush, his neck broken as if by an accurate hangman. His falcon rose in a blur of cruel hooks and steel feathers through the wet pine tops glittering in the wind. Diego never fastened the falcon's jesses. Just as he had never fastened Liliane's.

Liliane spurred ahead but reached Diego's side too late. Her tears fell upon his face as she cradled his old head in her lap, gently ruffling the childish down of his white hair. Even as she tenderly wiped away the blood that trickled from the gash on his temple, the crystal clarity of his mind and soul became less than the dew, with no more substance than the drizzle gathering on the pine needles to drop still, tiny weights upon the dark mahogany and green mosses.

Now Liliane's freedom as well as Diego's life were abruptly ended. With horrified clarity, she saw that in allowing Jacques de Signe the power to select her next husband should she be widowed, she had signed Diego's death warrant; that warrant had been executed without warning, without mercy.

Some of Diego's accompanying castellans had already ridden into the woods, searching with deadly concentration for a possible assassin. Other castellans dismounted to search the marsh. Although their faithful faces were as familiar to Liliane as her own, they suddenly seemed to be far-away strangers. Except for Pedro, his eyes hot and desolate as he stood over her with his crossbow, ready to defend her. Soon Jacques de Signe would wrench her away from Pedro and the rest of them, but most painfully from Diego.

My darling Diego, she grieved, brushing a soft kiss across his forehead. I came to you as a child, and now you leave me so, as if you were the baby we longed for, sleeping at my breast. My child, my darling, my husband. I am but twenty years old and my heart is shattered. Now I shall be forced to leave you and our beloved Spain and return to France, to the gray fortress of the monsters who swore to kill you. . . .

1

The Deadly Bargain

They were quick enough to come to her. Sitting in Diego's chair in the great hall, her pale, fine-boned face starkly beautiful against the black velvet wimple of her widow's garb, Liliane impassively studied their faces. Louis de Signe's blunt features were weak in their brutality, suggesting muscle going soft. His large, heavy-lidded pale blue eyes were restless in his yellowish face. He was liverish, she noted with an apothecary's practiced eye. Louis was careful with wine by day, but the servants reported that he sometimes stumbled about his room at night.

Cousin Louis, his short, deceptively quick body bulky beneath his black woolen surcoat, was suspiciously quiet about Diego's death. He might well have been the one who had felled Diego, probably with a rock from a sling. Louis liked to hunt; he was good at it. No one knew for sure why the horse had bolted; the trackers had found no trace of footprints among the flattened reeds and marsh grass. Diego might merely have gashed his head upon one of the stones on the ground. Still, on a damp day, the marsh was a good place to snare a falconer.

While Louis might be the hunter, Jacques had probably loosed him on the quarry. Almond-eyed Uncle Jacques, with his lethally quick brain mounted atop slow fat. Ponderous in jewel-trimmed velvet, he swayed gently as he offered sonorous condolences upon Diego's death.

Unholy slugs, Liliane thought passionately. If you have murdered Diego, I shall teach you the taste of bitter salt. You know

3

not justice, but the galled taste of your own blood you shall discover.

Liliane longed to order her men to kill Jacques and Louis, but to do so without proving their guilt would be murder. Also, she could not risk the lives of her loyal castellans, outnumbered as they were by Jacques's armed men at the castle gate. Five Norman mercenaries stood behind Jacques and Louis while she kept only Pedro with her lest a command for additional bodyguards rouse the castellans' suspicions. At the slightest evidence that the Signes had assassinated Diego, the castellans would attack them like raging wolves and be slaughtered for it.

Above her widow's black, Liliane's face was chiseled ivory; her brows and lashes were gold, hinting at the color of her covered hair. Her amber eyes were tranquil, no longer translucent with sorrow or red from nights of weeping for Diego. Possessed by her private devils of guilt, rage and remorse, Liliane had ridden the hills surrounding Malaga these past weeks: weeks that seemed both too brief and too long.

Liliane loved Malaga and pine-studded Andalusia. Along this coast, at once rugged and sublimely seductive, she had adventured freely for seven years, until the time came when Diego had no longer treated her as a son, but as his wife and a woman. In most ways she had been ready to be a woman, but she chafed at the restraints that came with womanhood, in particular the long skirts that hampered her even as they flattered her slim curves.

When she was fourteen years old, Liliane had suffered the brutal loss of her parents in a raid by a neighboring baron. Afterward she submerged herself in convent life but encountered more superstition than solace. Instead of submission, Liliane learned rebellion.

She had been at the French convent for six months when Jacques, Baron de Signe, the titular head of her family, had claimed her father's lands and brought her to Paris. He arranged a marriage; Liliane was packed up again and sent to Spain. Despite her uncertain future, she had been relieved. Paris was a pesthole, but Jacques's house emanated evil and intrigue. She particularly hated her cruel, licentious cousin Louis.

In Spain, she had been presented to Count Diego del Pinal, a graying man who had sacrificed much of his modest wealth to gain her. Diego soon made her see her good fortune. Not only had he been dear to her parents, but he was also a valued advisor of Almansor, the Moorish ruler of Southern Spain who had once been his enemy. A wise and sensitive man, Diego helped her explore the practical possibilities of her rebellious nature.

At the time, Diego wanted a lively, youthful companion far more than he wanted a wife. With his encouragement, Liliane often dressed like his castellans when they went hunting. She learned to ride with the best, also to use a scimitar and light weaponry to defend herself against the dangerous amirs who roamed the countryside.

Diego was not the lover she might have imagined from the songs of the troubadours, but she grew to love him and would have given him her body and soul had he wanted to claim them. Diego, however, was too wise to take all she had to give. He was aware of his age and had not the heart to leave her emptied.

Although some time had passed, his death still made her feel like a bird with a shattered wing. She had lost Diego and must also lose Andalusia with its wild coast and lemon-scented courtyards, its lovely palaces and fountained pools that shimmered turquoise in the sun. Diego and Andalusia sang in her blood. Here were her people; here her heart. And her heart had been trampled by a pair of greedy, vicious men who were no better than the baron who had destroyed her parents. Now the tears were dammed in her soul and she prepared to face her relatives.

"Liliane, dear niece," murmered Jacques with feigned compassion, "I commend your strength of will. When we heard the distressing news, we made all haste back from Cadiz, but you seem to have made an admirable recovery from your husband's death."

What you mean, she thought, is that I do not weep, therefore I neither grieve nor fear your power. And without that fear you suspect I may not be trusted to serve your purpose. "Diego was old, Uncle," she replied softly, then rose with a sigh of velvet. "His end was mercifully quick. He died a happy man." A gold and sapphire filet gleamed on her alabaster brow as she inclined her head. "Do you know of another with such rare fortune in these uncertain days?"

"Then, Cousin," Louis paused, his eyes hard, "you attribute Count Diego's death to accident? You blame no one?"

"No one," she replied simply, betraying no trace of her suspicions. "Who can be sure what happened? It is useless to speculate. I am grateful that you have returned to lend me your

strength and see me safely from this place of sad memory.''
Liliane looked about the graceful Moorish arches of the hall, the
fine mosaics and brass chandeliers. Two months ago, she reflected, the pair of you stood in this room and threatened Diego's
assassination. You needed a rich widow to placate a bloodthirsty
French count back from the crusades who had threatened to split
your gullets for poaching on his land. This count had won your
French king for a friend, and you had no brides to offer as a
token of peace. And now you cannot trust the one bride you
have, Liliane thought, smiling inwardly.

But her secret triumph crumbled when she remembered how
foolish she had been to submit to their blackmail. In an attempt
to save Diego, she signed their scrap of vellum, relinquishing
her right to choose her next husband, giving that power to
Jacques. Diego's estate would be given into the guardianship of
Almansor, while she and her rich dowry would once more become Signe property to be dispensed as Jacques saw fit.

Years ago, Diego, the closest friend of her parents, had mercifully married her to prevent Jacques from selling her off to the
bidder with the most land and influence. He saved her from the
legal robbery of her property and childish virginity, and he kept
her spirit from being crushed by some uncaring lord.

All Diego asked of her in return was that she bear a child to
replace the heir he had lost in the early Christian wars against
Almansor's father. Patiently he waited those last, precious years
when he might have more easily sired a child, so that she could
experience her own childhood. When she was seventeen and had
learned to love him, he attempted to consummate their union.
Humiliated by his failure, he had not come to her again. Instead,
she went to his bed, where she stayed not as his lover, but as
his companion and comforter. Those years were happy.

Diego had learned much from both Christians and Moors, and
all of it he taught to Liliane. From the Christian world, she
mastered history and languages; from the more tolerant, enlightened Moorish world, she acquired knowledge of mathematics,
astronomy and medicine. From the great Moorish libraries in
Cadiz and Cordoba, she read in the original Arabic book, untouched by the narrow mysticism of the European Christians.

By sharing what he had learned from book and sword, Diego
gave Liliane weapons for survival. In a man's world where a
scholarly woman was undesirable, even suspect, she had culti-

vated a brain so sharp and deft, that few strangers were aware of her intelligence. Also, not trusting the amirs, Diego had taught her how to command the defense of their lands.

At times Liliane had felt like a ghost: not quite a wife, not quite a woman; not a Christian, not a Mohammedan; not a Spaniard, a Moor or a Frenchwoman. Her only allegiance had been to Diego. His love was her anchor and now she had none. She was being forced to go to France to marry some brawny, blue-blooded thug named Alexandre de Brueil to placate Uncle Jacques and Cousin Louis—and buy her time until she could determine their guilt and claim revenge for Diego. Somberly, she stared at them as they hovered like vultures. Already she knew too much about their various crimes for them to risk losing control of her. As long as she was useful, they would let her live, but the instant she crossed them, she would die. She wondered if her unlucky bridegroom, Alexandre de Brueil, had the wit to know that the Signes had numbered his days, as well.

"I place myself willingly in your hands, Uncle," she told Jacques as she came down from the dais to take his hands. "Diego was like a father to me, but with all respect, he had not your political and financial acumen."

Jacques's piglike eyes gleamed and she knew she had struck a note he understood: cold, calculating practicality. "You flatter me, my dear," he murmured. "I shall strive to meet your high expectations."

"I am sure you will, Uncle. I trust you will protect my interests as your own, thereby we shall all prosper." She paused and, with a deliberately careless air, added, "This Count de Brueil is young, you say?"

Louis laughed mirthlessly. "Never fear, Cousin. You will not find another father in Brueil."

She matched his smile. "Do not misunderstand me, Cousin. I am not gauging Brueil as a lover, but as an opponent. Better to disarm him than cross swords, *non?*"

Chuckling, Jacques embraced her. "Welcome back to the bosom of your family, my dear. Your father may have been something of a disappointment to me, but blood always tells. I think you will prove a sharp match for Alexandre de Brueil."

And for you, she thought grimly, *though you do not yet know it.*

2

The Flute in the Wood

A forest east of Toulon, the southern coast of France
April 1189

Alexandre de Brueil perched above the spring stream that was frigid with run-off from the snow-capped Alpine highlands. Poised lightly on the balls of his feet, he waited for a flash of silver among the black rocks. A winter of dry venison, and before that, searing months of near starvation with the defending crusaders during the siege of Jerusalem, had made him dream nightly of fresh trout in running water. He had imagined water pouring through Jerusalem's sun-baked streets, cascading off the city walls, down, down away from him to the enemy who flaunted water-filled goatskins at the trapped Europeans who were dying of heat and disease in their burning armor.

Alexandre forced the image from his mind. Chilled by the shade of the hillside's overhanging pines, he shivered slightly as he watched the frothing stream. Since leaving Palestine, he had piled his bed with furs and willing women, but had yet to be warm. The desert sun had thinned his blood; the siege, his body. He now had the hungry look of a wiry greyhound. After the siege, the overwhelming desire to gorge himself had been quickly quelled when he found that his shrunken stomach was unable to tolerate large quantities of food. The idea of greasy mutton and potatoes revolted him. He craved the fresh vegetables and fruit of the Crescent, pictured one exquisite yellow Lebanese lemon slice riding atop the trout now leaping among the rocky stream beneath him. Then he saw it: a shimmer of silver streaking through the shadowy current. He uncoiled his slim body and poised his light, forked lance above the frothing water.

A short while later, Alexandre's flute could be heard over the sizzle of roasting fish. Pausing briefly to sprinkle a pinch of aromatic Eastern spices onto his catch, Alexandre resumed playing an Arabic bazaar melody. His contentment was marred only by the nagging reflection that this would likely be his last moment of freedom for a long while. On the morrow he must marry; the thought affected his digestion like rancid meat. He already knew the discouraging details: Liliane del Pinal was the twenty-year-old widow of a Spanish nobleman and was reputed to be clever. That made her used, nearly past her prime, and practically foreign. As was typical of Spanish matrons, she was probably a religious fanatic and a shrew of less learning than presumption. She was also a Signe, and the Signes had all been weaned on treachery and greed.

Alexandre's lips pursed on the flute. Still . . . whatever Liliane del Pinal's bad points, the notorious Signe greed had made her rich. And at this point, money was the bargaining point he could ill afford to ignore. The Signes were afraid of him, he thought with contempt. In fact, it was Philip they feared, who shrewdly and ruthlessly ruled them all. Since the age of fourteen, a year before his royal father's death, Philip had governed France. Even then he'd been a match for the sly Plantagenet brood sired by England's dangerous lion, Henry II. Now twenty-four, Philip could play Richard the Lionhearted, the dead king's eldest son, like a harp. Philip was going to be a strong king, and if the inclination took him, he would crush the Signes as if they were mere cockroaches.

I helped Philip put down the Flanders uprising, Alexandre mused, then escorted the French banner to the Holy Land. Now, I am Philip's friend, and that has cost me my blood, my ideals and the near ruin of my neglected estate, upon which the Signes have gnawed like rats. Well, by all the Saints, thanks to Liliane's fat dowry, I shall at least rebuild my estate. Alexandre smiled mirthlessly. Besides, if my new bride is too sharp a bone, I can always pick her clean of money and toss her back to her greedy uncle. His smile broadened wryly. Ah, perhaps I have a few scruples, after all. If I followed Philip's example, I would stuff the wench into a tower as he did his first wife, blandly marry another woman, and watch the papal feathers fly. . . .

* * *

Astride her Moorish mare, Liliane herd a flute. Silvery as a cool beam of light, a wistful melody shimmered about the wood. I wonder if Pan haunts this place, she mused with a spark of playfulness rare to her since leaving Spain. The journey first by sea, then two days overland, had been a strain, her revulsion for Jacques and Louis increasing with every mile. This past week she had stayed at Castle de Signe while Jacques had briefed her on what he expected from her coming marriage to the Count de Brueil. For the time being, she was simply to keep him informed about everything that went on in the count's demesne. "Other than that," he had told her benevolently, "just enjoy yourself. Be pretty, wear your jewels. He will be smitten with you in no time."

Jacques's meaning was clear enough. She was to seduce Alexandre de Brueil into trusting her. If only her uncle knew how inexperienced she was at seduction!

Liliane had come to France to guard both Alexandre de Brueil and herself. She might never prove that Jacques had killed Diego, but sooner or later he would try to kill Brueil, and that she must prevent. If she could not prove Jacques had committed one crime, she might expose him in attempting another.

She had tolerated her relatives' escort as far as the edge of the Brueil demesne, then she easily lost the lavishly dressed wedding party in the shady forest. Anywhere else, Louis and a few of the party's armed escort would have swiftly retrieved her, but here in the threatening shadow of Count Alexandre, he and Jacques were confused, anxious and hesitant. If they wandered off the trail, they risked being shot for leaving their agreed route. They must be itching to throttle me, she thought, and laughed shortly. Let them stew. She would show up at the wedding, but not without a few last hours to call her own. She had always been someone else's property: her parents', then Jacques's, and finally Diego's. Now, for a brief span of hours, she would follow the sun-warmed wind and the mysterious flute that mesmerized with its lure of ancient temptations and elusive delights. . . .

In a small glen of pines nestled among the hillside rocks, Liliane found the flutist. The player was no Pan, yet he so resembled the errant god that she was frozen in fascination. He perched above the stream, a lithe, young ruffian. His worn woolen braies and chainse were topped by a fox-lined cotehardi.

His sun-streaked hair and beard were trimmed short, his face and hands a deep bronze. Although he was probably born a serf, his musical skill was bewitching, and she saw that his hands were fine-boned for a common plowman. His face was hard, with rapier-sharp features, but he also had a sensuous, full-lipped mouth. He was a thief, she decided, who survived by his wits. She had best keep her distance. Those fingers playing so quickly upon the flute might be as quick with a knife.

Alexandre sensed he was being watched and thought instantly that it was a Moor, but that was impossible. Oak leaves stirred in the breeze, obscuring the motionless watcher. His knife was at his belt, but the new foliage blocked the path of his bow and javelin. It would be impossible to notch the bow quickly enough to keep the stranger's arrow from his throat. He must lure his silent observer into the open.

Alexandre lowered the flute. "I have fish enough for two," he said casually, having not the slightest intention of sharing his precious catch. "If you remain shy, *mon ami*, you will shortly dine on cinders."

For a long, breathless moment, no sound came from the tangle of trees. Then he heard a voice as mild as his own reply, "Better to swallow a choice cinder than a javelin."

The stranger's French was Poitevin, which puzzled Alexandre; it was also cultivated, which puzzled him more. An assassin brought in by the Signes? However, unless the fellow was of a lethally playful bent, Alexandre would now have been stretched upon the ground. "I have no wish to cut your throat, merely to eat my lunch," Alexandre countered smoothly. "Will you be kind enough not to delay it?"

"By all means, dine at your pleasure. You need fear no interference from me."

"I confess to a dislike of anyone, particularly a conversational bush, staring at me while I chew," Alexandre tossed back, becoming genuinely irritated. His fish was starting to look overdone. "Kindly show yourself or be gone."

"No need to be prickly," returned the bush calmly. "May I have a small slice near the tail?"

Damn the cheeky varlet! thought Alexandre. "Whatever you please," he lied, "so long as I am relieved of the role of Moses."

A golden-haired youth warily stepped from behind the oak

cluster, holding a javelin loosely in his hand. Alexandre, familiar with the seemingly careless stance and latent quickness of hunters and warriors, made no move toward his own weapons. The boy was handsome, richly dressed, with soft, fair skin. His smoky eyes were those of a seducer. He was too pretty for Alexandre's liking. Probably some foppish page who had wandered away from a hunting party. Probably one that belonged to Jacques.

"Are you a Signe?" he asked abruptly, watching the boy's eyes.

Those eyes widened, then the boy smiled pleasantly. "No, just a member of the entourage. The seigneur was hunting boar today. I prefer fish to pork."

Alexandre pointed his flute. "There is the stream."

The youth cocked his head. "You are retracting the luncheon invitation?"

Alexandre shrugged with little regret. "Only have one fish. So sorry."

"Because you still think I am a Signe . . . or because you are a liar?"

"Because I think we are both liars."

The youth's derisive laugh told Alexandre that he did not much care what a ragged man thought. "Then we are in excellent company." He grinned recklessly as he clambered a few feet up the rocks, but he was careful to keep Alexandre in view. Finding a flat rock across the stream, he poised his javelin.

If that unweaned brat catches something, vowed Alexandre, I shall eat my boots.

Within minutes the brat was spitting a sleek trout to roast, as Alexandre ignored his boots and began to pay assiduous attention to his own dinner. So, this boy is more than a fop, he decided, his suspicion whetted.

Seeming to read his mind, the boy eyed him mischievously. "I begin to understand your wish to keep your dinner to yourself. You eat with the appetite of a starved bear."

He may know who I am, reflected Alexandre, if he refers to the Palestine siege. He smiled without humor as he pried the last morsel from his trout's spine. "At least I keep to my own forest."

"Yours?" The boy raised an ironic brow at Alexandre's tattered garment, then gazed at the lush greenery about them. "Do these woods not border the demesne of the Count de Brueil?"

So he had not guessed. Alexandre's smile widened as he tossed the trout bones into the stream. "Does a squirrel deed out his burrow? This wood will belong to foxes and weevils like me when Brueil is dust. Besides, have you seen me take a stag, even a rabbit, that would blight his hunting?"

The boy nodded at the fish bones rapidly floating downstream. "Surely, you agree that Milord de Brueil could hang you for this encroachment?"

Alexandre shrugged. "Why would he bother?" He patted his slim middle. "I eat less than one of his hounds."

The boy turned the spit. "Some seigneurs value men less than hounds." The smoke rose in a savory, pungent spiral.

"Is Alexandre de Brueil so hard of heart?"

"I know him not; I have heard only that he has a fondness for fighting."

"Brueil?" Alexandre laughed shortly. "I assure you, having had a tour of battle in the Crescent, he has no such appetite. Given leisure, he would be little different from you, with scarce more on his mind than choosing between fish and pork."

The page's smoke-colored eyes caught the fire's hot, orange glow. "You suppose me a lap dog?"

Alexandre grinned. "Do you find that irritating?"

As the page unspitted his fish, he shrugged. "Gold-collared fleas are more so; the Signes have a wealth of them."

Alexandre laughed. "Fie, to speak so of your masters."

The page's eyes narrowed as if he saw evil genies in the fire. "Aye, my masters . . ." Silent for some moments, he neatly partitioned his fish. "Tell me, is this peace-loving Alexandre de Brueil so fond of the Signes?"

"He will marry one tomorrow," replied Alexandre dryly.

"Marry, to marry is to marry, is to marry, as our good King Philip would say," purred the page, plucking up a bite of trout. "Is the lady beautiful?"

"I doubt it" was Alexandre's flat response as he propped his back against a log. "But you should know that better than I."

"I have no great interest in women," responded the page lightly. "In any event, the demoiselle is too tawny and immodest for my tastes."

Alexandre's ears pricked. "Immodest?"

The page yawned. "To meet her, you would scarce know her from a boy."

"Oh." Alexandre's disappointment was evident. "Well, perhaps her lack of sex has preserved her virtue."

"I wonder," mused the page, his cheek full of fish and his expression faraway. "Free for a night, with none the wiser, what fancies and allurements might any woman entertain when bound to an unwelcome match?"

Alexandre stretched out his long legs. "After all," he speculated, "she was married to an old man. The demoiselle may know much of men or nothing; for want of a vigorous bedding, she may be either wizened or wanton."

The page flushed. "I daresay the lady would dislike having her honor scorched over coals not yet lit. Who is to say her new groom is not wizened or wanton?"

Alexandre's lips twisted wryly. "In truth, he is a bit of both."

Beneath his sloped, gold-trimmed cap, the page grimaced. "Then the lady must envy your weevil's carefree existence; weevils do not marry much and are the wiser for it." He tossed the last of his fish to Alexandre. "Enjoy the rest, weevil, and count yourself rich. My appetite has been ruined by civilized fare, rich with sauces of money and marriages."

Alexandre had developed much the same aversion. They stared at the half-eaten fish with its treacherous bones. A water drop flattened on the trout's dulled scales. Another plopped on the page's plumed cap, another on Alexandre's bare head. "We had best look for shelter," observed the page. "Is there any nearby, sirrah?"

"I know of a dry den." Alexandre gathered up his weapons and flute. "Unless you've grown too civilized to tolerate another man's droppings."

The page's laugh had a girlish but attractive ring. "You may rest easy on that score. Even lap dogs know when to trot out of the rain."

The page untied his horse and let Alexandre mount before him in the saddle. They wound through the wet wood until they were drenched, but there was still no sign of a cave or dry shelter. Alexandre's teeth began to chatter, his hands turning blue on the reins. The page pulled a fur-lined mantle from his saddlebag and flung it over them both, but he made no effort to share his body warmth. By the time they reached the Brueil hunting lodge and dismounted, Alexandre knew why. The downpour had soaked the page's linen chainse and molded it into a surprisingly delightful shape. His companion was a girl.

He had been imagining assassins but never, even remotely, a female wood sprite. The young woman's contralto voice was low enough that she had easily disguised her sex. A suspicion as to her identity grew in his mind. Was this lithe, sultry-eyed "boy" his bride to be? The provocative possibility of probing her secret teased his mind. Surreptitiously, he watched the rise of the lady's chainse as she unleashed the saddlebags and flung them over her shoulder. Then he quickly undid the crimson saddle cinch and hauled the saddle into the back of the wooden lodge.

Like a mammoth tree stump, the lodge blended into the wet green wood. Its western wall bounded a small lake, and some of the stones had tumbled into the water, while on the other side, the stable was little more than a tumble-down wooden slant of roof.

At this moment, Alexandre's black destrier trotted up to welcome him. In order to rebuild the strength he'd lost in Palestine, Alexandre had wandered the wood on foot this morning, leaving the stallion to graze the far side of the lake. As he stroked the stallion, he noted that its training and magnificence were not lost on the girl; her sardonic cool gaze told him that she assumed the animal was stolen.

After tethering his horse, Alexandre retrieved a rusty iron key from beneath a nearby pile of rocks. As the key screeched in the worn lock, his companion observed with a hint of sharpness, "Never a rabbit do you take, eh? For a villein, you treat Alexandre de Brueil's property as if it were your own, and your speech is smooth as Cathay silk. Come, sirrah, are you poacher or proprietor?"

"I am a common bastard with a highborn tongue, and I have some claim to this place," Alexandre answered smoothly. "Is that answer enough?" He did not know why he lied; unless for pride that this beauty should not think him a worthless thief. He saw that she was stunned.

"You are a brother of Alexandre de Brueil?"

"We share a trifling resemblance about the jaw." Alexandre picked up the saddle. "Then again, we have another similarity. Neither of us has a livre to his name, but I am a free weevil whereas he is a dutiful flea." He shouldered open the heavy door and they entered a dusty, bare room with a stone fireplace glutted with leaves, mullioned windows cloudy with age, and a lively family of mice. A common table and ornately carved wooden chairs centered the room. Into the rounded stone fireplace was cut the leopard and unicorn emblem of the Brueil family; at its sides were stone griffins mounted on balls, which had lost most of their detail to soot. A greenish light suffused the room. Alexandre carelessly dumped the saddle. "Seigneur Alexandre rates none of my envy. He must take a bride to support this dog-eared legacy, while I wear no woman's collar."

Liliane suddenly disliked this man's taunting air and his bold, brilliant blue eyes. She knew his arrogance was empty, tinged as it was by bitterness. His mockery of Alexandre de Brueil seemed aimed at himself as well. Like many lone wolves with noble blood, he saddened her. Right now she had too many problems of her own to welcome those of a stranger. This wiry buck might have made a very handsome lord, but instead he was merely a poacher stretching his luck. Eventually his luck would run out and his neck would stretch as well. That would be a great pity, for he was quick and keen. His movements as he lay the fire were deft and agile, and his mobile face intrigued her. He resembled one of the lean and hungry young amirs always preying on Almansor's power. The amirs often ran to fat and dissolution by middle age, but she could not imagine this man weakening. His thick auburn hair and ink-blue eyes, startling as star sapphires against his deep tan, were the only indications of his European heritage.

Aye, he was a very pretty lord of hedgerows and snares. She was not altogether sure he was not a snare himself. This might be sunny, southern France, but he was brown as a currant and shivered as if the damp spring were alien to him. Jacques had told her that Alexandre de Brueil had just returned from Palestine. Might he not be expected to be brown and sensitive to the cold? "Sirrah"—she sauntered to the fireplace and leaned against it—"have you in your freedom passed all your life in Provence?"

Continuing to arrange the logs of wood in the grate, he held up a bronzed hand. "Obviously not." He glanced up at her, a knowing look in his blue eyes. "I trailed the Count de Brueil to Palestine, for which I was not thanked with loot but saddle galls and flux."

"Yet you saw the Christ's Holy Sepulcher?" she pressed. "Was that not some recompense for your pains?"

Alexandre arranged wood chips atop his meager pine stack. "Aye. I saw the Sepulcher . . . through a whining, lying scrabble of peddlers with bolts of cloth from Christ's shroud and forests of splinters from His cross. I could fair build a cathedral from His bones and roof it with the palms He kissed." He carefully placed the last chip. "God has left that place and gone into the desert." He was silent for a moment. "Jehovah strides that wilderness and leaves the cities to hypocritical vermin."

"So, you have faith, after all," she said softly.

With a brief laugh, he flicked flint against steel. "Not enough to go on quests. I shall not linger here, but venture to the north where the king fights the English and there is gold to be had. Then I shall go to England and bribe my own land out of Prince John." His eyes challenged hers. "Why are you wandering about the woods? Surely not to seek a dragon?"

Liliane began to toss off a careless retort, then she suddenly paused and said gravely, "I do pursue a quest, perhaps for a dragon, or perhaps I seek myself. It is as if I am lost in a hall of mirrors that turn, and warp, and cast back the sun and clouds in strange shapes. Your flute in the forest bewitched me and led me to follow its call." Her light laughter held a touch of uncertainty. "You have a very fine forest, but I confess some fear of a dragon."

He rose, standing half a head over her. "I will protect you," he said quietly. She was startled by his sober tone, but more by the unsettling expression in his blue eyes. He was looking at her like a man might a girl who beguiled him. She suddenly became afraid that he saw through her disguise. A shiver ran up her spine. She was alone with a vagabond thief whose nearness stirred her with strange anticipation. Never once had she allowed herself to look at a man other than Diego, never once had she imagined another man touching her body, filling her with that secret flame that Diego in his fading virility had left unkindled. The intense blue eyes searching hers filled her with uncertainty. As if deceived by mirrors, she saw in those luminous pools her own white body entwined in his dark one, his hands hidden in her golden hair. His mouth . . . so near . . . parted as if he could see her vision, and his breath caught.

"Who are you?" he whispered. "Tell me . . . you have nothing to fear from me."

Nothing? A cold chill seized Liliane. She was the pawn of murderers, the promised bride of the lord of this demesne who in his power might seek harsh revenge for any impingement of his honor. However, she was less afraid for herself than for this rugged drifter without land or power to protect him. She feared that this mysterious stranger might stumble into peril if she did not use her wisdom to save them both.

Liliane tried to regain her common sense. Why assume that this man had discovered her disguise? For safety's sake she had dressed much the same way by ship and coach, thereby journeying from Spain without discovery. At times, Diego and his men nearly forgot her sex, so expert had she become in passing as a boy. Why then, she wondered uneasily, did this poacher's stare seem so intimate? Was he fond of boys, as were so many Moorish males? Perhaps she had even led him on by pretending to be a fop, uninterested in women!

She stepped hastily away from the young Frenchman. "Protect me, sirrah? I can find my way about well enough." Pretending boredom, she walked across the room. "Tell me, as you seem to know this place, is there nothing we may drink to warm ourselves? The rain has given me a slight chill, but you are shaking."

"There is Italian brandywine," Alexandre answered thoughtfully.

Liliane heard the wet plop of his sodden cotehardi as he slung it over a chair, and she turned abruptly in alarm. She watched him pull his wet chainse over his head. His shoulders and arms were better muscled than she would have assumed. In the dim light she could see scars marking his fine, lean torso. Despite his scars, he was beautiful. Determined to maintain her own guard, Liliane had no wish to see him naked. As his damp curls disappeared through the hanging laces of his chainse, she protested uneasily, "Come, man, this place is as drafty as Gibraltar in a gust and your fire is feeble. Do you see me as a nursemaid if you take ill?"

"I have few illusions about the skill of maids, and if you dislike the fire, cut your own wood." He flung away his boots, which were followed by his wet braies. Catching a glimpse of his slim white flanks, Liliane hastily averted her eyes. Padding from the room, he tossed dryly over his shoulder, "By the way, my name is Jean and I do not commonly make love to boys."

Rain or no, Liliane decided that it was high time to leave. Before she could reach the door, he had returned with an armload of dry clothes. He tossed her a pair of musty braies and a chainse, then stood by the fire to don his clothes, possibly to preserve her modesty, she thought ruefully, since he obviously had none.

Rain drummed overhead, rattling the leaking roof. Liliane sighed and inclined her head at the door he had just used. "Is that the bedroom?"

He raised a brow. "Zounds, I have met snappish lap dogs, but rarely a modest one." Then ignoring her, he pulled on his dry braies. "Suit yourself. That is the bedroom and I am sure the mice will be fascinated."

Liliane hurried into the room. Jean had not exaggerated. A field mouse scampered into its hole at the sight of her, then peered out again, its whiskers twitching. The room was simple yet beautiful. An ancient chest stood in one whitewashed corner. Greenish rain-softened light slanted across the room from the deep casement window. The window's heavy, irregular glass held tiny bubbles, reminding Liliane of a rising sea. Beyond it, wand-like emerald willows melted lushly into an amber lake. The bed was white and downy. A simple pottery bowl filled with wax served as a lamp; beside it lay a worn, illuminated book of Persian poetry.

Liliane was overwhelmed by a sense of stillness. It was as if she had waited to walk into this room all her life. In her mind a small chime sounded a single, caressing note. Alexandre de Brueil has slept here, she thought. This room is too well kept, the bed too fresh, unless this Jean the poacher has kept it so. Still gazing at the room, Liliane pulled off her cap and her mantle, and slid out of the rest of her wet clothes. What she had thought were braies were actually Moorish pantaloons, which swelled full to gather at the ankle. She was reaching for the tunic when a soft laugh at the door made her catch the garment to her chest and whirl around.

"Lucky mice." Jean's amused, admiring gaze dropped to the tunic she clutched to her breasts. "You have a splendid back," he observed lightly. "Certainly strong enough to cut your own wood."

"What do you mean by spying on me?" she demanded, frightened and furious.

At her flushed cheeks and smoldering stare, his own eyes grew hot. "I thought you had finished dressing; you took long enough. Why play at being a boy? You are lovely." His gaze swept to the silky fall of her hair, then down to the pale swell of her breasts, and his voice grew taut. "And ripe. Alexandre de Brueil is a lucky man."

The fire in Liliane's eyes flared. "Why do you say that? I have never seen him!"

"Come, are you not the lady he is to wed—and bed 'ere the morrow's moonrise? His bride is fair, I hear, yet"—his voice lowered—"I knew not she was gold as a mote of sunlight and fair as a spring-dewed morn. Nay," he breathed, "thou seem wizard-spun, a changeling maiden with such sorcery in her eyes and form that may lure mortals and magicians alike to folly."

Liliane was reasonably accustomed to flattery, but no man had ever spoken so to her, not even Diego, who had surrounded her with love and friendship. Although she was not vain, she suddenly knew that in many ways she had been a stranger to Diego. He had not sensed the secrets of the sensuality she was beginning to realize lay within her. Not so this Jean, with his alert, penetrating gaze. He watched her as if awaiting a mistake, a revelation . . . something she must not give him. She was to be chatelaine of this demesne, the wife of his half brother. Already he knew too much and was rapidly guessing more. She must confuse him, escape this place and go to Castle de Brueil as quickly as possible. "As you say, why play games? I see mine is up," she forced herself to reply coolly. "My name is Pilar and I am meant not to marry your Alexandre de Brueil, but my cousin, Louis de Signe."

His eyes became so hard and flat that she stiffened. She could not tell whether he was contemptuous or somehow disappointed.

Bitter and angry, Alexandre was galled to the core. This lovely, tantalizing creature was not to be his on the morrow, but go to a pig of a Signe. He knew Louis, who was nearly twice Pilar's age and dissolute as a baboon. In mounting fury, Alexandre stalked from the room.

As he waited by the fire for Pilar to finish dressing, Alexandre quickly made up his mind. This Pilar had a cool tongue, but she was shy of men . . . rather, shy of a man who openly desired her. Her uneasy blushes at his nakedness suggested she was yet unpracticed in love. Alexandre squared his jaw. Before dawn, he would see that she was experienced. She would know pleasure before she knew the pain of mating Louis. God knew what creature he himself was to wed on the morrow, but Pilar, with her hair caressing her slender hips, fired his blood as his rich widow was scarce likely to do. With charm and luck, he might persuade Pilar to be his mistress rather than marry her baboon.

But what could he offer her? He had no money to keep her richly, and he was loath to promise the wealth of a wife he had not yet seen. Alexandre had pleased many women, if he believed their passionate sighs, but he was not fool enough to consider himself so splendid a lover that a woman would exchange her future security for the pleasure he could give. Also, Pilar might well be far less delighted than he to offend the Signes. He frowned. Women were unpredictable and Pilar had shown herself to be particularly so; he might gamble on that unpredictability. Although the odds were stacked against him, he had won on less. However, given her current mood, she seemed bound to bolt at any moment. The rain was letting up and unveiling the twilight. How to keep her captive was the first problem.

Alexandre strode outside, untethered her mare and gave its rump a sharp slap. Her hair streaming over her back in a long golden plait, Pilar raced out in time to see her horse disappear through the dripping trees.

She glared at his innocent face. "Just why did my mare bolt?!"

"Wolves," he replied blandly.

"Wolves? Wolves who broke into full cry just as you bounded from the door, I suppose." She looked mad enough to spit. "What are you doing out here?"

"I came to fetch some wood." His smile was disarming. "The fire is low and I thought you would grow cold."

"There, my scheming lad, you would be right," she ground out, leveling the javelin at his middle. "Cold's the word, and that's all you will get from me this night. Lift so much as an eyelid in my direction and you will be fit only for the priesthood by morn." She backed into the lodge, jerked shut the door and bolted it, then slammed all the wooden shutters, leaving Alexandre to watch the last of the feeble sun sink.

Alexandre swore softly as he began to shiver again. As the woods grew dark, he debated kicking in a window, then thought better of it. By the end of twilight, the rain would resume and she would take pity on him. If she did not, he would be dog sick on his wedding day. Grimly, he figured that would probably be an appropriate condition.

For an hour, Liliane simmered. Soon the rain began again. The heavy drops against the shutters made her uncomfortably aware that Jean was being soaked by the cold downpour. Revenge was not quite as sweet as she had anticipated. But he deserves it for running off my mare! she argued fiercely with herself. Castle de Brueil is nearly nine miles from here. If I miss the wedding, all hell will break loose!

Her thoughts left the wedding. If I leave Jean in the rain, he is bound to get sick. And he has no one to look after him. She stared at the shutters shaking with the pounding rain. Jean is silver-tongued and handsome. Though he must have women about the countryside, he lives alone in the forest like an animal . . . like a magpie appropriating another bird's nest. He has as few qualms about usurping the bird's mate, as well.

After what seemed an interminable stretch, Liliane estimated that two hours had passed. Jean must be bitterly cold, yet after she had slammed shut the shutters, he had made no attempt to gain admittance. He might have sheltered in the leaky lean-to near the main entrance, where they had tethered her mare.

Why not let the miserable wretch inside? He had probably suffered enough. She had her poignard and javelin; also, the bedroom door had a hefty inside bolt beam.

As the driving rain raked the night's sullen sky, Liliane furtively opened the door.

Her javelin poised, she called, "Jean, come in and warm yourself! You may be a villain, but I shall not murder you by inches." The only sound that reached her was the cold slap of the rain on the forest floor. "Jean?" she called hesitantly as she stepped into the murk. The deepening mud was stiff and cold. By the time she had taken half a dozen steps, her shirt stuck to her skin. "Jean!" she yelled. "Answer me before I lose patience and leave you out here to drown like a cat!"

He must have been on the roof, for his weight nearly bore her to the mud. She had learned much of hand-to-hand fighting from Diego's castellans, but nothing of aerial assaults. With humiliating quickness, Jean had pinioned her arms to her sides with her javelin; it dug into her ribs as he hauled her, struggling, back into the lodge. Abruptly, he wrenched the javelin from her grip and shoved her away.

Whipping the poignard from her belt, she faced him with fury in her eyes. "Manhandle me again, you lawless churl, and you will be using your guts for braielaces!"

"I would not touch you again for pay!" Jean snarled. His narrow face was startlingly white with cold and anger; his quivering lips were purple. "You are entirely safe, mistress. Had I intended rape, my interest has long since withered, I promise you." As she began to retort, he put up his hand and snapped, "I only ask two things of you: be silent and do not block the fire!"

Warily, Liliane gave him a wide berth as he stiffly edged to the fireplace. Dripping puddles and leaving muddy footprints, Jean moved like an old man. Without looking at her, he hunkered down and stretched his shaking hands to the warmth. A violent bout of trembling seized him and he wrapped his arms about his chest. Liliane backed away silently. In an instant, the pointed javelin was aimed at her. "Where are you going?" he hissed.

"Something dry may be left in the bedroom chest," she retorted, "unless you wish to stay sodden."

"Ha! My only wish it to wring your neck, and yours is to bar that door between us." His arms tightened about his ribs. "For once we are in some agreement—in wanting to see the last of each other. Begone and cower in peace. Your chastity can shrivel like your heart."

Disgusted, Liliane thrust the poignard in her belt. "Were I heartless, you would yet be rotting in the rain. And as for chastity, look to your own tattered virtue before you preach at me." She stalked to the bedroom and rifled through the chest. Only a ragged pair of braies were left. She pondered what to do. She should just toss Jean the braies and bolt the door, but the wood supply for the fire was scant. To keep warm, he would soon be driven outside to replenish the wood, thus getting wet again. After their adventure in the rain, she was chilled herself. Finally, she went out to the main room and handed him the braies. He looked more miserable than ever, and she could see his shoulder blades jutting sharply beneath the wet chainse. "These are the last of the dry clothes. You said there was brandywine. Has this place a wine cellar?"

Alexandre laughed shortly. "You must think that this Alexandre de Brueil wallows in luxury. His cellar hold rotten potatoes and one jug of sour brandywine."

Lilian explored the cellar and found that he was right; however, after searching the dusty shelves, she discovered a few strips of venison remaining in a lidded crock. After lugging the jug to the fireside, she gave Jean the lion's share of the venison. "Chew that to ease the bile in your belly."

He regarded the salted strips with distaste, then began to gnaw one, a resigned expression on his face. Liliane unplugged the brandywine and took a swallow. Making a face, she handed him the jug. "It's nearly vinegar, but it will fight the cold."

Alexandre took a swig, and gasped, his eyes watering. "That's fit for imps!" Quickly, he stripped off his chainse and rubbed his arms and shoulders. Knowing that he would proceed to pull off his wet braies, Liliane hurried to fetch the bed's woolen blanket. He had pulled on the dry braies by the time she returned. Sagging well below his narrow middle, they seemed to be in danger of falling off him entirely. She threw the blanket over his bare shoulders. He muttered, "Solicitous wench," as he caught the blanket close about him and took another gulp of the brandywine. He choked and began to cough.

Consolingly, she patted his back. "Drink slowly. The devil will have you soon enough."

Alexandre shoved the jug at her. "See to yourself. You are as wet as I am."

Without argument, Liliane shared his brandywine. She had dry clothes in her saddlebag, but she couldn't risk getting them dirtied; she was to be married in them on the morrow.

Before long, both the woodpile and the wine were much depleted. Somewhat mistily, Liliane gazed at Jean. "Well, I am warm, but I am tipsy. In the firelight, you are beginning to turn a pretty lilac."

Solemnly, Alexandre inspected his hand. "I must be thawing." His blue eyes glinted with mild irony. "You have thawed a trifle yourself."

"Because I am not presently shoving a knife at your nose?" She laughed. "Do not entertain any ideas, sirrah. Just go on thinking of me as a lad and we shall get on well."

Lad. He had long lost that ability, thought Alexandre. The wet tunic caressed Pilar's breasts as his hands longed to do. Still angry, he had tried to forget his earlier desire for her, but the imps lurking in his heart were against him. He had sometimes been lonely in his youth and often in Palestine. With Pilar, he felt at peace, as if she were a companion with whom he had no need to be clever or prove himself. What he was seemed sufficient to her for the moment, as if she were an unquestioning child. Her eyes were gentle now, almost tender as she watched him, but she was no child. Although she was slender, her breasts swelled full, and their tips pressed hard against the thin cloth. Where the tunic wrapped, the cleft of her breasts was shadowed in a soft mystery that made his loins ache. Some moments ago, he had shifted the blanket across the swell in his braies.

He was fairly certain that she did not mean to tease him; she was merely unaware of her body's ripe display. He was tempted to make her aware, both of her body's riches and of his aching desire to plunder them; yet plunder it would be, if she were unwilling. The question was: how could he persuade her to melt into his arms, when thus far his forthright approach had roused nothing but her ire?

Feigning preoccupation with his venison, he studied her beneath the fringe of his lashes. Her beauty had all the subtleties of fine breeding, with none of the flamboyance one might have expected from a female who was masquerading as a male. She had the radiance of youth and expectation, yet he also sensed sadness in her and a certain cynicism that roused his sympathy. Who had hurt her? What had been her life—what marvelous fate had lured her to him in the forest? Was allurement the way to win her? Could he perhaps play upon the fancy that had drawn her to his flute? With some alacrity, he dispatched the last morsel of venison, then casually picked up his flute and began to play.

Unbeknown to Liliane, the melody Alexandre delicately fingered upon the slender flute echoed playfully, seductively in his mind as he drank in her softness. She seemed to sense his passion as she leaned back to rest upon her hands. Trilling low, then fluting with a nightingale's breathless freedom, Alexandre played as he never had before. He tantalized them both with the haunting music—an ancient Persian court poem of seduction. At length, he saw her half-closed eyes grow dark, and he glimpsed her stirred yet tempered passion. For now, that passion encompassed all men, all that was sensuous. . . . Somehow, with his exotic melody, he must bring her close to him.

Liliane watched Jean's fingers on the flute. They were now quick and teasing, now slow and caressing. The music was as exquisite as the sensual stroke of a cat, his fingertips teasing, their precise grace strangely enticing. She recognized the piece he played, having heard it more than once upon visiting the harem of Almansor. His audacity in choosing such erotic music first amazed her, then touched her sense of mischief. Why not let him go on with his pretty foolishness? After all, he was a much more entertaining player than the blind harem flutist, and vastly more handsome. How the Moorish ladies would giggle and flash their eyes at such a virile substitute for their wizened eunuch!

Indeed, Jean's dark, mobile fingers led her to entertain very unseemly imaginings. She remembered her fleeting glimpse of whiteness against his darkly tanned, finely shaped limbs. Of compact buttocks and, as he turned, darkness at his groin, and from that darkness rising, like a young stallion . . . Ah, Jean, her mind whispered, you are richly made . . . and no virgin. You summon me now as boldly as any animal ever called its mate, and the call is more potent to me—alone, untried and bereft of all love—than you can know.

Then, somewhere in her revery, she seemed to feel his hands upon her and her mind cried out, Jean, Jean, touch me so. . . .

As soon as the thought crossed her mind, she shunned it. To take this man as her lover would be sheer folly. As Alexandre de Brueil's brother, he must inevitably learn her identity. And yet . . . had he not said that he was bound to fight as a mercenary in northern lands with no intention of returning? After this night, he would be gone from her life. The thought both quickened her pulse and saddened her. After tonight, she would never again see him, with his beautiful, brown body and the smoldering sapphire eyes that watched her with a feline, deceptive carelessness. She knew what was in his mind; his song of seduction left no doubt as to his desire for her.

Liliane had known love in her life, but she'd never experienced passion. Once married, she would not betray her vow of honor by taking a casual lover from her husband's retinue. Before that vow, however, she owed the Signes and her enforced bridegroom nothing. To share a single night of love with a stranger of her own choice seemed to her less immoral than to marry perforce a stranger she might have to endure the rest of her life. None could expect her to still be a virgin after so many years with

Diego. Tonight she might find the secret part of herself that had always eluded her. In deserting the Signe party, she had embarked on some part of a quest and, in following the flute, found Jean. Jean, with his quick wit and fiery temper, the boyish vulnerability hidden beneath his cynical shell. Jean, who, but for her memories and those of women like her, might die unmourned in the north.

At some point, Liliane stopped fighting the flute, closed her eyes and became one with the music, surrendered to Jean's delicate play of hands and mouth. . . .

The flute's silence was brief, but the very real warmth of Jean's lips against her own seemed to last forever, causing the slow beat of her heart to quicken against his bare chest. His mouth was velvet, his hand caressing the sensitive nape of her neck, twisting the silken fall of her shining hair. His tongue teased the corners of her mouth, gently probing her underlip. Uncertain of what he wanted, Liliane caught her breath, only to have him claim the inner softness of her mouth, touching her tongue in a subtle, intimate caress. Hesitantly, she returned the tiny flick until his mouth melted to hers, his kiss deepening until he dizzied her. As her head fell back, her hands ceased to press against his shoulders, moving to the shaggy curls at his temples. His eyes burned with a smoldering passion, his breath was uneven.

"Pilar, I am on fire," he said huskily. "If you want me not, tell me now, else I shall carry you to bed and take what is promised to another man." His hand tightened slightly in her hair. "I am hard put not to claim you now in these scattered ashes."

"I confess I have not noticed the ashes," she whispered, "but when this night has passed, I wish only to be one among them. Touch me with your fire; make me know one single spark of its light before I return alone to the terrible cold. . . ."

Alexandre did not wait to carry her to the bed, but covered her with his body, arching over her as his lips found her throat. Quick with the impatience of growing desire, his hands slipped free the lacings of her tunic to bare her shoulders. As if only then realizing what treasure he had found, he cast aside his haste. With tantalizing languor, he began to cover her soft skin with slow kisses, lifting his head at each one to watch a rosy flush tinge the alabaster flesh his lips had touched. With those kisses alone, he eased open her tunic until it slipped from the peaks of her breasts. His lips parted with the swift intake of his breath.

"By all the angels, thou art fair as the delight of Solomon. . . ."As he slowly undressed her, Liliane shivered slightly and gently pressed her breasts high to fill his hands. His dark head bending, his lips grazed against their sensitive points until she gasped with delight. Warm as the rising sun, his mouth sought the buds of her nipples.

She had never dreamed of this sweet pleasure, this luring, erotic witchery. In the shifting firelight, her bare flesh against his was silk upon satin, spreading a glow of enchantment. "Ah, Pilar," he whispered, "you are ivory and gold and rose, lovely beyond my dreaming. Close not against me now, sweet." His hand carried hers to touch herself, share his discovery, guide him, follow him as he caressed the hidden place that made her tremble and cry out against his throat. As she arched, she felt the hard eagerness of his own desire, the impatient readiness. "I am your prisoner, sweet Pilar," he whispered. "Free me. Free me to love you, and my body will be a slave to yours."

She tugged at his braies with some hesitancy, and he laughed softly at her awkwardness. He guided her, letting her trace him through the cloth, letting her feel his length and strength. Then suddenly, his clothing parted easily to bare his manhood. Feeling his hard, heated flesh, she quickly drew her hand away. Startled at seeing a male fully aroused, she was hesitant to touch him again. Then, fascinated at the luxuriant mystery of his virility, she trailed her fingers down the curve of his groin to his firmly swollen hardness. The light pressure of her hand made his body tense. "Pilar, do not . . . ah, do not release me, but open . . . oh, love, open . . ."

He eased her thighs apart and his mouth covered hers as his lithe body poised. She knew what must come and, when it came, she welcomed the pain. He pierced her swiftly, surely as a blazing arrow, direct and deep. Tears of pain and joy filled her eyes as he tensed over her, filling her, and the stab of that first invasion gradually gave way to a throbbing ache. Then the throb changed to the pulse of his thrusting inside her, quickening, deepening. He moved with greater urgency, no longer bringing pain but unimaginable pleasure. Her body was floating, the sweet, forbidden heat rising and curling in incandescent tendrils that engulfed them in living flame.

Liliane's body gave a startled, trembling shudder. She then lay very still, trying to hold on to the wild, violent magic that was slowly fading, leaving a mysterious glowing warmth deep within her. Jean felt it, too: an iridescent glow that lingered in his cobalt eyes, lingered where his body was yet joined to hers. His mouth closed over hers, and he kissed her languorously. She sighed as his lips trailed lower. "Ah, Jean, if I had known . . ."

"You would not have banished me to the rain!" He laughed, then nipped her belly so that she gave a startled yelp. "Perhaps you would not have come to me a virgin." Sinuous as a serpent, he crept lower until he mischievously peered at her between her breasts. "Sly temptress, maybe you have pretended false innocence and lured me as a forest nymph would some goatish oaf."

Liliane giggled. "Goat you may be, but no oaf. I am untutored in love, yet splendid skill I recognize. Where did you learn such artistry, Monsieur Goat?"

"Stews, mostly," he answered laconically. "Paris and the Holy Land have as many whores as fleas."

The glow left her. "And now perhaps you think you must scratch again . . ."

Seeing her transparent shame, Alexandre flushed. "I ought to have my heedless tongue cut out." He touched her face. "Pilar, if *you* could only know . . . to have you here with me tonight, of all nights, is a miracle. Your gift of innocence is far more than I deserve. I have cherished little in this world. For most of my manhood, I have lived like a vagabond." His lips twisted with bitterness. "The future promises little more. If I could offer you luxury and—"

Her fingertips stopped the words. "I require nothing of you, Jean, especially gold. This sweet time we spend together is enough." Even as she said it, she knew she misled them both. She had not counted on the cruelty of sharing great intimacy with this man, then losing him.

Alexandre suddenly remembered that he had told her he was leaving, that she must believe they were to be lovers only until the dawn. Perhaps Pilar had counted upon his departure to guard her reputation. He tried to shove the suspicion back. She had been so entrancing, so open, so . . . what had she really told him? She was to be married to Louis de Signe, a man she did not love. Wait. She had not said that she did not love Louis. Since he found Louis abhorrent, he had assumed her distaste. A sharp, unfamiliar pang of jealousy stabbed him. "Pilar," he said slowly, "what if I did not go north?"

She turned in his arms. "What?"

Deliberately, he repeated, "What if I did not go? What if I stayed and you lived with me?"

Her voice filled with frozen panic. "You must go! I am to be married! I cannot stay with you!"

"And I thought you were beginning to enjoy all this rusticity"—his voice hardened—"or is it merely rustics that you enjoy?"

"Your place and your birth have nothing to do with it. Oh, Jean," she whispered miserably, "I never led you to believe—"

He abruptly pulled away and sat up. "No, in all fairness, you did not. The idiocy was all my own. Goats are not known for cleverness." He caught up his braies and dragged them on. "You have shown admirable patience with my bleating, milady. Fear not, I shall be off within the hour and none shall know of your hedgerow dalliance."

Liliane rose to her knees and clasped his waist. "Jean, do not torment us both. I am promised to another, whether I wish it or not . . . I must pay a debt of honor . . . fulfill a promise I made, even at the cost of my life." She leaned her head against his back. "Please, please . . . do not hate me. Remember that I have given you all that I am free to give. I have loved you."

"No!" Alexandre hissed. Whirling on his knees, he thrust his hips harshly against her. "This is what you love. You need not whisper honeyed words to flatter my vanity. Be honest, Pilar, you wanted pleasure as much as I, with no piper to pay on the morrow. Go now to your wedding, only while at the altar, do not tell lies of honor to your husband."

Liliane's yearning and anguish were supplanted by fury. "I cheat no one! Are you so honest that you can judge me? You, an envious parasite! What do you know of being sold as chattel? Of having your body and spirit pawed by some uncaring purchaser?" Tears of rage and pain streamed down her cheeks. She caught up one of her saddlebags and plunged her hand into its depths, then flung a handful of gold coins at his chest. "Take your pay! Take it and begone from my life! I want you not!"

Alexandre let the money fall, his face dark with hurt and fury as he caught her by the hair. "Nay, milady. I can claim my pay in another manner!" His mouth came down hard on hers, hurting her. Terrified, Liliane bit his lip. With a gasp of pain, Alexandre threw her down upon the blanket, forcing his leg between her thighs. "I can take you, willing or not . . . I can leave you without pride."

"As you think I have left you?" Tears of sorrow filled her eyes. "So our time together ends like this, with hatred and violence."

The anger slowly drained from him. He sagged away from her and sprawled upon the blanket. "No, it simply ends. I have never yet forced a woman. As for hate, I no longer know what I feel. Nothing. Empty."

"I do not believe that. I have done something very wrong, but not in making love to you. I have cheated us of any possible tomorrows."

He smiled wryly. "Could there have every been any tomorrows with a poacher?"

"Perhaps not." Her laugh was rueful. "I dislike rabbit!"

His own laugh sounded more like a stifled cough. "You should not joke. This is serious. Are we really never going to see each other again?"

"Never," she answered dully.

Alexandre shook his head in mock admonishment. "You are not being serious again."

"What can we do?" She curled away from him.

"We are going to change your mind." He turned her over and kissed her softly. "How do you like squirrel?"

Tears slid down her cheeks. "Jean, you do not understand. I made a promise, which leaves me no choice."

"Promises mean so much to you?"

"Particularly this one."

He was silent for a long moment, then his eyes seemed to darken. For an instant, they seemed filled with stark loss—a wistfulness and longing that made her heart ache. "You are far too particular . . . and much too much of a lady for a poacher."

"Please," she whispered, "the dawn is not far away. Make me forget being a lady for a little while longer. . . ."

Alexandre stretched out by her side and gently stroked her face, as if memorizing it with his fingertips. His blue eyes were as shadowed as the hidden, faraway lake of Lancelot. She had thought of chivalric romances and pretty tales. Now Lancelot and Guinevere, Tristan and Iseult became real, their unhappiness hanging in the very air, this firelit darkness. Jean's mouth was warm on hers, and when he came warm inside her, he could

almost make her forget the promises, the danger that haunted
her. Their passion was the only reality. And then they were
drowning in a wild, fiery current, a liquid tapestry that surged
tempestuously, sweeping them helplessly before it. She lost all
sense of time and place. The throb of her lover within her had
taken her into a swirling, wondrously colored dream, and she
never wanted to return to the world. For this brief, precious time,
Jean led them to a place of mysterious fascination where faery
lights, flickering and elusive, bathed them in a glow that grew
ever brighter until the shower of light blinded and seared them
with molten darts of rapture. Liliane felt she was dying of the
dream, longing to die of this unimaginable bliss. Jean's keening
cry rose with her own as his life leaped within her and branded
her forever as his own.

The ghosts of Lancelot and his queen, of Tristan and his lady,
smiled sweetly, sadly, then whispered away.

Liliane slept in Jean's arms. Her sleep was haunted by visions
that beguiled and taunted her with longing and fear of loss. A
cold wind chilled her as it wailed mournfully through her fitful
dreams. Since leaving Spain, she had felt that wind each night;
it was filled with terrible faces that pressed against hers, pressed
until she could not breathe. Jacques was a monstrous gargoyle,
Louis a creeping gnome. She flailed out desperately, reaching
for Jean, but the place where he had been was barren as a desert.
Her eyes flicked open.

Jean was gone. Heartsick with disbelief, Liliane stared at the
blanket where he'd lain beside her. Shivering in the damp dawn,
she sat up. The feeble light barely penetrated the gloom, but she
saw that Jean's weapons were missing. Her saddlebags were
neatly propped nearby; the gold she had flung at him was still
scattered across the stone floor. The fire had sunk into gray ashes,
and the barren cold of the stone floor had seeped into her bones
and entered her heart. Jean had left her without a word of farewell. She was alone with her nightmarish faces.

3

Ding, Dong: Oh, Doleful Day

Castle de Brueil
That same morning

Alexandre sneezed. Misery circled him like a vulture. He had
left his destrier in the lean-to for Pilar and run all the way to
Castle de Brueil through the sullen dawn showers. Now the
morning was as bright and fresh as a new coin, but he felt dull
and exhausted. Wheezing, he had staggered into the castle and
up to his room. He had called weakly for his manservant, Yves,
to bathe, shave and dress him for the wedding. Inert, he lay in
the bath water brought from the skullery. Through slitted lids he
watched Yves warily circle him with the shaving blade. Yves
was wise to be wary. Alexandre felt like cutting a throat—his
own. Miserable, he submerged himself in the cold water. Pilar,
as out of reach as the moon, must even now be riding to Louis.

Liliane rose in the saddle as Castle de Brueil came into view.
Rising high and gray upon granite, it towered above the rolling
fields of Provence. Even from a distance, the castle looked dilapidated. While its towers seemed to have been built fairly recently compared to the ancient keep, the castle must have stood
sentinel to the sea for at least two centuries. While not so stolid
in architecture as most Romanesque fortresses, Castle de Brueil
compensated for its vulnerable high towers with a broad moat
and craggy sea-rock base. A long sand spit ran southeast into
the Mediterranean Sea, which curved inland at the castle's back.
Wind-battered pines dotted the surrounding fields, ringing a

peasant village to the west and forming a large copse on the near side of the castle.

Liliane took the pretty copse as a hopeful sign; if the master of the castle had not cut it down for firewood long ago, he might not be a complete brute. He certainly had taken precautions for the Signe visit. His horsemen were mounted at intervals along the road and spaced through the fields. If any of the wedding party should wander or make a hostile move, the Count de Brueil would immediately be warned. Unfortunately, she could not say much for her own cleverness this morning. Riding in long skirts, she was late for her wedding. She had galloped until the horse was lathered, and she had probably left a trail of jewels from her embroidered mantle back to the hunting lodge.

She felt no guilt over her tryst with Jean, only a sharp relentless pang of loss. To make matters worse, he had left her his horse and tack. The black Moorish stallion was a fine animal and probably the only thing of value Jean had in the world. The tack was worn, but it was of good quality. He must know that she had no way of returning his property. Penniless, he had left her a kingly remembrance . . . in more than one way. She would remember his lingering touch and his engaging, mischievous smile until the day of her death.

When she saw that very same smile awaiting her among the gaily dressed assemblage in the courtyard of Castle de Brueil, she almost toppled off her horse.

Upon his first glimpse of Liliane riding steadily toward him, Alexandre's perfunctory smile froze. The left corner of his mouth twitched as his pulse began to pound. He was stunned, delighted and appalled. The wench had lied! She had played him for a fool again, not only lying about her intended, but by having bedded a poacher on her wedding eve.

Alexandre's gathered household was agog at his good luck. Even he had to admit that Liliane del Pinal was the most gorgeous creature he had ever seen, even among the odalisques in the Crescent slave markets and the haughty beauties of Philip's court. She was richly dressed in the stark, Andalusian style with sable-trimmed black velvet cyclas scalloped at the hip, over a yellow, long-skirted chainse and sorquenie with narrow sleeves extended over her slender hands. Her blond hair was caught up in gold filagree net on both sides of her head; the net filet that kept it in place was studded with emeralds, topaz, diamonds and amethysts. The smallest of the rings upon her fingers was larger than the simple gold band Alexandre had chosen for her from his scant store of Moorish booty. Despite her finery, the loosely braided hair beneath her filagree hinted that she had dressed in a hurry, and the hem of her black cloak was thick with dust.

Despite his racing thoughts, Alexandre made up his mind before his betrothed came within ten feet of him. Liliane del Pinal was as much a Signe as her odious cousins, and he had yet to meet a Signe who was not devious. Certainly, she had already proven she was an adept and ready liar. Last night, in the midst of all her lies, his bride to be had said she owed a promise even at cost of her life. That promise was probably to Jacques de Signe, and had something to do with this marriage. On top of her lies, she had enjoyed him as a lover, gotten rid of him and acquired his horse, all at no cost to herself. One thing she'd told him rang true: she wanted no marriage with Alexandre de Brueil. And last night, Alexandre de Brueil had behaved like a swain smitten with his first love. Well, until he took her measure, she was not going to get the upper hand with *his* ring on her finger. And by damn, he would have his horse back!

With shaking hands Liliane reined in the stallion. If Jean had a brother, he was Alexandre de Brueil. Brueil was finely clothed in a crimson tabard embroidered with his leopard and unicorn device over a gold chainse; his long horseman's legs were encased in olive-green hose with tawny ankle-length boots. His neatly trimmed, auburn curls glinted in the sun. He was also clean-shaven. Despite his rich clothes, he was Jean's twin—or was he? Could even brothers have the same vivid blue eyes, that irresistably reckless smile? And then she saw the difference in the smile: Alexandre de Brueil's was tight-lipped, as if he had swallowed a rusty horseshoe.

The mass of people in the courtyard were staring at her as she gaped at her bridegroom, and she suddenly realized that she must stop peering as if she'd been sold the wrong goods. "Count de Brueil?" she ventured hesitantly.

"I am at your service," answered Brueil, his gaze hard. "You are the Countess del Pinal, I presume."

Liliane saw no trace of recognition in his expression. He surveyed her coldly, then glanced about as if to look for her missing retainers. She saw that Jacques's eyes narrowed in irritation and Louis looked as if he would like to strangle her. He and Jacques must have searched for her all night before they had given up and come to make excuses to Breuil for her lateness. They must have feared that she would not come at all. Good! She'd had her first tiny ounce of revenge against them. She enjoyed thinking of their unease among so many armed castellans in an enemy camp. Six burly guards had intercepted her a short distance from the castle and escorted her across the narrow drawbridge into the cobbled courtyard. The Messieurs de Signe must have been received by a large complement of guards. Castle de Brueil was a tidy fortress and the castellans on the ramparts were sharp-eyed. The Signe party, shorn of their escort beyond the moat, must have squirmed for many an hour.

"We meet at last, *Monsieur le Comte,*" she murmured, watching Brueil. His uncanny resemblance to Jean still made her uneasy.

"I trust your journey was pleasant," Alexandre replied with a bland smoothness that only made her more uneasy. Why should he be annoyed unless he had been prepared to dislike her on sight? Was he piqued because she was late or . . . because he was Jean . . . because she had fooled him? But how could it be? How could he have come so far afoot in time to dress and greet Jacques and Louis?

"The journey was pleasant," she replied with feigned lightness, "so much so, I fear I dawdled. I do apologize for being late." She extended her hand to Jacques. "Uncle. Cousin." She did not bother to look at Louis.

Jacques, obliged to help her down from the saddle, wheezed slightly as he lowered her to the paving. "Dear Liliane. We were a little concerned at your tardiness. But, then"—he patted her hand—"we were sure that once you realized the time, you would ride as if your life depended on not offending the count."

Easing her hand from Jacques's, Liliane glanced up at Alexandre de Brueil. "I came on the wings of love and a very fine horse, Uncle. We Signes are great romantics, Count, particularly Louis. Sometimes I really believe he would kill for love . . . if he could just find the right girl."

Louis gave her a venomous look. She flashed him a bright smile. Then as if he were not worth her attention, Liliane turned to scan the de Brueil retainers standing three deep behind the Signe party. Brueil could not afford matched livery for them, but they looked alert and well fed, not dull-eyed and verminous as were so many of her uncle's servants, even in their celebration finery. She recognized Signe relatives in the crowd; among Brueil's people were only castellans and servants.

"My household," Brueil said, indicating with a sweep of his hand. "My mother trained them well. I believe you will find them courteous and willing." His tone said that he did not much care whether she did or not, only that he did not encourage her to meddle with their management.

Liliane nodded to the retainers who bowed en masse. Alexandre led the party indoors, and then Liliane was greeted by a stark great hall with the customary window slits replaced on one side by hallways; the larger one led to the bailiwick, armory and kitchens; the other small hall probably led to the upper chambers. Fresh reeds were strewn about the floor, and the place was scrupulously clean, but no bright banners and tapestries adorned the walls; no heraldry mounted the three huge, drafty fireplaces. The glassless windows on the eastern side offered superb, if narrow views of the Aleppo pines and Helm oaks dotting the meadows that rolled to the distant shore. At sight of the sea, the knot of anxiety within Liliane eased a trifle. She had lived within sight and sound of the sea for so long that she had dreaded brown inland silence.

A plump berry of a priest was waiting. Hearing the courtyard commotion, he had jumped to his feet. Although he was now composed, the tasseled cord at his waist was still swinging.

With few preliminaries, the service began. When the time came, Alexandre de Brueil's slim, brown hand upon hers felt strange; she tried to imagine it holding a flute. His rigid face did not seem that of a musician; instead she saw him at strategy tables or hidden behind a visor.

The priest droned on at length. Liliane had not heard so much Latin in years. Although it lent majesty to the service, the words grew monotonous as the sun waxed high and the onlookers began to stir in their hot garments. Liliane amused herself by translating the Latin into Arabic. A small smile teased the corner of her lips as she imagined the priest's horror, could he divine her heathen whims.

Alexandre caught her enigmatic smile. Why now, he wondered grimly, does she smile while last night she bewailed this moment? Was her dread of marriage but a sham to be easily rid of her hedgerow lover? His already tight temper was growing

frayed. He was definitely coming down with a cold. His head
ached and his throat was scratchy and sore. Right now, he would
give a good deal to be back baking his brains in the Holy Land
and bedding whores who bit his coins and gave him no trouble.

He should have considered the complications when he met this
demure-looking Liliane, but when he had seen her bare to the
waist in those Moorish pantaloons, her slim, white back curved
like an Indian *gupta* and her tempting breasts scarcely hidden by
his chainse, his brain had turned to suet and his loins to flame.
Now what in the name of King Philip and Saint George was he
going to do about their wedding night? Philip was an unabashed
libertine who would take his pleasure with Liliane, then board
her up in a tower come morn. And Saint George . . . well,
George's dragon-killing lance had a certain naughty charm.
Should he prod her with his own lusty lance and make her squeal
for more "amour"?

After the wedding ceremony had mercifully ended, Alexandre
was content to remain silent, leaving Jacques and the priest to
keep the conversation flowing during the modest wedding feast.
Shirred eggs with cream and leeks, roast pig and lamb with last
season's potatoes, and cabbage followed by good broth loaded
down the banquet table. Brandy pudding finished the meal. Alexandre had been able to afford only three musicians; they now
circled the tables providing a cacophony of harp, flute and horn
that heralded the bedding to come. Liliane's smile was gone; she
was white against the dramatic colors of her bridal costume.
Alexandre knew that he must be pale with tension, as well. His
eyes were watering with his coming cold, and the hand that
clenched his goblet was like ice. The music and cheers of the
assembled gathering resounded like the clamor of hounds about
cornered prey.

Alexandre took a deep breath and rising, held out his arm.
"My lady?"

Liliane stood, wavered for a moment, then rested her hand on
his arm. "My lord."

Amid the din of ritual catcalls and congratulations, they left
the hall and mounted the stone steps. The winding staircase was
narrow, the profound silence of the upper floors making them
seem very alone. Liliane preceded Alexandre, and he watched
her gently swaying as if mesmerized. His head suddenly felt as

if it were weighed down with bricks. He sneezed violently and the echo resounded through the drafty turret.

"Milord?" Liliane turned. "Are you unwell?"

She sounds almighty hopeful, he thought, his resentment mixed with sympathy. Does she think *I* relish bedding her? Damned right, I relish it; she has a shape out of paradise! "Madame need not worry. I shall perform my duty," he answered stiffly.

Her eyes lit with some amusemant. "Duty, milord? Faith, you are more romantic than my cousin Louis."

His head lifted in quick challenge. "Come, did you expect romance of this union?"

"Civility, at least."

"Ah, then, rest assured, civility you shall have aplenty." His hand went past her ear to push open his chamber door. Their faces were a breath apart.

"Have you a . . . less civil, less dutiful brother?" Liliane blurted with a hint of desperation.

Startled, Alexandre hesitated. He saw that she had not meant to question him so bluntly, yet to consummate her marriage with an unpleasant mockery of Jean was obviously distasteful to her. His eyes narrowed as he decided upon his tack. "Scarce two hours under my roof and you have the audacity to suggest my father has strewn the countryside with bastards?" His head tilted slowly as he gave her a wolfish smile. She suspected that he was Jean, but she could not be sure. He would make certain that she knew he was Alexandre, and only Alexandre. Jean was fiction; Alexandre was reality. And Alexandre would discover why she had agreed to a marriage that she deemed so repellent. He suspected that Jacques had put her up to something that could prove lethal. He could not imagine that her character was so black that she would make an attempt on his life, but she was undoubtedly Jacques's spy. Whether or not she was willing, she might give away information to feed Jacques's always dangerous ambitions. He would test her faith before letting her know how fully his heart had lain in her hand; he would not yield it again so lightly. "For all I know, a half dozen of my brothers may roam with the deer, *Doña*. I am the only legitimate one—the only one harnessed to duty. If you prefer another lover, I warn you not to take him too close to my shadow. My sense of honor is keen."

Liliane was both quick to cover her impulsive ploy and take

real offense at his implication. Her eyes narrowed with indignant
fury. "You mistake my meaning, sir! I merely suggest that you
would do better to approach me with something of a lover's tenderness. I am well aware that this match means naught but gold
to your coffers, but does that require that you greet me with
coldness and insults? I have vowed before God and man to be
your wife, and I shall fulfill that vow in every way. My honor,
too, is strong. Needs that my honor duel yours, thereby killing
all our hope for felicity?"

Alexandre had already learned that she was magnificent in
anger. Now, with her eyes flashing like her jewels, her breasts
heaving, she was a marvelous golden vixen, and he longed to
kiss her with a passion that matched her own. He also wanted
to reassure her, yet he feared she would recognize him as Jean.
Alexandre and Jean must remain separate entities until the time
came, if it came, to reveal that they had once been one for a
single, enchanted night. If he took her now, she would see
through his deception. They were too close to the memory of
their night together. He would end by whispering all sorts of
idiocies in her ear, telling her of his ridiculous gladness that
whatever she was, she was his. But she wasn't. He could never
let himself forget that she was Jacques's . . . and Louis's. She
belonged to them first and always.

"*Doña,*" he began, trying to think how he was going to explain not making love to her when she was so ravishing that her
very nearness was making him dizzy. Her perfume mixed with
the faint scent of the fresh meadows she'd galloped through. . . .
"*Ah, bella Doña . . .*" he breathed. As her eyes widened, a
tickling sensation seized his nose. He gave a violent sneeze and
heard his bride's faint, nervous giggle. He steered her firmly into
the room, backed rapidly out and closed the door. His last
glimpse of her face told him that she was dumbfounded but vastly
relieved.

A half hour later, Alexandre sauntered into the great hall, the
look on his face hiding the glum disappointment in his heart.
With the pact so obviously completed, Jacques and Louis went
quickly over the written contracts, then departed for their own
neighboring fief in the north. Alexandre politely saw them off,
then climbed the winding staircase to a turret window, where he
watched them file homeward. The Signes had been picking at

the Brueil borders for nearly three centuries. They would be back, one way or another, and they had left Liliane as their key.

That night, Liliane prayed that Alexandre de Brueil would not change his mind about consummating their marriage, that whatever his reasons, he would leave her alone. Sometime after midnight, she left off tossing in his big bed and began to wander about the spartan chamber. Pacing the cold stone floor she wondered why he hadn't come back. Eventually, she arrived at two possibilities: he was indeed Jean and he resented her lies and aversion to their marriage: or he was really Alexandre and he wanted only her money as revenge against the hated Signes. However it seemed that he could not possibly be Jean, who had loved her. Her Jean would not have left her alone tonight in such confusion and unhappiness.

Sleepless for the rest of the night, Liliane went to the southern window to watch dawn rise pink and dusky over the calm sea. Whoever he was, this cold man that she had married, she must try to reach him for his sake as well as her own. Alexandre de Brueil had reason to hate and mistrust her family. Louis had been vicious from childhood and Jacques . . . Jacques was a clever pig who wanted all he had ever seen. He should have been an Italian profiteer with his love of art, gold and deception. Having little interest in women, he was married to a sweet little simpleton who doted upon him and asked no questions. He was as faithful to her as one might be to a particularly comfortable, cushioned chair.

Louis was less predictable. She took care never to be alone with Louis.

And Alexandre de Brueil did not want to be alone with her.

Life would be much easier if he trusted her. As for love . . . She sighed, looking out at the dawn's elusive pink and gold playing over the gray sea. Better take one step at a time, she counseled herself.

After catching Liliane's Moorish mare, Alexandre was less morose than on his wedding day. He had not slept at all during the night, so at dawn he had gone riding in search of her white mare. The animal was far too valuable to let wander and be stolen; yet in his heart, he thought the return of the pretty mare might please his bride. He had not given her a very pleasant reception, after all. To be different from Jean the poacher was one thing; to be an ogre was another.

The sun had climbed halfway to noon before he found the mare grazing in a meadow near the shore. Luckily, she had not stumbled on her reins and damaged herself. She shied away as he walked his own black stallion near her, so he eased the stallion's reins and let it do the work of herding. He had little energy left, for his cold had settled into his head and chest now, and two nights of scant sleep had left him drained. Soon the stallion nosed the mare close enough to let him catch her rein. As he headed back to the castle, he toyed with the prospect of finding his new bride abed, fresh, rozy and drowsy. Should he amend his neglect of the previous night?

He had gone only a little way when he saw a rider on a sorrel destrier coming across the fields toward him. The rider was Liliane, dressed in her page's gear, her hair streaming in a long braid. His eyes alight with anticipation, he spurred to meet her, but as the couple closed on each other, he saw she was pale with suppressed anger. Scarcely another second passed before he realized why. Having saddled his stallion without thinking, he was riding "her" horse. Quickly reining in, he decided to put matters right. *"Doña,"* he said heartily, "what luck to meet you!"

"As a matter of fact," she replied in a taut voice, "I was concerned about my stallion. When I went to the stable, I thought he might have been stolen."

"No need for concern. I was just exercising your wedding present." With an innocent look, he paraded the mare.

"An uncommonly fine animal," she observed dryly. "Not the sort one encounters just wandering around."

"Indeed not," he agreed with a quirk to his lips. "I had quite a time finding her."

With an easy movement, Liliane dismounted into the budding furrow of the field. "I hope you did not pay too much. She has a cracked left hoof."

"Really?" He sounded convincingly dismayed. "How can you tell?"

Liliane did not believe Brueil's ignorance of the mare's condition any more than she did the rest of his tale. She had seen his skill with the stallion. As he had ridden toward her, he had been half asleep, yet his knees guided the stallion as if man and horse were one . . . as if they were familiar with each other.

Too familiar. Had he known where to look for the mare? "I know horses," she replied evenly. "Particularly those from Andalusia."

"Andalusia? I only buy horses like this one from the Cresent." Aware of the direction her thoughts were taking, Alexandre affected a supercilious tone. "This mare," he lied baldly, "came from Damascus."

Liliane stroked the mare's nose. It whickered at her familiar touch. "The Caliph Almansor's sixth cousin once removed is also from Damascus," she said lightly. "Is that not remarkable?"

"As in coincidence?" Alexandre became stern. "*Dona*, are you accusing me of lying about this animal?"

Liliane's eyes widened with feigned innocence. "*Never*. I would not dream of wrongly accusing you of anything so dishonorable and common—"

"Never have I seen a woman more inclined to look a gift horse in the mouth!" Feigning indignation, Alexandre leaped off his stallion. "Ungrateful wench! Who are you to prate of 'common' when you lack the common courtesy to accept a gift generously given!"

Liliane felt a twinge of remorse. Count Alexandre *was* poor, after all, and he was trying to impress her. To be obliged to take a rich wife from a family he hated must be very damaging to his pride. She could at least give him the benefit of the doubt. She replied in a soothing voice, "Thank you, milord. I certainly do not mean to sound ungrateful. The mare is beautiful."

Alexandre had not expected so swift a turnabout. Had she seen through his charade? "Ah . . . then you agree she is not Andalusian?"

Liliane clamped her teeth. "No more than the caliph's cousin is from Damascus." She caught up the stallion's rein and began to mount.

Alexandre was loath to lose her company so quickly. Her hair was a shaft of sunlight, her eyes bewitching. He was impatient to make love to her again and would wait no longer than he must. Now was also a good opportunity to test her faith. His hand went quickly to her velvet-clad shoulder, halting her from mounting. "*Doña*, forgive my imposition, but I have taken a great fancy to the splendid stallion you ride. If you like the mare so much, particularly as she is more suited to a lady, perhaps you would consider giving me the black?''

Give him Jean's black? Liliane's anger rose. Give this petty, greedy, prideful liar the one remembrance Jean had left her—at great sacrifice to himself? How could this man be Jean when he antagonized her so? Looking up at Alexandre de Brueil, she said quietly, ''You must forgive me, milord, if I decline your offer. The stallion was also a wedding gift . . . from a dear friend.''

Unexpectedly, Alexandre felt his jaw tighten with an unreasonable surge of excitement and jealousy. Brief though her affair had been, Liliane remained faithful to Jean, a man she thought was gone from her life forever. ''A dear friend, you say?'' His voice held a sharper edge than he had intended, for her pensive, lovely face was filled with memories of Jean. ''Dearer than your husband, who stands so close to you now?'' He stepped impulsively toward her. He wanted to kiss her, to make her accept the reality of Alexandre and forget her forest lover.

As if burned by a flame, Liliane drew swiftly back. The revulsion she tried to conceal struck him like an unexpected, punishing blow. It was obvious that she wanted Jean; Alexandre was not at all to her liking. ''Then, by all means, keep the black.'' His words came out painfully, breathlessly. ''I have other nags.''

Liliane wondered if he was intimating that he also had other women. His handsome face was taut; he was startled and hurt by her refusal. The marriage was beginning disastrously and she would have given much to correct it. But she would not give him Jean's horse. ''I have planned a gift that may please you better, milord,'' she said quickly. ''It is a rich gift and one that will outlive this stallion.''

Alexandre grimly mounted the sorrel, leaving her to manage the restless mare. ''I will be much pleased, milady, if it but outlasts a Signe's affections.''

Liliane stepped back from the dancing sorrel's path. ''What has my family to do with this?''

''That remains to be seen, milady.'' With that, Alexandre spurred his horse and galloped back to the castle.

Liliane slowly followed him. Matters were quickly going from bad to worse. She was not accustomed to handling men, perhaps because Diego had not required the usual feminine machinations; he had seen too much in his life to be influenced by his pride or social tradition. In comparison to Diego, this Alexandre seemed a prickly boy. Diego had readily given her freedoms beyond her sex, and she'd enjoyed a position that commanded respect. She was intelligent and fair and she'd been comfortable with servants, castellans and visiting gentry.

What was this Alexandre like? How would her treat her? He did not impress her as being especially tolerant.

Be fair, she told herself. You don't know him at all. Why not tour the demesne and see if he is at least a tolerable manager? You have given him control of your fortune, my girl; and you would do well to discover what he means to do with it. She mounted the stallion and whistled to the mare. As the horse trotted after her like an obedient dog, Liliane smiled impishly. If Alexandre could only see his Damascus mare now!

Stopping briefly by the stable, Liliane handed the mare over to a hostler with grooming instructions, then she proceeded to cross the field. If upon her return, the mare's coat shone properly, Liliane would have gained a foothold in her new domain. If not, she would cuff the hostler's ears.

Liliane was eager to explore the coast, but she thought it best to accustom herself to her prospective duties as soon as possible, as well as see to the future of her dowry. Reaching the crest of a hill, she paused to gaze over the fields toward the deep green forest where she had met Jean. Although only a few miles away, it seemed very far. The way north to the Aquitaine was still farther. How easy it would be to turn the stallion's head north!

With a sigh, Liliane brought her attention back to the problem at hand. She knew the perimeters of the Brueil demesne, for Jacques had shown her maps. Except for the encroaching Signe fief which bordered perhaps fifteen miles from Castle de Brueil, Alexandre's fief ran northeast in a finger from the sea nearly to the French Alps, east beyond the village of Cannes and west over a day's ride toward the Italian kingdom of the Lombards. Squabbles with the city-states of Italy had many times changed the western border, but the Brueils, who were invariably fighting someone, had always retrieved their own. Scrappers, she judged, and Alexandre de Brueil was the worst!

During her ride, Liliane tallied up repair costs in her head. Due to Alexandre's absence in Palestine, many of the fields were overgrown, the vineyards were parched and one of the nearby village wells had caved in. He had made a valiant beginning, but all the work would cost a fortune: a generous share of *her* fortune. Oh, he needed money badly enough. From a practical standpoint his marriage investment would be a good one. The greening land which swept to the seas was lovely and fertile, the forests were thickly timbered and not too much depleted from centuries of wood fires. Most of the serf gardens were plowed for planting. The villagers, like the castellans, were reasonably well fed and not surly from mistreatment, although they were naturally wary of her. They had heard that their master had married a Signe, and like him, they had no love for their predatory neighbors. Anxious to assure herself that Alexandre was a humane ruler, she had greeted them pleasantly and introduced herself. While the serfs were polite, she received few smiles and a good many sober stares. She was sure that the news of her visit would soon reach the castle.

Indeed the news of her roving reached the castle before she did. Tired and dusty, Liliane went to her chamber with just enough time for a bath before dinner. The maids were disgruntled. All these baths were a bother. The master had acquired the habit of excessive scrubbing in the East; must they now lug water for their new mistress, as well? Perhaps when the novelty of her honeymoon wore off, she would be back to a sensible schedule of one or two a year.

Tossing off her riding clothes, Liliane ignored their muttering as they placed a yellow cloth screen between the copper tub and drafty windows. She was relieved that Alexandre kept sufficient provisions for bathing—she had expected no more than a wooden keg and lye soap. Both the patterns stamped on the tub and the one woven into the screen fabric were Moorish, and the fine soap was scented with sandalwood. He had probably found these things in the Crescent markets. In a castle where she had seen little furniture other than the great hall's carved chairs, benches and truncheon tables, to have such spendid bath equipage was a great luxury. However, she now noted that Alexandre's bed was big and comfortable with a few scattered Eastern pillows. Two Roman-style chairs rested by the fireplace, and a wonderful Damascus rug covered the floor's cold stones.

In truth, Liliane thought as she settled into the water, the gray stone set off the bright Eastern colors beautifully. The room exuded a sophistication that she had long ago discovered in Andalusia with its wonderful architecture and splendid mosaics. She missed Malaga's pine-softened crags and surf-pounded beaches. She missed the lemon-scented vales and twisted olive trees; the dark-eyed, ivory-skinned people with their flowing Moorish robes and intricate customs. Sniffing Alexandre's lovely soap made her remember the scents of the bazaars and perfumes of veiled women and . . . *Dio,* she wanted to go home.

Wishing the serving women would go away, Liliane closed her eyes. When she opened them again, the women had left and Alexandre was staring down at her. She had not yet used enough soap to cloud the water, and she had to force herself to lie still under his brilliant gaze. His eyes held a fierce hunger and he seemed to be holding his breath. He was poised between flight and fascination as if he had been surprised by some danger.

Alexandre was her husband and she must make him so in fact, thus they might make a beginning. That they should live separately was wrong. If she could seduce him, soften him with womanly wiles, they might have a fruitful life together, if not the passion of chosen lovers. They might have children . . . and hope. She must lure him into forgetting his reservations. Strangely, the intensity of his blue eyes disturbed her as Jean's had done, made her feel that she was looking at Jean. She wished fervently that he was Jean so that he might take her, wet and slippery, up into his arms and kiss her with that velvet mouth and make her forget . . . that she had married Alexandre.

Alexandre wondered what Liliane was thinking as she lay there so still and silent, her hair hanging in damp strands to the floor. He wanted to wind it around his fingers, kiss her soft, blooming mouth and watch her eyes change, their smoky fires shimmer and flare. The water surrounding her pale body was glinting in the setting sun's long shafts of rusty rose and gold. She was softly rounded, blue-shadowed, mysteriously enticing. The peaks of her breasts glimmered just beneath the amber water. You are mine, he thought: by law, by your own consent and by your heart whose warmth I have known, whose racing pulse I have kissed when I made love to you. You are mine, mine. But even when he started to reach out to her, he knew she irrevocably belonged to Jean.

Alexandre's jaw tightened as he tore his gaze from her, searched for some distraction to block his mind from his body's urgent demand. His attention was caught by her small pile of clothing. "A fair long ride you had today," he commented tersely. "As you do no know the land, I had thought of sending out searchers."

Although Liliane yearned to wrap herself in the towels nearby, she managed to remain still and shrug casually. "There was no need. I am accustomed to finding my way in unfamiliar terrain."

Alexandre fidgeted, still not looking at her. "Apparently. I should not have thought the Andalusian Moors so forgiving of ladies wandering unattended. Do the women there not go in veils?" Somewhat perturbed that she had made no effort to cover herself, he gave her body a thorough perusal, a mocking glint in his eyes.

"In veils," she replied evenly, "and often accompanied by eunuchs."

Alexandre flushed at her inference. "You will find few eunuchs in King Philip's France, milady," he shot back. "While my fief is fairly safe, you would be wise not to go without escort." Glancing at her piled clothes he added, "Also, I do not know your habit in Spain, but in France, ladies of birth do not flaunt their charms in male dress."

Liliane sidestepped the challenge. "So you think me charming, milord? I confess I had begun to wonder." With a deliberately arch glance, she rose from the bath and held out her hand. "As my ladies are unavailable, would you mind giving me my robe? The silk one, over the chair."

He was sorely tempted to catch her hand, throw her over his shoulder, haul her to bed and tame her impudence. Was she *trying* to seduce him, to bait him into bed and whatever snares she could devise? "You do well enough, Madame, but do not take on airs." He tossed her the robe. "I may have married you, but I have no reason at all to trust you, only to end some night with your poignard in my gullet."

Liliane slowly stepped into the gold-embroidered violet robe and wound it securely about her. "Blunt words, sir. Do you propose to evade my wicked schemes by celibacy till death do us part? Surely, a more congenial arrangemant might be devised."

"Celibacy?" His eyes full of her, Alexandre laughed without mirth. "I am not the one with a foul reputation, *Doña*. I shall not suffer unduly for company."

She swept the trailing robe into her hand. "And what do you propose *I* do?" Her lashes flicked up teasingly. "For entertainment, that is?"

Alexandre, angry at her attempt to play the wanton, snapped, "Why not try being a lady for a change?"

Liliane's temper kindled and her eyes flashed with anger. "You have no cause to assume me unchaste!"

His eyes narrowed. "Have I not? Even your uncle and cousin do not know where you spent your wedding eve. Would you care to enlighten us all?"

Liliane paled. Had Alexandre somehow talked to Jean? How could he know? Unless . . .

Alexandre saw by her distraught expression that he was pushing too far. He had to retreat unless he wanted her to guess the truth. "Do not worry," he said slowly. "Your secret, whatever it is, is safe . . . for the time being. But I warn you, play me false and you will regret it. That you are my wife matters naught; I will brook no traitors."

"Perhaps you see traitors where none exist," Liliane whispered, turning away. Alexandre knew that Jacques had given her orders to spy, but he could not know that she had no intention of serving Jacques's ends any more than she must. Achieving justice for Diego's murder was proving much more of a burden than she had anticipated.

Aware that he had hurt Liliane, Alexandre wanted to comfort her but he knew that she must be warned not to meddle in his affairs on behalf of her family. He did not want to be forced to punish some treacherous act, and the idea of sending her back to her relatives was repugnant. If only he could tell her how glad he was that, devious or not, *she* was his bride.

He came up behind her, his lips close to her ear. "Prove me wrong, Liliane, and I will make you happy. You will want for nothing that is in my power to give."

Liliane wanted to turn to him, for he sounded so much like Jean that her heart was torn. "But how long will you trust me, Alexandre, when any passing breeze might rouse your suspicions? I foresee nothing but your disillusionment."

He touched her hair. "Do you suggest I trust you?"

"I suggest you do not judge when I have done you no ill."

No ill, he thought. When you have brought me nothing but confusion and a troubled heart? And yet . . . and yet . . . I had not thought to know love in my life. So much time has passed, so many weary roads have I traveled in fighting other men's battles. And when I so desperately needed peace, I was forced into this marriage, one that promised only emptiness with a stranger. Then you come, my bride and temptress, my eternal torment. If this is love, my hope of peace is forever gone. He stroked her hair. Stay. Stay and take whatever peace I have left. Make my days restless with longing, turn my ambitions to dust; only kiss me as you did one rain-swept night when the fire and the moon were spent, and ancient lovers danced round us. . . .

Liliane thought that Alexandre was about to make love to her. She hoped for it and at the same time dreaded it. Ah, the cruelty of being doomed to live with a man in the haunting image of her lover. But Jean's spirit was gone, gone forever like a far-off hawk. Liliane became breathlessly still when Alexandre touched her shoulder. When he turned her around to face him, she offered no resistance.

Alexandre saw the waiting in her eyes. She was soft in his arms, but the waiting was terrible. If he kissed her now, the passion within her would be lost forever. Although she did not hate him, she was ready to endure him and this knowledge cut him to the core.

Tell her! *Par Dieu*, tell her the truth! But he could not. For the sake of generations of his family and the defense of their demesne, he could not. If she knew he was her Jean, she would know her very nearness made him go weak in the knees. He must first test her loyalty and prove her useless to the Signes—they must give up any idea of using Liliane to undermine the de Brueils. If he could also persuade her to like the part of him that was Alexandre, he might reveal himself entirely. Not bedding her gave him a valuable way to manage her. If he did not consummate their marriage she knew he could always get rid of her if she gave him too much trouble. She did not have to know just how much trouble it would cause him not to pull her into his arms—and into his bed. "Shall we go down to dinner?" he murmured. Liliane looked startled, then dismayed. Not for want of his attentions, he warranted.

"Milord. If you will give me a moment to dress?"

The robe dropped to the floor and his resolution almost went with it. She could not continue to bait him if he was to keep his hands off her tonight and the nights to come. His mind in a whirl, Alexandre adopted a tone of prudery. "Madame, if you know not modesty, pray learn its virtue or I will send you for instructions to the Sisters of Avignon!'' Nearly driven to desperation, he swiftly left the room.

With a low, heartfelt cry of frustration, Liliane kicked the bath bucket over.

4

The Intractable Lady

Liliane was up at cockcrow to continue her inspection of the demesne and to explore the beach. To her chagrin, when she went to the stable for her stallion, two castellans mounted to accompany her. An attempt to dismiss them would avail her little; they took their orders from Alexandre. By noon, she had completed her tour but refused to ruin her first enjoyment of the beach by towing a pair of burly bodyguards with her. Demurely pleading a call of nature, she directed her stallion into the small woodland bordering the village near the castle. In minutes, she emerged from the other side of the wood and galloped down to the shore.

The castellans waited for some time before sheepishly reporting to Alexandre. They found him troweling mortar and resetting stones in an old byre, and their reception was blistering. Leaving them to finish the byre with its muck and stench, Alexandre rode off to find his errant lady.

When Liliane looked up to see Alexandre pounding down the beach on his big sorrel, she knew she could outrun him on the black; but to do so would only be foolish. She wanted no one with her now, wanted to hear no human voice. For this brief moment, she had harkened only to the singing voice of the turquoise sea, the same sea that touched Malaga, her home with Diego. Across the shining black pebbles, Alexandre came surely and swiftly. The shore line was irregular, not so rocky as Malaga's, but with steep cliffs rising above calm inlets, protecting the smooth beaches from the fierce storms. This gold and blue shoreline was giving her a peace that she was not eager to have disturbed.

Alexandre reined up with a clatter of pebbles. "Why did you leave your escort?" he demanded curtly. He was flushed and perspiring, more so than the early spring warmth warranted.

"I wanted privacy, milord," Liliane replied, waving a hand at the foaming surf and low wind-shirred white clouds. "Your castellans are polite but not poetic."

"My castellans are not obliged to be poetic but to be guarding you."

"For what purpose, milord?" she countered. "To keep me safe . . . or you?"

He ignored her implication. "Hereafter, milady, you will go nowhere alone. The castellans have been punished, so I warrant you they will be less easy to lose next time." Alexandre leaned over his saddle pommel, "And if there is a next time, you will be confined to the castle."

Liliane's crimson cheeks matched his. "Do you intend to treat me as a prisoner, sir?"

"I will be obeyed, lady. How you are treated is entirely up to you." His eyes took in her boy's attire with a scathing glance. "I told you I would not have my wife appear before my people in unseemly dress. Wear that garb again and I will burn it!" With that, he sharply motioned her to ride before him back to the castle.

The hard glint in his eyes warned her not to try his patience now. She wondered if he was ill. He sat gingerly in the saddle as if it hurt him. In no mood to be sympathetic, Liliane pelted past him.

Alexandre left her in the castle courtyard and rode out again to resume his unfinished task. She wondered briefly where he was going; he did not look well enough to go very far. No doubt he was just angry, for his cold seemed to have passed. She had not heard him sneezing and coughing since their wedding day.

Once he was gone, her anger began to subside. After all, she grudgingly conceded, her boyish attire and lack of chaperonage *was* unconventional, and her new husband appeared to be an exceedingly conventional man. She would gain little by flying flamboyantly in the face of his social prejudices. Certainly his retinue was equally conservative, and she wanted their respect, as well. Until everyone grew accustomed to her, she must play the decorous lady. And so, to keep peace with Alexandre and his retainers, Lilane donned a smoothly draping blue bliaud that laced at the sides over a white chainse.

Properly clothed, she set out to inspect the castle. As she descended the winding staircase, she ran her fingers along the inside wall. Upon first entering the castle, she had been determined to discover a hidden escape route. Every old castle had secret tunnels and exits in the event of a siege. She had soon noticed the stair's curve did not encompass the entire width of the tower. Another private staircase might well wind within the first. When she had been alone in the turret chamber, she had searched for a door to the secret stairs, but so far she had found none.

Upon reaching the courtyard, Liliane headed for the less frequented part of the castle. The rooms she had seen on her arrival were virtually the only ones intact; most of the ones on the south side at the rear of the castle were damaged. There, countless sieges and wars had left pocked walls and cascading rubble where a band of masons clambered on new scaffolding. Alexandre had wasted no time in repairing his defenses. Two of the workers noticed her and waved furtively to their foreman. By the time his head swiftly turned, she had disappeared from his view, but she knew he would inform Alexandre that she had been watching their work. He would undoubtedly think she was spying.

Putting aside that chilling thought, Liliane went to the kitchens; they were huge, the fireplaces so sooty and poorly drafted that the food cooked unevenly. The cooks were willing and knowledgeable, but they were hampered by their inefficient facilities. While they greeted her politely, they clearly did not welcome her presence. The sturdy maids also performed their work with reasonable diligence but steadfastly avoided her. All the servants eyed her now with open suspicion, and why not, Liliane thought, when they were expected to follow their master's lead? At dinner the previous night, Alexandre had scarcely said a word to her.

That night he did not even appear at dinner. A wave of anxiety washed over Liliane. No one else appeared to be disturbed; they seemed to take his erratic habits for granted. Had he gone wandering like his brother Jean? As the hour grew late and the fire's glow crept low upon the castle walls where she sat alone in the hall, Liliane doubted if Alexandre meant to return that night. If he did, he would not come to her chamber. The castellans were now abed and he would not hear of her "spying" until the morning.

Lost in her thoughts, she tapped her fingers on her chair arm. The night was hers, if she cared to take it. If she were to go out alone, she must do so at night. She could not pass through the guarded gate, but there were places in the battle-scarred wall where a clever climber might wriggle through. Aye, best try her luck tonight, for she knew Alexandre's mind now. The castellan guards were just the beginning; he would make sure she saw no one alone, sent no messages to Jacques. She must see if she could get out of the castle and saddle her horse, if only for a brief ride. Tonight, her sole desire was to escape through the castle walls and return without discovery. In the future, she would have to repeat tonight's performance.

Liliane went up to the turret chamber and, holding her candle high, minutely examined the stones of the inner tower wall. After nearly an hour, she finally found a stone near the floor that was unlike the rest. By candlelight, its shadowed lower edge was set a little higher into the mortar than the other stones. She pressed both ends individually, but nothing happened. She gave the stone a hard blow with her hand on the right side, then the left. With a faint grind from behind its stone face, the wall developed an irregular crack from floor to ceiling. She hit the stone again and the crack groaned open until it could accommodate a body only a little wider than her own. From the look of the well-oiled leverage workings, the stairs had been recently used.

After she changed to dark hose and a short, hooded cotehardi, Liliane took a long silken cord from her wardrobe. Before she had left Spain with Jacques and Louis, she had made her preparations. At her shoulder, an iron mantle pin was mounted with a decorative brass stud; about her waist, a heavy braided silken cord was many times wrapped with knots every span or so.

After glancing out the window to make sure the courtyard was empty and the guards preoccupied on the ramparts, Liliane took the candle and stole down the secret staircase. The stairs were only an inch or two wider than her body and ended abruptly against a stone wall perhaps seventy-five feet down. Assuming that the stairs continued beneath the castle wall and led to some point outside, Liliane looked for another opening, but without success. Finally, giving up and exploring the outer wall, she needed only a few minutes to find the sister mechanism that would open the door to the courtyard. Dousing the candle, she shivered slightly in the murky darkness that filled the stairwell. Hastily, she struck the stone and the door ground open. The sweet, pungent scent of newly sprouting vegetables and flowers drifted into the stairwell from the courtyard garden. She slipped outside the door, then fumbled to close it before the guards took notice of her. She ran carefully over the stepping stones in the garden, guarding against leaving telltale footprints in the moist earth.

Beyond the garden lay the rear wall. Liliane climbed a rubble pile to the lowest of the gaps that would accommodate her body. On the other side, the wall dropped away some fifteen feet to the craggy base of the castle. She unfastened her iron pin and angled it between two solid stones, thrusting it inward, and testing it with a hard jerk. The pin slipped and, on the second jerk, worked loose. Liliane bit her lip nervously. If the pin gave while she was dangling from the wall, her fall would be sure to break bones. She found a new spot, angled the pin until it resembled a fishhook, drove it in and jerked it. The pin held.

Liliane smiled in the darkness. The Moors had many tricks, and she had learned several of them well. The guard watching the wall had his back turned, as he was looking for someone trying to enter the castle, not leave it. In moments, Liliane had slid down the wall. The moat was easy enough to cross, although it was smelly and unpleasantly chilly. Dripping, Liliane scaled the rocks on the moat's far side and crept toward the smithy on the edge of the small market beyond the castle gate. When Alexandre had brought her back that afternoon, she had noticed several destriers and peasant plow horses outside the smithy: too many for the smith to reshoe in an afternoon. She checked the string of horses. The destriers had been shod and were now stabled at the castle. The remaining unshod plow horses were plodders except for one likely prospect with an unfinished shoe.

Liliane was good with horses. After wrapping woolen rags on its hooves, she had the mare untethered and cantering into the darkness without the drawbridge guards noticing more than a slight shuffling among the string. Soon Liliane was beyond the castle, its black bulk rising against the moon. She and Jacques had designated a place to leave messages near the Signe border, but she had no need to go there tonight. Jacques would not expect her news for at least a month. As Liliane rode toward the sea, she felt giddy with glee at her escape.

Liliane would have been far less self-satisfied had she known that she had been watched from the moment she crossed the courtyard. As every ship had a rat, so did every castle have a malcontent. Mentally composing his report of the castle's activities, he had been sitting idly in his window watching the guards' movements on the wall. A stealthy figure under the garden trees had drawn his notice. He did not recognize the figure in the shadows, but once it ventured into the open courtyard, he readily guessed from its undisguised walk that the person was a female despite the male costume. Also, from what he had been privately told of her purpose at Castle de Brueil, he was reasonably sure that the woman was Liliane. With an intrigued smile, he watched her wriggle through the hole in the castle wall and anticipated the pleasure her adventure would give his master.

Liliane rode along the shore toward the spot where Alexandre had intercepted her on the beach. She saw no sign of him. The sand and water were pale, the tumbled rocks echoing the wind and sea. She thought longingly of the forest where she had met Jean, but it was too far away to go there and be back before dawn.

She did not expect to encounter Alexandre prowling about. He probably had a mistress among the serfs, but this thought did not arouse her jealousy. Only Jean could make her jealous. After all, Alexndre had a life before her arrival. Indeed, they were virtual strangers!

Still, she was concerned about his appearance this afternoon; he had looked ill. He had also been filthy, with drying mortar on his hands. She had not seen him working on the castle, and as she quietly passed the few outbuildings that were being repaired, she looked surreptitiously for him. As might be expected at this late hour, all was still and dark.

After checking the last dilapidated byre, Liliane decided to head home. Her clothes had begun to dry, but she was shivering and eager to seek her warm bed. After all her exertions, her ride of freedom was proving less enjoyable than she'd anticipated. Some three miles from the castle, she trotted along a worn path winding near the river that fed into the sea. Beyond a fringe of

trees and down a steep bank, the river gurgled and murmured
. . . with a voice that sounded almost gutturally human.

Liliane instantly halted the nag and went breathlessly still. The
moon shone down through the trees, and flickering leaf shadows
played along the path. The water ran below the trees through a
long, winding black gully. The rush of water crashing down rocks
surrounded her. Liliane strained to listen above the churning
river, and she could almost swear she heard someone moaning.
She slipped from her horse and tethered it, then drew her poignard from the sheath concealed within her sleeve. Silently she
crept down the bank. On the edge of the river, she crouched,
waiting for her eyes to adjust to the darkness. Soon, she was able
to define the shapes of the trees towering above the underbrush
and bracken, the sharp rocks of the higher river, and the pool of
quiet water below them gathering before it formed another rocky
cascade. Among the reeds along the bank lay a dark form that
could easily have been mistaken for a log.

The limp body was breathing fitfully with a soupy rasp. A
hand stirred in the reeds, plucked at a bit of river debris, then
fell limply. Liliane crept forward like a squirrel. She might have
happened upon a drunken serf, who was in danger of either
drowning where he lay or being drawn into the river's current.
To help him was to risk discovery and its nasty complications;
she might well be packed back to Jacques or something even
worse if Alexandre felt so inclined.

Liliane's eyes narrowed as she peered at the body on the bank.
To leave the man would be committing murder, and that she
could not do. She tossed a pebble at him, but he remained motionless. She eased down the bank to his side. He lay on his face
in the mud, his arm and lower body submerged in the rushing
water. Her poignard poised near his ribs, she turned him over.
It was Alexandre, his face nearly covered with mud and leaves.
He gasped in pain at the movement, and his eyelids flickered but
did not open. The water was cold with melted snow runoff and
his skin was icy.

Madre de Dios, Liliane thought with pity and dismay. Better
a drunk! Alexandre must have fainted sometime in the afternoon
while working, then recovered his senses long enough to mount
his horse and try to reach the castle.

Panting with effort, Liliane dragged him up the bank, then she
began to rub him briskly until he coughed and stirred. She re-

trieved the gray plowhorse, then, gathering all her strength, placed his foot in the stirrup and, pulling, forced Alexandre to lift himself into the saddle. While both relieved and perturbed that he did not seem to recognize her, she took care not to stimulate his memory by talking to him. When she finally had him securely upon the plow horse, she led it wearily up the bank.

Suddenly the nag whickered. An answering neigh sounded from an upper glade. Just as Liliane debated retreating into the brush, the shadowy bulk of Alexandre's destrier materialized through the trees. This was luck—she would have to ride double with Alexandre to keep him mounted, but she had another use for the sorrel. After luring the horse near enough to snare him with her cord, she mounted behind the mumbling Alexandre, nearly pitching him off in the process, and headed home at the fastest pace he could tolerate. Dawn was close; she was already pressing her luck. The trip was difficult—Alexandre's large body was limp and she could scarcely keep him conscious enough to maintain his balance. Finally, she let him lie along the nag's neck. The stars were paling when she came as close as she dared to the castle drawbridge. She let him slide off the horse, not bothering to hide the noise, and immediately a demanding shout came from a guard.

"Who goes there?"

In a flash, Liliane had wrapped the sorrel's rein about Alexandre's lax wrist, vaulted onto the nag and disappeared into the darkness.

The four guards looked at one another. "Something's out there; I heard it," insisted the one who had called out.

"As did the rest of us," another guard replied calmly. "Want to go out and take a look?"

Not past his teens, the first guard flushed. He could not yet see the horizon, and to venture beyond the walls by dark might invite an attack from whatever was wandering beyond the bridge. " 'Tis a short while until dawn. We'll see what it is, quick enough," he muttered.

The other guard laughed derisively. "We've the makings of a veteran, lads."

Dawn had scarcely brightened the sky when a pounding came at Liliane's door. She stripped off the last of her garmets, shoved them under the mattress, then pulled on her sleeping shift and slid under the covers. "What is it?" she demanded breathlessly.

"The count is desperate ill, milady!" came the urgent reply.

Her fingers dug through her forgotten braid, unravelling it as she went to open the door. Fortunately, she had thought to pile her hair atop her head under the hood of the cotehardi; otherwise it would now be suspiciously wet. Alexandre, unconscious and borne by two men, looked worse by gray daylight. His closed eyes were smudges in his white face; his clothing was sodden. "Put him on the bed," she commanded. "What on earth happened to him?"

"We don't know, milady," the head guard answered as he and his companion lowered Alexandre to the bed. "We found him fallen off his horse near the drawbridge at first light. Looks like he's been in the river. He must have tried to make it back, but fainted en the way." He started to thrust back the cover.

Fearing he would notice the unrumpled linens, Liliane intervened quickly. "I shall do that. If you will see that the servants bring hot water from the kitchen . . . also more linens and enough cord to string them high about the bed."

Seeming relieved that she had her wits about her, the guard nodded and went to dispatch his duties. The other guard, a broad young man with fiery hair and a stubborn jaw, did not move, and Liliane had an idea why. "You require other instructions?" she asked quickly.

He held his ground. "I think I should stay, milady. You need assistance."

"With milord's clothes or with poison, sirrah?" Her eyes held a sympathetic understanding that belied her ironic tone. "You need not be concerned. I am neither overly shy nor a murderess. My first husband lived to a ripe age."

"You will forgive me, milady"—the young man's head came up—"but one might observe that your former lord's demise fit well with your uncle's ambitions."

Angered and amazed at his gall, she stared at him. "Do you propose, sir, that *I* dispatched my husband?" When he simply looked back at her, she wanted to explode with exasperation. So this must be the castle gossip. And why should Alexandre's retainers not think Diego's death quite convenient? It certainly had been timely, and damnably so.

Liliane glanced at the bed's inert occupant. No wonder Alexandre was reluctant to bed her; he would rather tangle with a scorpion. She sighed. "You are to be commended for your loyalty, guardsman, if not for your deference. Come, help me with my lord Alexandre. While we debate, he freezes."

After they had quickly stripped Alexandre of his wet clothes, Liliane was glad of the guardman's presence. Alexandre's body was identical to Jean's, arousing all her memory and longing. Like Jean, he was brown all over except for the pale band at his loins. However, now his skin had an unhealthy, grayish tinge, and his labored breathing boded ill. Liliane was worried. His illness had the look of lung fever; if so, he might easily die. If he did, she would be free of both him and Jacques, but not free of her debt to Diego . . . or her compelling attraction to Jean. However unlike him in spirit, Alexandre was inextricable from Jean, and she had vowed to stand by Alexandre in sickness and in health. Now helpless and in danger of losing his life, he deserved her best care. She leaned over and gently covered him.

The guardsman was watching her closely. She looked up at him. "What is your name, sir?" She supposed he was not used to being addressed so courteously by anyone, far less a titled lady. Under his shock of flaming hair, he looked at her speculatively, as if he suspected she might be trying to flatter him.

"Charles."

"Just Charles?"

"Just Charles."

So, she decided, with that name, his fine speech and features, he is another noble bastard . . . who might well be acquainted with Jean. "How did you become sworn to my lord Alexandre, sir?"

Charles seemed to become slightly less wary. "I was appointed his father's squire when I turned thirteen, milady. The old count was a friend of my father's."

Wisely, Liliane did not inquire further about his father. "And you became Alexandre's squire when he was knighted?"

"I did, milady."

They both heard the rattle of buckets accompanied by grumbling outside the door. Liliane rose. "Well, sir, you appear to be my husband's friend. I will tell you frankly, there's a chance he may die. I shall do my utmost to see that he does not. To that end, Alexandre and I will both need your help. Be as suspicious as you like, but I warn you, do not fix too entirely upon me.

You may become like a blind hound with a fine nose wasted upon his own familiar hearth when the woods are lively."

Charles smiled quizzically. "I will remember, milady."

At Liliane's orders, the servants hung sheets about the bed, then brought braziers to boil pots of water to steep the rose hips and herbs she had brought from Spain, until pungent steam filled the room. The lung fever, gathering its forces for days, now seized Alexandre with a vengeance. By midnight, despite massive drafts of rose-hip tea, his breathing was a gurgling rattle that had the servants crossing themselves and blaming the infernal, sweltering steam. Without the steam, Liliane knew that Alexandre would suffocate.

His restless ravings were incoherent, mostly in Arabic the servants could not understand, for they would have found his curses on Palestine to be blasphemous. Charles, however, understood more than a little, Liliane believed. Most of the European fatalities in Palestine had not been due to the sword, but to disease and the relentless sun. Shocked and saddened, Liliane listened to Alexandre, until without thinking she took his hand, that he might dimly know he was not alone in his hellish memories.

Charles's eyes widened at her gesture, then narrowed in suspicion. Although she noticed increased antagonism, Liliane was not much worried by it. While she might not understand Alexandre, she understood Charles. He would be a hard nut to crack, but once she gained his trust, he would be soft and as priceless as gold.

Three days passed with little sleep for anyone, particularly Liliane, who was trembling with exhaustion. She did not know when Charles slept, for he was continually at her side tending Alexandre. Charles saw right through her, Liliane thought. He sensed that she was merely performing a duty, with no love and little affection. He was wrong, but Liliane was unsure just how wrong he was. She missed Jean terribly, more because he seemed to be with her in the form of Alexandre. In some strange, distant fashion, she loved Alexandre, but where that love began and stopped, she could not begin to say. She only knew that she wanted to love Alexandre, who could give her a full life and children; she did not want to keep hopelessly loving Jean, whom she could never have.

Liliane found it easy to love Alexandre when he awoke and looked at her with the eyes of a child. She stroked his brow and felt its coolness. She touched his lips and found her name upon them. "Sleep now," she whispered, and he closed his eyes and slept peacefully.

She looked over her shoulder at Charles. Expressed in his face was both gratitude and dismay at the unguarded trust for her he had witnessed in Alexandre. He smiled crookedly. "I am not sure whether to thank you or cut your throat. You are much more clever than I anticipated."

Liliane's eyes closed wearily as she lay back on the bed. "Do you really think anyone here will ever trust me? One *needs* a clever head in this place. Everyone else is befuddled with fear of my family."

"We do not fear the Signes, milady," Charles replied sharply. "We merely know them."

Her eyes opened. "As you do me? May your God protect you for you *are* deaf and blind." She closed her eyes again. "No matter. Cut my throat and count yourself prudent. Perhaps my lord Alexandre will reward you from my dowry."

Charles stepped forward to retort, but he could see that she was already falling asleep and beyond caring whether or not he dispatched her.

Weary as she was, Liliane was lovely, with her shining blond locks so near Alexandre's dark curls that their hair tumbled together. Because of her cleverness and beauty, they will soon think as one, mused Charles. Struggle as he may, Alexandre will become besotted with her and that will be the death of him.

And what of you, Charles? he asked himself. Are you, too, already besotted with the wife of your liege lord? Cut her throat and be hanged for it. Alexandre can live and hope for happiness.

Charles fully understood Alexandre's susceptibility to Liliane. At five, Alexandre had lost his mother and two-year-old sister in one of the plagues that repeatedly scourged Europe. His father, Henri, was rarely at home. He was usually involved in some military campaign, either for King Louis or his own adventurous ambitions. When he was at home, he overwhelmed his lonely son with hearty, bullish affection and demands. He expected the shy, slender stripling to be strapping and aggressive. "Scare off the dogs, boy. Roar at 'em like a lion and give 'em the back of your fists." Fortunately, Alexandre was strong, both in his wiry frame and his will. The old man had not broken him, but he had left several dents. Alexandre, who never cared to be a soldier, was thrown headlong into the violent adventures his father adored. He hated slaughter, the waste, the stupidity; yet all along, he had remained loyal to his one bond of love—his father.

Alexandre and Charles became closer than most boyhood friends. When old Henri shoved his fist down a dog's throat once too often in Burgundy and had it fatally bitten off, Alexandre inherited the estate he had run from the age of thirteen. Alexandre had shrewdly stretched Henry's war booty further than his clerk thought it could possibly go. However, Alexandre made the mistake of applying to King Louis for monies owed his father for loans and knightly service, and when they were not forthcoming, he went to Paris to demand them.

In Paris, he met Philip, who at the tender age of fifteen had already governed France for a year in his ailing father's place. Brilliant and dangerous both in intrigue and war, Philip meant to unite all the warring factions of France under his rule. He was in the midst of recruiting officers for a fight in Flanders when he met the audacious, stubborn Alexandre. Finding the young man charismatic, attractive and persuasive, he allowed him to pry from the royal coffers a portion of the monies due him, and thereby lured him into service to the crown. "As I am raising a campaign and cannot pay you the total now, help me put down the rebels," he cajoled Alexandre, "and you shall have all your gold and more."

To Alexandre, the offer had been irresistible. He would gain the active battle experience necessary to all landed seigneurs and enough money to allow him to spend the rest of his days without having to use that experience.

Alexandre performed valiantly in the Flanders campaign, yet somehow he did not earn enough in booty and pay to return to his fief; Philip shrewdly saw to that. Alexandre was no idiot; after another campaign, he perceived Philip's ploy. By then, however, Philip had infected him with the fever of duty, patriotism, friendship and the desire to see France unified and strong so that her safety would be insured. Time and disillusionment had killed those dreams. In strength lay a margin of safety, but there was no guarantee. One battle led to another, and at last he knew that the fighting would never end. One day, Alexandre found himself frying in the Holy Land for no reason other than to uphold Philip's reputation.

Charles, although trained as a squire and ambitious to win a knight's spurs, had not accompanied Alexandre. Alexandre left him to manage the Brueil demesne. Honored, Charles was adept at his task, but he never told Alexandre that he longed to be in the military. Each time Alexandre came home, Charles found him more withdrawn, torn as he was from the roots that gave him sustenance and strength.

Liliane could have no idea how dangerous she was to Alexandre now. Alexandre desperately needed a home and children and, most of all, a woman to love who would love him in return with all her faith and strength. Liliane's beauty was breathtaking; she was the sort of woman a man dreamed of in deserts and high places. Wildly desirable, she would be all too easy to love. In the last days of Alexandre's illness, Charles had seen she was also strong, intelligent and resilient. She was the wife Charles would have chosen for Alexandre, except for the one fatal flaw of her birth and upbringing. Charles had sometimes dealt with the Signes in Alexandre's absence; they were vipers who wouldn't rest until they saw Alexandre dead. Now one of them lay in his lord's bed. Charles strongly suspected that Liliane had merely saved Alexandre for another day in order to gain his trust. She might simply be ensuring that he completed the worst of the repairs on his fief before her family appropriated it.

Charles half slid his dagger from its sheath, but one thought made him hesitate. What if Liliane had acted honorably? She professed little love for Alexandre, yet she'd spared nothing for his care. Such dispassionate diligence might be expected if she had an ulterior motive, but what if he was wrong in his assessment? At times, he had glimpsed a tenderness in her, almost as if she wished for a like response from Alexandre. If Liliane were good, to destroy her would be heinous wickedness, yet to let her live posed a great danger to himself. She now knew that he was her enemy. If she gained sway over Alexandre, she might bring about his dismissal, even his destruction.

Finally, Charles shoved his dagger back into its sheath. He would give her a little time to show her spots before he flayed them off her.

Liliane awoke to find Alexandre's blue eyes gazing drowsily upon her. His heavy black lashes had subtle lilac glints that made his irises such a deep blue, it was as if he regarded her from an underwater grotto. Those eyes were so like Jean's, with the same sleepy intensity, that she jumped as if she'd seen a ghost. "I am sorry; I did not mean to startle you," he murmured.

Liliane gave a slight laugh. "I am just unaccustomed to being stared at while I sleep."

"It is rude, I know . . . but you are an extraordinarily beautiful woman."

She smiled. "One you seem well able to resist."

He grinned. "You are not quite real to me as a wife. I might resist you less as one of Philip's mistresses."

"Wouldn't seducing one of Philip's mistresses be dangerous?"

"Very . . . but worth the risk, perhaps, in the case of a woman who could dazzle Merlin."

"You are certainly complimentary this morning."

"I am alive this morning. Finding that one has escaped being fertilizer to a colony of mushrooms cheers one up." Thoughtfully, he tucked his hand under his cheek. "My nose tells me I have you to thank for my affability. No one else would have thought to put such stinking herbs in steampots. A Moorish remedy, is it not?"

Liliane put her hand on his forehead. "Do not talk so much. You are not up to it."

"I am not up to a great many things just now; however, only one is regrettable." His blue eyes followed the long curve of her, then slowly closed.

As his breathing grew regular and steady, Liliane eased the covers higher about his neck. Like Jean, he was boyish in sleep, very quiet. Although his face was worn and gaunt from the fever, he captured all her attention. When he was not suspicious and supercilious, he was most appealing. Liliane smiled wistfully. She had not expected to have the rare fortune of finding a new husband as enlightened as Diego. Alexandre was merely acting as an average male. She and Alexandre both had adjustments to make, especially since they now realized that neither of them was a fool. Still, Alexandre must have a weak spot, otherwise Charles would not have been so afraid that she might gain control of him. If Alexandre proved manageable, her task of foiling Jacques would be much easier. However, she found the idea of a manageable husband quite repellant. She might as well be wed to a sheep! Liliane peered down at Alexandre. He had survived years in the military service with Philip, the murderous brazier of the Holy Land, and now half a night in an icy river. Such feats did not speak of weakness. With growing affection, Liliane gently ruffled Alexandre's hair. He might even survive her and Jacques!

By evening, however, Liliane began to wonder if Alexandre would survive his own overzealous castellans. The overseer of builders came twice to inform his master of Liliane's perfidious spying upon their inadequate defenses. The second time she sent him away, she advised mildly, "Given rest, your lord will see you two days hence. I much doubt that my uncle will break the peace in that time. Your defense is King Philip, not tumbledown walls."

The master builder was sufficiently offended to bide his time for three days, and Alexandre rested peacefully, particularly after Liliane stationed Charles at the door to quell the servants' worries. Fortunately, despite his suspicions, Charles was sensitive to Alexandre's condition and gave his full cooperation.

By the third day, Liliane had to contend with Alexandre. His wiry body had been toughened to rawhide in Palestine, and it was that, as much as her nursing, that had saved his life. He had responded well to rest and quickly became impatient at being confined to bed. When he insisted upon getting up, Liliane, used to letting Diego venture beyond his strength, made no argument. Her unspoken opinion was justified when Alexandre's knees buckled at his third step. However, Alexandre was undaunted; too much work had to be done on his fief for him to lie idle. If he could not work on his feet, he would do so in bed. He ordered the clerk to bring up the demesne accounts. Liliane was impressed that he could read and write, also that he managed to do so for more than an hour.

The master builder's visit soon interrupted Alexandre's efforts. At the burly man's request for privacy, Alexandre asked Charles to escort Liliane to the courtyard. "My lady is becoming too pale from being cloistered in a sickroom. Fresh air will do her good."

Upon reaching the courtyard, Charles studied Liliane's pensive face in the bright sunlight. "I take it you know why the builder is with the count?"

She started to walk along the old stone wall bordering the cobblestone yard. "I know."

"Then why stay? Why not return to your family? Surely you realize that the accusations are just beginning."

"Return to Jacques? For resale? Without a dowry?" Liliane
turned to Charles, her eyes alight with anger. "Why should I not
just tie a stone about my neck and jump into a millpond? No,
sir. For better or for worse, I have bought my place here. I am
the *Comtesse del Pinal et de Brueil*. What you and your compatriots think is your affair, but be prepared to either prove your
slanders or answer for them."

Charles straightened. "Do you think it wise to sound threats
at such an early date?"

"Do you think it wise to bring discredit upon me, particularly
over trivialities?"

He smiled grimly. "I see your point; however, the count's
people are far more willing to believe you evil than virtuous.
They will see you as they wish to see you."

Liliane leaned against a column. "My only concern now is
Alexandre. He is not as well as he thinks. You have far more
influence with him than I, so I hope you will assist me in seeing
that he does not push himself too far."

"A neat sidestepping from the issue, but yes, milady, I will
try to convince the count to spare his strength, if not to share
his power."

"Oh, so you think I wish to divert part of his responsibilities
to myself?" Liliane cocked her head. "No, indeed. I wish to
divert them to you, if but temporarily."

"Perhaps you do not realize that I am already the count's
seneschal, milady."

She looked startled, then laughed. "That is true, since you
were not at the wedding. I take it you were away attending to
Alexandre's affairs. Well, that is good. Alexandre should accept
your help quite naturally."

"The count is his own man. To predict anything about him
may be courting trouble."

Liliane pressed Charles no more. She understood his reasoning well enough. He thought she meant to win him over by offering him power as well as her favor. She looked up at
Alexandre's tower window. Charles was right to be wary—her
favor might soon prove a liability to him.

Alexandre was quiet when Liliane returned to the tower. She
already knew that he was sensible enough to realize she could
not live in the castle without being aware of the vulnerability of
its fortifications. Nevertheless, she had expected him to turn

against her for her covert investigating, but he had not and for some reason his quiet courtesy saddened her. Accuse me, she felt like crying. Accuse me wrongly so I will feel less guilt in wishing that Jean was here in your place!

Had she known Alexandre's thoughts, Liliane would have been far more uneasy. He vaguely remembered falling from his horse as he rode from the byre, then tumbling down the riverbank. He did not recall remounting his destrier, or any horse for that matter. The guards had found the sorrel with him, but in his dim recollection, he remembered clutching the mane of a gray horse at some point that night. Someone had been riding behind him. Now, considering his status and ability to reward his rescuer, who would have saved his life, then not lingered to be thanked? His saviour must have recognized him; otherwise, why bring him to the castle?

Alexandre watched Liliane take up her embroidery, his mind still upon his mysterious rescuer. Few serfs had horses and the only gray belonged to a former serf named Pierre le Blac, who lived in a stone hut five miles up the shore. Pierre, whom he had freed with his family for military service, just might be his man.

"Do you sing?" he asked Liliane suddenly.

She laid down her embroidery. "A little. Shall I find my lute?"

"Do, please. I have ever been a restless patient and am apt to require entertainment. The cracks in yonder wall have begun to pall."

Fetching her lute from her chest, Liliane laughed. "When you have heard my singing, you may prefer the cracks."

Alexandre shook his head. "No fear of that. When I first occupied this chamber, I was but thirteen and still fanciful. Often when I was alone, I studied those cracks." He pointed. "That long crosswise one is the road to Cathay with its rare silks and jewels and spices. That lump is the palace of the cruel Dragon Emperor, and the shallow dip beside it is the Willow Tree Garden wherein dwells his lovely daughter."

"And is she wicked, too?" Liliane asked softly.

"No one knows." His eyes were ink-blue beneath their shadowing lashes. "She has never been seen by any living mortal. Only the nightingales sing of her beauty. By moonlight, she is a wand of ivory with jeweled eyes and gleaming hair intricately woven into lovers' knots by attendant silkworms."

"She sounds a bit unreal, as if she were the creation of a clever artisan."

Alexandre smiled wryly. "That is quite possible, for she is a temptress. Any man who attempts the garden wall and looks into her eyes is turned into a lion dog of marble."

Liliane was puzzled. "A lion dog?"

"A tiny, wheezing, ridiculous creature blinded by its own hair. The Chinese keep them as lap dogs."

Liliane pensively stroked the smooth inlay of the lute. "So, the princess is cruel, after all."

"Perhaps she is a prisoner, under a spell."

Liliane cocked her sleek, golden head. "Who can break the spell?"

"A prince who sees past her cold eyes into her heart, yet still loves her more than his life. If she is without a heart, he will lose both his manhood and his life."

Her smile was wistful. "Poor prince. Better he should stop his ears against the nightingales and keep his heart."

"Then he would be a poor, cowardly prince, doomed to wander forever alone, longing for the lady of his dreams." Alexandre lifted his hand in a graceful gesture of both resignation and beckoning. "Come, then, nightingale, sing thy song. What is life without risk?"

Liliane was almost reluctant to begin playing. Alexandre's tale was mere fancy, yet the image of Jacques's gargoyle face grinning above a crimson dragon's body filled her mind. Danger stalked her, and Alexandre was better warned away . . . yet, he would never believe her if she told him the truth now. First he had to believe *in* her, see into her heart and love her, just as the prince of his fancy must win his mysterious princess. Knowing this, Alexandre probably had contrived the tale to let her glimpse something of the longing for love in his own heart. For the first time, Liliane wanted to reach out to Alexandre, not some absent ghost like Jean. And so, for Alexandre, Liliane sang an ancient Andalusian song of love, a Gypsy *canto hondo*, or "deep song."

Alexandre had never heard such a song; it was mostly in Spanish, but many of the words were unfamiliar. Liliane's voice was lovely, strong and vibrant, with a passion as wild as the storm winds of the coastal crags of El Andaluz. The pitch of certain notes was Eastern, and the rhythm and tapping of her fingers against the body of the lute was exciting and exotic.

In the song, a young *gitano*—a Gypsy—fell in love with a noblewoman who seduced him into killing her husband so she might marry a powerful duke. The jealous *gitano* stabbed her, and in dying, she swore her endless love for him in a beautiful *lacrissima*, as well as her eternal vengeance—promising to haunt him in every whisper of the wind and rustle of the leaves, in every sigh of the sea and crackle of his nightly campfires.

Liliane's singing fascinated Alexandre. Not everyone appreciated the earthly, unconventional style of the *canto hondo*, but he found it both terrible and exhilarating in its moodiness and passion. The teasing, taunting ardor of the two proud, wary lovers made his body tense with anticipation. The alluring, treacherous woman who captivated the *gitano* with empty promises became a victim of her own desire. Her surrender was furious and complete; his possession of her was filled with both wild triumph and foreboding defeat.

Liliane's hair had loosened from her chignon and fell across her bare ivory shoulders. Her breasts swelled beneath her cerise bliaud as her seductive voice rose in a song throbbing with passion. As she reached the crescendo, Alexandre wanted to drag her into his arms and sear her mouth and body with kisses. In the music, he heard the scream of a stallion and imagined his own cry of triumph as he at last claimed her as his wife, feeling again her softness, experiencing the strangely wanton innocence that had so maddened him at their joining.

Without thinking, he half rose from the pillows, only to hear the *gitano*'s lament.

" 'In the burning embrace of hell, I am lost to heaven. This devil woman is my love and destruction. Ah, I embrace her as one damned does the ashes of his hopes and honor.' "

Perspiration chilling his brow, Alexandre fell back upon his bed. Liliane might be inviting him to take her, but she was also warning him that having her might exact a terrible price.

As if she sensed the strength of his temptation, her eyes, wide and misty, held his. Whether she challenged him or pitied him, he did not know, but his desire was like a compelling, maddening sting that might only be assuaged in her flesh. He suddenly knew he would never want another woman as he wanted Liliane. That she might feel nothing for him, that her response might be silent mockery, was unbearable.

When she stopped singing, he lay tense as a tightly strung

bow, silent but ready to release all his pent-up emotion at the
first touch of her hand.

Liliane listened to the growing silence after her voice no longer
filled the air. She had expected at the least a polite murmur from
Alexandre, if not the ardent response she had increasingly hoped
for as she had come under the spell of the *canto hondo*. She had
seen the *gitanos* dance, the elegance, the passionate attraction
that mounted to fiery abandon. She had known that abandon
once with Jean, and now she wanted to experience it with Alexandre. With his sun-glinted hair tousled and chainse falling
open upon his muscular chest, he was most appealing. His skin
was so smooth, so vulnerable and touchable. His eyes had turned
that strange, disturbing shade of blue that stirred her, made her
believe that he wanted her to caress him, to ease that chainse
back from his shoulders and kiss him, have him slide away the
covers so that she might kiss his naked body until he was wild
for her. His eyes told her he wanted to see her unclothed, too;
to see her hair swirling about them both as she molded her body
to his and began the fierce, sinuous dance of desire together in
search of another of love's endless mysteries.

When his eyes beckoned her so, why did he still look so rigid,
so unapproachable?

Had her song offended him? The *canto hondo* could only offend a prude; the song itself was a work of art, and she thought
that her voice was pleasant enough. She began to grow uncomfortable. "I take it that you find the wall cracks preferable to my
singing, my lord?" she said a bit faintly.

"I assure you that I was far from bored, my lady."

In the golden afternoon light, Alexandre's expression was so
like Jean's, that of an eager boy alive with a man's ardor. So
often, she was certain he couldn't be Jean, and yet at this moment all her senses cried out that he *was* Jean, and she wanted
him to take her in his arms. After so many weeks of uncertainty,
both longing and frustration compelled her to cast aside caution.
"Yet you appear unhappy, my lord," she murmured, her own
heart in her eyes. "Perhaps you prefer the flute?"

Liliane had hoped for a reaction, but certainly not the one she
received. Alexandre might have turned into a different man.

He was taken completely off guard by her question. His desire
cooled abruptly as he was sharply reminded that Liliane still
thought of Jean, and that her beauty cloaked a swordsman's mind.

To discover his weaknesses, she knew to probe for openings, and Jean provided a major one. Hurt and angry, he instantly became Jean's opposite. "I am not unhappy, Madame," he replied in a deliberately peevish tone. "I am merely weary. Pleasant music invariably puts me to sleep. Unfortunately, your heathen song of lecherous adultery has achieved the opposite effect. Do me the kindness of learning a few decent French songs that will spare us both embarrassment." He sank into the pillows and gave her a sour stare. "Also, call upon the priest this afternoon and make confession. Your moral education is sadly lacking."

Torn between fury and disbelief, Liliane gaped at him. She knew the hypocrite wanted her. Sanctimonious popinjay! She could scarcely imagine that only moments ago she had contemplated going to bed with him! She should have left him in the river to turn completely to ice; his brain was already as frozen as his stifled manhood! Stonily, she rose. "You need no music to put yourself to sleep, my lord; let but your serious nature have its sway. All creation will disappear into the maw of one great yawn."

Liliane saw Alexandre's mouth twitch as if he might laugh, but then he said sternly, "You are impertinent, milady."

"Children are impertinent, sir. You are in no danger of drawing ridicule from babes. Before your heir tries his teeth on your finger, you will be gumming gruel." Liliane stalked out and slammed the door. She flew so quickly down the turret stairs that she missed the muffled laughter that echoed through the upper tower.

A week later, Alexandre rode out to Pierre le Blac's hut. The gray horse he thought might have carried his half-drowned body to the castle was grazing in the meadows nearby, but Pierre swore flatly that he had played no samaritan. "The nag was not in my keeping on the night you describe, my lord, but strung on the smithy line to be shod."

Alexandre accepted his story. After all, why would Pierre lie, particularly when a few questions to the smithy would expose him?

Alexandre had Pierre bring over the big mare, then he examined its hoofs; the left front one was notched from a loosened nail. "That's why I had her reshod," explained Pierre. "She was beginning to favor that side."

Alexandre thanked him, then set out for the riverbank he had tumbled down. As he did not remember precisely where the fall occurred, well over an hour went by before he located the spot a half mile below the old Roman aqueduct that spanned the river to the northwest. Several rains in the fortnight of his illness had washed away footprints, leaving only faint marks where bracken and undergrowth had been trampled. With a hunter's patience, he finally found a horse's hoof print with a crooked notch; also a human footprint, nearly as small as a child's. Serf children sometimes played on the bank; perhaps an older child had made the mark. Still, he was right about the gray.

As he was still weak from his illness, he rested on the bank for a few moments. Sunlight sifted through the new oak leaves to play on the rushing water. It made him think of fishing by the forest stream and his first encounter with Liliane. She had not come near him for days and he did not blame her. Fancy, his recommending a priest to curb her "lusty" spirit! He was delighted by her defiant response, less so by the alienation to which it must lead. Startled by her knowing mention of the flute, he had overreacted, seeming more of a martinet than he had intended. Liliane was also probably annoyed that he was using her dowry money without legally having a right to it, since the marriage was unconsummated. As a woman, even a wealthy one, Liliane could make little trouble on that score; however, if she solicited Jacques's assistance, she could force the issue. It was ironic that he should have to be forced to bed a woman for whom he was fairly panting, yet he was too well aware of his susceptibility to enter that snare too quickly.

The next day, feeling stronger after his foray in the fresh air, Alexandre rode out to the byre to finish resetting the wall. He had been in haste to finish the work the night he had been overcome by lung fever. With satisfaction, he found the project undisturbed. Making certain that he was unobserved, he entered the byre and pried three large stones from the wall where he had lowered the dirt floor a foot below the outside ground level. An iron box containing Liliane's dowry—gold dinars, silver dirhams and the titles to her lands—was wedged behind the stones. Whatever happened to him, the Signes would never retrieve Liliane's money. By much scrambling in the courts, she might regain her Spanish lands to buy her next husband, but any spying would cost her dear.

He took a pouchful of coins and replaced the box behind the stones, but as he turned to leave, he noticed a small, familiar footprint in the damp earth. It was nearly lost under his own prints, but had been undisturbed by the weather. He found similar prints by the door and outside the byre, as well as faint traces of a notched hoof. Whoever had ridden the gray had been both at the river and the byre. The byre was ruined, nearly roofless and empty for a decade; no one had reason to come there, except to look for him . . . or the money. The money he dismissed—he had been too careful in disguising its hiding place, even to the point of sending workmen out to various sites about the demesne so that his own work at the byre would not draw attention.

Why then would anyone come looking for him? If foul play had been the object, he would certainly have been left in the river. Besides, the footprints belonged to a person too small to have considered assaulting him. The castellans were used to his spontaneous forays that sometimes lasted for days, so they would not have looked for him. Bit by bit, he narrowed down the possibilities. When he had not returned to the castle, someone, perhaps noticing he was growing ill, had set out to search for him. That someone had stolen the gray mare from the smithy string. His rescuer was either a small man, a youth . . . or a woman. The first two possibilities indicated a loyal retainer too lowly to have his own mount; the last was highly intriguing. Did he have a female admirer?

His paunch spreading across his broad knees as he shifted his ponderous weight, Jacques de Signe did not bother to rise for his guest. While he had no particular contempt for spies, having often been one himself, he had no interest in nonentities, although he knew that nonentities made the best spies. The spy he had assigned to Castle de Brueil was reliable, dull and inexpensive. "Well?" Jacques folded his heavily ringed fingers over his gold-sashed middle.

"Your neice, the young countess, is enterprising," murmured the spy. "Although never allowed abroad without guards, she has already discovered a way to leave and enter the castle without detection."

Jacques smiled at Louis, who sprawled in a nearby chair. "So you were wrong, Louis. Liliane will have more than one use."

Louis, his stubbled face made no more attractive by the hazy candlelight, shrugged sullenly. "I still do not trust her. She is too clever for her own good. Women like that always try to play both sides."

Jacques laughed. "She is a Signe, after all." His attention shifted back to his spy, whose eyes were modestly downcast. Sometimes, the balding little man carried his mild-mannered demeanor too far, trying to convey his absolute trustworthiness. He was undoubtedly making his own puny, amateurish effort to advance his private profit. Jacques was presently unconcerned, but if the turncoat scuttled too far into the light, he would be crushed like an errant roach. "Tell me, Monsieur, how are the count and countess getting along?"

"With all respect, milord, the count trusts his new bride no more than your nephew." The spy bowed to Louis. "In short, he appears loath to touch her."

Jacques grunted. "That will pass. Liliane is too fetching to be ignored and Alexandre too hot-blooded not to try her. She knows better than to become with child; heirs do not serve our interests. See that she is discreetly advised by a midwife."

"The countess needs little advice in that respect, milord. She is an experienced apothecary," the spy replied dryly. "The count would have been dead of lung fever in his wedding week had she been less expertly devoted in nursing him."

Louis leaped to his feet. "You see! I told you she would play us foul!"

Jacques eyed him patiently. "Liliane has more sense than you. Had she let Alexandre die so soon after the marriage, she would have been blamed, fairly or not. Philip would be at our throats. What better way to gain an enemy's trust than to save his life?" He tossed a jingling pouch to the spy. "Has my niece spotted you?"

"Of course not" was the offended reply.

"Good. Keep it that way. See she gets the note in the pouch."

While riding back to Castle de Brueil, the spy read the note, which was in English. He was not supposed to speak English, but he did, far better than England's ruling Plantagenets. English was an ugly language, but to the point. Jacques de Signe required information about the Brueil defenses from his niece. He would then compare her report with the ones he had been getting. If they did not match, Jacques would know that someone was giving him false information. He carefully refolded the message and replaced it in the pouch. Then he wondered briefly how long it would take him to learn to forge the countess's writing and shove her neck into a garrotte.

Liliane soon became thoroughly disenchanted with Castle de Brueil. In the weeks that followed Alexandre's illness, the place was practically a prison. She was firmly advised that the ruined part of the castle was unsafe for exploration and she was never allowed past the castle wall without an escort. The servants accepted her orders readily, and because she had always been accustomed to a relaxed household, she required no major changes. Also, she was sensible, considerate and deft at handling servants. Her success in preserving Alexandre's life had quickly won her a respect that might have taken years to achieve. Still, although the servants were obedient, they were reserved and suspicious. Some whispered that Liliane was a heathen witch, particularly as she never attended Mass in the chapel and never confessed to Father Anselm.

Liliane received no outside guests and was very seldom in Alexandre's company upon his recovery. He slept in the small turret chamber beneath hers and avoided her except at evening meals. She did not miss him, for his reference to her spiritual health had galled her to the bone. She was convinced that his prim virtue would wither any woman's desire. By the month's end, she was more than ready to venture through the wall again for her appointed visit to the message tree. This time she took no chances on finding a horse, but instead had a page take the black out to the smithy just before dusk when the smithy would have no time to attend it.

After an hour's ride, she reached the lightning-scarred tree that Jacques had pointed out near the Signe boundary. A narrow, ivory cylinder wrapped in oiled cloth had been placed high in a burnt-out hole. Standing up in her stirrups, she plucked it out and trotted into the moonlight to scan it. Jacques's request for information on Alexandre's fortifications was exactly what she had expected. If Jacques knew how poorly the castle was equipped to deal with a determined attack, he would have long ago attempted one. The Signe party had been watched closely during the wedding festivities; she was sure that Alexandre had let none of them see the damaged wall.

Liliane quickly reached for the writing materials in the pouch at her waist and wrote several lines on parchment. In her note she expressed her admiration at the number of armed castellans, praised the ample water and food supply, and marveled at the sturdy walls. Bedrock expanded under the castle and new weapons appeared in the armory. She described Alexandre and Philip as being not only friends, but virtual brothers. She warned Jacques that her ability to leave the castle would shortly end, and he must soon make a decision about Alexandre. On the last point, she sincerely hoped Jacques would be discouraged.

If he went ahead with his plans, she only hoped to catch him in a move that would prove his guilt in Diego's murder. She was certain Jacques would involve her in any attempt to kill Alexandre, thereby insuring his total control over her. If Jacques proposed a plan, she could not only warn Alexandre, with any luck she'd also have written evidence to present to Philip. But she doubted that Jacques would provide her a weapon by committing his plans to writing.

After returning the message cylinder containing her reply to the tree, Liliane headed back to the castle. The sound of the sea's murmur, however, proved too strong a temptation. Several hours remained until dawn, and she might not be out of the castle alone again for some time. She would certainly have the beach to herself at this time of the night.

Before long, Liliane spotted the stretch of beach she had found the day Alexandre had interrupted her ride and ordered her back to the castle. This part of the beach was unbroken by rock. The moon was high, the surf low, sighing sweetly on the smooth, shining pebbles. Liliane gave her horse free rein and for an hour she managed to forget that she was a virtual prisoner, far from her beloved Malaga coast. Finally she dismounted. Part of her hair had slipped from her cotehardi, and after looping the horse's reins about her wrist, she let him tag behind her at the surf's edge as she walked along, absently tucking in her hair.

Without warning, the clatter of falling rocks startled Liliane as a rider surged down the pine-topped outcropping above the beach just ahead of her. Within seconds, Liliane had swung onto her horse, wheeled him around and headed inland. Her pursuer was aboard a good destrier, and her pulse pounded in her temples as she used the looped rein to drive her stallion up the loose shale bank.

She dared not be caught, whether the rider was a marauding

thief or a castellan. In the first case, she had only her knife and might well face rape or worse; and if the rider was a Brueil castellan, she would be in a great deal of trouble with Alexandre. She cracked the rein against the horse's flank.

Alexandre was almost sure his quarry was Liliane. He had seen the quick gleam of her long hair from the top of the outcropping. How the hell had she gotten out of the castle without passing the guards? Angry and determined to find out, he gave chase, but his sorrel could not match the black.

Alexandre arrived at the castle to discover that the black destrier and its blond rider were nowhere to be seen. He hailed the guards. "Has anyone passed through the gates since dusk?"

The reply was negative. Liliane must have another method. Alexandre circled the castle, but he saw nothing save black gaps too high for her to reach. She might have mounted the rubble against the inside wall when leaving the castle, but then she would have had to climb down the sheer outer wall and swim the moat. Wasting no more time, he ordered the drawbridge lowered, galloped into the courtyard and slid off the sorrel. Grabbing a torch, he raced up the turret stairs and pounded upon Liliane's door with both fists. "Open the door, Madame!"

A sleepy mutter answered him, and after a long moment the door opened. Disheveled and drowsy, Liliane looked adorable with her night shift slipped off one smooth ivory shoulder, her hair in soft disarray. "You knocked, milord?"

Alexandre seized her elbow and steered her back into the room. Without a word, he passed the torch low over the floor. Then he saw what he had expected: wet footprints. To his amazement, they were exactly the same size as the ones at the byre and river. Fury and confusion crossed his face as he turned to stare at her. Having seen the same thing as he had, Liliane stared back, no longer looking sleepy but cool and wary. Her hands were behind her back and Alexandre guessed they were locked around a dagger. "Well," he demanded hoarsely, "what explanation have you, Madame, for disobeying my orders and riding abroad at night?"

"I was bored," she returned flatly.

"More than bored, I would say! How did you get out?"

"I applied to the priest, as you suggested. He suggested I pray for a miracle."

Alexandre let out a snort of exasperation. "I shall turn Mohammedan if the Lord grants miracles to Signes! This is not the first time you have gone out at night. You were the one who dragged me out of the river!''

The flicker of surprise that crossed her face betrayed her, then she shrugged. ''Had you drowned, I and my family would have been blamed. You would have been in no condition to deny that you had been clapped on the head.''

Her blunt, apparent indifference made his blood run cold. ''You are in a dangerous position, milady. For saving my life, I owe you a fair hearing, but do not tread too heavily upon my indulgence.''

She lifted her chin defiantly. ''If I defended my disobedience with wifely concern for your safety, would you believe me?''

Now Alexandre was startled. He would have given his horse to be certain that she cared for him, but everything he knew of her decreed that she was a liar. He was silent for a long moment, then he said slowly, ''Your solicitude presents an entrancing idea, but I'd sooner believe a camel would rather kiss than spit.''

Her face became even more guarded. ''Well then?''

''Well then, tonight I was hale and hearty upon riding out. Did you assume I might land in another river?''

''Why not, when my uncle is apparently so enterprising?''

''He is not so stupid as to come for me while the honeymoon linens are scarcely rumpled. A far duller mentor than Philip might consider suspect your becoming my heiress so quickly.'' He thrust the torch near her face. ''Your demise, my good wife, would cause considerably less clamor. Now, what were you doing out tonight?''

Alexandre knew she considered him a peevish boy, but he saw his false threat had quickly altered that impression—now she judged him as dangerous.

''I told you I was bored. I am your wife, not your prisoner. Indeed, I am not even your wife, yet you spend my dowry and insult me when you have no proof that I have done more than seek respite from an intolerable existence.''

Alexandre remained implacable, particularly as a black thought had just occurred to him. Most likely she had been on some Signe errand, but what if she had gone looking for Jean? ''Did that respite include meeting a lover?'' he snapped.

Liliane went white. ''My crimes mount apace! Why not accuse me of conjuring spells over the sea to wash Castle de Brueil into its depths? Would that I had a lover, at the least a man who does not perpetually look at me as if I am a demon in female form!''

Alexandre let out a short sound of exasperation. Liliane would roast before she told him more than she wanted. For the time being he must stew in his own juices of jealousy and suspicion, but sooner or later she would make another slip. He was sure that Liliane had carried out some kind of rendezvous. His surest tactic was to provoke her into sneaking out again, so he could follow her. Her purpose in leaving the castle might be innocent, but if she was indeed bent on treason or infidelity, it would mean the end of them; a realization that sickened him. ''I owe you my life, Liliane,'' he finally whispered. ''For that I give you tonight. If you cross me again after tomorrow's dawn, you will sorely regret it.''

She did not doubt him. His expression looked fierce in the flickering torchlight. ''Then do not imprison me,'' she said evenly. ''I cannot live like this.''

''Yet you *are* alive—better that than drawing an arrow in the back from an edgy castellan.'' Suddenly feeling weak as he realized the risks she had been running on her nocturnal forays, Alexandre left her before she could detect his vulnerability.

The next morning Alexandre examined the castle base beneath the breaks in the wall. He found Liliane's tracks on both sides, and some holes and scratches in the lowest gap. As his fief bordered near the Alps, Alexandre was no stranger to mountaineering. Liliane had obviously used some sort of rappeling tool. Had he not once seen her expertly spear a fish, he would not have believed a woman to be so audacious and capable. Searching her chest in the master chamber, he found nothing and returned the contents so that they appeared undisturbed.

After giving the derelict wall guard a ferocious dressing down and a six-month bout of armor polishing at dawn with the squires, Alexandre summoned Charles. ''I need someone I can trust to keep his eyes open and mouth shut on the north wall night watch for a time. Will you take on the task?''

Charles's brown eyes narrowed. ''Of course. Do you expect trouble?''

''Indirectly.'' From the tower window, Alexandre pointed out the gaps. ''I want all the holes filled except for the two lowest ones at right. If anyone tries to get in or out of them, don't try to stop them, but come posthaste to me.''

''Done.''

The snare was arranged; now for the bait.

Four days later, Alexandre had a scullery boy slip a message to Liliane while she was working at his mother's old loom. The boy nervously twisted his grimy hands. "The gentleman said you would give me a silver penny, *Madame la Comtesse*.''

''What gentleman?''

''A dark, rich gentleman about so high''—he indicated—''with shoulders so.''

Louis, Liliane decided. Except that Louis would not send a message this way. Jacques claimed that he had no agents in the castle, which might well be a lie, but he had also insisted that the tree would be their sole vehicle of exchange unless he heard differently from her. She handed back the message unread and gave the boy his penny. "Take this, boy, but bring me no more messages from strange gentlemen. Give them instead to my husband, the count, with my compliments." Whether Alexandre or Jacques had sent the note, she would not be caught in the middle of their maneuvers.

Alexandre, having half expected her to refuse the message, rewrote it, then invited her to a private dinner in their room. For the occasion, Liliane wore her finest garments and maintained a steely composure even when he served her the opened ''Louis'' message upon her plate. ''A gentleman wishes an assignation,'' he observed laconically.

''Indeed?'' Liliane daintily removed the message from her plate. ''No doubt you will discourage the reckless fellow?''

''I leave that to you, milady.'' Alexandre lounged back in his chair with feigned carelessness.

Liliane took up her goblet. ''Surely my refusal to accept his petition should be discouragement enough for this mysterious suitor, milord.''

''Were I susceptible to your charms, milady, it would not discourage me.'' Alexandre smiled humorlessly. ''I bid you read the letter, milady, and answer as you see fit.''

With a patient shake of her head, Liliane did as Alexandre ordered, only to feel as if the parchment had exploded under her fingers. It was not a ''Louis'' note but a message from Jean! In

French was scrawled, "England looked cold, after all, so I shall wait where it is warm. Come fishing."

Alexandre watched Liliane's fingers tremble. "Afraid you will catch a shark?"

I live with one, Liliane thought angrily. Why should I be afraid of another? She tossed the note back on the plate. "This note makes absolutely no sense and it is unsigned. It might have been sent by anyone."

"Anyone who can read and write that is. At Castle de Brueil, that would include Charles, who is far from fond of you; my clerk, who loathes women in general; and Father Anselm, who loathes only deceit—and spies and faithless women would seem to fall into that category."

Outside in the turret, Jacques's spy placed his ear closer to the bedchamber door. An unknown element had come into the game! He had altered his own report to Jacques so that it matched Liliane's. Had either of them told Jacques the truth about Alexandre's defenses, he would shortly have had to seek new employment. Having but lately come to his treacherous trade, the spy was not yet expert, but he was steadily becoming more adept. To successfully doublecross a master of intrigue as seasoned as Jacques de Signe took solid skill which he was diligently trying to acquire. He was delighted by Liliane's arrival, for she could be used to keep Jacques dangling; that she was betraying Jacques as well was of no consequence. He could easily ensure that Liliane appeared trustworthy to Jacques for as long as it was to his advantage, then he'd trip her up and raise his price.

If he discredited her now, she would be useless to him. The spy listened carefully. Alexandre seemed to think that Liliane had a lover, and he was now baiting her. Just as Alexandre started to speak again, the spy heard Liliane rise from her chair.

"If you fancy duplicity at every turn, milord, you will fret yourself into an early grave long before any enemy can put you there!" With that, the spy heard her go to the window, swiftly followed by Alexandre. A rousing quarrel ensued, the words flying so quickly that they were hard to make out. The spy sighed. At this rate, Liliane would not long be married to Alexandre.

Over the next few weeks, the hostility between Alexandre and Liliane hung like a thundercloud over the household. The couple never fought before the servants, but many a battle raged behind closed doors. Jacques's spy was a trifle perplexed. Alexandre seemed convinced that Liliane had a lover, but so far, he himself had seen no evidence of her dalliance. Was Alexandre sharper than he'd thought, staging a jealous show to pave the way for formally accusing Liliane of infidelity to the Church and Crown—and ridding himself of her?

5

The Irresistible Bait

Castle de Brueil
June 1189

As the golden balmy days of early summer passed, Liliane became increasingly miserable, and it seemed that Alexandre was bent on making her so. Not that he continued to bait her. After the first few days, he withdrew into himself with a brooding tension that promised ill when he finally exploded. All that she might have accomplished in her marriage was now lost. She was off balance, her hopes for a happy marriage dashed. Nothing remained for her but deadly duty.

Liliane was especially wretched now that she knew Jean had returned. Although her entire being longed for him, she dared not go to him. Not only was she too aware that to be discovered together was a terrible danger, but her strict sense of honor prohibited her willful pursuit of him. Outweighing her moral and practical reservations was her fear that she might weaken in her determination to win justice for Diego. Yet day by day she endured Alexandre's bitter silence, his wordless accusation and reproach, and she wondered with growing despair how she would ever make matters right. With Philip's influence and support, Alexandre might very well divorce her, whether or not he could prove just cause. Women had few legal rights—even less against a royal favorite! Without her dowry, which Alexandre might well retain, Liliane was powerless.

Liliane anxiously awaited the monthly word from Jacques that might give her the means to ruin him. Then she would either prove her loyalty to Alexandre or, if he continued in his hostile treatment of her, she could complete her mission of gaining justice for Diego, then seek a divorce and return to Spain. One faint hope illumined that prospect, but to think that Jean might accompany her into poverty was foolish. Besides, in Alexandre's present frame of mind, he might well have answered Jean's note with word of her death . . . and it would be better for Jean if he had! At that thought, Liliane's heart twisted like a broken harp string as she bent over the tapestry she had begun for the barren great hall.

While she worked, another terrible possibility taunted her. What if Alexandre had forced the messenger boy to reveal the man who had sent him? What if he had devised some way to lead Jean into a trap? If so, Jean might already have been discovered! What revenge would Alexandre take for her infidelity with his own brother? A sick fear haunted her. Had Jean been found in the lodge? Had Alexandre killed him? She should have immediately warned Jean to fly from danger, yet she would have most certainly been caught, and Jean would have been more at risk than ever.

Liliane knew that she was being watched, and not just by Alexandre's two aunts, who plied their needles at her side. To visit and inspect the bride, the women had paused on their annual jaunt to Arles. Their dislike and general mistrust of the Signes were barely masked by chill politeness. The way their needles stabbed the long expanse of the tapestry made Liliane think they wished they were stabbing her. It was obvious that her rich wardrobe and striking beauty had excited their open envy and disdain. Liliane was unaware that Alexandre had forbidden them to criticize her to him and his household. She knew only that she was miserable and that Jean's life was probably in grave danger.

Two days later, Liliane's heart jumped to her throat when Alexandre burst unannounced into her room while she was brushing her hair. Since there had been few female servants in Diego's essentially male household, she liked to braid and pin up her own hair. The sun was setting, gilding the distant forest treetops that beckoned daily to her. Alexandre wore a fixed smile that seemed incongruous with the odor of brandy that clung to him. He moved with taut restlessness around the room, his chainse open to the waist and stuffed carelessly into his braies. He gave her a sidelong, curt nod, seeming to look for something, yet his eyes fixed upon nothing, not even her. His gaze seemed drawn to the west turret window and its waning sun. His unexpected entrance and distracted air made Liliane uneasy. "My lord," she murmured, pausing with her brush in her hair, "did you want something?"

Alexandre half turned to stare at her. "I want a wife," he said bitterly. "I do not want an opponent. I do not want a woman whose soft flesh might as well be made of armor, a woman who yearns for another man and lies with every breath!"

"I have been faithful beyond all duty. Why do you yet accuse me?" she whispered.

Alexandre moved to stand over her and, grasping a lock of shining hair, began to slowly twist it in his fingers. "Because at long last, I know what is in your heart." His eyes were as dark as ink. "Poor Alexandre, hope and connive as he might, has never had a chance. Your heart was gone before you ever set eyes on him. Given the whisper of a chance, you would fly from him as if he were stinking carrion." His fingers tightened, pulling her hair painfully. "To whom would you fly? To a lover who offers a delusion of ecstasy? Why dream of a phantom when you can be touched by reality?" His fingers locked in her hair. He drew her roughly to him, forcing her head back and arching her throat to his slowly lowering mouth . . . searing her white flesh with the brand of his kiss. His hand drew down her robe, caressing her neck and shoulders, stopping at her breast. She gasped and went rigid, her heart pounding. There was passionate excitement in his touch, yet a frightening ferocity, too, as if she were an obstacle to be conquered, possessed. As he pulled her up against him, gone was the moralist, the martinet; in his place was a man whose blue eyes burned with desire.

"No!" Liliane gasped, twisting away from his broad, muscular chest, the hardness that pressed demandingly against her. He abruptly released her and she stumbled, nearly falling against the bench.

"Save yourself, then," he growled, his words slurring angrily. "Let all that beauty and passion turn to dust while you wait for a man who no longer exists!"

Dazed with pain at her rejection, Alexandre stumbled blindly from the room. Although he had half anticipated her refusal, he'd still pursued her like a doomed bull taunted by a red scarf. He should not have had so much wine; he should not have crashed

recklessly into Liliane's room. But his savage need for her had
driven him on. He had let his devious secret and the resulting
misunderstanding go on so long that everything seemed tangled
into a hopeless knot. Although he was cunning and successful
at planning battles, he'd contrived a tactical mess at home. He
might sever the knot once and for all by telling Liliane the truth,
but now he doubted if even the truth would help them. While
Liliane might betray Alexandre, he had learned that she would
not betray Jean. At first he had thought she was merely protecting herself, but now he realized she wanted Jean to get away
safely. She loved him! Alexandre thought grimly how ironic it
was that his alter image had practically sabotaged his marriage.

As Alexandre wandered listlessly in the garden, he found it
hard to believe that he had once made love to this cool stranger.
To believe that she had melted like honey in his arms, that she
had been passionate, innocent—his love alone. It was a love he
had to find again or risk losing his sanity. If she would not come
to him as Alexandre, would she come to him as Jean?

A choked laugh escaped from his lips as he stared down into
the rose-covered well by the garden walk. His reflection rippled
as a pebble from the well wall fell into the water. Perhaps he
was already losing his mind! Alexandre had become as much a
fiction as the fey Jean. Who was *he*, this shadowy man, scarcely
more real by sun than by moon? He no longer had substance; he
had become an empty pretender, moving from one pretense to
another.

Alexandre remembered sitting late one evening with Liliane
before the fire in the great hall perhaps a month after the wedding. Their silences were long; her finely chiseled face wore a
remote expression. "Have you ever been in love, I wonder?" he
had asked in a sardonic voice covering the longing he felt. Her
eyes had widened; she seemed startled, frightened, almost sad
for an instant, and he had wanted to take her in his arms, to
reassure her with his gentle caresses. He'd wanted to show her
that real love was not as elusive as she thought—it would come
again.

She had then startled him. "I loved Diego."

Not realizing how unhappy she must have been, he frowned.
"Was he not old enough to be your grandfather?"

"He was a great man. A good man. So kind and patient I
could never imagine his having savagely fought the Moors for

twenty years." She smiled slightly. "According to his castellans, he was ferocious in battle, with strong arms that could wield a battle-ax and swim across the Quadaquavir River in armor."

Alexandre poked at the logs in the fire. "He sounds formidable, but what did you ever talk about?"

"He saved me from being married off at fourteen for barter. Had he been the dullest man in the world, I would have hung on his every word. As it was, he was a fine scholar and far from dull."

"Pity you have had to step down in life," he remarked dryly.

"I did not expect another Diego, but"—her eyes twinkled mischievously—"neither did I expect to have to reassure a man of twenty-six about his comparison with a man of sixty-eight."

Alexandre flushed scarlet. "I assure you I am not jealous."

But he had been. He had been jealous of the soft glow Diego's name brought to her eyes, the gentle tenderness that slipped into her speech. An old man and a lowly poacher had been able to touch her heart while he, Alexandre, could not. He felt more alone with this lovely woman at his side than he had felt even in the sighing desert wind of Palestine's nights.

Upon taking her as his bride, he had begun to dream of Liliane as once, his lips cracked with thirst, he had dreamed of white-foamed rushing water during the siege of Jerusalem. Now he saw her dancing in white and silver veils so gracefully that his throat grew dry, his hands reached out to touch the silky warmth of her, only to find the cool stone of the courtyard well. In its deep, dark depths, he was the only illusion.

The last of the sunset was disappearing, casting the castle walls in rust and gold, just as it must now be turning to russet flames the forest of Jean and Liliane. If he became Jean once more, he might lure Liliane there again. However, if she gave herself to him, he'd have won a hollow victory—he'd know for certain that it was Jean she loved, not Alexandre. Foreboding and despair overwhelmed Alexandre. Catching up a stone from the cobbles, he hurled it into the water. His image shattered, swiftly fading into gathering darkness.

Near midnight, Liliane slipped into her dark cotehardi and hose, then tucked her long hair up into the cotehardi hood. Just as she was strapping the silk cord about her waist, she heard a faint scratch at the door. Her heart seemed to stop for an instant, then its quick pounding reverberated in her ears. Another scratch, more insistent, sounded at the door. She stood frozen. A final scratch came, then an ominous silence reigned.

Liliane waited for nearly an hour before she opened the door a crack. No one was in the tiny hall. She eased the door open and stepped out, only to feel something brush against her foot. She stooped to pick it up, then stepped back into her room and rebarred the door to examine her find by candlelight. Two hawk feathers were bound together by a fine, black strand that looked like silk; it was horsehair. She frowned, puzzled, then smiled as she realized her mysterious gift must be from Jean. The hawk feathers symbolized their brief freedom together; the horsehair came from the mane of Jean's black stallion. Liliane's spirits soared. Jean was alive!

But the next moment, her spirits sank. Nothing had really changed, for all that lay ahead was the promise of empty years. To keep her honor, she must not see Jean . . . and yet he must be warned that his brother suspected her of having a lover and that further communication between them might prove disastrous. Jean *must* leave.

Some time later, Charles made his report to Alexandre. "Lady Liliane has gone through the south wall. The watch spotted her just after I did, when she was climbing down the outside wall. I had to stop him from putting an arrow through her." His tone suggested that he had been sorely tempted to let the arrow fly.

Alexandre clapped him consolingly on the shoulder. "You did well, *ami*. Do not worry; this will be milady's last night to prowl abroad. Have the workmen seal those last gaps in the wall at dawn." He headed for the stable.

Eyeing Alexandre's sheepskin vest and ragged clothing, Charles tagged after him. "Going fishing?"

Alexandre flung a saddle blanket on the sorrel. "In a manner of speaking. A goldfish may not be sporting game in a garden pond, but"—an odd smile played around his mouth—"in the wild, it is another matter."

Charles handed him the saddle. "You may not find your goldfish alone, you know; sharks are likely to accompany this one."

"Not tonight," Alexandre replied shortly. He cinched the saddle and checked the bridle. For once, I am going to have my wife all to myself, he thought grimly.

But as he galloped off into the night, Alexandre was not as confident as he had pretended to Charles. Uncertainties darted like startled deer through his head. His concerns were overshadowed by one overwhelming fear—what if he could no longer *be* Jean? Jean was carefree, with a light tongue and light touch, while Alexandre had become suspicious, humorless and quick to take offense. Pulled this way and that by his bewildering emotions, he had adopted the role of a sober lord of the manor as his only security. How could he be able to play the rustic Jean convincingly enough to deceive Liliane? His appearance tonight before Liliane might well be disastrous. Muttering an oath of exasperation as he entered the forest, Alexandre suddenly spurred his sorrel, effortlessly jumping a fallen log. He had better be waiting for Liliane at the lodge, not galloping in late on a horse she'd surely recognize. That was his last thought before the sorrel slipped as he landed, dumping him into icy nothingness.

A shiver crept along Liliane's spine as she spied a faint light glimmering through the dark trees. In moments, she had reached the clearing of the old hunting lodge, leaving the safe canopy of the forest behind her. Although the July night was warm, she suddenly felt cold and exposed. The stars were clear and close, the trees scarcely stirring in the gentle breeze blowing across the moonlit lake. She could hear only the lapping of the water on the shallow shore, the faint crackle of sparks from the old stone chimney. The snapping fire and the sighing wind brought back vivid memories of the night she had spent with Jean—the warmth of his body, his mouth as they lay by the fire. Her heart knotted painfully in her breast. Tonight, there must be no blissful joining of their bodies; there could be only parting and a loss even harsher than before.

Liliane dismounted and tied the black to a branch with trembling hands. There was no need to stable him; she would not stay long. If Jean would see her to the edge of the wood, she could walk the rest of the distance to the castle by daybreak, thus leaving him his stallion. Liliane hesitated. Far from having her longing dulled by time and distance, she had missed Jean more with each passing day; now her anticipation was unbearable. As she slowly lifted the door latch, she wondered, with the world to wander and new women to divert him, had Jean missed her half so much? She took a deep breath and opened the door.

The face that turned to her from the fire wore an expression that was bewildering. Anguish, relief and passion distorted his features so that for a moment she wondered wildly if this could be her Jean. He had aged; his boyishness was gone. He was as distraught as she. Relief mixed with pity as she saw that their brief tryst had cost him as much unhappiness as it had her.

"Oh, Jean," she sobbed brokenly. "Oh, my darling, I am sorry!" In another moment, she was in his arms, pressing kisses upon his face, clinging to him as if the world might crash from beneath her feet if he should move away. With a stifled groan, his mouth came down on hers. His kiss was harsh, urgent, taking her breath, her tears, making her need for him soar like the night's bright new stars. His hands that had tangled in her hair now roamed feverishly. His desire enflamed her; the roughness of his beard-stubbled jaw as he buried his face against her throat filled her with raw excitement . . . and the gradual, needling thought that only short hours ago, Alexandre had kissed her so, with the same demanding hunger. With a gasp, Liliane pulled away. "Jean, no . . . we must not! I came only to warn you—"

"Of what?" His voice was hoarse and muffled against her throat. "What more need I fear when my soul is gone?" He lifted his head only to bend down, giving her another kiss that made her faint with an intense longing to forget everything but the warm hardness of his body, the heat of their desire. His lips grazed her ear. "You have taken my sanity, my honor . . . witch, witch . . . adorable, hateful, faithless witch . . ."

In desperation, Liliane turned her head away. "Were I faithless, I would not have come tonight. Oh, Jean, you must go! He knows . . ."

His hands dropped from her as if he had been burned. She suddenly realized that his clothes were nearly soaked, his left shoulder and back smeared with mud. A trickle of blood appeared just above his hairline. "He knows what?" His mouth twisted in a wry smile. "I assume you mean your cuckolded husband, Alexandre?"

Distraught, Liliane ran her hand through her hair. Why was he so muddied and hurt? Why did he stare at her so strangely, almost as if he hated her? "Please do not tease. What's happened to you? Your head? Your clothes?" She caught at his sleeve. "Has Alexandre set his men upon you?"

He laughed shortly. "Why should he? I am no one. I might as well not exist."

"To Alexandre, you are very real. He does not yet know who you are, but he will soon, unless you leave."

He studied her. "Oh, I think Alexandre knows me well enough. As if he walked in my skin, I wager he imagines every silky inch of yours that I have touched. In his dreams you lie in his arms, he caresses your soft hair, your breasts so pale and smooth, traces the curve of your smile . . ." He turned abruptly away. "Alexandre may be sometimes difficult, but he has a name, position. Why the hell are you here with me?"

Liliane bit back the fatal, useless words that sprang to her lips. If Jean knew how she had missed him, knew how unhappy she was, he would not want to go away and leave her again. But leave he must. "We shared a night I shall never forget," she said softly. "When I am old, I shall remember a beautiful youth who took my innocence and left me the poetry of his passion. Tonight I came only to warn you that your life is in danger. I owe you that little, at least."

He cocked his head, his blue eyes sharp and spearing her with his intense gaze. "Do you care nothing for Alexandre?"

"Before God and the law, he is my husband; that bond may not be broken."

"I did not ask you that."

"My life with Alexandre," she replied softly, lowering her eyes, "is none of your affair."

A wild frustration seized Alexandre. His warring emotions were like pincers tearing him apart. When he first saw Liliane standing in the doorway, he was Alexandre, confronted by proof of her betrayal. Then she flung herself into his arms, and he knew only that now he might finally have her, that he had to have her. Yet, when she pulled away, it was Jean she rejected; Jean, who was jealous. He was quickly losing his sanity! "What affairs are mine?" he snarled. "This sort? The sordid sort? Will you play the lady for Alexandre and the world, yet moon in your heart for the sinful bed of a thief? Will you cheat all and leave none in peace by being a hypocrite?" Liliane had become deathly pale, her eyes wide and pleading, but he could not stop. "Does being a whore in your thoughts and dreams add a certain fillip to your superficial virtue?"

She slapped him then, an expression of horror and disillusionment upon her face. What had come over her Jean, the man who had once beguiled her so? Choking back the tears, Liliane whirled and stumbled toward the door. He caught her before she could take another step, his hands hard on her shoulders, pulling her close. "Do not go," he whispered. "If I lose you tonight, it will be forever." He turned her to him. Unresisting, she was limp in his arms, her face wet with tears. "Stay," he pleaded hoarsely. "Stay a little and leave me not so quickly to the hideous, lonely years. If you will not let me love you, at least talk to me. Without you, this fleeting spring has seemed a century of frigid winter. All that was once dear to me is now frozen and remote, all my hopes an empty waste. . . . Liliane, look at me. . . ."

She finally raised her head, her lovely, amber eyes filled with yearning and sorrow. "How little did we think that one heedless night might lead to so much unhappiness! Did some cruel fairy bewitch us and haunt our deams with ephemeral visions? And now even sweet memory has turned bitter! We have come to hate the very cause of our distress."

Alexandre knew then that the impostor Jean could not, must not, survive this night if he and Liliane were to have any chance for the future—yet to destroy Jean was to destroy the part of him she loved. There was no choice; he had to risk everything. "Have you so little hope for happiness with Alexandre?" When she did not reply, he pressed further. "Tell me, Liliane. Alexandre is not a monster, but a man who needs love like any other. How could he not care for a woman as entrancing as you? If he seems slow to respond, give him time. He has much to overcome because of his hatred of your family. How can he be sure that you have not come to destroy him?"

"I mean no harm to Alexandre. As I have sworn fealty and faith to him, I would protect him with my life, but I . . ." She hesitated, as if afraid to say too much. Turning toward the fire, she continued, "Alexandre is a jealous man, Jean, and he has just cause; that much you must already know. Our first message was intercepted; it brought me wild delight, but stronger fear. Alexandre has power, Jean, which you have not. He can destroy you."

"And you," he added quietly.

"And me, though not with a sword, perhaps." She took a long breath and went on, her voice steady, "Have you ever considered what might happen if Alexandre divorced me and I were returned, dowerless, to my uncle?"

"A third marriage in a backwater village?"

At his sardonic tone, Liliane looked up at him. "A good deal worse. I much doubt that my husband Diego died by accident."

He frowned. "You think Jacques will kill you?"

"If he considered me not only useless but a threat to him."

Alexandre studied her. She had not mentioned the danger she had run in braving the castle wall again to meet him. He had noticed her damp clothes, and the thought of her difficult escape filled him with awe. She had also said nothing of her sterile, loveless marriage. Obviously, she feared he might linger if he knew too much. He wrapped her in his arms, tucking her head beneath his chin. "Do not worry; after tonight, you will have naught to fear from me. 'Tis time you and Alexandre had a start without a ghost hovering between you."

"Where will you go?" she asked brokenly.

"I do not know. Wherever ghosts go, I suppose—oblivion."

Liliane's eyes widened with apprehension. "Oh, Jean, you will do nothing foolish?"

"No, no," he soothed her. "I will simply fade from your life. But no matter where I go, I will not be far away. Some part of me will always linger with you . . . unless"—he tilted her chin up—"you forget me."

"How can I forget?" she whispered, then could not stop the words. "I love you."

Feeling as if his heart might break, he touched her lips. "Love Alexandre. We are not so very different, he and I. Do not waste your life living in memory. Alexandre is real; he is your present and your future. I am but a passing whisper of yesterday."

You are nothing like Alexandre! Liliane wanted to cry. I have tried to love him, but 'tis easier to love a lump of metal. You are human warmth and tenderness, and I shall freeze outside your arms! Involuntarily, she moved closer to him.

He hesitated, then his arms tightened as his lips grazed the side of her neck. "*Ah, Dieu,* 'tis hard to be noble," he whispered harshly.

When he kissed her lips again, Liliane knew she could deny him nothing. His lips devoured her like a flame run wild, her body molten where they touched. At her moan of defeat, Alexandre's breath came hard against her flesh. In one movement, he swept her into his arms and carried her to the bedroom. He set her gently upon the bed, then with feverish fingers loosened her

clothing, sliding it swiftly off her body. His mouth sought her
bare flesh as though he were starved for her eager warmth. Liliane locked her arms about his neck, her passionate response
banishing any last thought of restraint. He broke away for an
instant to undress, then embraced her again. She felt his manhood press hot and rigid against her body in the darkness. He
buried his face against her pearl-white breasts, trailed burning
kisses across her smooth stomach. Then, unable to wait any
longer, he entered her. His gasp of pleasure mingled with hers.
So many nights of wanting each other had culminated in this one
wild moment. Alexandre's lips played over Liliane's throat and
face as he filled her. She was so soft, fit so perfectly—it was as
if their souls had joined as well as their bodies. An unearthly
music seemed to spin away the harsh world. Their hearts and
blood pulsed to that impatient music. Their driving rhythm
quickened to a high pitch, a piercing vibrato of naked desire that
swept to a dazzling crescendo. The after-echoes of their passion
drifted over them like a faraway, lilting harp.

Liliane touched her love's face with a lingering, wondering
caress. "Can our delight be a sin when it is so fair and sweet?"
she whispered sadly. "All the happiness I shall ever want in the
world is within this room. I shall never come here again, yet
wherever I go, your flute will sound in the wind, and I'll hear
your elusive voice in the sea's murmur. For my sake, live by
some distant shore whose waves may someday play upon this,
with fingers of soft foam that I may touch. Live not alone, but
take a wife and have children, that I also may hear their bubbling
laughter in the sea." Her eyes glistened with tears she longed to
shed. "Ah, the years, the heavy years press down upon me even
now. Hold me, my love, and keep time away for a little. Like
some puny Atlas, I am too soon grown weary. . . ." A wistful
smile curved her mouth. "Tell me of the days before I knew you
so that I may have memories without burden. Tell me of your
adventures, the desert on a dreamless night when the stars were
gleaming crystal globes, cool fountains and singing houris . . ."

Cuddling her close, Alexandre spun her stories of beauty and
danger, but it was not long before she slept. By moonlight, he
saw the smudges of fatigue beneath her eyes. Because of his false
messages and her concern for him, she had not slept for many
nights. Feelings of guilt and tenderness overcame him. With a
feather's touch, he stroked her hair. Even if I be damned and die

for it, he thought fiercely, I love her! She has freely given me the greatest happiness I have ever known. Whatever brief delusion this may be, I shall not wreck it with more suspicion. You will not be sorry to be the love of Alexandre de Brueil, my sweeting, nor will you become weary longing for another who was kinder and more boon companion than he. I shall be all to thee—with a boy's innocent ardor and a man's knowing gentleness. Sleep, my pretty Atlas; you have found one to take the world from your slight shoulders.

Alexandre realized later that his own restless nights must have caught up with him, when he was startled awake by Liliane's muffled cry. She struggled in his arms, flailing out in the throes of a nightmare. "No! Do not cage me! I can bear anything but that!" she sobbed. "Lonely, lonely . . . oh, Jean, where are you?"

Alexandre was profoundly shocked. She had appeared so cool, so unaffected during her confinement at Castle de Brueil, that he had not realized what torment his restrictions had caused her. He pulled her close and kissed her softly. "I am here, my darling. Do not be afraid. You are not alone."

Liliane's eyelids flickered, then her amber eyes opened dazedly. She gazed blankly up at him for a moment, not recognizing him, then drew him down to her. "Love me," she whispered. "Take my soul lest it wither with the summer's flight. Love me. Carry me into that heaven for lovers that is earthly paradise." Her kiss was intoxicating, so sweetly nectared a flower beneath his lips that he drank deeply, savoring with the leisure of a browsing bee. His slow caresses ignited a fiery excitement within her as he bared her body to taste the silken undercurves of her breasts, the smoothness of her stomach and the sensitive warmth of her inner thighs. The buds of her breasts were fragile pink blooms against his lips. As Alexandre made love to Liliane, their sighs and whispers became one with the breeze over the pond, their kisses lingering like moonlight drifting through the forest darkness.

They lay on the large white bed, their slim bodies intricately entwined. Alexandre explored his lover, finding the tiny, hidden rose of her sex, tasting, persuading, delicately arousing her until she quivered, crying out to him, for him. With tantalizing slowness his shaft slipped between her petals, lightly sliding across her velvet softness. Slowly, moment by moment, he prolonged

the aching pleasure of pleasing her. Then her dewy moistness
enclosed him, her magic swirling about him, her body a steam-
ing garden with lambent, glowing flowers that lured him with its
scarce-touched mysteries.

Liliane wrapped her golden hair about Alexandre, stroking
him, shyly touching between his thighs with the light, bewitching brush of a firefly. Her lips were at his throat, his chest, her
body translucent as the moon on water, flowing into him, a silver
shimmer of desire. He became lost in her, no longer resisting
the swelling rhythm that carried them both into a darkness deeper
than the forest night. They discovered a new night, intoxicating
in its secrecy and splendid sensuality. Their quickening bodies
were shining now, wreathed in dampness and desire. At the
height of their ecstasy, the firelights amid the myriad flowers
exploded and fell to lie aglow upon the musky earth within the
lovers' twilight garden, where Liliane slept like Eve, her innocence too freshly and sweetly lost to be yet missed.

When Liliane awoke hours later, she found that her paradise
had disappeared, and with it, her forbidden Adam. Just as he
had done upon their first night together, Jean had set silently
upon his way, leaving her to awaken alone. As she sat up and
saw the moonlight waning upon his empty pillow, Liliane involuntarily moaned, heartsick at his desertion. Why? she thought,
angry at herself. Why do I so miss Jean's bidding me farewell?
He is right to avoid such pointless agony, and yet . . . ah, you
unforgiving saints, he is gone—as if death had stolen him in the
night to leave me mourning like Magdalene.

In the damp darkness, a final cold memory chilled her—Jean
had not asked her to go with him this time. Had he known she'd
refuse, or did he foresee that in the guilt and hardship of their
escape they would in time turn on each other? In her despair,
the bleakest of all thoughts seized her—was she merely a com-
plication in his life that he was already relieved to leave behind?

Liliane didn't know how long she sat numbly wrapped in their
sheets, but too late she realized that the dawn was dangerously
near. Coming to her senses, she quickly dressed and checked
the shed, relieved to see that Jean had left her the black destrier.
With a final glance at the cabin where she had known such happiness, she mounted and galloped off toward the castle.

In the wooded copse outside Castle de Brueil, she slid off the
black and slapped his rump, sending him off for Alexandre to

find browsing. Then she turned and raced through the copse. Breathing hard, Liliane crouched at the edge of the forest and intently scanned the castle battlements; luckily none of the five guards were paying attention to the copse. The sky was growing lighter by the moment and the first of the village cocks began to crow. In less than a minute, Liliane had covered the ground between the wood and moat, slipping into the water and swimming silently to the wall's rocky base, where her knotted silk rope still hung down.

After sliding through the hole in the wall, she dashed across the courtyard to the northwest tower. As she swiftly mounted the tower's first few steps, she froze, horrified to hear someone coming down the upper staircase. They were already looking for her! Fortunately, last night she had taken the precaution of barring her bedchamber door on the inside before she had left, but she would need a good excuse for not opening the door this morning. Someone must even now be hurrying to tell Alexandre or searching for an ax to break into the room!

Liliane retreated back to the tower door, casting a quick glance over her shoulder to make certain that the guards were still occupied. Seeing that they were all headed for the west wall, she crept into the garden, pulling the door open to reveal the secret passage, then easing it closed behind her. Feeling her way along the stone walls through the impenetrable darkness, she ran soundlessly up the staircase. She pressed the release and let herself into the bedchamber, sighing in relief. Before she had a chance to turn around, she found herself yanked abruptly into the room. Knuckles dug painfully into her armpits, and Liliane looked up to see Alexandre glaring into her flushed, horrified face.

"You crazy, little idiot!" he hissed, his eyes flashing with fury. "Do you want a damned arrow in your back? All one of those guards had to do was turn around!"

Charles stood behind him, wearing an expression of both exasperation and amused fascination. "A chit of a female, by God, and she's queen of the beggars and spiders!" he cried. "I've half a mind to see how well she does going over the wall *without* that cord of hers."

Liliane, her nerves taut with fear and desperation, jerked sharply away from Alexandre, flashing her poignard in deadly

warning at Charles. "Shall we see how well that half mind works
with half a belly?"

With a muffled oath, Charles started for her, but Alexandre
quickly blocked him. "I shall see to Liliane. You attend to those
guards who were so blind this morning."

Charles nodded reluctantly. "Just watch *your* belly, *ami.*" He
gingerly sidestepped Liliane and her ready knife. A moment later,
they heard his boots echoing on the stone stairs.

Alexandre was not about to take any chances with Liliane.
Her pale face was set with a determined harshness that was totally unlike her. She seemed capable of killing him and anyone
else who might threaten her life. Aware of how cornered and
hopeless she must feel, Alexandre felt a surge of pity for her.
"Liliane, you may as well give me the knife. With all your un-
common expertise, you must know that you cannot escape the
castle now."

To his dismay, Liliane edged toward the window. "Perhaps
not," she replied quietly, "but you will not have the satisfaction
of tormenting me."

Alexandre held his breath as she neared the window, then let
out a low, frustrated sigh. "Satisfaction? Good God, do you
think I have gotten satisfaction out of your misery? That I would
enjoy picking you up from the courtyard stones?" He ran his
fingers through his hair in exasperation. "Look, I am not going
to hurt you; neither is Charles nor anyone else. Just . . . move
away from the window. I only want to talk to you."

Liliane remained where she was, watching him with distrust
in her wide eyes. "I can hear well enough from here."

Alexandre had known that reaching an understanding with Liliane would not be easy, but he had not imagined negotiating at
knife point. He conceded that the blame was entirely his, for he
had let their communication disintegrate to this sad state. Finally
he said, "I don't blame you for not trusting me when I haven't
trusted you. Perhaps we are right not to trust each other, but
does that not kill any hope of making our marriage work? I did
not realize that soon enough—I have been cold and you have
been conniving, and where has it all gotten us? To your threatening to stick a knife in me!"

Alexandre moved away to sit in the opposite window. He pensively stared out at the bright morning sun, then looked back at
her wary face. "I do not know what expectations you had of this

marriage, but I doubt if they were much more than mine. I did not want a wife; I wanted money. On the other hand, as a free and well-dowered woman, you could have wanted neither marriage nor gold from a nearly penniless minor noble on whom you had never set eyes. Jacques de Signe must have forced you into this marriage. What weapon did he use?"

"One that is now blunted," she answered cryptically.

"Did he send you here as an assassin?"

"I do not know. I rather doubt it."

"Why?"

Liliane smiled grimly. "Like you, he is unsure of my reliability."

"Are you reliable?"

"When I choose to be."

"But you do not like to be forced."

"Neither do I like to be caged."

His face was taut, his features sharply defined in the angled light. "And at the moment, you like me little better than your uncle."

Liliane nodded. "Very little; however, my uncle is more dangerous than you."

"Is he?" Alexandre gave her an odd smile. "Still, perhaps I might achieve more by persuasion than he has by force." He saw the dubious look return to her eyes. "Before I waste my time, I want to know—would you kill me if your uncle commanded it?"

"I am no murderer," Liliane replied curtly.

"But are you a traitor?"

"You have nothing to fear from me; my uncle is another matter. Upon our marriage, I swore you fealty. Any obligation I might have had to my uncle has long since ended; I owe him nothing."

"As you do me, if one wishes to be legally correct. My 'failure' to visit your bed leaves you morally free to leave me to whatever fate I deserve, indeed to leave me entirely." He slid from the stone sill and came steadily toward her, as if oblivious of her weapon. "Do you want an annulment, Liliane?"

Liliane backed away, lifting the poignard. "To live in poverty while you spend my dowry?"

He stopped suddenly. "I am no thief. Your property would be

returned to you, and in time, total repayment of what has been spent."

She clenched her jaw. "I do not believe you."

"I daresay you do not." He smiled crookedly. "Still, your cage door is now open. Will you fly or not?"

Liliane stared at him. She trusted him not a whit . . . and yet, his fair, thoughtful behavior was so different from his usual severity. . . . She craved to flee Castle de Brueil and find Jean, yet while she might owe Alexandre nothing, she was still honor bound to prove that her uncle had murdered Diego. And it was only at Alexandre's side that she might repay the debt.

As she hesitated, Alexandre added softly, "If you stay, I will keep no part of my soul, mind and body from you. You will become my wife in every way."

Liliane did not need to ask what he meant by "every way." He would bed her and expect her to bear his children. The thought now left her cold and numb. Her mind no longer seemed to work. "Why do you make this offer now?" she at last managed to whisper. "You have caught me in flagrant, repeated disobedience—even suspect me of treason! I might have been confiding all your secrets to my uncle last night."

"You know very few of my secrets, milady. Only by staying with me can you learn them."

"Are you *tempting* me to destroy you?"

"Perhaps I hope to intrigue you."

"And by so doing, trap Jacques."

"Believe me, your uncle is secondary in my mind at the moment."

"What do you want from me?"

He laughed softly. "Rather more than before I met you, I admit." He eased the point of the poignard away. "I want to love you as you should have been loved from the very beginning. I also want to break Jacques's hold over you."

She shook her head distractedly. "So you can exert your own? I do not wish to be under any man's control. Why should I trade one set of shackles for another? At least, Jacques's tether is a long one; yours is tight about my throat, so tight that I cannot see the sky without walls of stone to block its clouds, or walk by the sea without the shadows of your guards to dim the sun. Your love offers me not happiness but a stifling prison."

"I will hinder you no more, Liliane. Hereafter, you will be

free as a forest sprite." The intent, searching look in his eyes made her suddenly unsure of what she wanted.

Not once had Alexandre asked her where she'd been last night . . . unless he knew. That possibility was horrible but highly unlikely. Alexandre could not possibly know she had been with Jean and still offer her his love; yet she was uneasy. He was so like Jean now, with the same wry, beguiling charm. He wore Jean's smile, with its fleeting, boyish wistfulness, the hint of mischief that might have been coquettish in a girl, yet in Jean was so unpretentious that it was utterly disarming. Thinking of Jean made her heart ache. Last night she had known love rich and fulsome as she would never know it again. Whatever Jean felt, she knew her love for him would endure as long as she lived. He seemed so far away, and yet, as Alexandre's blue eyes gazed into hers, so tormentingly near. "What if I refuse your offer?" she murmured.

The hope fled from Alexandre's face, and his eyes looked past her to the woods outside. "Then," he said slowly, "I should have Father Anselm begin annulment proceedings. You may leave at tomorrow's daybreak just as you came, with your dowry and jewels . . . and the black stallion to go where you please."

Liliane stared unseeingly at the jewels winking in the poignard hilt; their brightness seemed to mock her plight. Whatever her personal longing, she was bound by duty to Diego. "Beside bright honor," Diego had once told her, "all else is dull dross, and God's honor is first." By the last, Diego had not meant the petty bickerings of religion, but the uncompromising demand of human ethics that soul and conscience must mirror, whatever one's vision of God. The wars that mattered were not of the world but of the soul. In honor, she must give Alexandre the benefit of doubt and with that her trust, as he promised his own. To refuse that trust would be to fail him and Diego, as well as herself. If he was lying, she could hardly end in a worse situation that she was now in, unless she wound up in the castle dungeon. With a lump in her throat, Liliane handed him the poignard and whispered hoarsely, "I shall accept your offer then, my lord. I pray you make it in good faith."

As if he had not dared to hope, Alexandre's face lit up with a bright, quick glow. He tossed down the poignard and caught her firmly by the shoulders. "By all I hold sacred, you shall not regret remaining my wife, if aught I may do will please you.

You need not fear that I shall force you to my will or my bed.
Come to me as you will, only do not close your heart and mind
to me. Believe me when I tell you that I have paid sorely for the
distress I have caused you. 'Twas not ill meant, and was a bitter
trial to me.'' Gently, he touched her lips. "Believe that I find in
you all that is lovely and desirable and fascinating.'' His lips
curved with Jean's endearing touch of mischief. "Perhaps at dinner you will tell me where you learned to climb with such agility—perhaps from the monkeys of the Moors?''

"At dinner, my lord?'' Liliane asked uneasily. "Am I to pass
the afternoon in this chamber?''

"If you desire. However, I thought you might like to ride
along the beach.'' His eyes glinted with sapphire, like sunlight
on the water. "Alone.''

Liliane's spirits suddenly lifted. "I would very much like to
ride, but''—she smiled sheepishly—"I fear that I am rather tired.
I had better nap until dinner.''

His mouth twitched with suppressed humor. "Of course.''
With roguish gallantry, he took her hand in his and kissed it.
"Until then.''

After he left, Liliane flung herself wearily upon the bed. Fa-
tigued as she was, she found that she could no more close her
eyes than an owl could ignore mice. Ah, how her doubts and
confusion skittered and squeaked like mice! Where was the old,
sardonic Alexandre?

He certainly did not come to dinner. Her new, bewildering
husband was suave and charming—courtesy itself. He was also
very funny, which startled her more than anything else. The old
Alexandre had no more sense of humor than a cobblestone. Liliane had never seen him laugh, but then she had rarely laughed
herself in the past months. Tonight, Alexandre was brimming
with infectious high spirits. Liliane relaxed, relieved that she did
not have to endure another of their usual dull, noncommunicative
dinners. She alone proved susceptible to his gaity: the surrounding castellans obviously did not share their master's ebullience.
Their suspicions of her had been confirmed, and they considered
the dungeon a more fitting place for her than her seat at the head
of the table. Alexandre's aunts were white with stifled fury and
Charles scarcely lifted his accusing gaze from her face. Finally
she whispered to Alexandre, "This is never going to work. They
all believe that you have lost your wits.''

Alexandre grinned. "Perhaps I have. Sanity was becoming a burden."

"But, my lord . . ."

"Please, call me Alexandre or Alex, or whatever you like, but not 'my lord.' I am beginning to feel as though I ought to have an attendance of priests to merit such perpetual deference."

Liliane was dumbfounded. Was this the severe man she had married? "Alexandre," she began hesitantly, then she continued more firmly, "Alexandre, surely you must see that your family and retainers will never accept me."

"They will accept what I accept," he said flatly, and for a moment she glimpsed the old, determined Alexandre.

"But I am not sure that I can ever be happy. . . ."

He took her hand. "You promised to trust me. Where is the fiery courage and defiance that you brought from Spain? Leave our people to me."

Our people? He had never before suggested that anything in his demesne might also be hers. She gravely doubted if human hearts and minds could be casually allotted her like sticks of cordwood. "Alexandre," she said patiently, "whatever you dictate, they will never love me."

"But they love *me*. Although my aunts, who love only themselves, are another matter, my people will wish to see me happy. In time, they will see that you make me happy and, in perhaps a longer time, that you wish me well."

Liliane lowered her eyes, her expression grave. "Can you be so sure of that, when I might so easily turn on you at any time?"

"If I cannot be sure," he replied quietly, "I may as well go to the devil now. I should not want to live to see you faithless."

Liliane was both touched and bewildered. Gone were his demands that she be true, his threats if she betrayed him. All she saw now was his quiet trust in her. Although she was grateful, she was also frightened by the enormous responsibility he'd placed upon her.

Suddenly she noticed the clerk's face. As if Antoine Fremier could sense what she was thinking, his usual bland expression was belied by a peculiar brightness in his pale blue eyes. That brightness faded so quickly that she thought it must have been a trick of the candlelight. The clerk peacefully chewed his stew as if he were a browsing ewe lamb. Even his face resembled mutton, shapeless and pinkish gray. His mouth and chin were weak, his hands pudgy and useless for much besides tallying figures. Liliane had never paid much attention to him, and now only that fleeting, diamond brightness in his eyes had drawn her glance. His interest did not disturb her, for she assumed that a man who worked at mathematics would naturally be inclined to analyze her in her present situation. In fact, everyone around her was watching her, only more obviously than the clerk.

Alexandre had ordered entertainment to follow dinner. One of the guards juggled, and a group of the village peasants performed a round dance. The performances lacked enthusiasm, but Alexandre seemed not to notice, vigorously applauding everyone. Because he had gone to the trouble of planning an evening she might enjoy, Liliane tried valiantly to look as if she did, but she found the pretense difficult amid so many hostile faces.

Oddly enough, her discomfort was eased by the priest, Father Anselm, who was last to take part in the entertainment. She was surprised to see a priest participate in so worldly a display, particulary in a recitation of romantic Angevin poetry. The poem was long and beautiful, benevolently delivered by the rotund father as if he were unaware that the heroine's favors to her hero included more than tourney ribbons. Was Alexandre trying to show her that he and Father Anselm were not as stuffy as she thought?

She glanced at her husband, half expecting him to be either staring with boredom or sound asleep. Had he not professed that entertainment of this sort left him cold? But, no, he was wide awake, with an expression of alert interest that made her uneasy. Everyone in the castle normally retired shortly after sunset; the hour was now near midnight and many were openly yawning. Alexandre ought to be tired; she had noticed lines of fatigue about his eyes and mouth in the early afternoon. She prayed that lively energy had nothing to do with his private plans for the hours before dawn. At this thought, Father Anselm's poem progressed too quickly for her liking, and it seemed to be finished in moments.

A trifle unsteady, Liliane stood with Alexandre to thank the entertainers and bid a warm good-night to the gathering. As Alexandre turned to lead her to the stairs, Charles's furious expression made her glad that her husband was between them. In the darkness of the stairwell, a cold panic seized her. She could not go to bed with Alexandre now! How could she pretend to love him after Jean, whose very ghost seemed to be at her side?

She soon found that Alexandre had no intention of making her endure him. At the top of the staircase, he kissed her cold fingers. "Good night, my love. May all the stars smile upon your dreams and bring you peace. If you want me, I shall be nearby."

The intensity in his sapphire eyes suggested that he was available to provide more than a drink of water! To her horror, Liliane noticed that a pallet had been laid beside her door. "I thought you said there were to be no guards!" she protested. "You vowed that you would trust me!"

"You, I trust"—his eyes glinted mischievously—"but my loyal retainers may be overzealous."

"Will you not be very uncomfortable?" she asked, a doubtful expression on her face.

"Very." His voice was soft; his eyes held a seductive light.

She eased awkwardly around the door. "I am so sorry." A moment later, her pillow peeked out. "You may want this . . ."

Alexandre grinned ruefully. "I daresay I shall. Ah . . . do not mind any groans and thumps you hear; 'twill be just my pommeling away."

"You will be safe?" she asked, concerned.

"Stiff, but entirely safe."

She could not resist. "Shall I sing you to sleep?"

"Tonight," he replied with a meaningful smile, "I think your singing would have the opposite effect." Then his eyes brightened. "However, I am fond of having my back rubbed."

"For that, perhaps you had better apply to Father Anselm. Your good priest must be an expert—his old hound dotes on having his back scratched!" Laughing, Liliane closed the door.

6

The Truce

The next morning, Liliane discovered that although Father Anselm was not around, his old hound had acquired more company than the friendly hunting dogs that lay about the great hall. Charles had mysteriously adopted two huge, surly mastiffs, which he was training in the courtyard. Liliane's eyes narrowed when she saw them snarling and lunging at the other dogs. Strongly suspecting that the mastiffs were intended to curtail her nocturnal roaming, she turned abruptly to Alexandre, who was walking along the rampart wall at her elbow. "Did you . . . ?"

"No," he said quietly, "I did not."

"They are dangerous, Alexandre."

He sensed her unspoken request. Leaning over the parapet, he called, "Charles, when those beasts learn manners, they are welcome within the walls; until then, chain them outside."

"Of course, my lord." Charles quickly led the mastiffs out, but Liliane distrusted his easy compliance. She had seen enough to know that he was a good trainer. The mastiffs would shortly be "controlled" enough to obey his commands and be "exercised" at night when he often supervised the guards. Even if she could get over the wall, the dogs would be waiting on the far side. She knew that Charles would be slow to call them off.

Alexandre studied her pale face. "Would you care to take that ride now?"

"Alone?"

"If you like."

Liliane had to give Alexandre credit; he did not do things halfheartedly. Before, he had guarded her like a hawk; now, by giving her free run, he was risking not only her uncle's scheming vengeance, but the loss of his retainers' confidence, as well. He looked worried as he went with her to the stable. Was he afraid that she would run all the way to Jacques, or that one of his people might turn assassin and relieve her of that temptation? Whatever the risk, she was determined to test him. A wimple and chainse were not her favorite riding attire, but she was too impatient to change. She ought to send a reassuring message to Jacques while she had the chance, but she dared not take the risk today. She might well be followed. Alexandre might have merely pretended not to know that Charles had acquired those mastiffs. Despite her husband's concessions, he certainly was testing her, as well.

However, this game could be played both ways. "Would you like to come?" she asked brightly as he saddled the black.

Alexandre looked faintly amused, clearly aware that the last thing she wanted was company, particularly his. "Another day, perhaps, when I have less work." His blue eyes twinkled. "But thank you for the invitation."

Oddly enough, halfway to the shore, Liliane found herself actually missing him. In his current mood, he was not nearly as dreary as he had been; in fact, he was charming! Of course, this remarkable change might well be just a performance to knock her off guard. She took a deep breath of fresh air and spurred her destrier onward. She had no wish to brood about intrigue on this bright morning. The green meadows sparkled with dew, and the distant beach and brilliant turquoise sea beckoned. Low cloud puffs drifted over the Mediterranean, whose sleepy morning breakers spilled lazily over the black rocks as she reached the beach. The shoreline was empty. Unable to believe that she was not being watched, Liliane twisted in the saddle to look back over the way she had come. Only low, scattered pines and rippling grass met her searching gaze.

For a half hour's westward ride, Liliane saw nothing more but lovely, barren hills carpeted with morning-glories and thistles, until she spied a couple of children. The boy, who was perhaps eight years old, and a younger girl rode a driftwood "horse" partly buried in a patch of seagrass a hundred or so yards up the beach. They were probably harmless, but she had seen too many

Moorish children who were adept spies to dismiss them completely. Her suspicions were confirmed when farther along the beach she came across a lonely figure. Like a humped, brown tortoise, Father Anselm was perched on a high rock jutting into the sea. He was fishing with a string attached to a short peg, which he held in one hand while he wound the string about it with the other. A small fire was kindled on the beach. He is after *langoustes*, she thought, but he may also be making sure I do not wander too far. She rode up to him, pebbles scattering beneath the black destrier's hooves. "Good morning, Father. I hope I am not disturbing you."

The old priest stood, a broad smile splitting his plump face. "No, no, my lady. I am having poor luck this morning. I fear that I rose too late and my quarry has already breakfasted. The Lord is reproving my laziness."

"We all retired too late last night to eagerly face the sunrise. You are wise to try for your own *langoustes*. Old Doucette is a fine cook and clever with spices, but she grills seafood nearly as long as mutton."

Father Anselm looked surprised. "Is that it? I have always been disappointed by Doucette's shellfish, but mine are invariably as tough as hers."

Liliane glanced back down the beach. Another fire glimmered where the children had been playing; it was unnecessarily high for cooking. "Why not summon your accomplices, Father," she suggested softly, "and with luck, we shall all have a fair lunch."

The priest flushed. "Signal fires were not Alexandre's idea, you know, but Charles's . . . and mine."

"My lord Alexandre is fortunate to have so many devoted protectors," she replied lightly.

"We mean no offense, my lady, but . . ."

"None is taken. You all have good reason to doubt me."

Father Anselm played awkwardly with the fishing cord. "We wish it were otherwise, my lady, but you see, your riding alone poses certain difficulties."

She dismounted. "I can imagine."

Father Anselm had shuffled forward to assist her. Observing her agility, he hesitated, then tentatively extended his hand. "I wonder, my lady, if you really can imagine the whole problem."

She grasped his hand and he hoisted her up onto the rock. "If I may ask, did Count Diego del Pinal allow you to ride alone?"

"No," she admitted. "A castellan named Pedro always accompanied me, although he rarely interfered with where I went."

"Then you had escort for good reason, you will agree?"

She smiled. "If you mean that Moors are not accustomed to encountering females alone and unveiled, I will agree. That is why I often wore male clothing so that I might pass as a boy. Also"—her smile grew impish—"Christian raiders like my uncle, Baron de Signe, sometimes rode down from the north."

The priest was undaunted. "Here they also raid from the east. The Lombards have never been content with their borders. Adventuring *banditti* have often wandered this far in the past few years."

And King Philip was too far away to lend assistance to Alexandre, Liliane mused. Suddenly she saw how Jacques might destroy Alexandre without provoking the king's retaliation. "How long has it been since my uncle wandered this far?" she asked with beguiling innocence.

"Too recently to ignore his ambitions." Father Anselm's voice took on a stern note. "If you have no regard for your husband's welfare, my lady, I hope you have the common sense to protect yourself. While my lord count has asked us all to preserve your safety, there are *some* limits to our power."

Liliane's smile faded. "Alexandre asked you to guard my life?"

"Did you not persuade him to do so?" countered the priest dryly.

"No," she said slowly. "I knew nothing about it." She settled on the rock and looked out to sea. "I do see your point—this is not just a matter of propriety. If anything happened to me, Alexandre's position would be damaged, particularly if one of his retainers were the culprit." She glanced up at the priest. "Are you sure it is wise to tell me this? The information could be a two-edged sword."

"Whatever his outward behavior, Alexandre cared for you from the first," Father Anselm said quietly. "We all knew that when he gave you his stallion."

Liliane was startled again. "*His* horse? The black destrier?"

"He raised it from a foal."

For a moment she was bewildered. Why had Alexandre not

told her that the stallion was his? Then an awful thought flashed through her mind. *Dio*, had Jean *stolen* the stallion from Alexandre? No wonder Alexandre had been set against her from their first meeting. No wonder he was jealous and refused to touch her! He must have known where she had gotten the black! Had Jean enjoyed some private, perverse revenge in sending his brother an impure bride on his own horse? Had humiliated pride prevented Alexandre from telling her the truth?

Liliane shivered in the warm sea breeze. How could Jean betray his brother *and* her? Now that she considered it, such a perverse joke might not be beyond his ironic sense of humor. So foul a trick would have turned any husband into a monster. When one considered all he might have done, Alexandre had shown the restraint of a saint. Jean probably never even left, but hung about to hear the explosion. When she had not been destroyed in it, he had had the gall to seduce her again! Her eyes squeezed shut with fury and humiliation. How willing she had been!

"I have been a beast!" she blurted with such vehement, heartfelt contrition that a less charitable man than Father Anselm might have thought it false. At her barely suppressed rage and pain, Father Anselm watched her warily, taking a careful step back. "Now, now, I hope not . . ."

Liliane gazed up at the priest in mute frustration. He had not the vaguest notion of why she was so upset. Taking a deep breath, she recovered her self-control. "I am sorry, Father. I was thinking of something else." Like wringing Jean's neck. For months, she had been tearing her heart out over a . . . an unscrupulous prankster! She felt utterly disillusioned and alone. Jean, whose memory had lingered so strongly with her, must be now banished once and for all, she decided. She would be damned if she ever thought of him again. She brooded silently for a moment. "Father, did Alexandre's half brother, Jean, accompany him to the Holy Land?"

Father Anselm looked puzzled. "Count Henri was a worldly man, but I know of his having but one child. Count Alexandre took ten castellans to Palestine. At the time, he could not afford more."

Liliane smiled faintly. "I take it that none of them looked like him."

Still confused by her line of questioning, Father Anselm shook his head. "Count Alexandre's looks are hardly common."

No, Liliane agreed grimly, one does not see those ice-blue eyes every day. Jean had certainly constructed a detailed lie. He had probably picked up his information about Palestine while hanging about the coastal inns and brothels, then fabricated a tale of war-weary valor to spend on whores and naive maidens like herself. She had given her heart and soul to a lying, lecherous thief. Disillusionment and depression weighed upon her like a boulder.

Father Anselm's worried look was back again, she noticed. He must wonder if Jacques had pinned his hopes on a lying pretender, a heretofore unknown bastard of old Henri de Brueil's. She had better relieve the old man's consternation before he questioned Alexandre and roused a hornet's nest. She forced a careless laugh. "You are undoubtedly right, Father. When we arrived in Toulon from Spain, some taproom drunkard bragged of being a Brueil back from the wars. Ten minutes later, he was a cousin of the *Duc d'Orleans.*"

The priest smiled hesitantly. "Thanks to the benevolent favor of King Philip, Count Alexandre has gained some fame of late."

Yes, she thought, with a bastard brother trading on every facet of that fame. Sitting here feeling sorry for herself would do no good for any of them. Everyone who lived on the fief was affected by a rift between their lord and lady; the sooner peace was made, the sooner all would be more secure, if not necessarily happy. Would she ever know happiness again?

With a sudden rush of nostalgia, Liliane gazed at the fire on the beach, recalling roasting shellfish on the shores of Malaga. Abruptly, she stood up. "If you do not object to my inviting myself to lunch, Father, why not summon your young friends and I shall show you a good way to lure *les langoustes.*"

Father Anselm's face lit up in an eager smile. "Why, of course. I should be delighted."

Half an hour later, the squealing, laughing children had overcome their initial suspicion and shyness. Hip high in the water, Liliane and her companions were ranged along the waterline, where they had smeared bait on the rocks. The spit was soon strung with roasting shellfish, which had been attracted to the heavy, irresistible fish scent. For the next two hours, Liliane forced herself to forget the pain Jean had caused her, remembering only the carefree life she had once known in Spain.

She was good with the children, disarming them easily with

her tales of adventure in Spain as she cinched up her skirts for wading in the tidal pools. She loved the children, loved their prattling, mischievous company, and they knew it. Once she caught the priest looking at her with a gentle, much relieved countenance. He was an absurd sentimentalist and naively shared confidences to the point of being dangerous to Alexandre, but he was also a good, loyal man. She liked him.

They spent a leisurely lunch and glutted themselves with shellfish, folktales and joking. Afterward they tried a game of blindman's bluff but were too full to play long. As the children gamboled in the low surf, Father Anselm and Liliane sat on the beach. They chatted companionably for some time, and as Liliane finally rose to return to the castle, Father Anselm told her quietly, "You seem happy today, my lady. While I do not flatter myself for that, should you ever need my help as a priest, I am at your service. I fear difficult days lie ahead for you."

Liliane touched his hand. "I should be grateful for your friendship and advice, Father, but do not fear for my soul." She nodded to the children poking their toes in the sand. "With their hope and innocence, they symbolize my religion."

He was unoffended, but let her go with a small admonishment. "Even children do not find it easy to be good, and perhaps they blame themselves more when they are not. Be kind to yourself as well as to others. Often you will find good where you least expect it."

Wondering if he were referring to her or Alexandre, Liliane bid him and the urchins a reluctant good-bye. She did not relish leaving their lively company for the tense atmosphere of the castle. Alexandre would be bound to wonder where she had been for so long, but if he lost his temper, this time she at least had a verifiable excuse for her tardiness. Nearing the old Roman aqueduct, she was not surprised to see him riding out to meet her. She *was* surprised to find him uninquisitive and pleasant.

"I hope you had a good ride." His blue eyes held amusement at her wet skirts and bare feet. He patted a saddlebag. "Doucette has grilled us a brace of doves for lunch. I thought you might be hungry."

"I have dined, thank you, and very well, too." She explained the impromptu picnic with Father Anselm and the children.

Alexandre looked envious and disappointed. "I have been laying stone on the east wall and perspiring all morning. I wanted to roll like a pig in the mortar and cool off.''

''Why not take a swim?'' She nodded toward the river in the shadow of the aqueduct. ''If you have wine in that saddlebag, I will keep you company afterward while you eat.''

He brightened considerably, then gave her a roguish grin. ''Why not join me for the swim?

She could not help grinning back. ''Perhaps another day, thank you.''

''At any rate, the swim must wait. I am expected at the village to present a christening gift to a new babe. The boy's parents will be much honored by your added presence.''

Liliane doubted if the serfs would be so delighted, but as she had already accepted Alexandre's company, she could not very well decline it now. Also, such simple ceremonies were an important part of her duty as chatelaine to the people.

As she had expected, the villagers were not pleased to see her, but Alexandre's warmth and delight with the newborn and his generosity to the parents greatly thawed the chill. Watching Alexandre tenderly hold the child in his arms, Liliane felt an unexpected wave of warmth for him. She sensed that his fascination with the babe was not pretense, that the glow of affection in his eyes was real. He will be a good father, she thought, if ever I give him children.

After returning the child to its parents, Alexandre did not immediately leave the village. Leading his destrier, he walked among the serfs with Liliane at his side, pausing to talk to many of them. He asked about their concerns and comfort and whether they thought the sprouting grain needed more rain and if the rabbits were plentiful. Although she had never accompanied him on his regular rounds of the estate, Liliane now realized that he was as familiar with the serfs' daily lives as his own; he shared their ailments, complaints, loves, bereavements and prosperities. She doubted if they confided so much to Father Anselm. She could sense that they were not so open today as they must have been on other days, and she stayed back at first to encourage them to speak freely. However, Alexandre often drew her forward as if to make clear to the peasants that she was as responsible for them as he was. Sometimes they fell silent or responded to her questions with a trace of defiance. Count Alexandre has earned his place with us, they seemed to say to her. No Signe will ever deserve the allegiance we pay him. Liliane sighed—she had anticipated no other reaction.

Alexandre gave practical advice on several problems and promises of assistance where warranted, then he handed Liliane up into her saddle. As they rode out of the village, she was pensive. No priggish martinet could have won the affection she had seen that the villagers held for Alexandre. Diego's people had also followed him with a loyalty that bordered on fanaticism. Diego had given her a place in their hearts, but if she were to be happy among Alexandre's people, she must win them herself.

Upon their arrival at the ancient aqueduct, Alexandre stripped off his clothes without coyness. When he saw her surprised expression, he challenged, "You saw me unclothed when I had lung fever, did you not?"

"A limp flounder is scarcely comparable to a lively salmon," she retorted lightly. She could not deny that Alexandre had a beautiful body, particularly in the green shadows of the river woodland. Lean, brown and compact, with long legs and fine shoulders, he had a tight, perfect rump, and moved with a careless, fascinating grace. For a prude, Alexandre was certainly unconcerned about his nakedness.

He waded into the river, then dived into the deeper midstream below the aqueduct arches. He was as agile a swimmer as an otter, his brown skin glistening as he shot through the water. He must swim a good deal to keep so sleek, Liliane mused. Most knights developed knotty, heavy muscles, broadswords requiring great strength and endurance. Also, for one who had spent the past eight years at war, he had very few scars. A sword had scarred the ribs beneath his heart and another slash had marked his left forearm. A shield battered down had likely left him open to any enemy attack. Despite his scars, he was beautiful. He must be quick and deadly with a sword to have survived so long, she decided, for he had not the bulk to sustain the usual extended hand-to-hand combat required by broadswords. Alexandre's best weapon would be a scimitar capable of slitting a man's gullet before he could swing a heavier European weapon.

Alexandre rose from the rushing stream, pausing to shake his wet, dark auburn curls. The current foamed about his groin, and with a start, Liliane realized that he was aroused, his manhood rising from his body. He laughed when he saw her face. "Sorry, my titillation is due to the water bubbles." Then he added, just audible over the sound of the rushing water, "but you do look lovely, sitting in that chartreuse light. Simple garments like the blue chainse and wimple you wear become you better than elaborate ones." He emerged from the water and slowly walked toward her. He hunkered gracefully down in front of her and touched her left ear. "One day, I would like to put a single pearl . . . there . . . like a teardrop."

Liliane was uncomfortable, keenly aware of Alexandre's bare skin, his mesmerizing blue eyes and the open invitation between his thighs. She flinched, a small, startled gasp escaping her as he traced the soft skin beneath her jaw. "I ought to replace at least one of your tears," he said softly. "I have made you very unhappy, haven't I?"

"You are not altogether to blame," she whispered, then hesitated. "I think I understand more now than I did at the beginning. Why did you not tell me the black was your horse?"

A startled flush suddenly stained his cheeks. She could tell that he was casting about for an explanation; when it proved elusive, he looked away and his voice grew soft. "Ah . . . I thought you might be embarrassed. You could have had a fall from your own horse and found mine grazing . . ."

"Wearing a bridle and saddle?" she prodded gently.

Alexandre was silent for a moment, then he sighed. "You have nothing to explain, Liliane. We were not married then, and besides, the whole marriage arrangement was not of your choice. No matter how you rode into my life, I am grateful to have you here."

She searched his eyes. "Even when you must know that Jean gave me that horse?"

A blank look came over his face, perhaps a shade too quickly. "Jean?"

"Your half brother."

"Liliane," he said slowly, "I have no brothers and that is God's truth."

Strangely enough, Liliane believed him. Quite possibly he did not know about Jean . . . or did not want to know about him.

As if to avert more questions, Alexandre rose quickly and put on his braies. Silently, she watched him pull his chainse over his damp shoulders. It stuck to him and, rising from her seat on the moss, she helped him ease it down. "Alexandre, at the time I married you, I was in love with another man."

He paled slightly. " 'Was'?"

"I learned he was a thief and a liar."

He blanched even more and his voice grew dull. "And you want nothing more to do with him?"

She wondered why he sounded so disappointed. "No, I will not see him again . . . but I must apologize for having cheated you of the bride you must have expected."

Now he looked relieved! "Oh, that is no matter," he returned with a curious smile. "In fact, I was in love with another woman."

Liliane's heart gave a painful lurch. "Is that over?"

"In a way"— he gave her a wry smile—"it scarcely began." His eyes captured her. "But now that I have you, you will find me both ardent and faithful."

If Liliane had some doubt of the latter intent, she was left little doubt of the former. Before she could protest, Alexandre pulled her close and kissed her, softly but with stirring resolution. She felt an unexpected tingling, and just as she realized that his kiss seemed painfully familiar, he released her. His blue eyes were dark with promise.

Liliane wondered what might have happened if he were not already dressed. Afraid that he would not quickly dispense with such an inconsequential obstacle, she moved hastily out of his reach. "Are you not going to have your lunch?" She hurried to his horse and pulled food and a bottle of wine from his saddlebag. "Oh, a good brandywine," she chattered as she fished for the crockery mugs she had spotted deeper in the bag. "I had nothing to drink with the *langoustes*. This looks wonderful." She thrust everything into his arms.

With an amused smile, Alexandre laid napkins on the bracken and spread out the small picnic. "Why not have a taste of the doves, as well? *Langoustes* are little more than an appetizer."

"Oh, no, thank you, I ate far too many of them this morning." Feeling like an awkwardly polite child, Liliane seated herself a short distance away.

He sat down, poured a little brandywine in his mug and tasted it. "So-so," he commented with a faint grimace. "Doucette doesn't believe in wasting our best on saddlebag jaunts."

Or me, thought Liliane.

Alexandre poured a cupful for her, then himself. She did not notice anything wrong with the brandywine, but then her palate was not accustomed to Italian wine. She was more accustomed to Spanish *aqua vini*, but usually drank only water and strong tea in the Moorish manner. Feeling unaccountably nervous, she drank the wine too quickly. He glanced at her cup, then suggested as he refilled it, "You have quite a thirst . . . still, it is hot today. Do you not think you should savor your wine more slowly?"

"Oh, I am used to it," she replied quickly, then felt foolish, remembering. If she had not drunk so much brandywine that first night at the hunting lodge with Jean, she might not have been so easily seduced. Fortunately, she need not worry about Alexandre; he filled her cup only half full.

As he ate and made light conversation, Liliane sipped her wine slowly, yet she already felt its heady effects and the noon heat. Staring at her cup and simmering in her wimple, she sat for some time, scarcely listening to Alexandre. At length he reached out suddenly and pulled the wimple off, then swiftly unfastened the throat of her chainse. When she looked at him warily, he grinned. "You have never bowed to propriety before; why suffer for it now?"

"I thought you demanded propriety. You have disapproved my lack of it often enough," she replied a trifle tartly, tossing back the honey-blond hair that curled around her shoulders.

"I was a prig, was I not?" he replied easily, then he leaned back and laid his head in her lap. His expression was trusting and a little wicked. "You will continue helping me to relax? Good behavior can be wearing, *non?*"

In answer, Liliane poured more brandywine and quaffed it. Soon she was not only relaxed but nearly incapable of thinking clearly about anything but Jean's perfidy. She knew he had loved her, and that his pain at leaving her had been as real as her own. Had his vengeful joke turned on him and left him as bereft as herself?

Dizzy with brandywine, Liliane wanted Alexandre out of her lap. His comment about being good had piqued her. It was so difficult to be good. She did not think she could be really bad. She had been bad with Jean, but at her worst, she had been wonderful, her body and mind floating when he touched . . . as he was touching her now with his gentle, teasing fingers, kissing her lightly with his soft laugh. She was looking into his blue, fathomless eyes, then falling into them, and he was ink-blue all around her, darkly enveloping, making her senses sing as he caressed her. His mouth was growing hot, hotter than the wine, and that hot wine was coursing through her veins, bubbling like the bubbles that had teased him in the coursing river. His lovely, long manhood was eager and wanting her.

"No!" Dazedly, desperately, Liliane pressed him away. "Jean, we must not—" She took a sharp, horrified breath, trying to clear her head. Alexandre's caresses had stopped; he was lying back, his head propped on his hand, staring at her with a look of passion and quizzical frustration.

Liliane closed her eyes. She was still disoriented, but shame had swallowed all but one realization. "I called you Jean," she whispered. "I am sorry. I meant to put him out of my mind."

Unexpectedly, he gently touched her hair. "Do not be sorry. I would not have you faithless to any man, so that should you ever smile at me, I shall know that you smile for none other."

Liliane opened her eyes, and studied him carefully. "I am beginning to know why your people love you," she said softly.

"I love them," he said simply, "and you."

"A little time ago . . . *was* that you . . . loving me?"

"Did your lover seem to be a dream?"

"Yes."

"Then he could not have been me," he replied sadly, "for I have only reality to offer. I pray that honest day and near delight will soon prove sweeter than your elusive night of phantom memory."

Liliane touched his face and then, resting her hand on his arm, stood up slowly. With his assistance, she tried to steady herself. She could barely lift her head, for it was still spinning, yet at the center of her growing perception lay a certain knowledge. She knew of but one way to exorcise the phantom of Jean. From the steady look in Alexandre's eyes, she saw he knew of but one way, too.

Their ride back to the castle was silent, and when Alexandre helped Liliane to dismount in the courtyard, she was still unsteady on her feet. Even so, her voice was sure as she looked up at him. "Tonight, I will be yours . . . if you still want me. Be certain of that, Alexandre. I would not have you court more unhappiness for some illusion. I came into your life but a short time ago; my yesterdays belong to Diego. Although he is dead, I carry old loyalties. Whatever may pass between us after tonight will alter nothing of the past. I will never dishonor you, but if ever I must choose between allegiances, know that I must be true to the one who first gave me life and protection.''

''Then Jacques's hold on you is through Diego,'' he murmured. ''That explains a good deal.'' He put his hands on her shoulders. ''I agree to your terms, but ask only one thing. Never feel that you cannot turn to me in difficulty. Come to me before you go to Jacques.''

''I will,'' she answered gravely, then added to herself, *if I can.* Jacques had a viper's stealth and quickness; he also had Louis, who was scarcely less deadly. If Alexandre were ever caught between the two of them, she might not be allowed the luxury of discussing defense.

''Wait for me at sunset,'' Alexandre whispered as he walked her up to their chamber. ''I want to see its blaze in your hair.'' Just inside the door, he kissed her—a tantalizing echo of the kiss they had shared by the river. Then he left her.

Liliane touched her lips. Far less assured than she outwardly seemed, she was afraid, bewildered. How could she have loved Jean, yet be so quickly captivated by Alexandre's touch? Was she going to Alexandre's bed out of duty to Diego or for another reason that made her flush with guilty excitement?

Alexandre had dinner brought to their room that night. Dressed in pale gray velvet that made his eyes seem startlingly vivid, he arrived just as the maids finished arranging the little table he had ordered set up by the window. Liliane saw him catch his breath as he looked at her, and she was glad she had worn the gold-trimmed cream samite Almansor had given Diego for her. A rose mantle of gold- and pearl-embroidered samite was gracefully draped over her shoulders. The airy chemise was the most graceful garment she owned. Her hair was caught up in a pair of ivory pins and cascaded down her back to her waist. Long, gold Moorish earrings jingled like tiny chimes in her ears; aside from those, she wore no jewelry except the gold ring Alexandre had placed on her finger at their wedding. The maids gave her sly peeks and whispered to one another that she looked heathen, but they were also greatly impressed . . . as was Alexandre.

Giving an appraising glance at the table and nodding his approval, he dismissed the servants. Then he stood, gazing for a long moment at Liliane as if he were closeted with a beauty worshiped by the Persian poets. Her hair and the gold that touched her body shimmered with the sun's last slanting russet rays; her amber eyes were liquid honeyed fire, her lips palest coral. She saw that he wished their dinner were finished and their night of discovery richly upon them. His impatience passed like a quick breath between them as he murmured, "You are fair as lilies upon the water of wishes men make in their most still and desperate moments, until their dreams gain a quivering, fearful clarity. Thou wonder . . . thou woman."

"I thought I had lost poetry when I came to France," Liliane murmured faintly, "yet I find it again on the lips of thieves, priests and warriors. You make me such fair compliments, sir, as harpers sing. I wonder that any mortal maid can be worthy of your sweet words."

Alexandre laughed softly. "Fear not. Whether bakers or bishops, we Frenchmen love poetry and women. If our loves are somewhat overscented, their flaws beflowered and pasted o'er with mirrored gilt, we are fond of them no less. True angels must prove tedious, while earthly creatures are warm and quick and varied as the wild birds that herald our springs. Welcome to France, my lady." He kissed her fingertips. "May love's summer soon show its fair sun so brightly that winter will prove shy and spend its force in a distant clime."

A twinkle glinted in Liliane's amber eyes. "At the very least, as far away as my uncle's demesne. Imagine his surprise at being up to his third chin in hoarfrost."

At mention of Jacques, she sat that Alexandre was considering questioning her about him. However, he obviously thought better of the idea, probably because he knew she would give him no answers. The less he knew, the more freely she could maneuver without his interference. If he were aware of all she intended, he would most definitely intervene.

As he had done that afternoon, Alexandre made sure that the wine was to his liking. He poured Liliane's brandywine and served her much as the courtly Diego had always done. She enjoyed his pampering and the familiar, little touches of a man's concern. At the last moment, Alexandre diluted her brandywine with water. "Until you grow accustomed to our wine, we had best not dizzy you before the soup course is ended." As the soup was turtle laced with more wine, she was glad of his foresight, yet curious.

He noticed her quizzical look. "Is something wrong?"

"No, nothing, only . . . most men . . . well, do you not think the brandywine might make me more . . . acquiescent?"

"I need not leave that to the wine," he replied calmly. "I want nothing to come between us tonight: no haze of wine, no memories, yet much of this must be left to you. A man's possession of a woman comes not through her obedience, but her desire. All others become shadows beyond the flame of the beloved."

"Have you loved so deeply?" she whispered with a touch of sadness.

He was silent for a moment, then he answered gravely, "I have loved so. My heart is fed upon by longing and the nearness of one who may mean my destruction, yet from whom I can no more turn than the wind from the first promising sparks of a holocaust."

Liliane felt a tremor of fright at the growing intensity in Alexandre's eyes. Sharply aware of her sudden uncertainty, he frowned slightly, then carefully folded his napkin and rose from his chair. "I will leave, if you like. You will be forced to nothing."

Anxiously, she stood and moved swiftly to him. Almost without thinking, she took his hand. "Alexandre, for your sake and that of your people, send me away. I am wrong to put innocent people at risk, whatever my reasons. I believe now that I may bring you only disillusionment and unhappiness. You ask too much from me that I may never be able to give. I promise nothing, yet you would offer me all. I cannot in good conscience accept so much."

" 'Tis already given"—he gently pressed her hand—"yet if you wish to leave now, I will not hold you."

Liliane shook her head in distress. "I made a solemn vow upon Diego's death to undertake a mission of great importance. I cannot in honor abandon this demesne of my own wish with my mission unfulfilled, yet I would not bind you to that duty, as well."

"So you seek to escape on a technicality." Alexandre laughed softly. "Nay, my sweet, I shall not make your choice easy by sending you away." His hands cupped her face. "Hold this one certainty in your uncertain mind. If you stay with me this night, I shall never willingly let you go."

And then he kissed her, his mouth sealing her decision like a

brand. His arms held her surely, yet did not tighten, still allowing her the freedom to move away. His lips held both heaven and
the devil. Bewildered by the *déjà vu* of his embrace and her fiery
reaction to it, Liliane's mind made a last struggle of resistance
and lost. As if she were melting, she swayed, her mantle sliding
to the floor. His arms closed hard about her, his kisses now
merciless in his knowledge that he could make her his.

His hands caught the back of the chemise, tightening its filmy
samite against her breasts, then his mouth seared against her.
The lacings parted beneath his quick fingers to leave her shoulder
bare, porcelain-white against the heat of his mouth. The samite
slipped still farther, offering the undercurve of her arm and a
shadowed, mysterious vale where he roamed ardently to find the
full swell of her breast. His breathing came fast, his heart pounding under her trembling fingertips. "Ah, my love," he breathed
against her flesh, "I am too much in haste. What folly not to
savor the riches of our joining."

Reluctantly, he put her away a little. "Come, Liliane, slowly,
slowly; come to me as I will to you. Cast away our first restraint." He eased away the covering of her shoulders, and the
samite slipped low to barely conceal the full-bloomed tips of her
breasts. "What sweet, shy flowers," he whispered, "to remain
yet unseen, yet pout at their neglect." With a slow slide of his
tongue, he bared a high peak, and his mouth closed upon its
flushed crimson. Liliane gasped at his delicate, knowing torture.
The peak of her breast felt his teeth as he sent a current of liquid
fire coursing to her belly. Suddenly, she wanted to feel his bare
skin, to touch and explore him as he did her. Her fingers lingered
beneath his collar.

Realizing her wish, Alexandre slowly stripped off his tabard.
The tanned skin of his wiry, finely formed torso was irresistible,
even where white scarlines clawed its smoothness. As she tentatively traced a scar to his breast, his manhood swelled, yet he
made no effort to undress further. His intent gaze locking hers,
he pressed her chemise to her hips, then let it fall to the floor.
The rigid thrust of his arousal brushed the vee of her thighs,
teasing with a slight, undulating lift of his hips.

Half startled by her own rising eagerness, Liliane slid her
hands down his buttocks to caress their firm undercurve, then
pulled him against her.

"Liliane," he whispered, "Liliane, I want you. Free me

now.'' As her fingertips brushed against his swollen shaft, her lips parted at the promise of him. At her wondering touch, he groaned, ''Ah, please . . . please . . .''

Her fingers fumbled at the fastening of his hose, then she felt his virility spring forth, warm and ripe. She kissed his chest lightly, ardently, as she explored him, caressed him until his head rested upon her shoulder and he trembled with desire for her. He lifted his head, his eyes inky with passion. His mouth came down hard upon hers, his tongue probing until she felt faint. Then he swept her up and carried her to the bed.

He cast aside the last of his clothing, and she thought he would finally take her, but as he lay with her upon the cool linen, his mouth found her between her thighs. Startled, Liliane tried to close her legs, but he pressed her open, his tongue probing her. She was burning, burning, and yet the scorch of his mouth was relentless. . . . She cried out, shuddering, but still his wildfire played over her bare body, her breasts, until she could bear waiting no longer. At that moment, Alexandre plunged within her in a single, deep thrust that drowned her in a wave of ecstasy and desire. She heard moaning as his body moved over hers and realized dimly that she was making sounds like a pleading animal. She only knew that she wanted him to fill her again and again. The slow, sensual movement of his slim hips was sweet agony. All life, all existence seemed to issue from him and become powerfully imbedded in her. The tantalizing glide of his sex was elusive, his brown body imbued with a primitive grace. His muscles were corded with his effort to control his own need as he strove to fulfill her so utterly that she would never want another lover.

Like Jean . . . who was inside her now. Liliane was not quite sure when she knew, but inexperienced as she was, she was certain that two men might be physically alike in every way, but not the same in bed. They would not, simply could not be identical in the way they kissed and felt inside a woman's body. After she parted from Jean that last time at the hunting lodge, Alexandre had seemed increasingly like him in manner and speech to the point that had she closed her eyes she could not have told them apart. Now her eyes *were* closed and the lilting drive of his hips, the passionate urgency of the man who was making love to her was as familiar as her own racing pulse. Her body arched beneath Alexandre, her senses singing, scattering her dazed fury even as it bubbled up.

Then, fragile reality was shattered as he moved deep within her, taking them both to a high, brilliant place where lightning raged and the firecloud of their desire engulfed them in a roiling burst of passion.

Afterward, Alexandre lay with his head upon her breast. Blissfully contented, he was at peace, while Liliane, her mind clearing, was increasingly, vehemently at war. Alexandre had lied to her from the beginning! He *was* Jean! She wanted to rip his hair out, strangle him, hit him until he howled! She was so furious she did not dare speak, but lay there under him and considered a thousand ways of revenge. After finding that forty-two of them would work nicely, she began to calm down. After all, even a guilty man deserved a trial, did he not? Then, in good conscience, she could torment him at her leisure.

Curling a tendril of his hair and toying with the idea of ripping it out, she judiciously considered Alexandre's probable reasons for lying. They were complicated and various, but finally Liliane had to admit there were several points that mitigated his guilt. Oh, she could make him pay for his perfidy, *if* she wanted to make the next twenty years as unbearable as the last three months. If she had learned little else from their time together, she had found that pride and suspicion exacted a terrible price. The wicked slant to her lips softened as she finally reached a decision. With rueful fondness, her fingers wove through his shining curls. No, she had not the heart or the stupidity to punish the deceitful rogue as he deserved, but she would exact one pleasant tweak of revenge. She would not tell him she knew.

Alexandre stretched luxuriously and rolled over on his back. "You were magnificent," he whispered.

Liliane moved atop him and softly bit his underlip. "And you, darling, were never better." Beneath her lashes, she saw his eyes widen in confused alarm, and she kissed him as she had never kissed him before.

7

Kings May Meddle

Castle de Brueil
Fall and winter of 1189

For Liliane and Alexandre, the last days of summer were like a garden of flowers, each a fresh revelation of love's blooming. They were careful to take the time for themselves to let their love grow naturally and fully. In stolen moments from their duties as lord and lady, she and Alexandre picnicked, fished and hunted, although they never returned to the hunting lodge. Then fall winds stripped the trees of their leaves, touching their branches with winter's first, light snows. Winter closed the castle upon itself, with only a rare visitor or wandering merchant stopping at its doors. The distant wood rang with the sound of falling axes as the woodpiles of the villages and castle rose high against the biting winds from the Alps. In the highest turret of Castle de Brueil, the fire in the grate always burned brightly late into the night.

The castle folk saw the affection between their master and his lady, and although some distrusted the glow in Liliane's face, others swore that she loved their liege lord and would be faithful. At Alexandre's side, she worked among them, tending their injuries and sending them food. She was happy—happy as she had never been, and Alexandre was as proud as a young stag who has at last come into his own, with his chosen mate and a peaceful mastery over his domain.

As the months passed, even Jacques de Signes's cloud hardly darkened their horizon. Although she usually rode with Alexandre, Liliane was now able to roam without hindrance. "I believe that no man of yours will harm your lady now,'' Father Anselm assured Alexandre in September. "They will not risk their souls as well as your disaffection.''

Taking care not to abuse Alexandre's trust and the serfs' tolerance, Liliane went to the message tree only three times all that glorious fall and dark winter. No doubt Jacques's man, who normally visited the tree every other sabbath afternoon, had more trouble during the winter snows, and she found nothing after the first visit.

Upon that visit, she found Jacques's brief inquiry. "Is there trouble?'' Her answer that the problem had been solved seemed to satisfy him, for in November the cylinder was empty. She was not surprised that Jacques had heard of her being caught after her foray to the lodge. Castle gossip might be expected to travel; on the other hand, someone might have carried the news to Jacques, yet so far, he had not contested her lies about Castle de Brueil's defenses. If Jacques did have an observer in his pay, the spy might either be playing him foul, or Jacques could be playing her.

Liliane became doubly careful. She was strongly tempted to confide in Alexandre, yet she knew he could not permit her to keep playing such a dangerous game. No doubt his inclination would be to bait Jacques, quickly ending the game, yet the risk of an open attack on the undermanned castle was becoming increasingly possible as spring drew close. Alexandre had seen enough of war; he wanted no more of it. Word drifted down from Paris that Philip planned to leave on crusade with King Richard in the spring; if so, he might soon be years absent from France, leaving Alexandre without him as a vital ally to contend with Jacques.

Liliane needed to devise a plan to discredit and ruin Jacques before Philip departed for Palestine. After much thought, she decided upon a possibility. Father Anselm had mentioned that minor Italian princes sometimes led bandit raids into Alexandre's territory. Why not persuade Jacques to disguise some of his men as Italians and conduct such a raid? She might logically persuade him that Philip would blame the Italians for attacking Alexandre. Once Jacques took the hook, all she had to do was warn Alexandre to prepare for an ambush. If he caught a few "Italian" *banditti* and forced them to provide confessions for Philip, Jacques would be meat for the royal dogs. Jacques would take the bait because he badly wanted direct access to the sea to lower his mercantile expenses. Unlike sullen Louis, Jacques had no love of petty brawls; money was his chief concern.

The slippery point was the possibility that there was a spy in Castle de Brueil. If Jacques guessed that she had been lying about the defenses, he might wrap her neck in her own rope.

In May, Liliane left the suggestion of the *banditti* in the tree cylinder; however, before she reached the castle, she feared that disaster had already struck. Serfs were whispering and hurrying about the villages like bees whose queen has died. When Liliane inquired, they told her in dismay, "The French and English armies are camped only a day's ride away. King Philip has come to the castle. His escort is enormous!"

And he has come without warning, she thought, their anxiety becoming hers. Philip and Richard must already be on their way to the new crusade. Within a few days of departing the castle, he and Richard would sail with the armies from Massilia for the Holy Land and leave Jacques the leisure to move on Alexandre. Another dangerous, disheartening possibility occurred to her. What if Philip re-enlisted Alexandre to help him fight his new war?

Her white mare became sweat-flecked from the speed Liliane urged on her. As she expected, the castle environs were scattered with tents and strings of horses; soldiers tramping about her spring fields stared at her in open admiration as she galloped past them. After tossing the mare's reins to a hostler in the castle courtyard, Liliane raced up to the turret chamber to change. Her one weapon with Philip would be persuasion, and women were most convincing when they were dressed in their finest. As she pulled on a yellow chainse, from the turret window she glimpsed Alexandre leaning against the old, ruined wall arguing with a tall, dark-haired young man she knew must be Philip. Looking hot and bored, his retinue lounged idly among the rubble. Armor, gear and supplies were piled in the far courtyard and twenty horses crowded the smithy string. About fifty chargers were penned outside the bailey wall. Liliane gave her hair a few short strokes and shoved its honey mass into a long gold snood. Then, wearing her yellow chainse, a pink bliaud and jeweled filet, she hastened down the stairs to the kitchens.

The cooks were scurrying about, trying to find enough knives and trenchers to serve Philip's retinue. Pickled salt bacon was steeping in crocks. Several pigs and mounds of last season's wizened turnips were roasting on the grates as Doucette and three other women turned out pastry for apple and egg pies. From their size, the pigs were probably old ones, but in a day or so, the cooks would be forced to take mother sows and sucklings. The rest of the food being prepared would cut a wide hole in the supplies they needed to last until the crops were harvested at summer's end. Please, let Philip depart soon, Liliane prayed silently. His nags are eating the forage for our animals, and his men are tramping the young seeds into the ground.

Doucette caught her eye. "You do not approve, my lady?" she inquired.

"On the contrary, Madame Doucette," Liliane replied, "you have done admirably. Will sunset be convenient to serve dinner?"

Doucette nodded. She had no love for Liliane, but Liliane accorded her personal and professional respect. Liliane also would accept no nonsense about rudeness and slipshod work. Malcontents were sent to work the fields.

"What will be put on the tables at sunrise, I'd like to know." Doucette wiped flour off her face and whacked out another crust with a twirl of her knife.

"Fish. Send out the village serfs and let them keep a fish for each member of their household if they turn in eight from the catch to the castle by cockcrow."

Doucette swatted a scullery boy with a floury hand. "You heard. Off with you to the villages and tell 'em it's fish." She squinted at Liliane. "Should I ask about lunch?"

"Soup from leftovers, and as for dinner, let Philip's men hunt for it themselves. They will be wanting entertainment in the afternoon. A stag and boar or two should be turned up at the very least."

"And the next day?"

"Plain porridge," Liliane said firmly. "That should urge them on to Massilia."

Her gimlet eyes betraying her suspicion that Liliane might be trying to discredit Alexandre, Doucette put her hands on her hips. "It won't do. The king would be offended."

"From all accounts of him, he is not idiot enough to be offended. Royal retinues are like locusts. Too long in one place can ruin their hosts. Philip must be aware Alexandre is more vulnerable than most in that respect.''

"Milady might ask your uncle, the baron, to invite His Nibs for a week," slyly suggested the old cook.

"That is an excellent idea," Liliane agreed calmly. "I may even offer my uncle your services as cook for the king's stay."

With an appalled grimace, Doucette subsided. She would have been grimmer yet had she known that Liliane was seriously considering the older woman's suggestion. Jacques would be both thrilled at the king's notice and horrified at its expense, particularly as Philip would also certainly ask him for a hefty financial contribution to his campaign. Still, before she urged Philip onto Jacques's doorstep, she had best make certain that the king would not be susceptible to her uncle's bribery and blandishments.

Liliane summoned a harper from the village for the night's feast and had children gather flowers for the high table. Finally she ordered that all the serf women and girls go to the hunting lodge for the evening so that they would not be obliged to accommodate Philip's troops. Only those who wanted to make themselves available were free to remain. Nearly a dozen stayed— no prizes most of them, but enough to cheer the soldiers.

As Liliane sent out a servant to buy extra trenchers from the market outside the wall, Alexandre and Philip strolled into the hall; that is, Philip strutted, while Alexandre moved as tensely as a leashed leopard. Six of Philip's retinue drifted in behind them. Two were richly dressed courtiers who disdainfully glanced at the barren walls and plain furnishings; one was a sharp-eyed, balding little man in brown surcoat whose expression gave away nothing; the other three were hard-bitten bodyguards.

Philip posed a striking contrast to his companions. A shade taller than Alexandre, with the same wiry quickness, Philip exuded charm and energy. Clad in green and yellow velvet tabard, he was handsome and knew it. His narrow green eyes appraised Liliane with a connoisseur's appreciation, certain of her reciprocal approval.

Liliane gave Philip a lovely, welcoming smile, but she was definitely not attracted to him. He might be Adonis himself, but she had strong reservations about men who locked up one wife to enjoy another. She sank into a curtsy as the men approached. Then, as Philip bade her to rise, she exchanged a quick, sympathetic look with Alexandre. From his tight-lipped expression, she gathered Philip was either deserting or appropriating him. Her heart sank, even as he introduced her to Philip.

Philip, seeming blithely oblivious to the newlyweds' dismay, conveyed his approval of Liliane with a flirtatious grin. "Alexandre, you have found a very pretty countess. I envy your luck." He caught up her hand and kissed it. "How do you find life in the country after the sophistication of Andalusian cities, my lady?"

" 'Tis most pleasant, Your Majesty." Liliane smiled up at Alexandre with particular brilliance in a vain attempt to fend off Philip's attention. Within her was the growing certainty that Philip was going to cost them their happiness. "But, then, I should find life fair with my lord even in a barren desert."

As if disappointed, Philip arched his left brow and laughed softly. "By Saint Michael, Alex, your beautiful wife's in love with you. 'Tis unfashionable but a splendid relief from the calculation of most grasping vixens. Fortunately, Countess, you will not be obliged to follow your husband into the desert; instead, you shall remain in Provence to grace France."

"Remain?" she echoed numbly. "Am I to understand that Alexandre is . . ."

"To accompany His Majesty to Palestine," Alexandre finished flatly. He looked at her as if he wanted to cut his own throat.

Liliane could not conceal her stark dismay. At her stricken face, Philip murmured, "Aye, she does love you, you poor cockerel. If I were jealous and wanted revenge, this would be it. If I could, I would reward you better for your past service, *mon ami.* I need you, Alexandre. That infernal roasting spit across the sea may turn kings and heathen to my taste, but my appetite will be satisfied only upon a whole and suzerain France. France, not your mother, birthed you. You were bred not from your father's seed, but from those vast pine forests blowing northward of here to the sea-battered rocks of the Aquitaine." Philip grasped Alexandre's shoulders. "I am a clever fellow, *ami;* I am very good at being king, and you know that not another like me is going to come along for another hundred years. England has a blowhard bully boy on the throne and a pimply coin counter in the larder; Spain is being gutted by Moors; and Italy by its greedy lords and the Church. *This* is France's golden hour, and if I have to squeeze your marrow blood and that of a thousand others, I shall use every last, glittering drop. I shall do it"—he shook Alexandre slightly—"and you will damned well smile while I squeeze."

Alexandre was silent for a long moment, then his lips curved in a weary smile. "I have been your man since the Flanders rout; only a pile of rocks over my bones will ever keep me from answering your call. But grant me one boon, if you will, sire; leave the last trump to God."

Philip laughed heartily and threw his arms about Alexandre. "I knew you would not fail me!" He held Alexandre at arm's length again and, to Liliane's surprise, she saw his eyes were glistening with tears. "You are the best of my knights, and my most faithful friend. With you at my side, I cannot fail. Glory awaits us both, *ami!* History follows in our very footsteps. We will bring back the days of Charlemagne and make France so strong that none will dare challenge her integrity."

What has all this to do with the invasion of a distant country whose integrity France ought to respect? Liliane wondered, but such a question was not only impolitic, but virtually incomprehensible to a monarch preoccupied with *la gloire de la France et du roi*. Philip might love Alexandre, but he was mercilessly willing to use him to the death, see his home lost through abandonment and neglect, and deny him family and children. As with most kings, his favor was two-edged. Unfortunately, the edge that might have benefited Alexandre was proving dull, indeed.

So far, all Alexandre had gained from Philip's friendship was flattery and a short reprieve from Jacques de Signe's open attack. Philip's flattery was worth nothing and his reprieve would end the instant he left France. If Jacques used her *banditti* plan now, without Alexandre and his best knights as defenders, the Brueil lands might well be lost, and it would be her fault.

Dinner that night proved quite a success. Doucette jumped at the opportunity to prove that her cuisine could please a king, and her efforts had never been more artful. Had she known that Philip was normally no trencherman, especially when he was fired with a new campaign, she would have been less boastful of his royal compliments in the kitchen. Despite the king's disinterest, every morsel was devoured by his less abstemious knights and retainers, that so to the end of her life, Doucette had a fine tale to tell—one that gathered splendid additions to its menu with every passing year.

Alexandre and Liliane might as well have been served bread and water, for both had lost their appetites. For Alexandre's sake, Liliane was as charming as possible to Philip, who reponded as if he were not married. After Philip's first queen had died, he virtually imprisoned his second wife, the Danish Princess Ingebörg, and had his bishops annul their marriage so that he might marry his mistress, the Tirolese Lady Agnes.

For dinner, Liliane had worn her wedding dress, which Philip much admired. He also admired her skin, her hair and her eyes. She noticed that he was careful not to make Alexandre *too* jealous, but her husband seemed to play little mind to the conversation. His mind was miles away, probably already in searing Palestine. He laughed at none of Philip's witticisms, but Philip appeared oblivious to Alexandre's humorless distraction. Such was not the case, Liliane soon discovered.

She learned several things about the King of France that evening, primarily that he had a mind like a razor and missed nothing. Philip was capable of presenting whatever face he chose to get the reaction he wanted. Liliane concluded that Alexandre had already learned this. Short of being rude when he was around the king, Alexandre retreated into himself and waited Philip out, aware that sooner or later Philip would make his case. As a result, Philip usually wasted little folderol on Alexandre, most likely relieved to have a simple relationship. All he wanted to know was that Alexandre would give his life for France. Tonight's gallantry was mostly for the sake of Alexandre's bride, but his manners did not extend to allowing her to be present when he closeted himself with Alexandre for two hours after dinner.

Too restless and anxious to go to bed, Liliane saw the household settled and went to walk in the garden. The perfume of primulas, verbena and yarrow reminded her of the Moorish gardens where Alexandre would soon be in the Holy Land. More than Jacques's wolfish ambitions, she dreaded being separated from Alexandre. They'd had too little time together to really know each other beyond their flowering passion. Now they might be separated for years. She had perceived that Alexandre needed something from her she could not yet give him—a womanliness beyond the body she so passionately yielded him. And if Oriental females had a superlative skill, it was at using their mysterious femininity.

Liliane did not expect Alexandre to be a monk; he would be gone too long to sleep alone. And yet, much as she was already becoming jealous of the Eastern women who might enter his life, she was aware too that the refined women would be closely closeted. He would have to turn to unfeeling street whores. Although Alexandre had spoken little of being lonely in his first experience of the Crescent, she sensed that he dreaded being isolated in a hostile land almost as much as he dreaded another brutal, pointless war. Philip did not strike her as being the foil of anyone, including the Church he had blatantly ignored when he neglected the impediment of divorce and took a second wife. In time, the Pope pardoned him, but why would Philip, of all men, bother with a Holy War, particularly in the company of Richard, whom he thought reckless?

Suddenly, she saw a tall figure watching her from the shadow of the wall. Her hand moved to the poignard concealed beneath her sleeve. Although she was Alexandre's wife, she still never went unarmed.

"Never mind, Countess," the figure said softly. "I have but come to enjoy the moonlight."

The voice was Charles's, but Liliane did not relax. While she had not run afoul of his mastiffs, she and Charles were no more friends than they'd ever been. "I would prefer you left, Charles," she said quietly. "I wish to be alone."

He stepped away from the wall and came toward her. "I can imagine that you would, Countess. All your bright smiles at the king aside, you seemed rather glum at dinner." His big shoulders were imposing in the dim light cast by the courtyard torches, and he smiled oddly down at her. "Strange, I should have thought that you would be delighted. With Alexandre gone, what is to stop Uncle Jacques from descending upon this place like a wolf on a pen of sheep?"

"I have encountered very few sheep loyal to Alexandre," she replied flatly, "and you and I must stop Jacques. Take what is left of my dowry and hire mercenaries in Avignon if you must."

"Brave words, but I really do think you hate to see Alexandre go." His tone was mocking, but not so much as usual. He sounded too defeated to want to bait her.

"I love him. If I had a choice, I would send you to Palestine in his place. I have seen you training the castellans. You know what you are doing. You would love war; it suits your suspicious nature.''

Charles laughed. ''Would it suit your uncle's suspicious nature to discover you are so loath to see your husband leave?

''Go,'' Liliane said tiredly. ''I am in no mood for your idle taunts.''

''Idle?'' He turned serious. ''Was your dowry offer idle?''

She eyed him narrowly. ''I can supply castellans, perhaps six unlanded knights for a goodly time, *if* we find them quickly. Unless''—she could not hide a note of anger and contempt— ''Philip sends the entire country to the desert.''

''Who would govern those mercenaries?'' Charles challenged. ''You? Then have them betray the castle in a fight?''

''Choose your own men, but be prepared to answer for your decisions upon their employment to me. I would have you as an ally, Charles, not as my governor.''

''With six armed knights at my command, you might not have a choice,'' he drawled. ''I could pack you into the keep until you lost your beauty . . . and your hold on Alexandre.''

''Alexandre would kill you.''

''When he returned, perhaps; but he would have his land.''

Liliane laughed suddenly, softly. ''You are his bulldog to the bone, are you not?'' Her hand left the poignard and plucked a primula. She handed it to Charles. ''Choose your men and lock me in your keep when Alexandre is gone. I may lose my youth there, but not my faith to him. You may learn that he cares for more than my beauty.''

Charles silently took the flower, murmuring, ''If you put yourself and your fortune into my hands to protect Alexandre, you shall not regret it.'' His voice lowered to a whisper. ''But betray him and the dogs will spurn what I leave of you.''

''Fair enough. Now I state my bargain. Crush the primula upon your pillow tonight. I have brought Alexandre as much happiness as he has given to me. Wantonly destroy that happiness and until you die you will see my face whenever you smell a flower or look into Alexandre's face.'' With that, she left him in the garden and went to the tower chamber to wait for Alexandre.

He was late in coming. When he did, he pulled her quickly into his arms and kissed her. ''While Philip rests his men, we have tomorrow and another night. By God, I shall waste no more of this one!''

His hands traveled urgently over her body and she answered him with the same abandon. A thousand nights were in his touch, with all their fevered longing, and his kisses were hard and hot. Even as he pressed her upon the bed, he was baring her. His mouth claimed hers again as he pulled quickly at his own clothing. When they were joined as one, she felt herself falling with him into the rapturous bloom of their vanishing spring—its flowers scattering as if by a blinding, relentless wind. The blossoms whipped against their faces, their fiercely driving bodies. The skies ran scarlet with fast-flying clouds, and when they soared together into the vast red sun, Alexandre's cry was like a hawk's scream.

When at last they were both still, Liliane looked up into Alexandre's face. He wore a strange expression and his eyes were an almost eerie violet. He caught her hair tight in his hands. ''I could kill him,'' he whispered. ''Forswear faith and kill Philip. He has a thousand men, younger, braver men than I, their eyes still shining with untarnished, untried faith in him. Let him turn to them, for I am weary of him and all the rivers of blood that follow him. He still believes that nothing can come between him and me, not even the woman I love. But you, this land—by God, peace!—all deny him. . . .''

His eyes held their wild light for another moment, then he laid his head upon her breast. ''All, *all* deny him, yet I will never say him nay. Why? For my children, that he will not wrest away their inheritance? I know not. I know only that I fight no more for pride.''

Liliane held his face in her hands. ''You cannot deny Philip unless he first denies you. Before all of France, he has put you at his right hand and he cannot let you relinquish that position without having his pride and friendship publicly slighted. Turn from him now and he will destroy you.'' Her hand pressed hard. ''But know this, my darling: go to Palestine and you will have Charles and me at your back. You are no longer poor; you have a wife and friend who love you, as well as the favor of the king. You do not go to war alone this time. My every waking thought will be with you.'' She kissed him. ''Come home to me, I beg you.''

''Marry how many wives he will,'' Alexandre breathed,

"Philip will never find such a one to love as you. If only you could come with me, I would show you the desert on a starry night when all the sands seem to heave in a white sea and the palm trees whisper their dry prayers on the unbroken wind. Come to me in my dreams, my beloved Liliane, and we will be one again as the doves of Solomon."

Then they were one, man unto woman, as the first mating of living things upon the earth, that eon upon eon extended creation.

The next morning, as soon as the men left for their hunt, Liliane rode to the oak to leave another message in the cylinder. The first note was still there. Deciding that the *banditti* idea had best wait, she removed the note, then noticed that the parchment was of a lesser quality than the one she had used. Upon a close examination of the note, she discovered that it was not her own. The script and wording were similar, but the suggested date for the attack had been moved up, possibly to take advantage of Alexandre's absence before the castle could be reinforced.

Liliane had been right about the spy, and now she knew it must be someone who could write. Any one of the castellans could be hiding his scholarship, but the obvious suspects were Father Anslem, Fremier and Charles. She dismissed Father Anselm and Charles, but the cleric was a possibility.

She would let Jacques take care of the problem, by telling him the message had been altered. Assuming the spy was his, her loyalty would be affirmed and he would be forced to recruit a new infiltrater. A new face in the castle would instantly come to her notice.

Liliane added a line to the note in the cylinder, which Jacques's man was due to pick up that afternoon. When she had finished, the message read, 'The king has arrived. An invitation to Castle de Signe might be in your favor. If such an invitation does not arrive at Castle de Brueil by sunset, I shall assume my message has been altered as were the rest of our communications.'

Jacques's invitation to Philip arrived at sunset while Liliane and Alexandre were closeted alone with the king for an aperitif before dinner. "The ingratiating, self-seeking weasel," muttered Philip, throwing the message into the fireplace grate. Apparently, Alexandre had assured him that Liliane had little love for her uncle, since he took no care to hide his contempt.

"My uncle is an exceedingly rich man, Your Majesty," Liliane observed softly. "Possibly he will offer a contribution as well as armed men for your campaign."

Philip peered at her, then his mouth curved in a vulpine smile. "Never make your wife angry, Alexandre. She has a brain as well as a pretty face. She will either make you rich or cost you your head." Casually, he sipped his aperitif. "I had already planned to visit your uncle, Countess. Kings cannot be particular about the purses they pick. I had intended to surprise him . . . but, then, I have an idea you reminded him of his manners."

Liliane and Alexandre glanced at each other. Philip's contempt of Jacques had been just another empty show, a pandering to their emotions. Certainly the pockets Philip picked were rarely repaid. That he now made his real intentions clear was a warning not to toy with his favor. "Do not fear, Countess," Philip drawled. "I am not angry, so long as you remember that men, particularly kings, like to lead, not be led"—he stroked her cheek—"be the carrot ever so lovely."

Alexandre rose silently to his feet and gently drew Liliane from Philip's reach. "This is one carrot for whom I would fight even a king."

A cool glint entered Philip's green eyes. "I will remember that."

With a cold chill of foreboding, Liliane knew that he would.

Philip paid his call on Jacques de Signe. To Alexandre and Liliane's dumbfounded delight, Philip returned a week later with the hastily equipped Jacques and Louis and twelve of their finest knights. "Recruits," Philip explained lightly, waving his doffed gauntlets at the Signes' dour faces. "Not only Signe gold, but their strong armed men shall accompany us in this Holy Crusade against the infidel."

Liliane looked up at Jacques. "So you have made peace with the king, Uncle?"

"I am honored to prove my loyalty to His Majesty," rasped Jacques. From his flat tone, Liliane surmised that the proof had been expensive. Jacques was not pleased with her.

As Philip watched Liliane standing beside Alexandre, his eyes held a calculating glint. "I regret that we will not be enjoying your hospitality tonight, Countess, for we ride now to join Richard. Your husband will attend us in Palestine."

Liliane wondered if Philip enjoyed the eloquent pain in her eyes as she turned to kiss Alexandre. Jacques and Louis would think her distress at his leaving a sham; Philip would guess it was agony. "Farewell, my love," she whispered to Alexandre. "I pray for a quick victory and your safe return."

He clasped her tightly. "I *will* come back to you; now I have more reason than even my life to do so. I want to spend the long years with you. . . ."

"Take them now," the eavesdropping Philip added casually. "One, at least." He pulled on his gauntlets, smiling without warmth at Liliane. "Your husband asked a year's leave of me with his promise to meet the army in Palestine. Did he not tell you, my lady?"

Hardly daring to hope, Liliane caught Alexandre's arm. "Is this so, my lord Alexandre?"

"That I made the request is so," Alexandre replied slowly. "That it has been granted, I have dared not hope."

"You should entertain more faith in your friends, my lord," rebuked Philip, his green eyes mocking. "With a good navigator and few men to transport, 'twill take you no great time to sail to Acre, Alexandre. A king encumbered by position and army must sail in sight of shore, for a lost ship may cost a hundred fighting men and near half that number of horses." He smiled wryly. "Naturally, Richard and I will attend a great number of entertainments while we battle over tablecloths with our hosts to establish policy that will be ignored the moment our sails are out of sight. 'Twill be a damned tedious trip that will waste a year at least. I shall look for you this day next spring in Acre."

"Thank you, sire," Alexandre replied quietly. "I shall not fail you."

"No," Philip replied expressionlessly, "I do not suppose you will." He doffed his cap to Liliane. "My lady, look after your husband well. I want him in fighting trim to meet the Saracens."

"I will, sire," Liliane said softly. "I thank you for your gracious generosity." Although she knew that Philip's concession was calculated to hold Alexandre's loyalty, she was nonetheless grateful to him.

Philip kissed her fingertips. "You are more than welcome, lady." Then he added impishly, "Will you not bid so sweet a farewell to your uncle and cousin? After all, they must brave a great distance to try their courage against the heathens. 'Tis a voyage even the hardy do not always survive.''

All eyes turned toward Jacques. Liliane went swiftly forward to curtsy before him. ''Godspeed, Uncle''—she looked up—''and to you, Cousin. I know that you will comport yourselves bravely.'' Like trapped rats, she mentally added. And as such, God willing, may you meet your just deserts. He sees into your hearts when I cannot. Liliane tugged a yellow ribbon from her sleeve. ''This favor was meant for my lord Alexandre, but as you go now in his stead''—she tied the ribbon to her uncle's gauntleted wrist—''wear this and remember that I think of you.''

Jacques patted her head with his heavy hand. ''The year will pass quickly, my girl, and will be over before you know it.'' He unknotted the favor and returned it to her. ''Keep this for your husband, who will soon join us.''

Liliane forced herself to accept the ribbon with a smile, pretending that his words held no threatening promise. ''Thank you, Uncle. I shall do so. As for the time passing quickly, I shall waste none of it.'' She eyed Louis demurely. ''Guard our uncle well, Cousin, and see that he does not suffer unduly from the desert heat.''

Louis grunted sullenly. ''None of us will escape the heat, were the Devil himself to protect us.''

Alexandre could not resist grinning wickedly. ''Do not dismiss the Devil's favor too lightly, kinsman. Men become none too particular of allies when frying under the enemy sun of Palestine.'' He held up his hand to Philip. ''God save you, my liege. Please offer my respects to King Richard.''

Philip touched his cap and spurred his destrier to the northeast. Like squat black toads in their saddles, Jacques and Louis followed, their retinues falling in behind them. As the riders picked up speed and their pennants flapped in the sea breeze, Liliane clasped Alexandre's arm. ''Jacques is right, my love. Our time together will be brief.''

Alexandre swept her up into his arms and headed for their turret. ''Then we will not spend it in chatter. I will show you a rare place to tie your yellow ribbon.''

She giggled. ''Alexandre, you are shameless!''

'' 'Tis spring, Madame!'' he crowed, then whispered in her ear, ''I would wear a pennant upon my standard to celebrate!''

8

Monkey in the Marketplace

Castle de Brueil
February 1191

Jacques's sober prediction proved all too true. The seasons came and went like ephemeral wraiths, and the winter, usually so sere and long, prematurely gave way to the melting snows and mud that promised the first new buds of spring. Alexandre spent his free time reinforcing the castle against his absence, yet time grew short and much remained undone.

As Alexandre had only ten knights and twice that many castellans to accompany him, he meant to sail from Massilia directly to Acre. Two lords who would meet him in Massilia had pledged to conscript for Philip another two hundred men. As the damp blasts of early February blew across Provence, Alexandre dared wait no longer to leave for Massilia. In a bitter rain, with his mounted men dripping in their saddles and his foot soldiers shivering among their weeping women, he bade Liliane farewell, and upon her finger placed a gold signet ring that duplicated his own. No greater mark of trust could he offer her, for it gave her power to act in his stead, whether to his good or his ill.

Liliane drew him into the great hall to kiss him. "Take great care, Alexandre," she whispered in the shadow of the cold gray walls. "Jacques and Louis are more dangerous to you than any infidels."

"Nay, you are the danger," he murmured. "In leaving you, I leave my heart. Will you wait?"

She was dismayed that he could doubt it, then she remembered that he still did not know she had guessed he had once pretended to be Jean. "I love only you, my darling. Nothing will separate us; I swear it on my life."

His mouth claimed hers, passionate with bitter loss, and she remembered the long night and how the sadness of their love-making had drained them. Finally, they had simply held each other and waited numbly for the sun. Before Alexandre had gone down to his men, she placed a medallion about his neck. "If ever you are in mortal danger from the paladins of Saladin, show them this and say it was given you by a friend of Almansor. You will gain either freedom or . . ."

Shaken, she could not finish, and Alexandre dryly finished for her. "A quick death."

"Saladin is an old comrade of Almansor. I believe he would be merciful."

He ruffled her hair affectionately. "What shall I do with a wife who is friend to all my worst enemies?"

Liliane laughed. "Heed Philip and do not drape yourself with too many sloe-eyed concubines." When he started to protest, she gently laid her finger across his lips. "Nay, promise nothing. Only guard your life. You have seen that Jacques is not loath to use women to gain his ends."

She smiled with forced brightness when she waved off Alexandre and his troops. Her apparent cheer did not go unnoticed by Charles, who stood at her side in the courtyard. "So," he commented laconically, "now you have the place to yourself."

"That I do," she replied quietly. "Have you made reconnaissance of the force left at Castle de Signe?"

"By Alexandre's order. Twenty men at arms and two knights remain."

This time her smile was genuine. "Bless Philip. He stripped them to the bone."

"It suited his purpose."

Conceding nothing, Liliane met his gaze. "And ours." She tossed him a pouch from her kirtle. "Still, we are undermanned, as well. You will take these gold dinars and hire mercenaries in Avignon. Also buy weapons and post a border patrol at the old hunting lodge. You are now not only my seneschal but also my military commander. Six of the dinars in that pouch are yours to cover your first three months pay."

He stared at her. "At that rate, I could apply to the king for my own land in three years."

"In three years, Alexandre will be home and by then it will be high time you had a place of your own." She cocked her head. "You are a very intelligent man, Charles. I would be foolish to let you become dissatisfied, as well."

"Not everyone has your means of betrayal."

Refusing to take offense, she watched Alexandre's pennant fade into the distance. "Do not protest too much. You may soon find that I have reason to reward you."

By tomorrow morning, in fact, Charles would understand all too well the reason for his high recompense.

At dawn, as the meadow mists rose about her, Liliane looked back at Castle de Brueil; it was her home now and she would only see it again with Alexandre at her side. Under her indigo blue cloak, she was dressed as a royal page in gray velvet, courtesy of one of Philip's fops whose snobbery did not preclude his selling some of his clothing to a beautiful countess who professed a wish to richly garb a page of her own. Under the cloak she also carried a light crossbow used for bird shooting.

Accustomed to her sometimes riding alone, the guards made no inquiry as she crossed the drawbridge with her disguise well hidden from their notice. Her comfortable relationship with them would soon have been ended by Charles, who would awaken this morning to his role as sole governor of the castle. Liliane had no misgivings about him; he would guard the place with his life. Were she to linger within his reach, he'd put her to the sword if her uncle killed Alexandre in Palestine. Charles made a superb friend, but a relentless enemy.

Just now, Liliane had enemies enough and they could not be fought at Castle de Brueil. Once in Palestine, Alexandre would need someone behind him. What easier way for the Signes to take the Brueil lands than to make certain that the sole Brueil heir never returned to his ancestral home.

Philip was an equally dangerous opponent. He saw Liliane not only as an enemy Signe, but also as a rival for Alexandre's fidelity. He would make every effort to turn Alexandre against her; and ruthless and clever as he was, he might just succeed. Liliane knew that a tiny doubt about her still lingered in Alexandre's mind. Lonely and frustrated in Palestine, he might in time give heed to Philip.

No, Liliane dared not molder under Charles's thumb at Castle de Brueil. After a year's hard debate, she had made her decision. Alexandre needed her now more than ever, but in a way that might tear them apart. To follow him to Palestine would never have entered her head had Jacques and Louis not been destined there. Women were nuisances and liabilities on campaigns. Alexandre would have good cause to be furious if she tagged after him; therefore, he must be unaware of her presence. He was about to make a steadfast new friend: one Jefar el din.

Audacious as Liliane might be, she was not foolhardy. Even a knight traveling alone tempted bad luck. Massilia, or Marseilles, as some now called the old Roman town, was about a three days' ride westward along the coast. From Massilia, Alexandre would embark for Acre. Liliane found a rock sheltered hideaway that she could use to observe the coastal road. With the horse hidden, neither searchers from the castle nor passersby could spy her. Just before dusk, a search party rode past her with Charles at their head, his eyes squinting at the sun shafting through the clouds. A short distance beyond her vantage point, she saw the riders split up, most of them heading inland, while the rest continued west.

Merchants and travelers often used that road, but nearly two days passed before she spotted a likely group of pilgrims accompanied by monks. Despite the clerical robes, she was slow to approach their band—monks were not always peaceful, and were usually armed. Some abbots were no better than robber barons, and ruthlessly raided their neighbors. She held her crossbow at the ready, cocked beneath her cloak. When she appeared, mounted on the barb, no one advanced to meet her. The band formed a tight phalanx behind a burly monk who towered above them on a roan destrier. Liliane halted warily before him and addressed him with her contralto voice lowered, "Good Brother, I journey to Massilia to join the Holy Crusade. May I ask your blessing and seek safe passage in your company?"

The group eyed her dubiously, the big monk most of all. "You have my blessing and welcome, young sir, but you have more the look of one accustomed to gentle pursuits than to war," the monk said bluntly. "The way to redemption need not be taken by force of arms, but by worthy deeds. I beg you to reconsider, sirrah, and live to grow old in charitable works."

Liliane was a trifle taken aback. This was no proselytizer who cast men off, young and old, bent and whole, to the hazards of the Holy Land with exhortations and threats of hell. "As you are a practical man as well as a holy one, good Brother, I am grateful for your advice; however, my way must lead to Palestine. I trust that Heaven will give me guidance and protection, and yet"—she uncovered the bow—"as you see, I do not propose to weary Providence with unnecessary effort on my behalf."

The monk regarded the small bow with a wry smile. "Providence will be hard put to see you drop more than a quail with that quill."

"Think you that force is preferable to accuracy?" Liliane gestured at a distant pine down the road. "Yonder mid branch is overladen with cones." Taking careful aim, Liliane fired a quarrel at the pine. A single cone was neatly severed from its limb and landed in the road mire.

"I grant you that pine cones do not have the retaliatory ability of the Saracens," Liliane said quietly, "yet I believe that I will not be entirely useless to King Philip."

The monk shrugged. "As you will. You may join us as far as Massilia. We journey to Avignon." He nodded at the crossbow. "Keep that where you can get at it."

Liliane nodded. "That is advice I will readily take. Lead on to Massilia, good Brother, with my thanks."

He waved her to a spot near the rear of the phalanx amid a cluster of women pilgrims. Meekly, Liliane accepted her assignment. One did not argue overmuch with giants.

In three days, they came within sight of Massilia, a triad of small towns perched upon a rocky hill above the sea on the Gulf of Lions. The highest town was joined to the ship-dotted sea by a creek. To the south was the port of Les Catalans looking toward Cape Croisette, and below center was the Vieux Port. Brother Marcus, the huge monk, looked enviously at the cathedral rising above the narrow streets. "Yonder church is not long built and I would give much to see it," he commented to Liliane, "but the town is foul and methinks the wise course will be to pass it by. Road brigands pose less hazard than the streets of Massilia." He shifted his saddle. "We leave you here, then, young sir. Fare you well and may God look after you and the pine cones of Acre."

Liliane laughed. "Thank you, Brother. May you one day see the Cathedral de la Major without risk of your neck."

The big monk grinned. "I worry less for my neck than my virtue. Look to yours. Many a villain in Massilia will have use for a pretty boy."

But the boy who waved the monk and his companions adieu was not the same fresh-faced creature who wandered the streets of Massilia a few hours later.

No one paid attention to a slim, slight Berber in black aba with cobalt-lined haik. Once Liliane's pale hair was concealed by the haik and her brows stained, her dark-lashed amber eyes easily passed for Moorish. She kept the haik high over her face and she would acquire a tan within a few days of Mediterranean sun. If her choice of disguise was unusual, it was also practical. She was not tall and strong enough to pass as a European soldier, but Christian Moors sometimes fought on the side of the crusaders. Being alien, they were not chatterers and held themselves apart from other Moors.

Her Berber attire had been easily devised. The monk had been right: wet-eared pages were attractive game in Massilia. After sharp haggling, Liliane purchased a good scimitar and dirk in an armory, but kept the crossbow strung at her back. She also traded the bay barb for a deft gray Moorish mare that resembled the fine animal she'd left behind at Castle de Brueil. The mixture of coffee and grease staining her face and hands would last until a deep tan turned her into Jefar el din.

After a half day of roaming the harbor port, Liliane discovered a real problem in her original plan to befriend Alexandre; he was quite unlikely to be open to making a new acquaintance. Only an idiot would be convivial in Massilia, a teeming hive of seamen and human vermin. Fights were rampant and the harbor bars and brothels were particularly vicious. Whores squalled from the windows and, if necessary, accommodated their clients in alleyways. Sailors, merchants, slaves and criminals of every nationality crowded the grimy narrow streets. On street corners Liliane saw North African Moors conducting auctions of terrified blacks, usually sold in groups to be resold elsewhere.

Finding Alexandre's group was more simple than she'd imagined. The winter storms had ended and Philip wanted reinforcements. The crusaders' every move was discussed in the city and probably relayed to Saladin. Alexandre's men were housed with him and those of another French noble, Lisle, in one of the largest inns near the waterfront. Three lateen-rigged ships had been collected for transport and idled at anchor while knights bought slaves to serve as hostlers and foragers. In Malaga, Liliane had seen that slaves were not worth the trouble. Besides, once in Palestine, they would run away at first chance only to be retaken by the Saracens, to whom they'd blab information the Europeans had chattered in front of them.

Philip might be good at his profession, but she had heard that Saladin, outnumbered as he was, was better. He was well informed and a magnificent tactician. According to Alexandre, Philip rarely misjudged an opponent, yet his recruitment policies seemed careless and overconfident. His officers took in recruits with scant examination, often pressing into service street refuse who would be little more help at war than chickens. Liliane faintly smelled a rat, but was not sure where it hid. To find out, she applied for a position with the rat keeper.

The sergeant Liliane approached for admission to Philip's army was big and blundering, flatly disapproving of Moors in general, and the army in particular. When he demanded proof of her Christianity she produced from under her aba the Byzantine cross she'd purchased for such occasions. Unimpressed, he grimaced. "Trade your god and you'll trade anything."

"All gods may be the same," Jefar el din murmured, "but my parents were Christian."

"Can't go home for some reason, eh?" The sergeant grunted. "All right, sign here. The king'll take any man on two legs that doesn't spit on the cross."

Just as she started to sign the recruitment roster, a shadow fell over the parchment. Glancing up, Liliane was dismayed and overjoyed to see Alexandre. What if he recognized her? She was almost relieved to see that his eyes were those of a stranger, a fighter who had warred with the Saracens. Skeptically, he eyed the cross about her neck, then said in good Arabic, "Your zeal is commendable, my friend, but you would be better off joining the blue-eyed Richard at Acre. He is more of a purist than our good King Philip. You would be less likely to have your throat cut in your sleep."

"I sleep lightly, *effendi,*" replied Liliane in Arabic. She made her voice low and husky. Her accent was Andalusian, but she doubted if Alexandre would recognize that fact.

She was shocked when he did. "Where is your tribe? You dress like a Saharan Berber, but you are not Tuareg."

"I have no tribe, *effendi*. Once my parents dwelled with the Berbers of the Siwa Oasis in Egypt, but they became outcasts after their conversion."

"Your sisters and wives; are they Christian, as well?"

Aware that Alexandre's slight was deliberate, Liliane drew herself up with a flat-eyed stare. Moorish men did not discuss their women outside the family. "I have no blood kin, *effendi*. They were massacred with the Christians of Jabal Nefusa."

Alexandre was unrelenting. "If you have a bone to pick with your people, take it up with *Melek Richard*. Personal blood feuds have no place in my lord Philip's plans." He shook his head at the sergeant and turned away.

Liliane was perplexed. What was she to do now? She had not expected Alexandre to be more particular than the other nobles about recruits. Resignedly, she touched her forehead and left the inn. She knew better than to argue with Alexandre in military matters. She must find a way around him.

Recruitment stations had been set up at several points along the waterfront. Many sergeants kept at hand a preaching friar and holy relic under embroidered cloth to make the oath of allegiance more binding. Liliane went to a station at the mouth of La Joliette creek and reapplied for enlistment. This time she received little argument. With a triumphant smile, Philip's newest soldier strolled to the marketplace to purchase a few items for her kit.

The market was bustling. Oriental rugs and brass, weapons from Spain and foreign souvenirs were sold outside the ship chandleries and food stalls. For the sea crossing, Liliane bought flat pita bread and felafel, lemons, dates and an eggplant purée called ganoush. She also found extra tallow to maintain her dark complexion, a striped wool blanket, medicinal herbs, a metal water flask and a small bowl. Finding a vacant spot, she seated herself in the Moorish style and ate some of the felafel, fresh fruit and wilted endive. While she ate, she tried to think of a way to approach Alexandre.

Just then, a female monkey danced down the overhead awning of a high window and hung upside down to grimace at her. Liliane held out a bit of pita bread. The monkey peered at it for a moment, then leaped down and sidled toward the bread. When the small creature would not take it from her fingers, Liliane let the bread drop. The monkey grabbed the bread and ate it. Then, with a sidelong, bright-eyed look at her, he began to roam curiously among her purchases. Suddenly the creature snatched the bright bowl and tried to make off with it. Liliane, who had been watching to make sure the monkey stole no fruit, tossed the bedroll over it. Forced to drop the bowl to scramble free, the monkey raced off screeching across the market. Liliane laughed. The little beggar was a trained thief, taught to steal shiny objects that might be gold or silver.

Still pondering the problem of Alexandre, Liliane continued to wander the market. Near dusk, she noticed the monkey again. This time the audacious creature was picking pockets. Just as Liliane started forward to warn a plump gentleman that he was being relieved of his pouch, she was struck by an inspiration of how to employ the monkey's dubious talent. She darted a quick glance around, hoping that she would not encounter a confrontation with its owner. Just as the monkey's paw darted out for a snatch, she sidled up behind it and grabbed it by the scruff. When the creature gave a horrible screech and tried to bite her, Liliane gave an apologetic smile to the startled man. "A thousand pardons, Monsieur. This mischievous creature is not yet resigned to becoming a pet for my eldest son."

The plump man blustered, "Then you should keep better control of him."

"Be assured"—Liliane gave him an obsequious smile—"I shall."

Liliane then took the monkey, which she named Kiki, to a campsite outside of town. She could not abide the idea of sleeping in one of the city's grimy inns. For two days, she soothed the half-starved monkey and spoiled her with food until Kiki realigned her loyalties; the capricious monkey also learned a couple of new tricks.

The day before the crusaders were to set sail, Liliane returned to Massilia with Kiki perched on her shoulder. Kiki wore a tether in case she proved troublesome. Upon reaching the market, Liliane tested Kiki at an orange stall. The animal had become extremely wary after being twice caught, but she soon returned with an orange. Liliane rewarded her with a fig, then quietly returned the orange to the stall as they passed into the Street of Angels.

The next time she unfastened the tether, Kiki performed beautifully and returned promptly. Kiki was a little too prompt for safety, Liliane decided as she stroked her and gave her another reward. The monkey must learn not to make a beeline for Liliane. Magpies, ferrets, parrots and monkeys were often used as thieves, usually to be eventually caught and punished cruelly for their innocent loyalty to their masters. And Liliane had no wish to lose a hand under Moorish law if Kiki were apprehended in Palestine.

She set up watch outside Alexandre's inn. When he emerged with Lisle, she followed them at a safe distance down to the harbor. There the pair stood for some time looking out over the bustling harbor, watching the dockworkers load the ships for debarkation at dawn. After the two men parted, Alexandre continued alone to a dockside inn which specialized in spicy *couscous*. Liliane waited until he left the inn at nightfall, then followed him into the winding street that led back to his lodging. The streets were still crowded, and at an intersection, Liliane pointed out Alexandre to Kiki, jingled the money in her coin pouch and let her go. Kiki scampered off through the crowd and in minutes was back with Alexandre's pouch. Liliane swept the monkey up onto her shoulder, then strode off after Alexandre. She had to trot two street lengths to catch him. Although Alexandre had not seen the culprit, he had felt the pouch go and was casting about for the thief. Liliane approached him as he followed a suspicious-looking pair up a side alley.

"*Effendi,*" she called softly, "I must speak with you."

Without stopping, Alexandre shot her an impatient look. "I told you, take your case to *Melek Richard.* Now, begone."

"I believe yours is the trouble, *effendi.*" She shot a glance ahead at the two characters who had now turned with unpleasant interest. "A matter of a pouch."

Alexandre, also noticing the pair ahead, halted. "Not here. Come with me."

They retreated, the ruffians following. Alexandre headed up another alley, then, nodding to Lilian to take a shadowed doorway, pressed himself into the shadowy recesses of the one opposite. Kiki scampered up onto a crumbling balustrade. The two ruffians, their knives drawn, entered the alley.

Liliane's heart began to pound. Only once had she been faced with the prospect of killing a man. A Moorish raiding party had attacked a band of Diego's castellans with whom she had been riding to Cadiz. As Diego had not been present to protect her, she soon realized why he had taken the precaution of teaching her to protect herself. The castellans had been outnumbered, the fight brief but vicious. Although beaten off, the raiders had driven away two mules loaded with supplies, and they might have taken her as well to please their amir. She had been terrified and clumsy in the fighting, but she had learned never to merely injure an opponent; doing so had nearly gotten her strangled. She learned that killing was the best defense.

Now, when the moment came in the Massilia alley, her knife slid in neatly under the scoundrel's fifth rib without a sound. Her hunter was dead before he knew that his game had reversed. Alexandre dispassionately wiped his own knife on the other thug. "Now, what about the pouch?"

Liliane swallowed hard, not looking at the dead men. "Shall I explain in a less compromising spot, *effendi?*"

Alexandre nodded grimly. He led Liliane to his inn and waved to a table in the common room. Liliane sat gratefully, her knees still weak. The killing had been so quick, so quiet . . . so horribly impersonal. "Brandywine?" Alexandre asked, probably noticing that she was pale under her brown face stain.

Liliane declined his offer. "My habits are still Moslem, *effendi.*"

"And eminently practical in a hot climate." Alexandre waved away the innkeeper approaching with a bottle of his best rotgut. "So. You are . . ."

"Jefar el din."

"And what do you have to tell me?"

For answer, Liliane dropped his pouch of gold on the table. Kiki chattered excitedly.

In an instant, the pouch disappeared under Alexandre's cloak. His voice came hard. "Where did you get it?"

"I noticed two men, not the ones we dispatched, following you. I thought they meant mischief but they passed into a brothel. At that point, a boy picked your pocket and I sent Kiki to relieve him of his booty. Unfortunately, in that time, you had fixed on the pair in the alley."

With skeptical perusal of Kiki, Alexandre took a couple of coins from the pouch.

"No, *effendi.* I do not want your money."

"See here," Alexandre said quietly. "Whatever your pet's part in this, I will not admit you to my banner. With all respect, I have fought Saracens too long to relish one at my back in battle . . . or in the street. You handle yourself well. You will find a place . . . but not with me." He rose and pushed the coins across the table. "Take the gold and Allah give you luck."

"Keep your gold, *effendi*," Liliane replied coolly. "I do not kill for pay but to survive. Honor also can be a luxury." She lifted Kiki to her shoulder. "May you have a safe passage to Palestine."

With narrowed eyes, Alexandre watched Jefar el din leave. Something was very familiar about this Berber fellow with his proud, graceful carriage and walk. He was not quite effeminate, but the use of his hands . . . Alexandre could not pin down his memories. He certainly did not believe the street tale. The Berber had probably put the monkey up to nipping his money just to make another try at joining the army. Moors were masters of deceit and particularly enjoyed gulling infidels. Yet . . . there was something steady about Jefar el din. He had noticed the Berber's distaste at being obliged to kill the thug, yet he had done so without quailing. He was determined, too, with none of the false obsequiousness many Moors practiced on Europeans they privately despised. Alexandre had a feeling that he would run into Jefar el din again.

Liliane spent the night on one of the troop ships. Deciding that the ship would be cleaner and cheaper than one of the local stews, she showed her army admission to the shipmaster who could not read and bribed him to let her aboard. She and Kiki burrowed under the bow among the stow of canvas, where they slept soundly until the first soldiers boarded at dawn. She had been discouraged when Alexandre had proven unyielding the night before, and she was horrified to hear him board the ship. There were three ships and he had to pick hers! Muffling Kiki's chatter, she burrowed deeper into the bow and kicked the canvas aft so that no attention would be drawn to her when the crew hoisted sail. Curling up, she pulled her haik over her head and covered Kiki so that they appeared to be a bundle of stowage. Preoccupied with seeing a hundred men, their gear, and horses being properly stowed to keep the ship balanced, Alexandre took no notice of her. Some time went by before the ships were loaded, due to some of the soldiers' reluctance to board. If the men had not been conscripted, the army would have attracted few volunteers. Almost none of them had been to sea; they feared every calamity, from wild storms to sea monsters. Liliane smiled sympathetically. They would be wretched soon enough without seeing dragons.

With squeaks of wood echoing the many rats scurrying about the hold, the pitch-caulked ships glided into the bustling harbor. At the slap of the water against their hull, Kiki's eyes became wide and frightened, her tiny hands digging into Liliane's arm. Liliane cuddled her and whispered words of comfort she could not share herself. Already very fond of the little monkey, she was unwilling to leave her behind to be starved and used badly by her former master. Kiki could learn virtue as well as vice, but meanwhile her current versatility might prove useful.

Liliane peeked out at the soldiers huddled in the creaking ships. Although the sun had just risen, they were sweating and miserable with fear. She was startled to see that Alexandre was white as a sheet in the stern. He looked less afraid than ill, and with dismay she realized that he was going to be seasick before they were beyond the harbor.

She was right. Five minutes out, Alexandre was retching over the side along with three other men. More soldiers were turning green from the heaving swells. With a sigh, Liliane settled down to wait until the next morning. They were nearly a day's sail from land before she crawled back to Alexandre. He was weak, parched and utterly miserable. She fished in her medical sack for herbs and ground them into her bowl with water from her flask; then she helped him sit up. His eyelids fluttered as she held the brew to his lips. "You!" he whispered hoarsely. "I ought to haul you back!"

"We are too far out now," she assured him calmly. "Besides, I have my papers. I have joined Count Lisle's banner. Drink this; you will feel better."

He eyed the bowl suspiciously, then, at its stench, looked as if he would be sick again.

"Come, *effendi*, do not be foolish; the bowl does not contain poison to keep you from causing me trouble in Acre. Once there, I will fight Saladin whether King Philip keeps me or not. If you are too stubborn to accept my help now, you will feel like mule dung for the duration of the voyage."

Alexandre drank the stinking brew. He silently vowed to hang the Berber by his thumbs later.

Through that day and most of the next, Liliane felt Alexandre's bloodshot eyes on her as she attended the men. His stare became even more intent when once she caught herself from falling overboard as the ship pitched and rolled. She realized that when they landed in Acre, she had better get out of his reach until his temper cooled considerably.

Unfortunately, Alexandre's temper did not wait until Acre to explode, but only until the ship's passengers were asleep. One of the four aboard who did not become seasick, Liliane was peacefully sleeping in her spot near the bow when a hard hand closed about her throat and another over her mouth. Her eyes flying open, she uttered a muffled, terrified squeak. "I am going to strangle you," a low, furious voice muttered from the darkness. "Then I am going to keelhaul you and twist your scheming little head off!" A hand shifted and Alexandre's mouth came down in a brief but forceful kiss.

"How did you know?" Liliane gasped when his mouth lifted.

In answer, Alexandre grabbed a strand of blond hair escaping her haik and flattened it across her nose. "The sun is fading your stain, and when you lose your balance, you catch it like a woman," he hissed. "What the hell are you doing here!"

"You need me!" she whispered back. "Do you suppose Louis and Jacques are going to let you sail home in glory?"

"I can take care of my own ass, *merci!* How do you think I managed without you for twenty-odd years?" He let out another exasperated oath. "You *shived* a hulk in Massilia, *par Dieu!* How did you spend your childhood? Slitting your dolls' throats!"

"That ruffian was after *me,*" she retorted, then held her breath as a nearby sleeper stirred, "not the other way around. Diego did not want to leave me helpless in the world so . . ."

"So he taught you gutter fighting." Alexandre grabbed his hair with Gallic fervor. "Helpless? He turned you into a little monster!"

At that, Liliane went cold. Hurt filled her heart, closing out whatever else Alexandre was saying. The worst she had feared was happening. Alexandre thought her unnatural; she was no longer a woman to him—certainly not his love that he expected to wait quietly at home for him so that he could fantasize about her in pastoral peace. Silently, she tucked her hair away, pulled her haik across her face, then curled away from him.

Alexandre was quiet now and she could feel him staring at her. The drowsing Kiki pushed into her neck, and her tears were wet against the monkey's soft fur.

Alexandre touched her shoulder. "Liliane, I am sorry." He was silent for a moment. "I did not mean for my outburst to be so unfair. If you were a man, I should have praised your courage and skill. As it is, all I can think of is the danger you risk, that you could have been killed by that street thug and that you have been venturing alone about those foul Massilia streets." His grip tightened. "I appreciate your concern for me, but the army camp at Acre will not only be exposed to the risks of war, but be teeming with disease and hardened womenless men. I should worry far more about those threats to you than any from Jacques."

"You do not know him as I do," Liliane muttered.

"You must not know me very well, either." He nuzzled her neck. "Enjoy your sea voyage, darling, because the moment we reach Acre, you are going to embark upon another voyage home."

But home is with you, Liliane thought stubbornly.

Alexandre settled down to sleep with his back against hers. Although he scarcely moved until morning, she sensed that he was wide awake.

For the rest of the voyage, except for sleeping near her at night, Alexandre was careful not to pay undue attention to her. She suspected that his reticence was as much due to not wanting to alert the other men as to his lingering shock and dismay at her presence. Aware that she was causing him a very real problem, she would have given much to ease it, but she was not prepared to return to France. Jacques was wickedly patient and Louis was relentless. Better for Alexandre to endure injured pride than a terminally injured skull.

Yet, oh, how keenly she felt Alexandre's disapproval! She longed to curl up next to him and have him put his arms around her. He might think her brave and resolute, but she felt like a nervous mouse when she thought of the street thugs. The idea of seeing war at close hand filled her with dread. She had been lonely as Jefar el din for she dared not risk discovery by exchanging more than a few sentences with anyone. Alexandre's quick

penetration of her disguise made her feel vulnerable. When un-
recognized, she had foolishly envisioned herself as his guardian
angel, which lent closeness to their relationship. Now he knew
her identity and his anger isolated her.

On the night before sighting Acre, Alexandre watched Liliane
stir restlessly. He was aware of her every movement . . . and her
deep hurt. He slouched gloomily against the gunnel. He could
not even make love to her; to do so now would be to say good-
bye twice, and he could not bear that. He wanted to comfort her,
but he knew that if he forgave her too quickly, she would fasten
herself like a crab to him. Her acquiescence at being sent home
deceived him not at all. She had no intention of returning to
France, but she would do so if he had to strap her to a wine
cask!

Near dusk of the next day, they sighted Acre. The best port
on the Palestine coast, the city lay in the shallow northern curve
of the bay of Acre. A vast white-gold desert spread inland from
Acre past Mount Carmel to the distant Galilean foothills that
shielded Lake Tiberias. The setting sun glinted off the great on-
ion domes and minarets that rose above the city behind its long,
heavy wall.

Siege machines had shattered most of the tall palms on the
highest city terraces; splintered stubs jabbed at the sky. The city
wall bounded the sea and wound above the harbor streets where
ramshackle shops still functioned. Several moored ships stood
offshore, and shelters constructed from dismantled ships strewed
the upper beaches above the tide line. Beyond the dunes, the
camp spread to the siege trenches, now emptied for the day as
were the ramparts of the city. Eastward, hidden in the great desert dunes, lay the camp of Saladin, who had come to give what
relief he could to the besieged city by raiding the crusaders.

Once in the harbor, Liliane had planned to jump overboard
and swim past the anchored ships for shore, but when they passed
the Tower of Flies, she had second thoughts. The water, though
clean enough offshore, was filled with floating garbage and ships'
debris in the harbor area. A thick sludge of sewage had gathered
in the coves protected from the sea breeze; eventually it would
edge out with the tide, but it rolled and stank. Alexandre's discouragement was quicker to the point. He slipped a rawhide
tether about her wrist and cinched it to his before she realized

what he was doing. "I could not bear to lose you," he quipped in Arabic, dropping her loose sleeve down to conceal the cord as he led her a little apart from the rest of the men leaning over the tilting gunnels.

As Liliane gave him an angry look, her free hand crept to her waist for her dirk. It was gone! He had stolen it! She jerked at the thong and Alexandre laughed softly. "Calm down, friend. You will miss little in leaving Acre. Sieges are much like that sewage; their stink never seems to go away but lingers long after the city is taken. King Richard may have his faults, but he knows how to conduct an assault. If the Saracens' will has not been broken by now, the day he does break it will be some time in coming and will be an ugly sight. Tomorrow will dawn hot and miserable, as will all the days that follow, and the army will grow meaner with each moment they sweat." His face sobered as he pointed to the Tower of Flies. "When Acre falls, you will not see the base of that tower because of the pile of bodies. Women and children will not be spared. I do not want you here for that."

"Alexandre, I am not a child," she replied quietly as the ship docked and the crewmen tossed lines to the quay. "I can endure Palestine if you can. Let me stay. If I take care, no one need know who I am.

"I knew, three days out. How long could you hide your sex from a sergeant or banneret? Twenty minutes in the field and you would be spotted. Besides"—the wrist tether tightened a notch— "I am damned if I will risk your neck. No more arguments." Once the ship was secure, he propelled her ahead of him up the creaking ladder. When they reached the quay, he did not bother to wait for his servants and belongings, but curtly ordered the shipmaster to see to them. Then he led Liliane toward the nearest loading merchant ship.

With the chattering Kiki clutching her neck, Liliane stumbled behind him. "Slow down!" she hissed. "Everyone will suspect something is amiss if you keep dragging me along like a puppet!"

Alexandre did not ease his pace. "I shall worry about that when you are in the middle of the Mediterranean. Pick up your dainty feet, my sweet."

The first merchant lateener was sailing for Rhodes. Alexandre applied to another one and was told Palermo. As he began to dicker in fluent Italian with the oily-tongued captain over the price of her passage, Liliane cast a quick, desperate look about the quay. In Alexandre's current mood, he would arrange for her to be stowed in the cargo hold until the ship was a day out. A few feet away, a sullen camel was being unloaded. Rolled rugs were stacked by the animal's feet on its near side; two rugs still remained on its back. Liliane eased closer to Alexandre, then loosened the slack loop about her wrist. Scratching Kiki's chest, she whispered in her ear, "*Allez!* Make trouble, Kiki!" That being one of her favorite orders, Kiki's small eyes gleamed, her teeth baring in anticipation.

The monkey leaped through the air to land atop the camel's neck. Scrambling to its head, Kiki screamed in its ears, then wrung them industriously. The camel exploded with pain and rage. The rugs still aboard the creature came flying off his back, and everyone, including Alexandre and the wide-eyed culprit who began the whole display, ducked.

Liliane had seen a camel in full froth, but never at so close a range. The spectacle was horrifying. His eyes rolled, teeth snapped, head snaked, spittle sprayed. The dockhands shrieked as spatulate hooves flayed with a startling reach at the nearest targets.

Liliane was so eager to distance herself from the beast that for the first few seconds, she forgot her purpose in arousing its ire. Then, observing the way Kiki bounced precariously atop the camel's skull, Liliane remembered haste, whether suicidal or not, was in order. With a quick tug, she slipped from Alexandre's loop and, her heart in her throat, bounded atop the pile of rug rolls and onto the camel's hump. The sensation was that of leaping into a tornado with teeth.

With a furious yell, Alexandre grabbed for the camel's bridle at the same moment its head snaked back for Liliane's leg. Alexandre missed and Liliane slammed her booted foot against the camel's bared teeth. She grabbed the startled animal's bridle, jerked its head in the direction of freedom and gave him a mighty whack in the ribs with her heels. Giving a ferocious shriek, he reared. Alexandre, with one arm shielding his head, grabbed at Liliane's ankle as the camel's cursing owner tried to drag her off from the other side. Alexandre nearly connected with an accurate hoof while the owner met Kiki's vicious little teeth. With a shout, the man grabbed his bleeding hand. When the camel's mad spin pointed his head to the quay entry, Liliane jabbed its rump with her steel brooch pin.

The camel exploded into a dead run. Trying to toss his rider off, he crowhopped and leaped dock cargo. Her spine ready to snap, Liliane screamed in Arabic for the quay to clear. She need not have bothered—everyone capable of running was in motion. She and the camel were called many foul names, most wasted on a non-Mohammedan and an animal preoccupied with murder.

Alexandre pounded off after the pair, but the camel had disappeared into the harbor alleys. For a few minutes, shrieks and howls from frightened pedestrians marked its passage. Finally, all Alexandre could hear was the rising note of panic in Liliane's fading shouts. Sick with worry, he stumbled to a halt with his chest heaving. Not only had he lost Liliane, but that crazy camel was apt to kill her.

Flattening Liliane was more the camel's intent. Although not clever, he discovered that walls, carts and people were not scraping her off. A low arch off the main street offered a new solution. Liliane ducked but not quickly enough. The arch scraped her painfully off the camel and onto the dirty cobbles. With the breath knocked from her lungs, she lay stunned, amid citrus peels and unnameable, slippery refuse. Fortunately, Kiki's chittering penetrated her rattled brain in time to realize that the camel had perceived the success of his maneuver and was gamboling back for a leisurely trample that would permanently add her to the general mess on the street. With a wheezing groan, Liliane crawled to a window lintel and dragged herself up. The camel trotted closer.

Mericiful heaven, she could hardly walk! What was she going to do? Overhead hung a tattered awning. Liliane grabbed for her dirk, then remembered that it was gone. She yanked the awning's cord; it snapped, but a corner of the awning tore. Dizzily, Liliane caught the edge and pulled hard. It ripped and fell down just as the vengeful camel came under the arch. She swung the awning hard against the beast's muzzle. The instant the cloth tangled about the camel's head, Liliane scrambled down, limping hurriedly away from where the camel was rending its new affliction. Kiki scampered after her.

Liliane scooped up the small creature to quiet its telltale chittering and set off down the first alley. Her head was clearing, but with every step her body protested more heatedly. Tomorrow, *if* she could escape that rotten-tempered camel, she was going to feel even worse. When she lurched around another corner, she heard no sound of pursuit—apparently the camel had been diverted to shredding the awning.

After walking some distance in confusion through the harbor streets beyond Acre's great wall, Liliane came upon the sweep of tents and makeshift huts of the joined camps of King Guy of Jerusalem and King Philip. Rubbing her bruised shoulder, she sank to a halfhearted squat. The camp was a warren of erratic "streets" strung aimlessly together. The fringes that caught the sea breeze were jammed with tents and hovels, while the ones that neared the siege trenches and desert dunes were open and empty. Saracen raiders would be roaming those dunes at night. Any crusader venturing far to relieve himself might be relieved of a working gullet, as well.

Odd bits of fabric, goatskins and horsehides patched together most of the tents; even by night, Liliane could see how the recently pitched French tents had already bleached in the relentless sun, the folds of their draping showing their original colors. A cluster of makeshift bordellos lay nearest the harbor town. The largest bordello was in a rundown two-story building with Moorish screens at its windows. Business was already brisk, and laughter spilled into the canvas-lined alley.

The camp stank. It was raucous with wandering soldiers, boisterous wenches and restless livestock. The usual disorder was aggravated by the arrival of Philip's army the previous week. French soldiers were already in scattered brawls with Guy's men, and the routiers were busy trying to maintain a boundary between the camp already established on the best site and the new discontented army of men. Liliane took care to skirt the chaotic French camp and the pole-mounted torches that cast a feeble, scattered glow over the allies. Fires and cooking pots sent up a greasy, sooty smoke that hazed the early evening air.

Liliane wrinkled her nose. She was hungry, even if the stench of burned mutton was unappetizing. Taking the Byzantine cross from beneath her aba and displaying it broadly, she ventured near a tent that gave off the odor of garlic and other savories. Unfortunately, the delicious odor was that of roast pig, and Liliane's experience was that converted Mohammedans did not usually convert to Christian diet. She prowled a bit farther, but soon thought better of purchasing a meal. Guy's soldiers, more wary of Saracens than the French, gave her dangerously suspicious looks. Being unarmed, she decided that her wisest tactic was retreat. With empty stomachs and without blankets, she and Kiki retired to a chilly night on the beach.

9

The Leopard and the Unicorn

Below the walls of Acre
April 1791

Liliane meant to wake before dawn and be off into the harbor streets, where she would draw less attention and be able to buy new weapons; however, she awakened to the rumble of siege engines and the sleepy challenges of King Guy's men to the Moors within the city. New to the game, the French scurried about like nervous fox terriers. King Guy was weary from badgering the Saracens alone for two years, and as he had broken a treaty with them to keep the peace, he was more dogged and desperate than fired by holy zeal. If the Saracens cornered him again, they would claim his head. He began to harass his enemy at first light.

Liliane ran along the shore to the harbor quarter to buy weapons and a few bland mouthfuls of *ganoush* for herself and Kiki. Unsure what martial experience she would face, she left the bitterly protesting Kiki with the food vendor. A few coins and a cold warning that she would slit the vendor's throat if he lost the monkey gave her reasonable assurance of retrieving her pet if she survived the next day. If she did not return by sunset, the vendor was to take Kiki to Alexandre de Brueil, the powerful French *effendi*. Kiki's delivery would assure Alexandre that he had no more need to worry about returning his errant wife to France. For her sake, he would care for the engaging creature.

When she returned via the dunes toward the battle, she saw that the siege lines were strung from south to north. Guy's flags flew over the south; Philip's white and gold fleurs-de-lis over the north. The bang of hammers and rake of adzes by carpenters laboring to build siege engines roused anyone inclined to loiter. Farther down the beach, squires and hostlers hurriedly led strings of horses to be exercised before the sun rose high enough to sear their skulls. As Liliane neared the battle lines, she saw she must leave the dunes lest she be mistaken for a Saracen scout. Not daring to recross the camp ditch by daylight, she wriggled and scrambled through the dunes to a patch frequented by the grooms. There she waited her chance, then fell in alongside the rear of a passing string as if she belonged to the group. Before the lead groom noticed her, she was back in the camp.

The archers with their wicker shields were already in place, while scattered knights gave directions to the siege crews and routiers. Alexandre was standing near Philip, who was examining scrolls on a folding table and issuing instructions to the foreman of several carpenters working on an odd-looking catapult. After a glance at the scroll, Alexandre appeared more interested in the points at which sappers were boring beneath the massive city walls. Occasionally, he looked around, his hunter's eyes sharply scanning the alleys of the siege camps, and with a jab of apprehension, Liliane realized he was looking for her.

She ducked behind a wine cask alongside a driftwood and plank tank near the looming Accursed Tower. Half a dozen doxies appeared with water jugs on their heads and baskets of bread to feed the troops already on the line. They drew immediate attention from the men, and aware that Alexandre's male interest would also be alerted, Liliane hastily deserted her shelter for one less open. A few laggards crawled from their tents to relieve themselves and grab a quick bite from the cooking pots before gathering up their arms and heading for their loosely assigned positions. Liliane was glad her haik hid her expression. She was no prude, but so many men squatting openly with dropped braies was a startling spectacle. So intent was she on not staring that she nearly ran into a large tent jutting into the path. Jacques's banner with his red boar fluttered in the morning breeze from the sea. Her spine pricked as she shrank back into a canvas alley. She was beginning to feel like a silly ewe lamb stumbling about a den of lions.

Several guards and men-at-arms were gathered about a low fire whose pot emitted a savory odor that knotted her stomach with hunger although she had eaten scarcely an hour before. The soldiers were fine-tuning their weapons as they awaited their master. As so few men were about, Liliane decided the others must have gone ahead to the siege lines with Louis. She soon found out that she was wrong.

Hearing steps behind her, Liliane moved hastily to clear the path, only to find herself eye to eye with Louis. Hastily, she salaamed, backing away with her head low. Louis flicked a signal to one of his men who snagged her sleeve. "What are you doing hanging about here, you infidel scum!"

Having learned as a child that Louis respected only strength, she drew herself up with a great show of outraged dignity. She snapped her sleeve from the guard's grasp, then shoved the thumbs of her trembling hands into her waist sash. "I am Jefar el din, Christian prince of the Siwans and counselor to *Melek Philip*. I go where I like, you insolent dog." She waved an imperious hand. "This tent protrudes into the thoroughfare. If it is yours, see that the error is corrected."

With tingling shoulder blades, Liliane stalked off. Several alleys away, she finally managed to draw a full breath. By tossing Philip's name at Louis, she had caught him off guard, but he would remember her. Anonymity was her best defense in Acre, but after less than a day, Louis's vindictive attention had been drawn to her. She might as well have angered a scorpion.

Glumly, she headed for the battle line. Few able-bodied men remained in camp and she would only draw more unwanted attention by wandering.

Showers of arrows flew from the archers' bows to rain upon Acre's defenders, their helmets glinting orange upon the massive ramparts. From those ramparts, Greek fire spiraled down upon the flimsy siege ladders thrown against the bulky walls. Liliane heard the heartrending shrieks of men falling off the ladders and the howls of burned men rising over the grinding racket of siege wheels, as the threats and curses of men lashing fearful draft animals forward added to the din. Only the veterans were used to the racket. Over the confusion, arrows hummed with the nasty, deep drone of crossbow quarrels.

Liliane covered her head as the first rock from a siege engine splintered against the Accursed Tower. Shards flew and dust clouded up as the rock's bulk dropped into the yellow earth at the tower's base. A fine ocher haze now hung over the middle line. Coughing, she looked for Alexandre. Philip's command post had been set up well behind the line, with its lily banners dainty and incongruous above the smoky din. She worked her way to an earthen wall near the post. Philip's crested helmet was occasionally visible above the wood-spiked, mobile barricade, but she did not see Alexandre. She might have known that the shelter of a barricade was not for him.

Although Liliane had heard that Philip was no coward, he seemed to be taking great care not to expose himself. The stories of two Palestine-bent Norman English nobles who had stopped at Castle de Brueil during the past year had shed light on Philip's eagerness to take up the Crusade. According to the nobles, Philip's motives in taking the cross were entirely pragmatic. Philip had once been close friends with Richard and warred with him against his father, Henry. Upon Henry's death, Richard, with an eye to his back, had strengthened his Angevin strongholds in France and, suspecting Philip of splitting his opposition, had ended their friendship. When Saladin took Jerusalem in 1187, Richard was determined to retake the city, whatever the cost to England. But he was not prepared to leave his Angevin possessions to the quick, ready claws of Philip. To keep Richard from declaring war and securing his claims before beginning the Palestine campaign, Philip took up the cross himself.

While making her morning purchases, Liliane had also heard a discouraging bit of news from the vendor keeping Kiki. King Richard had not yet arrived at the siege. En route to Palestine, he had decided to conquer Cyprus and make its ruler, Arthur, his heir rather than his brother John, a move Liliane thought was going to cause him a great deal of trouble back home. His absence from Acre would also prolong, if not cripple, the siege.

In a very short time, Liliane spotted Alexandre's position. His banners flew at center, his tiny force drawing the worst of the defenders' arrows and catapult stones.

Jacques's force, far more numerous and better equipped than Alexandre's, was on the curved south end, farthest from the risk of rear attack by Saladin's raiders. Jacques's position was probably as much due to his avoidance of risk as Philip's refusal to trust him at a more crucial point. She grimaced. Philip need not have worried. Jacques's concern for his own skin would incite him to fight like a weasel.

Liliane took up a strategic position a safe distance to Alexandre's right, between him and Jacques. Her new weapons included not only another crossbow, scimitar and dirk, but a round Saracen shield emblazoned with a Byzantine cross, and a tiny poignard concealed in the snug sleeve at her right wrist. Although her weapons were strong and light for a man, they were weighty for her. The pointed steel helmet and the padded gambeson that she had added to her haik and the used chain mail tabard also added unaccustomed weight.

She felt clumsy and miserably hot, although the sun was still more than half a span from noon. If not for the haik, perspiration would be streaming into her eyes. The sea looked cool and inviting, and Liliane cursed the pride that brought them all to swelter in the mounting heat. Acre's nearby marshes shimmered with a whir of mosquitoes and a stench of rotting plant life, refuse and a few corpses. The whole battleground was an open wound.

In 1189, King Guy of Jerusalem had laid siege to Acre until he had given his word to Saladin that he would desist. So much for chivalrous Christian oaths, Liliane thought wryly; the word given an infidel counted for naught. Guy had wasted no time in seeking an alliance with Richard and Philip. Now his pennants fluttered with the rest. Over the parched earth hovered the reek of death as battered bodies littered the ground. No dogs prowled to scavenge, as all of them had either been eaten by the crusaders or taken by the defenders to be devoured within the city. Even the desert jackals evaded the stretch between the city walls and the ditch.

This was the corruption Alexandre had endured in Jerusalem, except it must have been much worse confined in a city where food and water were nearly reduced to piles of dust. Liliane had never been able to coax Alexandre to speak much of the siege of Jerusalem; now she saw why. His experience had been unspeakable.

The sweltering day wore on as the siege engines pounded relentlessly at the walls. Aside from the helmets glinting on the ramparts, little was seen of the enemy. Sporadic crusaders surging up the scaling ladders were thrust away or doused with flaming oil. Having no bone to pick with the Saracens, Liliane fired only enough quarrels from her crossbow to keep from arousing notice and spent most of her time assisting the Knights Templars with the wounded along that section of the line. All the while, she kept alert to the whereabouts of Alexandre in relation to

Jacques's men-at-arms. At the moment, she did not think Jacques would send in an assassin from the rear. While there was much confusion and racket, the action was too directed upon the city for an "accident" to excuse an arrow or spear from any other direction. However, that situation did not last.

As dreamlike as a mirage, a group of horsemen approached the line from the vast gold sweep of the desert. A cloud of sand rising from the hooves of their dainty mares and sunlight glittering from their helmets, breastplates and weapons, the Saracen riders floated unswervingly toward them. The crusaders were being attacked from the rear!

Liliane's attention darted to Jacques. His fat bulk was stuffed into a hauberk that strained as if it had been twice let out. He wore a boar in gold atop his helmet crest. He looked massively uncomfortable and excited as he waved to Louis and snapped an order she could not hear. Without hesitation, Louis summoned a troop of twenty men-at-arms, and a few minutes later their horses scrambled across the far side of the ditch to encounter the Saracens. The Saracen troop met them with a volley of arrows that took out four riders, then wheeled and headed back into the desert. To the cheers of the watching ranks, Louis's men gave hot pursuit. Then, perhaps a mile and a half from the line, shrieking Saracens boiled over the dunes with eerie whistling cries. Louis's gauntleted fist went up, jerking back in the direction of the line, his men wheeling readily after him. The French destriers were strong and fresh, saving them from the reach of the fleet-footed Saracen mares; however, they were not swift enough to keep stragglers from drawing arrows in their backs. Louis, red-faced with anger and humiliation, led the pack.

Liliane noticed that Alexandre's attention, like everyone's, was on the chase. Then she saw that a Signe crossbowman was drawing a bead on the breastwork behind Alexandre's back. Her heart in her throat, Liliane swiftly nocked an arrow in her bow. Alexandre turned, redirecting his attention to the siege, just as the bowman fired and her own bow swung up. The bowman's quarrel ripped through Alexandre's breeze-whipped surcoat. He crouched, his shieldless arm instinctively going up. Liliane's quarrel took the bowman in the neck as he started to aim a second arrow. Paralyzed with fascinated horror, Liliane was unable to take her eyes from the man plucking frantically at the feathered missile, then, dimly seeing Alexandre's head turning toward her, she stumbled away down the embankment.

The flaw of her light bow was quickly evident when the bowman succeeded in plucking it out. As the quarrel had missed the spine and arteries, he was scarcely harmed. Flinging himself into the melee of besiegers in the trench, he fled back toward the Signe pennants through a rain of arrows from Acre. Praying that Alexandre would follow the assassin, Liliane scrambled toward the maze of tents. As she cleared the line, she heard feet pelting behind her—Alexandre had followed her! She ran into the nearest camp alley, diving into a battered tent. A flurry of shrieks and the clatter of cooking pots scattered a wizened Breton cook and an urchin child. "The infidel!" screamed the old woman. "The infidel is upon us!"

Ducking a pot leveled at her head, Liliane tore from the rear of the tent and down another alley. A flying lunge from behind caught her at the knees. She fell headlong into the dust. A hard hand dragged her up by the scruff and pitched her into a vacant hovel that stank of rancid grease and jumped with fleas. Before she could scramble up, Alexandre sat astride her hips, his fingers locked about her jaw. "Do you think this is a pigeon shoot? That damned toy bow is going to see you killed!"

"It stopped your being skewered!" she choked back.

With a short sound of exasperation, he dropped his punishing grip on her jaw. "My surcoat did as much as your shot. If you had missed him, that bowman would have pinned you like a plaguing moth."

"I did not miss," she retorted.

"This time." Shifting his grip to her shoulder, he rolled her over and kissed her firmly. *"Dieu,* I have wanted to do that for days!" Then, wanting far more than kisses, he swiftly unfastened her sash and threw up her aba.

Though Liliane's own blood had quickly fired, Alexandre's timing was unnerving. "Alexandre, we must not, not here! What if someone comes . . . those Saracens! What are you . . . you bastard!" Her protests turned to real anger as she realized his real intention of hobbling her knees with the sash.

Alexandre flipped down the aba and hauled her up. "I must return to the line. You have just enough slack to walk, but not enough to run anywhere, so mind your manners." He prodded her ahead of him out of the tent.

Liliane would not look at him on the way back through the line. "You need not sulk," he said dryly. "By now, even you could not pretend you adore Acre."

"Acre is disgusting," she retorted, "and while you are here, I am staying."

"I appreciate your loyalty, my love," he replied softly, "but not your impracticality. May I ask where you slept last night?"

"In the beach dunes."

"Where any jackal and Saracen raider might trip over you." He let out a colorful oath.

"Actually, I was more concerned with being mistaken for an enemy by one of the Christian guards."

"Our guards?" He laughed shortly. "A conscientous lot, that. More likely, a drunken routier would have wandered out and peed on you." He gave her bottom a less than affectionate pat. "A bit more haste, please. Your cousin Louis should be in a great fluster by now. I would not want to miss it."

Despite their heated conversation, both had been watching Louis's harried troop spill over the earthwork down the ditch into the camp. Their faces, Louis's in particular, were scarlet as Saracen jibes followed them. The Saracen horsemen reined up just out of bowshot and, jubilantly waving their scimitars and javelins, laughed and hooted insults. From the dunes behind them cavorted half-naked dervishes and perhaps sixty rearguard riders.

By the time they came in earshot of the rout, the fat had hit the fire. "There are not so many, sire," Louis was protesting to Philip, who had furiously come to deal with the troop sent off without his command. "Let me take a few more riders and go back after the dogs!" His gauntleted hand pulled his roan destrier's head around to turn back.

"Dismount, sirrah!" snapped Philip, who detested anyone looking down at him. "You have made fool enough of yourself and the rest of us for one day!" When Louis sullenly obeyed, Philip ordered curtly, "Fetch your uncle. Methinks he is due a share of the blame."

Louis dragged off his gauntlets and set off after Jacques. "Back!" hissed Alexandre, pressing Liliane behind him as Louis neared them, but she saw Louis's sharp eyes catch sight of her. He paused slightly, his eyes narrowing, then continued abruptly along the line. "The devil's luck," Alexandre muttered. "He has spotted you with me. Ten to one, his crossbowman's already been silenced with a spear to his ribs, but not before he sniveled to Jacques about your toy quarrel. Jacques and Louis will soon put together a likely tale of your part in their ruined attack.'' He grasped her arm. ''Come, you had best be out of here by the time Louis brings Jacques back.''

Liliane could not have been more in agreement, but then she had an idea that Alexandre's conception of ''out of sight'' was the first boat in the direction of France. ''Wait,'' she protested as he started toward the harbor. ''Jacques probably sent Louis after the raiders not only to impress Philip, but to provide a diversion so he might kill you. I am a witness. Why not bring me forward before Philip to confront Jacques and Louis now?''

''Because Philip would have to declare a trial, which spells delay. If I were willing to make you Jacques's target during that delay and if a Christian court would believe a Moor who has already turned his coat once, I would risk it. Unfortunately, Jacques still holds enough power to insure the dismissal of such a case. Like a tiger, he would be after you and even I might not be able to protect your pretty neck.''

''But everyone knows the animosity between your families. Besides, why should a strange Moor guard your life without cause?''

''Without the bowman, we have no proof of anything, only rumor as motive.'' He frowned. ''Unless . . . Diego's death was markedly convenient. Is there a possibility *he* was murdered?''

''A distinct possibility, but no proof. I believe that Louis startled his horse, but we could never find evidence.''

''Jacques is not one to leave tracks.'' He resumed his walk to the harbor. ''I shall see you to the quay.''

Liliane tried to think of some way to escape him again, but they had gone no more than a hundred feet when a shout rang after them. ''Ho! My lord Count de Brueil! You are wanted by the king. Bring your Moorish friend as well.''

''Every imp in hell must be about today,'' muttered Alexandre grimly. For a moment, as if debating some excuse for disobedience, he stared back at the burly Poitevin knight who had hailed them.

''We must go, must we not?'' pressed Liliane. Any risk from Jacques was better than being piled back on a homebound ship.

''Oh, yes,'' Alexandre said at last, his voice flat. ''My lack of enthusiasm for this campaign has been duly noted by the Crown. Philip wants not only my cooperation, but my total obedience. Crossing him now could be dangerous.'' He waved acknowledgment to the Poitevin, then looked at her. ''Buck up, sweet. I doubt if this interview will prove pleasant.''

Incongruously lightened of heart, Liliane accompanied Alexandre to the spot where Louis and his men now sweated and wiped their brows under the broiling sun. The Saracens, still cheerfully yipping insults, hovered on the fringe of the dunes, while the defenders of Acre perched on their walls and brayed like gleeful donkeys. Louis's face was crimson with controlled anger. Liliane grinned inwardly. He would be far more furious if he could understand Arabic. Alexandre's lips were twitching as if he comprehended more than a little.

Philip was taking grim delight in chastising Louis for going after the enemy without orders. Liliane had learned enough of the young king to know that had the raid been successful, he might have given Louis a mere public rap and rewarded him privately. Jacques, who was now puffing into view, must have had the same idea. Unluckily for him, he was new to Palestine and unfamiliar with Saracen habits of baiting the enemy into recklessness. Purple veins stood out at his temples as he labored up the breastwork. With cold detachment, Liliane observed that he might handily succumb to an apoplexy in the desert heat before he could return to France.

Chafing under Philip's harangue, Louis's eyes settled on Liliane and turned black with fury. Under the circumstances, her Moorish garb was a goad to his temper, particularly after their encounter that morning. Out to humiliate the Signes, Philip was sparing him nothing. As an added slight, Philip let Jacques wheeze in the sidelines for some time before he recognized him. Although Philip must also have been aware of Alexandre's presence, he took no notice of him. Alexandre seemed calm enough, but Liliane could not help being fidgety, for while Jacques's attention did not linger long enough to draw suspicion, he had perused her sharply, particularly her light crossbow. Alexandre had been right in guessing the bowman would describe the Moor that had wounded him.

Just then, Philip turned to Jacques. ''Well, Baron, what have you to say? This whelp is your responsibility, is he not?''

Jacques bowed submissively. ''The fault is entirely mine, Your

Majesty. My nephew is young and hot to prove his mettle in your service. I confess my old blood was fired by his ardor when he set out to avenge the insults the infidel enemy hurled upon the Holy Cross and your name. I had neither heart not want of spleen to restrain him." He bowed again. "I submit myself and my nephew to your will and just chastisement, asking only that you consider we are new to battle and to this hostile land."

He fawns so, thought Liliane, that one expects him to next roll over belly up at the king's foot.

Philip, weaned on hypocrisy, was cynically prepared to soothe the culprit into assuming himself forgiven. Such ambivalence tended to keep said culprit both cringing and fawning, too off balance to pose a threat in the future. "While I appreciate holy zeal and warlike fervor, Count de Signe will do well to immediately acclimate himself and his following to military procedure and deference to my royal command. Any further transgression of this nature must be punished severely. 'Tis not well for the infidel to observe division among our ranks. For this offense, your nephew will be fined one hundred livres." As Jacques winced, Philip turned with seeming idleness to Alexandre. "As for other matters . . . Count de Brueil, have you anything to add to this discussion?"

Jacques and Louis looked at each other uneasily.

"Nothing, sire," replied Alexandre.

"No? Some rumor floated to me that you have a grievance with your uncle-in-law this day. If so, animosities must be aired. I will have no brooding and ill will among my leaders." Philip gave a half paternal, half mocking smile. A young page, his eyes wide and wary as a hunted fox's, stood tensely just behind him. He was dust-covered with a scrape down his cheek, and blood trickled down his bare arm from a bandage high under his sleeve. Unlike the other young fops who hung about Philip's coterie, this one had seen fighting and possibly more. Jacques did not seem to have noticed the page; Liliane ardently hoped not, lest the boy run afoul of Louis.

"I assure you, sire, the Baron and I are on peaceful terms," answered Alexandre.

War has just not been openly declared, Liliane amended silently.

"That is good to hear," returned Philip easily. "Hereafter, it is my will that Lord Louis gain battle experience under your practiced command. I believe he will be less inclined to attempt ill-considered maneuvers.''

Louis whitened, both in anger at the assignment and fear at Philip's inference. Jacques's pudgy features had taken on the clammy pallor of a fish's underbelly.

Alexandre bowed, hiding whatever feelings he might have entertained on Louis's inclusion to his tiny force. "Gladly, sire, will I undertake to train my cousin-in-law. I have no doubt he will learn quickly to guard his rashness and bring credit to France.''

Louis, chafing at Alexandre's dig, jerked into a bow. "I am at Your Majesty's command.''

"Good," Philip replied pleasantly, "then the matter is settled.'' His interest swung around to Liliane. "Now we must attend to courtesy. Count de Brueil, will you introduce your friend?''

Alexandre, who would have much preferred his "friend" to be ignored, reluctantly motioned Liliane to step forward. "Sire, I have the honor to present Jefar el din of the Siwans, now a loyal defender of the faith.''

"A title our ally, King Richard, claims," murmured Philip. "Welcome to our service, Jefar el din.''

"With respect, *Melek Philip, effendi*, I am Prince Jefar," corrected Liliane as she salaamed. She disliked the look on Louis's face. He knew now that she had lied this morning about knowing Philip. Also, her company with Alexandre must suggest she had been spying upon their tent. Best she did not slip too far from an appearance of respect.

"You are far from your people, Prince Jefar," observed Philip. "May I ask what has brought you such a distance?''

Ignoring the cynical faces of the surrounding knights, she offered her tale of her family's conversion and ultimate massacre.

"I see," Philip said at last. "So your presence is due to personal as well as religious cause. May I ask how you became acquainted with Count de Brueil?''

"Prince Jefar rendered me a service, sire," Alexandre put in quickly, "when I was ill at sea." His voice lifted slightly. "He may have saved my life.''

"A grateful misconception, surely," Liliane murmured with a quizzical smile. "My lord was but seasick.''

A ripple of laughter went about the gathering at Alexandre's flush; Philip laughed loudest of all. "So, my lord Alexandre, it appears we all owe your friend a service. Prince Jefar must be ever at your side during this campaign to assure us of your continued good health." He grinned at Liliane. "Your Highness, are you willing to accept Count Alexandre's command?"

"Most readily, sire." Her lips twitched slightly in an effort to suppress her elation, for she was too well aware of Alexandre's discomfiture.

"So, my lord Alexandre," observed Philip puckishly, "you are twice fortunate today." He gave a casual wave of his hand. "Back to your posts, gentlemen. We have dallied enough and owe the infidel thrice a harrying for this respite." Briefly he turned with a murmur to Alexandre. "Take Lisle's place to my left, Alexandre, and keep sharp. Both my neck and yours may depend on it."

Everyone bowed as Philip departed for his barricade, then returned to their positions. The capable Lisle appeared to be ruffled at being demoted to a more distant position from the king, but all in all, took his reassignment with scant fuss. "He's privately relieved," observed Alexandre to Liliane as Lisle withdrew his men. "Philip's is the safest, dullest position on the whole line. Unless the Moors attack from the desert, we will be yawning the siege away until Richard arrives." He led her to the new position.

"Being appointed to Philip's left is a great honor, is it not?"

"Yes, and in these circumstances, the least welcome to a soldier. Still," he paused, "this position is best for your protection as well as his and mine. With the king so close, Jacques will not dare try another such attempt on my life. By being assigned to my command, Louis is now hamstrung, as well. Another 'accident' would be too obvious. You were assigned to me as extra insurance."

"So Philip has proven your friend, after all."

"He has use for me," Alexandre replied quietly. "A king cannot be a friend as other men, yet by his lights, he loves me."

Liliane looked up at him. "I love you, too, without Philip's reservations. Let me stay."

Alexandre's eyes filled with tenderness, then bleak regret. "No, sweeting. Your place is in France."

"My place is with you," she pleaded. "Please, Alexandre, do not send me away. Throughout history, many women have put on male dress and attended their men in battle. Who knows when you will return to France again or where Philip's whim will take you next? Shall we always live apart?" She touched his sleeve. "I should rather risk an early death than such long years of separation. I am not so brave as you may think."

"Nor am I," he replied softly. "I could not bear to see you die upon some bloody, wretched field as this. Be generous and kind as you have always been, Liliane, and press me no more about such dangerous folly."

Seeing the strain upon his lean face, Liliane fell silent, despair creeping over her as the day wore on. She had not admitted, even to herself, how afraid she was to return to France alone. The loneliness and suspicion that awaited her at Castle de Brueil seemed unbearable. Aye, she might have come to Acre to protect Alexandre, but she also craved his protection and companionship with an intensity she had not realized. She might endure living with the celibacy of a nun for as long as was required of her; but to live without him altogether conjured up a desert of such bleak horror that the wastelands of Acre seemed a lush garden.

The sun lowered, casting a bronze glow upon the city walls and the pale dunes. The sea was copper-flecked lapping at the horizon's lilac and russet clouds. Never had Liliane seen such a glorious sunset as in Acre, and she thought bleakly, that she never would again, for as the swiftly dropping night banished the twilight's brief whisper, Alexandre escorted her to the harbor. Just beyond the camp, he purchased a long, striped mantle from a vendor and cast it about her. "Keep to the walls," he admonished. "That camel drover and his friends will have clear memories of you."

While he took care not to choose the quay where they had encountered the drovers, they had not gone ten feet beyond shore when Liliane noticed that one of the men loitering on the quay belonged to her uncle's service. His obvious purpose gave her a desperate idea. After all, she would not be lying about the danger, but merely exaggerating it somewhat. She urgently tugged at Alexandre's arm. "Alexandre, that fellow over there is in my uncle's employ."

Careful not to display undue interest, he slid a glance toward the man. "Are you certain?" While aware Jacques might have set an assassin on her, he gave her a canny stare. "Or are you up to your games again?"

"Alexandre," she protested vehemently, "I vow that you may place me aboard whatever ship you like and that man will follow."

"We shall see soon enough." He took her arm. "Stay close to me." They strolled past the loitering man. As if on a pull string, he quickly followed them.

"Now do you believe me?" she hissed. "Jacques cannot afford to let me live. I saw his assassin try to kill you."

Without reply, Alexandre eased up to the captain of a merchant ship. Their pursuer drifted in behind them.

Alexandre's hand slipped to his sword hilt. Another man, in Portuguese dress, appeared from the shadows. Liliane's stomach knotted. She had not counted on having her story quite so forcefully confirmed. "Keep moving," Alexandre whispered through stiff lips. "We are just out for an evening stroll. When we reach the street, split."

Split! she thought fearfully. Why not serve me to them *au jus?*

Still, when they arrived back on shore, she obediently turned toward the camp, but took care to stay near shore. With the Portuguese trailing her, the silent alleys were no haven. The first man had followed Alexandre. Within the length of two streets, Liliane heard the pursuing footfalls grow quietly closer. Her heart hammering, she silently slid out her scimitar. A sound came swift and slippery behind her. She whirled to see Alexandre easing the dead Portuguese into a deserted alley. Looking about to make sure that no one had seen the assassin's disposal, Liliane followed Alexandre into the alley. He was neatly seating the Portuguese against a wall. "*Dio,* you did not stab him in the back?" she breathed, both relieved and horrified.

"I tapped him on the shoulder first," her mate replied laconically.

"Where is the other one?"

"As the day's crowds from Acre eased their rush to the Pit at sunset, he has reached hell by now."

Liliane surveyed Alexandre with new and uneasy respect. "You never waste much time accomplishing this sort of thing, do you?"

He cocked his head thoughtfully. "In truth, considering the peril of delay, I do not think I am overquick. My father, now, was hasty. At forty-one, he died old for a soldier in a squabble with a fellow knight over pillage. By the time he finished swearing at the rival and drew his dagger, the knight's poignard was sticking from his liver.'' He smiled grimly. ''A trifling prick, but to the point.''

''You did not much like your father, did you?'' she observed quietly as they scanned the alley's mouth, then went to check the shore's crumbling street.

''He was greedy and brutal, with no use for my mother except in bed when no more likely female was within reach. He had no liking for children, and home was merely a property to fight over. He hated kings and loved war.''

Alexandre's emotionless tone saddened Liliane immensely. How Alexandre must have been hurt in those early years! ''Your father expected you to be like him,'' she murmured as they watched the deserted street. ''Philip sees in you the same frightful boar, only sauced with intelligence and obedience.'' She moved into his arms. ''My poor love, you have never been free, have you?''

His arms closed about her. ''Bound by homage and honor, who *is* free? Richard's a slave to his temper and Philip is ruled by ambition. All men may be free one day, Liliane, but that day is not now.'' He kissed her softly. ''I should like to shock Philip very much this night by taking Prince Jefar el din to bed.''

Liliane giggled. ''I do not know for sure, but Philip might not be much shocked, I think, and Richard even less.''

''Shame''—he touched her lips—''for a lady to whisper such wicked gossip.''

But even as he kissed her, a tiny, troubling thought flicked through her mind. Gossip had long whispered that Richard and Philip had once been lovers. Philip had since proven his attraction to women, and yet . . . might he not only love Alexandre as his friend, but in some perverse way, *be* in love with him? Alexandre's passionate lips told her well enough that such an attraction would not be reciprocated, but love was so near to hate. Philip might not be fool enough to reveal untoward desire to Alexandre, yet what would Philip do if Alexandre thwarted him in some other way? A spurned woman could be more vicious than any man—and was not Philip now much like a rejected woman? He still had the ability to keep Alexandre bound to him, but if Alexandre should ever break that bond . . .

Alexandre's kisses were not letting her think. Her head was whirling and she clung to him, heedless of danger and discovery.

His hands moved freely, ardently upon the softness of her body beneath the aba, and she felt the urgency of his desire pressing hard against her thigh. Had he claimed her there in the dust, she could not have said no. She leaned close to him, felt his heart beating, racing, her own need matching his. "We cannot stay here," he breathed huskily. "I am fair to burst."

"Take me to your tent," she whispered eagerly. "I am burning, too, my love, and past waiting."

An expression of tense sobriety came over his face, and her heart sank. "You will not send me to France now?"

Slowly, worriedly, Alexandre shook his head. When at last he spoke, his voice was harsh, his desire laced with frustration and anger. "Now? No, I dare not. More of Jacques's thugs may be out around the harbor. Neither you nor I can know them all. The overland caravans will be watched, as well, and I will not send you alone in some cockleshell or caravan where Jacques may have set his villains. Foul as Acre may be, you are now safer with me here." Abruptly he lifted her chin. "But play no more games. You have caused me trouble enough. For your protection, my word will be law from this moment. Swear it!"

Her eyes looked into his. "When my safety alone is at risk, I shall obey you in all things, but if you are in jeopardy, *mon brave*, expect no docility."

He kissed her again, hard. "I will remember." Then he quickly led her through the harbor maze to his tent in the sprawling encampment. To evade the stench of crowded humanity and the nearby marsh, he had chosen a site beside Lisle on the fringe of the camp closest to the sea. Its placement afforded more privacy in their comings and goings, but was more vulnerable to Jacques's villains and Saladin's raiders. She was not sure which was more to be feared. Before they came in sight of the tent, Alexandre drew his sword and bade her unsheathe her scimitar. "I ordered guards set, but the place is bound to be watched by your accursed uncle's men. Keep to my right. If you spy anyone, raise enough racket to stir the dead."

Alexandre ventured forward into the shadowy, soft shapes of the massed tents. Without a moon, all grayed to treacherous monotones. The tents thinned, with wider patches of sand visible. To escape the stifling tents, a few sleeping forms lay like driftwood in the open stretches. Dying coals from faded campfires peered through the darkness like the hot, malevolent eyes of waiting demons—a single eye here, a colony there. Grown accustomed to the murkiness, Liliane was now better able to define shapes. Nothing moved. Only the sea rustled up on the shore. Then she sensed that a coal's light had suddenly been smothered. Her attention focused on the spot. When two more coals disappeared, she touched Alexandre's rigid shoulder. He had seen it, too.

"Yell!" he hissed.

Her nerves shot, Liliane yelled at the top of her lungs, with Alexandre's baritone clamor sounding as his sword lashed out. Toppling pots clattered and tent cloth tore as the startled assassin stumbled back. Thinking that Saracens had attacked, the sleepers on the sand reared up clumsily with furious oaths and fumbled for weapons. Warned by his master to absolute secrecy, the assassin fled now that all hope of secrecy was shredded. Liliane whirled as soft footsteps faded away behind her. She and Alexandre did not discover who else might have been lurking in wait, for the nearby tents were spilling their occupants, and the camp was rousing in a progressive wave of activity.

Alexandre briefly caught Liliane's wrist. "Come, follow me." In moments, they saw the guards stationed about Alexandre's large green tent emblazoned with his leopard and unicorn device. Too experienced to leave their stations, the guards held weapons at the ready. Alexandre called softly, *"Yves, c'est moi. I have a friend with me."*

The little Gascon relaxed, but others did not, waiting guardedly while he walked forward. "Advance, my lord. " 'Tis an unfriendly night. I am glad to see you returned safely"—his tone altered with a note of displeasure as he spied Jefar el din—"but if you will forgive me, my lord, this Moor will attract more unpleasantness."

"Prince Jefar speaks good French, Yves," Alexandre replied quietly. "You will all treat him with courtesy. He saved my life from a Signe arrow today. If he needs protection now, he shall have it."

Yves flushed as the others gathered round. "So that's what half that fuss was about when King Philip grilled the baron and his whelp. We are promised a lively time, milord."

Alexandre grinned. "Boredom ages a man, *non?*" He strode to the tent and drew open the tent flap. "Prince Jefar will be residing with us. You will obey him as you would me, and guard his life as you would your own. *Alors?*"

Grudgingly, Yves and the castellans nodded.

Liliane smiled at them as she walked to the tent. "I hope to put you to little trouble, gentlemen. I, too, should like to grow old."

As she ducked into the tent, she murmured to Alexandre, "Are you not going to tell everyone the attack was a false alarm?" Torches were flaring outside the tent as the clamor and bustle of the aroused crusaders continued.

"Not I." Alexandre followed her into the tent. A dry chuckle issued from the darkness as he prowled for a candle. "I have no wish to be sworn at for an idiot. Our neighbors will be as edgy as cats for the rest of the night: as fine a protection as we could want." He groped around in the dark for another few moments, then muttered, "Oh, the hell with it." His arms slid around her, his lips moving over her cheek to the corner of her mouth. "You are trembling."

"Am I?" Liliane laughed faintly. "I cannot imagine why." Desire for Alexandre and the fear she had been fighting for the last few days were welling up together. In a moment, she thought she might become hysterical.

"I have never seen you afraid before," he whispered, unwinding her haik and casting it aside. Finding the tension at the base of her skull, his hand massaged the back of her neck until the muscles began to unknot. "But, then"—his voice was warm and caressing—"I cannot see you at all . . . just feel . . ." His hands slid down her back to the curve at her waist, the swell of her bottom. His tongue lightly teased her mouth, probing her lips. Her head slipped back as she began to forget fear, forget everything but his sensual invasion.

In her mind, a unicorn and leopard circled, brushed each other. The leopard's coat was warm, rough; the unicorn's neck arched, its mane blown silkily over the leopard's back.

The hot night air touched her skin as her aba slipped away. Alexandre's hands were light and tantalizing as he softly traced her bare breasts, her belly, moving lower. Then his mouth was upon her, seeking the night flowers of her nipples, bringing forth exquisite pleasure, then trailing lower to her navel, over the curve of her belly to her thighs' joining. When he found her, her fingers dug into his hair, knotted as she arched, shuddered with a silent cry.

The crescent moon whirled about her, sweeping her high and swift until her legs melted from beneath her and she was spilled onto soft furs and silent rugs. Alexandre's clothing whispered about her, then he was bare and upon her, his mouth sweetly ravaging, his skin gliding over her body, the hot hardness of him strong and high. The silence seemed breathless as he poised, then he entered her, joining them with the pulsing, velvet heat of his claiming. Without hesitation, Liliane arched her body, opened her thighs to ease the ache, only to feel him go deeper. His thighs shifted, opening her impossibly. Deeper he pressed until she moaned against his mouth. Her hips moved so slowly, almost invisibly, the shaft of his sex touching, pricking from her whimpers of unbearable need. His muscles were rigid, his heartbeat heavy against her breast.

The dangers they had run that night acted upon them like an aphrodisiac. The stillness of him within her against the clamor outside the tent gave her a heady feeling of safety and euphoria. Surrounded by running, swearing, fearful men, they were alone, joined together as a single, insistent heartbeat, barricaded against the chaos outside, leaving a living, breathless silence within.

Then his hands slipped beneath her, lifting her, moving her upon him until the burning ache changed to an ecstatic throb. His body tensed, flexing as his hips moved in seductive undulation. Liliane held him closer, offering herself entirely. With a low cry of triumph, he thrust into her, closing her buttocks against his surge, tightening her to increase the wild sensation. Fiercely she met his thrust, wrapped about him, lifting with him, taking him as he took her.

Their mating was primitive, centered, as explosive as the emotions that had soaked the land beneath them in conflict for countless centuries. This was a private war, a private passion. Sweat sheened their bodies, and they reached the pinnacle in a flash of white light and a crash of brazen cymbals that sent unending ripples shivering across their night.

They clung together, listening to the running footsteps and voices in the distance. "We are conspirators now," Liliane breathed, "between two armies." She caressed his face lightly, probing his mouth with her fingers. "Alexandre, my Alexandre, I would not sleep, but lie lustful and melt thy heart and loins until the dew of dawn is but a distant scattering of their cooling fire.'' She rolled over to lie upon him, then kissed his chest and throat, her hair falling about his face. ''I have longed for thee beyond imagining, yet you conjure me to the height of that dreaming with the ease of a genie.''

Alexandre laughed softly. ''Poor genie. His conjuring is spent in pursuit of his enchantress. He would love her foolishly even if she were to pack him in a bottle.'' His lips teased hers. ''Tell me, temptress, how may I persuade thee to open the bottle every eon or so, that I may please thee and sate my longing?''

Liliane smiled bewitchingly. ''Oh, I will need no persuasion. And as for eons, I shall unstop the bottle each night . . . so . . .'' Her hair trailed to his groin, her tongue lightly flicking the warm, still moist tip of him. As he caught his breath in startled delight, she whispered before continuing her tender torments, ''Thy pleasure will be mine.''

10

Among the Lions

Dawn came early for the lovers who had wasted little of the night in sleep. With smudged eyes and dazed smiles, they answered the morning call to arms, but not before Liliane received a firm lecture on the preservation of her neck. As the day wore on, she discovered that safety generally entailed being steeped in boredom. As her crossbow's quarrels would not carry to the city rampart, and defenders within the sapper tunnels rarely spilled into the open, she had no targets. To boot, Alexandre would not allow her near the front, assigning her to a huge Poitevin sergeant who seemed capable of snapping the necks of any three fools who might assail her. She also discovered that the sergeant, whose nickname was Turko, was a good deal brighter than he looked. Although he wasted none of his sagacity in conversation, he missed nothing that went on around them and snapped orders to his charges as if he had eyes in the back of his head.

As the day's heat and dust mounted, the scaling ladders fell and siege engines repeatedly broke down. Liliane's frustration rose. She had not come to Acre to be mollycoddled by a gorilla. Louis was stationed closer to Alexandre than she!

Noting a pair of trollops dispensing water among the men, she directed Turko's attention to the girls and ventured a ribald jest. His stare fixed on the wenches, he grunted. Liliane quickly slipped over the rear embankment, but seconds later, a hammy hand descended up on her neck. "I am to be with Count Alex-

184

andre," she protested warmly. "*Melek Philip* himself assigned me there!"

Unimpressed, Turko shrugged. "Count Alexandre assigned you *here*. In the army, you obey. If you don't, you get people killed. Maybe you first!" His steady, beady gaze told her just how her demise might be accomplished should she err again.

Reluctantly, Liliane had to admit that Turko was right. She owed a responsibility not just to Alexandre, but to the men with whom he fought. Turko might have been shot coming after her, and had the Saracens mounted a rear attack just then, she would not have been in place to hold them off.

For several weeks thereafter, Liliane endured heat, monotony and ugliness. While no further assaults were made by Signe assassins, she was no less wary. The Christians were civil but made no pretense of trusting her any more than did Alexandre's castellans. Alexandre cut his social engagements to a minimum and saw only Philip and friends. Since he always took Liliane with him unless he was seeing Philip or another noble who had known her in France, invitations declined. These Christians were her own kind by blood, but Liliane became as increasingly alienated from them as they were from her. In all respects save birth, she became a Moor. Her only loyalty to the crusaders was tied to Alexandre. She was careful to make no mistakes, remaining obedient. And she kept a hawk's eye on Louis.

Louis was a good fighter, reliable, not flashy, but he took orders with a grim lack of expression that suggested he was biding his time. He had inheirited a good bit of Jacques's patience. I could learn from Louis and Jacques, Liliane decided at length. Everyone's patience was tried. Richard had not arrived, and rumor was that he was still bashing heads in Cyprus. Richard could never resist a fight. She wondered if his love of war would not one day prove his undoing.

Only Philip seemed unperturbed by Richard's delay. He was content to conduct the rudiments of a siege without making a concerted attack. Guy fumed against Philip's indifferent tactics. He wanted Acre taken and an end put to the sweaty tedium.

Alexandre did not complain, but in the evenings when they were alone together, Liliane saw the lines of weariness about his eyes, the grim tension and disenchantment. For appearance's sake, he had caused a tent for her to be set up next to his own.

Hidden flaps were stitched in the sides so that with a deft flick, they might enter each other's quarters unseen and visit privately.

At those times, Liliane gave herself completely to Alexandre's comfort. She made sure that any delicacies and good wines she could find in the market were placed before him at their evening meal. Usually she contrived to arrive at the tent before him to make certain that water was heated for his bath and oils readied for his massage. Save that she dared not wear women's garb for fear of discovery, she created a haven of peace and beauty for him in the midst of war. When the camp was silent, he came to her in her own tent. Her own limbs were bathed in scented water and oiled beneath his hands before quietly, fiercely, he made love to her.

In July, Richard arrived victorious from Cyprus, and all Acre heard the Red Lion's roar. "God's wounds, are we fighting a war here or drooling gruel!" With his legendary energy, he assembled new crews of sappers to tunnel under the Accursed Tower to either penetrate or collapse it. Contemptuously, he dismissed Philip's prized siege engines as lumbering woodpiles and set his engineers to build new ones. At dawn's first light, he was striding around the siege ditches in full sight of Acre's archers, rearranging troops and inspiring them to feats of glory. And glory he got. Within a week, Acre's walls were cratered from collapsing rock and the Christian assaults had tripled. Covered with blood, trench-digging sappers boiled out of tunnels ahead of Moorish raiders, only to wheel and return like ferrets after rats into their dark holes.

"Richard is a genius, is he not?" commented Liliane one evening to Alexandre. "The men adore him. He has to break Acre if he keeps this up."

Alexandre stretched out on the pillows. "Oh, Richard will press Acre hard, but Saladin is no fool. He has the patience and foresight Richard often lacks. Richard gives not a damn for next year; he can barely keep his interest in next week. England's future, the succession, is all negotiable, so long as he can enjoy the thrill of the chase."

"But what does he chase, if not power?"

"Personal glory, like a posy in his cap," Alexandre replied wryly. "Richard will get the glory and his brother John the curses for the mess Richard will leave behind him."

"How strange that a man can be so strong and so weak at the same time," she murmured. "I wonder what Philip is after?"

"Whatever it is, he will likely get it." He pulled her down to the pillows. "Now, Delilah, about this weakness in men . . ."

With a soft laugh, Liliane fingered his hair. "Your curls are becoming a bit long. Shall I trim them with my teeth?" Her lips drifted close.

"Will it hurt?" he teased.

"Oh, noooo." The last was a slow breath in his ear. "I shall think of something to distract you."

"For instance?"

"This." Her tongue flicked his inner ear. He squirmed slightly. "Restless, Samson?" Her fingers trailed up the inside of his thigh, and a slow grin widened on his face. He opened his legs invitingly. "I am yours to distract."

Straddling his open knees, she took a maddeningly long time to unfasten his braies. "They say Delilah sat addled while the temple crashed about her ears," she purred, gazing sloe-eyed at his rousing manhood. "What could she have been thinking of?" Feeling his muscles tremor, she trailed a finger about his groin. "I mean, a hero who slew so many Philistines with the jawbone of an ass, what *could* Samson have done to one delicate little courtesan?"

Her caresses grew more intimate, and Alexandre was soon gripping the sides of his camp stool. She lazily slipped off his chainse and began to tease his nipples with her tongue. In moments, he grasped her bottom and pressed her firmly down upon him.

Her bare feet levering against the rug, she moved on him, still tantalizing him with adroit nuzzles and pauses that were both delightful and maddening. Leaning forward, she let her breasts and hair tease his chest, her hands caressing him where he had entered her. With a harsh breath, he surged up within her, startling her with the raw, ripe power of him. He held her close down on him, inescapably captured, pinioned on his virility.

Victorious now, he brought her to eager submission. Liliane flowed with his driving movement, burning with it, melting with him until their bodies were incandescent, nonexistent but for the ancient, ringing pleasure. Wild, mystical music filled their skulls and senses, vibrating, humming until the piercing vibrato passed sound, whitened and obliterated.

Liliane was scarcely aware when Alexandre later carried her to the pallet and held her close against him. She shivered.

"What is it, sweet? What is wrong?" he whispered. When she did not answer, he stroked her neck. "You are very serious. I wonder if Delilah was so serious with Samson."

"At the end," Liliane replied pensively, "I think she must have been, unless she was heartless altogether. Did she know what her betrayal would cost him? What did she feel when she saw him blinded?"

He laughed. "If you keep to this bent, I shall think you are feeling guilty about something."

Liliane settled on his chest. "Not yet." Suddenly she smiled oddly. "Have you not noticed how well behaved I have been of late?"

"That is what worries me." He ruffled her hair. " 'Tis so highly unnatural, that I am beginning to stay awake at night."

She laughed softly. "Well, then, shall I do something wonderfully natural that will persuade you to sleep like a baby?"

His teeth flashed in the dark. "You are not contemplating a lullaby, I suppose."

Her tongue insinuated itself in his ear, then trailed to his mouth. "Not quite," she whispered. "I was thinking more of a duet. A few high notes"—she kissed him lingeringly, her fingers playing lightly, flutelike, across his groin— "and a few low, long, slow notes. . . ."

There was a long, luxurious silence, then a started cry of pleasure from Liliane. "Hush, now" came a lazy drawl from the darkness. "Baby has a few variations of his own."

Saladin attacked at dawn. The first bronze light needled across the far dunes, swelling like a subtle veil over the desert, casting away the shadow of night to split the crusader encampment with its haphazard geometrics of canvas tents and skeletal huts. From the dunes sifted dark-faced riders in trickles of milky sand with foot soldiers sliding almost beneath the slim-legged mares' hooves. Once the first wave was clear of the dunes, it furled into a trot, then a gallop gathering momentum and rolling swiftly toward the yet drowsing camp.

A few early-rising hostlers set up the first cry of warning. Pelting back to the camp with their strings of invaluable mounts, they howled loudly. Tent flaps flew open and men tumbled nude into the alleys. Cries resounded about the camp, echoed by the rising clamor of the enemy.

Alexandre threw the sheets back and ran into his own tent for his chain mail and weapons. As he dragged on his clothing and armor, he yelled to Liliane, "Stay here! If they break through, hide as long as you can!"

She swiftly tugged on her own tunic and ran to him. "But what then? What if they overrun the camp?"

White-faced, he buckled on his sword. "Then make a quick end, my love. Christian women are naught to the Saracens but butcher's meat and slaves." He caught her to him and kissed her harshly. "If they get this far, you will know I have gone before you. . . . I love you, for this earth's stay and any heaven or hell beyond. You will never lose me, whatever shapes eternity." Another hard kiss bruised her mouth, then he was gone.

Liliane felt a stifling fear and loneliness as if the encampment about the tent had sunk into the sand, leaving no human behind. Only steel-armored shells remained to fight, horribly animate as skeletal warriors sown by the dragons' teeth of Jason's legend. A horrid din had been raised outside, the tent walls writhing and jerking with the frantic movement of the men racing to the trenches. As she looked from the tent, Acre's mounted war machines pounded the camp, and the ground shuddered with the impact of great stones. The air hissed with Greek fire. Most of the camp was out of range of the fire, but dawn's rising breeze was beginning to blow brisk. A few tents were aflame like torches ready to spread.

Liliane knew from close experience with the Spanish Moors that Alexandre did not exaggerate the grimness of her fate should the attacking Saracens prove victorious. Beauty would gain her nothing but prolonged, hideous humiliation before the inevitable end. Most Arabs would not defile themselves by raping an infidel, but some were not so particular. Alexandre was also right about her being safer in the tent, but she had no intention of cowering in hiding while so many braved the fight. She would be useful on the line and, if humanly possible, to Alexandre. He would not die, if she could help it.

The ragged front ranks were already engaged with the charging enemy, the bulk of the defenders spilling in to block the main onslaught. Later, Liliane remembered little of the next hours, only her sickening fear and disgust and weariness. Unknown faces were severed masks, howling and demonic, surging forward, falling back, the shriek of steel raking through cries and screams.

For a time, she could not find Alexandre; when she did, he was near Philip, swinging his sword with a methodical deftness that seemed music next to the frantic hacking about him. His lean face was white, his jaw set. A scarlet handprint of blood masked half his face and his surcoat was blood-soaked at the hem. She slipped and slithered to him, then set her back to his in time to ward off a dervish whose manic, slashing attack unnerved her. The froth from the dark tattooed figure's mouth spattered upon her face, as did his blood moments later when his fever to kill her proved too hot. His guard became careless and one of Alexandre's castellans cleaved him from behind.

More and more Saracens spilled over the ditch to be pitched off and pushed back. Liliane was soon in awe of Alexandre's skill. No movement was rash or wasted; he had a surgeon's deadly control. Quickness was his edge, cold patience his deceptive lure. Philip, too, had lost his indolence. His green eyes narrowed, he was as vicious as a baited wolf. He and Alexandre were eerily alike now; they seemed a natural pair. Liliane wondered that two men so often similar on the surface could be so inwardly different.

Inevitably, Alexandre noticed her and the cold patience in his eyes became fury. His attention was fortunately distracted, for at that moment three castellans to his left went down almost simultaneously. Saracens drove endlessly over the embankment. Alexandre's sword slid beneath her arm up into a Saracen's diaphragm, lifting him slightly before he dropped. Liliane's scimitar sliced across his neck and her small shield crashed hard against her shoulder as the second Saracen swung his light mace at her head and missed. Alexandre saved her life, for she was too tired to move fast enough. She was a liability not only to herself but also to him. Let the attack end soon, she prayed. How could the Saracens keep coming with so many already sprawled dead in the trenches? Then Philip closed in with them to seal the gap, his green eyes dancing and teeth bared in a feral grin. "Harry the bastards!" he yelled. "To the squealing devils!"

Liliane was amazed and appalled. *Harry* the enemy? They were lucky to hold the Saracens off! And yet like a changing tide, she, Alexandre and the defenders swept forward, urged by

Philip's blazing audacity. Richard's rank was already pushing back the Saracens; now Philip's rank added its strength. The Saracens pressed back, but more weakly now, their counter-surges gradually ebbing until, impossibly, the front was empty. Something like silence filled with wafting cries of wonder and jubilation sifted through the moans of the wounded in the trenches.

Spent, Alexandre leaned on his sword. With a glimmer of fatalism, he surveyed the battered line of the retreating enemy. "They will be back. If not tomorrow, then soon enough."

"Not today, though," retorted Philip. When Alexandre said nothing, Philip gave him a brief slap on the back and went to find Richard.

Lilian read Alexandre's mind. How many tomorrows might they withstand such attacks? Before this one, they had already lost more men to disease than the enemy blades and bows. Many had died en route to the Holy Land and each day drained them more, for the stagnant marsh spread pestilence through the camp. The peak of the summer's heat was upon them, and the earth was like a hot brazier, the sun unrelenting as a vulture. Liliane looked across the lines' curve where Philip, his gauntleted hand outstretched, was triumphantly greeting Richard. But for the magic of these two men and the steady courage of those like Alexandre, the Christian army might have been slaughtered to-day.

Alexandre's harsh voice broke in on her thoughts. "You dis-obeyed me."

"You needed me," she replied quietly, then waved her hand toward the disorganized masses that wandered about them with dust- and blood-streaked faces. A few men slumped upon the bank; some were mortally wounded. "They needed me."

"You gave your word.' Almost idly, he scooped up a handful of sand and threw it across the ditch. "And your sworn word is not worth *that!*" His booted foot nudged a dead Saracen. "I was fighting men today, not your murderous relatives. I do not need or want you here. You have betrayed your vow." Rimmed with red, his blue eyes seemed faded. "In France, we agreed to trust each other, but in too short a time I have learned one thing: I cannot trust you."

She paled. "Is that all you see? Not that I love you?"

"What love can endure without trust?" His voice became a

hard whisper. "*My* needs, *my* hopes are nothing to you. You still live for Diego, dead needs, dead hopes. I need a home and a love to whom I may return—some delusion of hope that one day this kind of life may be over. When I see you here, stained with the stench and horror of this place and the war I hate, I know nothing but despair. . . ." When she put out her hand, he dully knocked it aside. "No, keep away. Just now I cannot bear to look at you." Bending, he wiped his sword on the *aba* of a dead Moor, then headed tiredly toward the pennants gathering about the kings' standards.

Heartsick, Liliane watched him go. His anger had gone deeper than she could ever have imagined. He had spoken so little of Diego and little more of how his love for Philip was now tied to her. This intertwining of their loving, warring spirits had grown complex. Her love had been straightforward, couched on solid admiration and the desire of one young passionate being for another. Her adoration and childlike awe, her dependence and idealism had all been given to Diego. She had once woven fairy tales about the long-vanished Jean but none about Alexandre. He was real and vital and she loved him with her whole soul . . . yet . . . did she?

Was he right in saying that too much of her still belonged to Diego? She knew that she had become Alexandre's icon as well as his fleshly paramour. Though he knew her faults, he still idealized her, and today however good her reasons, she had plunged that ideal into all he abhorred and nearly despaired of escaping. The ideal might be unrealistic, but it was all he had left. It would be long, if ever, before he was able to banish the memory of her amid the butchery of this day.

Liliane followed Alexandre to the pennants and stood at a little distance. Philip and Richard were elated, expansive; King Guy was noticeably less so. Conrad of Monferrat, Lisle, Alexandre and other nobles of Philip's court waited restlessy like stallions fired to racing peak, then reined back before their hearts burst. Derek Flanchard, a mercenary knight who had come to Acre with Richard from Cyprus, stood with a half smile at Richard's elbow. Dark-eyed and dark-haired with gray at the temples, Flanchard had a drowsy ease that was deceptive. Alexandre, having known Flanchard from the Flandrian campaigns, had described him to her as being the sort of man who thrived on fighting. He was charming enough at peace, but in battle he was in his element—a handsome wolverine loosed to slash and kill.

Of Richard and Flanchard, Liliane preferred Richard's forthright brutality. Flanchard would have been a murderer for hire had he not been a mercenary. He was the sort that had appeared at times seeking employ from Diego. The pay was the lure for these men, the killing field no matter but in evading the gallows. Diego taught her to recognize such wolverines. He always "tested" them against Pedro, who was wickedly quick with a mace. Rarely in Diego's domain did a wolverine escape burial for employment in an enemy's squadrons.

Suddenly, Liliane realized that Flanchard's smile was for Alexandre, who was speaking to Philip so quietly she could catch only a few words. Then, the last phrase carried. "Will Your Majesties hear a private proposal?"

"Of course," Philip agreed quickly.

She stiffened. Was Alexandre about to reveal her secret and send her back to France? The two of them headed for Philip's tent, a knot of men-at-arms threading after them. Behind her, she heard Flanchard observe mockingly to Richard, "That one has lost his taste for war. Let us hope he does not weaken his monarch's stomach as well."

Her loathing for Flanchard doubling, Liliane turned, a sharp rebuke on her lips. Richard spoke before she could open her mouth. "Brueil may take no more joy of this enterprise, Flanchard," he snapped, "but he will not shirk it, and King Philip is not for your gauging; hereafter, guard your remarks."

Flanchard subsided, but Liliane knew his cynical tongue would soon rattle again. She did not dare follow Alexandre and Philip when they rejoined Richard and went to his lion-emblazoned pavilion. An eavesdropping Moor about a royal tent was too reckless even for her. She retired to watch the tent at a distance. Biting her lip, she waited tensely. At length, a noble came to the pavilion's opening and summoned pages from the royal retinues. After a short exchange, the pages scurried off through the camp. Her skin prickled. Something was happening and Alexandre had set it in motion. She intercepted a page, the same one who had seen her shoot Jacques's assassin. "Have you not a message for me, young sir?"

The page looked startled. "Indeed, I have not . . ." Under Liliane's penetrating gaze, he fumbled, "King Richard bids all the lords and knights to attend a meeting in the royal pavilion in an hour.''

"Thank you,'' Liliane replied mildly. "I perceive my royal rank relieves me of that obligation.'' She strolled off through the camp. Outwardly, she wore the impassive face of most Moors who mingled with the Christians; inwardly, she was in a nervous quandary. In one way, she was relieved that Alexandre had withheld her identity; no meeting of lords was necessary to dispatch her to France. Why was the council declared? She knew better than to attend. Converted or not, no Moor was admitted to high war councils.

When Alexandre briefly returned to his tent to clean up for the council, she tried both to make peace with him and relieve her curiosity but was met with stony impassivity. He would discuss nothing but a change of linen. His mind seemed preoccupied with more than their quarrel on the battlefield. His continuing anger was understandable but his secretiveness indicated that he was initiating something in which he wanted her to take no part— something dangerous.

After his departure, Liliane hastened to Richard's pavilion. Knights and lords were slowly filing into the tent. She spied Philip's young page standing with a group of courtiers outside the entrance. When the council began, he sat down with his back to the tent to while away what might be hours of debate.

Thoughtfully, Liliane watched the boy as she waited in the shelter of the surrounding tents. From his position, he must be hearing more than a little of the conference. When the sun reached two handspans from the western horizon, the council ended. Most of the council members departed, but Alexandre, Philip and several other nobles lingered with Richard. A senior courtier said something to the page as the boy rose and stretched. The page nodded and set off at a trot into the camp; the courtier must have sent him on an errand.

Once the page had gone out of sight of the pavilion, Liliane waylaid him. "Young sir, I will take no more than a few minutes of your time, but I must speak with you.''

"Concerning what matter?'' the page countered warily. Liliane saw he had an inkling of her mission.

"I am pledged to guard the life of Count Alexandre de Brueil,'' she replied gravely. "Have I reason to believe that yonder council has put his life in jeopardy?''

"I may not speak of the council," the page said firmly, and started to brush by her.

No one was about, but to be seen talking alone with a Moor on such a day was unwise. Liliane gave the page credit for good sense, even as she put an arm across his path. "Wait, I beg you. I do not seek to spy upon the doings of your master and his allies. I wish to know only if there is danger to the young count."

The page put his hand upon his dagger. "See you here, milord, I may tell you nothing. Now, let me pass and be about my business."

Liliane held out her arms from her sides. "Take my weapons, sir, and fear nothing from me. If I must convince you of my good faith, it must be in private. Will you come to Count Alexandre's tent? His guards are not fond of me and you would have their willing assistance if you think me treacherous."

"I am not afraid of you, but I have no time for a conference," reiterated the page. "You must address Count Alexandre if you wish to know his plans."

"Count Alexandre has a concern for my neck, sir, and too often he risks his own. Please," she pleaded softly, "give me only that few minutes that I asked and you will understand my bond to the count; 'tis one that runs deeper than a sworn oath and I cannot shirk it."

The page stared hard at her for a few minutes, then waved her toward the beach dunes. He drew his knife and palmed it, then disarmed Liliane. "I have no use for traitors."

Liliane led the way into the dunes where the wind from the sea was ruffling a few dry shocks of seagrass. Once in a generous dip that bent away from the camp's view, she crouched down in the blowing sand and looked up at the page. Her hands went to the haik and tugged it free. The page gaped at the golden mass that spilled across her shoulders. "See you now, young sir, why you have naught to fear from a turncoat Moor? I am Liliane, Countess de Brueil, wife to Count Alexandre."

"But," gasped the page, "your uncle was the—" He halted, fearing he had said too much.

"My uncle was the villain who ordered my husband shot in the back. You have quick eyes and courage. That you are yet alive attests to your luck that my uncle has not guessed you saw more than you ought; it also speaks for your circumspect tongue. If not for the last, I would not risk your confidence now, for if

any should discover me, I should be sent back to France with
my lord Alexandre left to contest alone the treacheries of my
relatives.'' She put into her lovely eyes an appeal that might have
softened the heart of a crocodile. ''I beg you, have pity upon a
woman's love for her husband and help me now. Surely one who
has endured the doubts of his fellows because of his youth can
understand another who would be dismissed for want of strength
and a man's beard.'' She took his hand. ''You have seen that I
have courage and skill; believe also that I am faithful to my
husband and our liege lord, King Philip.''

''I believe you, my lady,'' he stammered, ''but I would not
see you join the enterprise your husband plans; 'tis for seasoned
warriors.''

''I have survived nearly as many battles as you, sir, and today
I was with Alexandre and King Philip. No weanling could have
helped hold back the Saracens. Tell me, what does my husband
propose?''

Reluctantly, he told her. He had not heard everything through
the tent wall, but he had heard enough. Alexandre, with Philip's
backing and Richard's interest, was proposing a series of coun-
terstrikes against Saladin, the first being scheduled for the same
night, while the Saracens would be celebrating their near success
in the day's attack. The aim was to disconcert and fatigue the
enemy with night raids, using a small, quick-moving crack force
like the Saracens' own raiding bands, a force that would not
greatly deplete the main crusader army should it be destroyed.

Liliane listened with growing depression. How like Alexandre
not to want to endure the humiliating, slow ruin of another siege
like that he had experienced in Jerusalem. He would rather fight
than rot.

Flanchard, the mercenary, led the many objections: the two
main ones being that if Alexandre were destroyed, he would take
with him part of the cream of the crusader forces, which they
could ill afford to lose; also that he proposed to arm them with
bows, light swords and scarcely more armor than jousting
squires, which Flanchard considered to be a mad idea.

'' 'Tis more mad to weight men like elephants,'' Alexandre
had retorted. ''Elephants may be impressive, but they also make
lumbering targets. We should be run down before we were well
away from Saladin's camp.''

The council wrangled for nearly another hour, with most siding with Flanchard. They might have continued until this night's chance was lost, had Richard not ended the discussion. His invariably grudging patience and his love of daring aggressiveness decreed his decision. "Choose your force, Brueil, and arm them as you like, but take no man unwilling. Such an enterprise will founder upon any hesitancy."

His dark eyes filled with irony, Flanchard rose. "If I may, Your Majesty, I should like to be first to propose my services to the count. If I am proved wrong about this venture, it still promises merit and adventure. If I am right, I confess a nagging, if perhaps fatal, wish to witness that justification."

"You are welcome, Sir Derek," Alexandre replied easily. "I shall need a good second in command to Baron de Lisle who earlier volunteered his skill."

Liliane was less sanguine. Alexandre liked Flanchard no better than she did. Flanchard was not to be trusted and he envied Alexandre's royal influence. His readiness to join the troop had not won him the lieutenancy he angled for, but he might attempt more devious ways to achieve that position . . . and more.

The sand swirled about her and the page, stinging them. "I must go," the page muttered, wiping grit from his face. "If I do not, the lord who sent me will set up an uproar." He blinked at her, then frowned earnestly as he backed up the dune. "I wish you good fortune, my lady, in your enterprise. You are brave, but I wonder if you would not better serve your husband as wives are wont. With all respect, I know I should not want *my* wife running about in heathen garb and risking her neck and virtue!" With that, he saluted her and took to his heels to resume his interrupted errand.

After redonning her haik, Liliane raced home. With the haik cinched high about her face, she ordered a bath of seawater to rid herself of her dirt and fidgeted while two servants filled the copper tub. Stripping, she jumped into the shallow water but had scarcely submerged her dirty face when Alexandre entered the tent.

He peered with alert fascination at her sleek form glistening beneath the water. The slender curve of her back rose gracefully above the surface. He trailed a finger along her backbone, and she snapped upright, improving his view considerably. "Fishing?" he inquired gently.

She flushed. "No . . . I am just dirty from the battle."

Alexandre studied her tangled mat of hair and the grayish patch of sandy dust about her face. "Odd, you pick up so much dirt beneath that *haik*. The only time you take it off is in the tent, isn't it?"

At the cynical look in his eyes, Liliane suddenly realized her mistake. The dune sand had dusted her hair. A reasonable explanation eluded her.

Fortunately, Alexandre seemed ready to let the question slide. Deftly, he plucked the slim bar of soap from the bath. "Shall I wash your hair?"

Ordinarily the offer would have delighted her; now it made her squirm. With luxurious laziness, he silently lathered her hair, his strong fingers working against her scalp. At length, she relaxed in spite of herself and her head slipped back against his hands.

Alexandre gazed down at the pale, enticing length of her. This softness, this fragile-looking desirable creature had fought at his side in battle. She bewildered him, frustrated him . . . fascinated him. How could any woman be so stubborn, so daring and heedless of her own safety, all supposedly in his behalf? He could not believe she loved him that much.

Perhaps she was thinking of Diego, he reflected cynically. Diego was at the core of most of her restlessness and mercurial moods. Was she driven by some guilt over Diego, something she had owed him or wrongly taken? Had Jacques somehow used her to bring about Diego's death?

And what was she up to now, with that startled blush that had greeted him when he found her in the tub? She had taken the haik off and not by accident, or she would not have fumbled for an explanation. He could think of only two reasons why she might have doffed the haik; either she had not wanted to look like a Moor or she had wanted to reveal herself as a woman . . . perhaps to a man—Richard or Philip? Jacques? A lover?

Alexandre almost hoped she had been playing spy again. Her pleading with Richard to send him home could only lead to public embarrassment. And what if she had entreated Philip? He could imagine the price the fair and lecherous Philip would demand of her. Alexandre forced that unpleasant idea from his mind.

Tonight he was riding out on a dangerous mission from which he might not return. As Liliane could expect little more than indifference and a skimpy escort back to France from Richard, her only protector would then be Philip. Banishing depression again, Alexandre resolved to make the most of the next brief hours with her; the last thing he wanted was to quarrel.

Her slippery hair was soft, like heavy silk in his fingers, her body white where the aba had hidden it from the desert sun and the eyes of men. His eyes. Sometimes he almost went wild imagining her bare under the voluminous aba . . . when no man knew but himself of its treasures, when all of them, reduced to prostitutes and buggery, would have been sick with desire for her. And she was his, so long as he could hold her.

He gently corded Liliane's wet hair about her neck and kissed her. Her tongue was pink, her nipples damp and rosy above the water, her lashes a swallow's wings closed over the high curves of her cheeks. He traced her elegant jaw, the shells of her ears, her throat and collarbones to her slender shoulders. Then he lifted her to him, bare and wet, and placed her upon the rug. Soap still glistened in her hair as he made love to her. Languorously, he kissed her armpits, pressed her breasts high to meet his lips and teasing tongue. He licked water from her navel, from her lower belly. She sighed as he moved lower still. He delighted in her pleasure, the quick response he could draw from her. These soft cries were his, this secret gateway to love. Her hands caught almost hurtfully in his hair and in turn he became merciless in his demand of her.

Only when Liliane begged for him, did he open his clothing and release his own arousal, sinking into her with slow luxury. She fitted to him with such delicious, maddening tightness that the slightest movement excited him to bursting. She was a whirlpool drawing him deeper into liquid desire. She shuddered, moaning past control as he quickened. A shattering tremor shook them, quaked in outward running splits that opened in a scarlet-streaked disorienting chasm of passion.

The glow snaked about their bodies, racing through their veins to blaze white-hot as if the desert sun had exploded there.

Alexandre, thou splendid liar, Liliane thought yearningly in the slow cooling aftermath. You fill me with life, even as you show yourself to death. With lips and limbs of flaming desire, you destroy me as if you would raise a phoenix in my place. What new creature do you think to leave behind you? What value is any life to me if you are gone from it?

Alexandre left her asleep with the lingering brush of his kiss

faintly stirring her hair behind her ear. She sighed, flung out a
hand as if reaching for him. He did not touch her, waiting silently for her to sink into sleep again. The tent was so dark he
could scarcely see the curve of her cheek, but just now he clearly
remembered her intent profile as she had perched over the stream
in Provence the first day they had met. She had been waiting, so
beautifully deft when she moved at last to capture her fish. She
had more patience than he, and perhaps more certainty of what
she wanted. Over the years, his own wants had grown simple.
He wanted her, peace, children. Tonight, those simple hopes
might be ended. When had his future really been different? Philip
invariably allowed him to go home just long enough to believe
that he might not be recalled to war. Since returning to Palestine, he had walked with death at his shoulder . . . and Liliane,
lovely, defiant and courageous, at his right hand.

"Aye," he whispered. "You will be a match for anything, my
sweeting. My golden hawk has claws enough for Philip, Jacques
and the whole pack. Fare thee well, my love. *Vaya con Dios*."

A short while later, Alexandre, Flanchard, Louis, Lisle and
thirty horsemen silently crossed the siege ditch that separated the
camp from the desert. The moon was a sliver, the dunes scarcely
discernible in its cold glow. Overhead the stars hung as brilliant
as the Eyes of God that the Saracens called them. The camp was
still, a jumbled mosaic of pale canvas, sharp-edged and temporary, while the dunes were smooth, curved and endless. Most of
the riders, unused to wearing only chain mail and helmets, were
fidgety. Their light swords and bows seemed flimsy, and the
destriers were bemused by the lack of weight on their broad
backs. The desert was cool now, almost chilly, with nothing to
break the wandering wind. Somewhere over the Mediterranean,
a storm was rising.

The horses' hooves left great pocks in the dunes as they
climbed. Almost instantly the pocks filled at the wind's ghostly
hands, and on the caps of the dunes the streaming sand blew in
pale shifting threads. Alexandre's big black led the way, his master's slim body supple as a reed as they negotiated the undulating
sands. Lisle came next, then Flanchard, with the rest fanning
loosely behind. Three scouts ranged well ahead.

In perhaps a half hour, the scouts sighted Saladin's camp and
waited for the raiders to catch up to them. The camp was a dark,
sprawling octopus of tents, the largest capped with pennants

bearing the Saracen crescent. "We will take that long left-handed
arm with the fat tents," Alexandre ordered. "Split and go in on
both sides. Take no loot, but quietly kill every Saracen you find.
Retreat instantly at the trumpet's call and ride to the wadi east
of Acre, then you ten"—he designated the far riders on his right—
"fan to the south and be prepared to harry and delay the enemy
for the rest to ride on to Acre." He looked at Lisle. "My lord,
you, with Flanchard as your second, will lead the main body to
Acre. Milord de Signe and I will be with the harriers."

Alexandre could feel Louis's eyes on him. Louis was well
aware that the harriers had the most hazardous assignment. Alexandre smiled grimly at him. He had not deliberately chosen
Louis to bait the Saracens, but he would have no regrets if Louis
was skewered and no longer able to harass Liliane. He only
wished that Jacques was available; *that* one was a plump worm
to dangle before Saladin's army!

Like deadly, vengeful spirits, they entered the Saracen camp
with only the whickers of tethered horses to greet them. Quietly
slashing the canvas tents, they turned long rows of sleepers into
blood-stained bundles that would never move again. Cries rose
as the canvas was jostled and ripped. An isolated scream rose
up to the moon, then another. Clatter sounded as the rest of the
camp was aroused. Men poured from their tents, slashing in
retaliation. The swords' rise and fall quickened to swift, urgent
hacking. Minutes later, Alexandre raised a smeared gauntlet and
the clarion called out over the slaughter.

In moments the raiders were remounted and pounding to the
west, leaving behind a furious uproar. The Moors appeared on
the horizon just as the raiders split. Louis was one of the first to
veer off, Alexandre among the last. The pounding of pursuing
hooves and the cries of revenge rose like the beat of a racing,
bursting heart. The visibility was short and the sensation was
that of a hideous, rushing mirage, overwhelming all in its path.

Two riders veered after Alexandre, as another part of the
Moorish band pursued the rest of the harriers. Alexandre wheeled
to meet the pair as they closed in on him. Digging in his heels,
he spurred forward. To his horror, his right stirrup broke. With
a fierce wrench at his ankle, the girth snapped, pitching him
sidelong onto the sand. Alexandre hit hard, rolling, the gritty
spray biting his face and blinding him. Stunned and disoriented
but still clutching his sword, he leaped awkwardly to his feet,

only to have the wrenched ankle cave under him with a burst of
pain. He stifled a curse, gasping as he forced himself upright
again. A shouting rider loomed from the darkness, slicing down
at him. Reacting with blind instinct, he desperately blocked the
attack with the flat of his blade, twisted his wrist to slide steel
on steel and thrust high to make contact with an armpit. The
Saracen shrieked and pitched forward, his flying weight dragging
Alexandre backward off his feet. The Saracen, far from dead,
was up first. His sword arm useless, the Saracen shifted his blade
to the other hand. Awkward and frantic to end a disadvantaged
fight quickly, he sliced and went wide. In seconds, Alexandre's
sword found his attacker's stomach. An instant too late. The thud
of hooves filled his skull as the second horseman leaned out in
space, javelin poised, its point trained on Alexandre's breast.

Then the Saracen leaned forward at a grotesque angle. He
hurtled off the horse, a feathered quarrel buried at the base of
his skull. In moments, another Saracen galloped from the darkness. Alexandre tightened his grip on his sword as the rider
charged him. As he drew back his sword to meet the assault, he
heard his name unbelievingly. "Alexandre!" The Saracen reined
in with a flurry of sand and extended a hand down to him.

"*Le bon Dieu!* What the . . . ?"

Amber eyes flashed in a flawless face. "Hurry! Others are
behind me!"

"Liliane! You spying little witch . . . !" Wasting no more
time on his startled fury, he vaulted onto her gray mare. "Come
on, to camp!"

She spurred the mare forward. "We shall never reach Acre
carrying two! The pursuit's too close!"

"Then head northwest. There is an oasis where we can try to
hide until they are past."

They were surrounded by the starlit night, the sand-shifting
wind and the mare's labored breathing as it struggled up the
dunes. Though Alexandre said nothing, Liliane could feel his
tension and anger. If they survived, she was in for trouble. Except for the dunes glimmering about them, they could see nothing beyond fifty yards. That meant they had to keep fifty yards
between themselves and the Saracens to remain unseen. She
feared that the jingles of the mare's bridle bit might carry; the
desert had an uncanny way of sometimes swallowing sound,
sometimes magnifying it. Just now, they were beginning to hear

the gallop of many horses closing from the east. Liliane urged the mare to hurry, but it was already straining. If they did not find the oasis soon, they would be run down. At that moment, the mare tripped, pitching them both forward to roll down a dune. Stunned, they rolled to evade the thrashing horse. As it floundered up, Alexandre scrambled to his feet to catch its rein. Trembling, the mare slid down the base of the dune and limped to a halt. "The devil," Alexandre hissed. "She has taken a wrench." He slapped the sorrel on the rump to send it lurching off, then caught Liliane's hand and dragged her after him. "Come on, run!"

"What about the mare?" she gasped. "Good horses are worth their weight in gold in Acre. She will cost a fortune to replace!"

"Which would you rather give up, a sack of gold or our skins?" he retorted. "We might as well try to conceal an elephant from the Saracens out here. The mare will head for the nearest water. We may be able to find her at the oasis."

Liliane had to concede his point. The hoofbeats were closer now, coming in waves that sometimes seemed to recede before they grew inevitably louder. Then, abruptly, they became thunder.

He thrust her toward the shadow of a dune. "Down!" The flat of his hand hit her squarely in the small of the back. She went down on her face in sand. A split second later, Alexandre landed atop her. She started to fight to clear her nose and mouth from the sand, then lay still as if she were shrinking. Hoofs threw stinging sand against her ears and cheeks. With bated breath, she waited for the horse to stumble and fall, waited for the next mount to pound them into bloody mush. . . . The ground shuddered beneath them, deafening them so that when at last Alexandre pulled her up, she scarcely realized that the Saracens were past.

Without a sound, Alexandre limped over a vast dune that swelled leviathan under the dim moon. The dune receded and another swelled. On and on they stumbled until she merely clung doglike to Alexandre's belt. Then, painfully, her forehead and nose connected with his mailed back. "There," he whispered. "See it?"

Liliane dimly saw a dull, silvery glimmer; a moonlit gleam. From what? Nothing lay in this desert but the hot sand beneath their feet. A pale female was the desert by night—undulating curves and sand whispering into the wind like a woman's hair. At dawn the sun would rise like the shield of cruel Mars, and they would wander at the mercy of both the broiling heat and the Saracens. The desert would become a Medusa with the deadly embrace of a hundred stinging serpents. Only now the desert was virginal, free of the envy of gods.

Alexandre caught her arm. "Are you all right? You look faint."

She smiled a little at his anxious tone. "I can keep going, but you must not let me stop to breathe so much; it goes to my head."

He gave her hair a little tug. "That gleam you see in front of us is the oasis, so we have not far to go now. Make no noise. Saladin may have left us a few surprises among the oasis palms."

Alexandre was silent for a moment, staring down at her. He touched her hair again, then fanned it lightly out to catch the wind's whisper. Like a golden spiderweb, it floated and fell, fragile, as if lying upon the water's surface before it sank. "The desert becomes you," he murmured. Then he drew her into his arms. His leather breastplate was cold, his arms hard, yet she felt only his heartbeat, the warmth of his mouth. They might have had the desert, the whole world to themselves. Danger, reality, all was merely an echo. She clung to him tightly, as if Acre had never been, as if the Saracens might not swarm upon them in moments. Not moving, their embrace held dancing and music, and they felt young as they might never be again. The desert threatened death but yielded life, as well. Their kiss was sweet, defiant.

After a long while, they parted reluctantly. "I ought to beat you," Alexandre whispered, "but I keep wanting to do it with your hair. *Dieu,* what a maddening, alluring creature you are. . . ." His head lowered as if he were going to pursue that allure, but then he released her with a sigh. "We are mad, both of us. In minutes, we could be slit to ribbons, yet here we are, playing like lovebirds." When she started to protest, he laid a finger against her lips. "Not another coo, *ma comtesse.* I want to enjoy more than a ruffling of your feathers tonight. Staying alive is a prerequisite to making love."

She giggled. "I have always wanted to see a pigeon's teeny, weeny—"

He swatted her bottom. "Mind your tongue, you minx. Teeny

weeny's all you deserve tonight; that and a gray old man. Your persistent pursuit of disaster is aging me.''

Creeping like centipedes, they finally arrived at the oasis. The dry palms rattled in the wind. Frayed, heavily listless but for the stirrings of their long fronds, the palms were high and thin, scattered among thick catalpa and thorn bush. A low gully led through the undergrowth to a pool of water at the center of the oasis. Motioning Liliane to keep low, Alexandre followed the gully, his feet silent upon the dry round stones at its base. A stirring of dark shapes ahead made them freeze. A long head lifted, tugging as if trying to be free of something. A low scrape of rock sounded.

''Two horses ahead,'' Alexandre whispered against her ear. ''Stay here. Use the bow if their riders show.''

Leaving her crouched in a cluster of thorn bush, Alexandre began to circle the fringe of the clearing around the water. Moments later, a slight thrashing occurred in the undergrowth. Liliane held her breath and readied the bow. A burnoosed figure reared from the brush only inches from her, grabbed at a horse's head and swung up onto its back. She fired a quarrel at the flash of white above the burnoose. The Saracen went down. To her horror, the man was not dead. With a long gash splitting his nose and cheekbone, he charged her, his scimitar a wicked blur. Then a silver band blocked his throat and a dirk's blur counterpointed the scimitar. The Saracen's hand clawed up, raked out, jerked and dropped limp. Liliane looked away as Alexandre pushed the dead Saracen away, then stooped to wipe his blade.

He glanced up at the nervous tethered mount and the edgily dancing companion mare. ''We are in luck. We ride back to camp. There is only one saddle, so the other horse must be a runaway.'' When she did not answer, he turned. ''What is wrong?''

''Nothing,'' she replied briefly. ''I am just a little tired.''

He eyed her keenly. ''Tired of walking or tired of splendid gore? Your stomach would not be beginning to rebel at your chosen profession, would it?''

''Do not be rotten, Alexandre.'' She slumped down on a low bolder. ''Do you really think I have been enjoying this marvelous, mosquito-ridden summer? Enjoy trying to slaughter men I do not hate, for a cause I find repellent?''

''Oh, I thought you were having a fine time,'' he replied sardonically. "Tonight was particularly splendid. A pity you missed the show at Saladin's camp. We killed most of the wretches in their beds. Very gallant and chivalrous, we were. If they ever capture one of us, I should not blame them if they buried us alive in scorpions."

"Stop it!"

"Oh, but then you did not miss all the show. You arrived for the finale, and I do owe you thanks for saving my skin." His head cocked quizzically. "Just how did you happen to arrive at so convenient a moment?"

"I joined the Saracen pursuit," she replied dully. "I was dressed like them. In the dark, they never noticed me."

He was silent for a moment, then his breath came out in a hiss of weariness. "I might have known. But, then, why not? Why do we not all dress like Saracens and end up fighting ourselves? What is the difference?"

"We are fighting each other again as we did this afternoon," she said quietly. "A little while ago, we were kissing."

Alexandre stroked her hair. "Come, let us walk by the water. I want to declare an armistice."

Her eyes slid over the Saracen. "I am not in the mood."

"I should think a man's death might put you very much in the mood to enjoy peace," he murmured. "For myself, I need to look upon water tonight. I hope, *par Dieu,* that it is clean." He walked off toward the glimmer in the darkness.

After a few minutes, Liliane followed him. The last thing she wanted now was to be alone with the Saracen—alone with herself. She saw Alexandre wandering about the patch of water. For a time, she followed him at a slight distance. The water was quiet, unlike anything she had seen in Palestine. Whatever muddy dregs the basin might hold, the pool surface looked clear at night. Beneath unnaturally large stars, it lay, a rare, liquid jewel where no fish swam among its facets, mirrors among mirrors. She moved close to Alexandre. "What if the Saracens come back?"

"They will not. We are too far north."

"What if they find the mare?"

"What if they do?" He turned to her. "Are you afraid now? Your mind is darting about like a worried gazelle."

"Afraid? Why should I be?" Liliane stared at the water, then shrugged uncertainly. "Yes. I am afraid. I have brought terrible differences between us, brought out monsters—distrust, lies, where we once had vowed to abolish deception. You still love me, but . . . you don't like me as much as you once did, do you?''

His mouth stopped her. "Hush," he whispered. "Would you have me entirely ungrateful? Had you remained safely at home, I would have loved you no less, but whatever the cost, can you think I want you there tonight?'' He kissed the corners of her mouth, her eyes, her ears. "Give me present delight and all your passion,'' he whispered huskily against her throat. "By day there is hell . . . by night there is you. . . .''

His hands found her shoulders, then beneath the aba, found her womanly body warm and resilient. Pliant against him, she let the aba fall from her shoulders, arching back to offer her breasts, pale and pointed, to his seeking mouth. He browsed, finding honey there, her flesh feeding his quickening hunger. He tugged at her lower clothing, finding warmer honey between her thighs. Her arms wound about him, her hips moving with a magic of their own in reply to his adroit teasing. His manhood, already hardened beneath his braies, responded with a ready surge.

"Damn,'' he swore softly, "this would be the time to be wearing armor!'' He tugged hard at his leather fastenings, then with a swift movement, dragged both light armor and chainse over his head. He pulled her to him, his mouth capturing hers. Her buttocks fit in his hands, her flat belly rubbed his swollen groin. No longer able to control her own desire, she caressed him, bared him and closed on him. With a low groan, he bore her to the sand. Her long legs parted as she arched her back, and in a single thrust, he filled her. His slow, almost languid rhythm matched hers as they tantalized each other, brought their bodies apart and together as if in a sinuous, exotic dance, writhing together on the sand. His dark flesh slid against her paleness, his arms stretched with hers. Bound by desire, the one enslaved the other, craving each other, withholding only to yield again and again with the tiny silver claws and bells of love. The music quickened, intensifying the vibrato of their slim bodies as Alexandre lured his lady. Bending, arching, the sultry-eyed Liliane maddeningly tempted and evaded him until he was driven to claim her. Their pulses became as drums, their kisses wild cymbals as their bodies joined and strained, singing a high, primitive, piercing note that trembled to breathless silence. For a long while, there was stillness.

His eyes inky, Alexandre looked down at Liliane, her perfect body pale, her blond hair spilled like shimmering light upon the sand. "Solomon was a great poet, yet I think he had no queen so fair as thou; Mohammed no houri. Tonight, I am as the kings and prophets, with all the possessions of earth and heaven in my arms."

"Within your arms lies my world, and all I shall ever ask of heaven," Liliane whispered. "If tomorrow finds our love's starry illusion tarnished, I beg you not to cast me away in this wilderness; I fear I should never find my way back to you."

His eyes narrowed slightly. "Would you do me dishonor? You are my lady wife. That I would leave you is unthinkable."

"I will never hold you to honor's bond, Alexandre. Where love is not, honor will not suffice. Once duty drove us together, but it must not become a strangler."

"What are you trying to say?"

"That if the day ever comes when I no longer make you happy, I will leave willingly. We need not quarrel and turn all our blissful memories to hate."

"By Saint Michael," Alexandre said with a trace of impatience, "what preys upon your mind tonight? Have I just beaten you? Do I take my ease in the camp stews? Why will you invite demons of discontent into our very union?" He caught her face hard between his hands. "Our bliss is *now*. We shall not mar it with grim and groundless foreboding." His mouth came down on hers almost brutally, so much so that she wondered if he were not wrestling with his own doubts. Her fears were beginning to fade into growing passion when a stealthy rustle in the undergrowth startled them apart. Alexandre caught up his sword from his spilled clothing, the weaponless Liliane crouching behind him. The bush stirred, then a low, skulking shape slunk across the gully. Alexandre let out his breath. "Hyena. We had better get out of here. More are likely to be around. They may be cowards singly, but in a pack they are vicious."

When they had dressed, he headed down the gully to the spot where they had left the Saracen and the horses. He dragged off the corpse's haik and tossed it to Liliane. "Here, you will need this. You cannot very well ride into camp with your hair flying."

Liliane fought the urge to drop the haik. It hung from her hand like a shroud. The thought of wrapping it about her head and face stifled her. Untethering the horse, Alexandre did not notice her white face as she slowly donned the haik. Then, a muted cry from the thicket riveted their attention, and he tossed Liliane the reins. In a whisper, with his knife drawn, he disappeared into the brush. The brush rattled as someone tried to scramble away, then she heard a shriek, which was swiftly silenced. Moments later, Alexandre emerged from the thicket, dragging a struggling figure by the scruff. "A Saracen?" whispered Liliane.

"Not quite," Alexandre replied dryly. "She is a Rifi. Round as an apple, with guts of jelly. Probably a slave, run off during the raid." He gave his squirming captive a shake to make her stand up. "If so, she has run far enough to have raw feet, unless the saddleless horse was hers. That dead Saracen on the ground must have pursued her." The girl was swathed in voluminous garments to the neck. A veil covered her face to her eyes, which were eloquent with fear and entreaty.

"We cannot leave her here."

"Why not?" Alexandre shrugged. "They will treat her like a pig in Acre. A Saracen patrol will check by here tomorrow and see her back to their camp."

"For a worse fate! Alexandre, she must have been desperate to run into the desert between enemy armies. God knows what sort of master she has! At the least, she is certain to be dreadfully punished."

The Rifi girl looked dolefully up at Alexandre as if to confirm Liliane's assessment. He sighed. "Oh, all right. We'll take her to Acre, but be warned: she is going to prove a nuisance."

Liliane was no longer paying attention to him. She was again all too aware of the smell of blood on the haik.

11

Trouble in the Tent

Acre
Same night

Just before dawn, the little band reached the crusader camp, which was in a turmoil. All night, fragments of Alexandre's band had made their way back with conflicting casualty reports. Alexandre himself was thought to be dead.

Philip met them at the ditchworks. "God's bones!" He seized Alexandre by his dusty shoulders. "You took long enough getting back! What the devil happened?" His green eyes flicked knowingly to the sloe-eyed little Rifi. "Or should I ask?"

Alexandre grinned wickedly. "Oh, the wench belongs to Jefar here. He could not resist her bottom. Threw her right over his shoulder and skipped out of an amir's tent." He flashed Liliane a mischievous glance. She smiled lazily back and gave the Rifi's bottom a pinch that dulled his amusement.

"Flanchard says you did not do much damage," Philip observed. "So far, you appear to have lost six men, among them two of my likeliest knights."

"We killed nearly fifty Saracens and spread havoc. By my reckoning, sire, that is a tidy maneuver."

"Can you establish your figures?"

"Most of my men are better at mathematics than Flanchard."

"They had better be. Richard is frothing for an accounting." Philip pushed through his hovering guards. "Come along, *mon ami,* time to recite your sums."

When Alexandre hesitated, Liliane gave him an inscrutably Eastern smile. "Do not worry. I shall see to the girl."

210

On the way to the tent, Liliane wondered if the Rifi had seen her back at the oasis without her haik and quite possibly without any clothes at all. If so, the girl might prove more than a mere nuisance and must immediately be sent out of Acre on an east-bound caravan. If questioned about what she had seen, she would surely lie. Liliane had a better way of picking her brains.

Once inside the tent, she examined the Rifi with a deliberately cold eye. By dawn's light, the girl was very pretty, with a ripely rounded body and the large dark eyes of a gazelle. She was also no more than sixteen and stiff with fear. "What is your name?" Liliane demanded.

The girl looked startled, then her brow furrowed in effort to understand Liliane's Spanish Arabic. "Saida," she whispered plaintively. "I was a slave of Idi ben Ibrahim. He bought me in Damascus when I was a child and mercilessly beat me."

"No doubt for chattering," Liliane observed tauntingly. The Rifi must be tested as to what she had seen and heard at the oasis; also whether she could be relied upon to hold her tongue. "I did not ask for the details of your life." She stalked around the chastened girl. "This Ibrahim must have been a beggar. You are on the skinny side."

For a moment, Saida lost her fear. "Idi ben Ibrahim was a great lord!" she retorted indignantly. "He chose me over forty other girls!"

"For what reason, I cannot imagine." Liliane sauntered over to a fruit bowl, selected a few dates and dropped comfortably onto Alexandre's pallet. She popped a date into her mouth, then muttered darkly, "Probably we should sell you to a brothel to make up for the trouble of saving you from the desert."

Terrified, Saida threw herself at Liliane's feet. "Great lord, I beg you have mercy! Do not let me be defiled by infidels!" A desperate, cunning determination came into her eyes. Crawling forward, she insinuated herself about Liliane's knees, allowing a generous view of her breasts in her low-cut bodice. "Lord, I know ways to please thee that thou hast not dreamed of. Let me prove my gratitude. I will take thee to paradise. Thy staff shall stand like the rod of Abraham. . . ."

Fighting to stifle her growing amusement, Liliane let Saida rattle on for a time. Clearly, the girl thought she was a man, so her identity was presently safe enough. Saida's awareness of her peculiar Arabic was another matter. Rifis were Berbers and Liliane spoke little of the Berber dialect that should have been native to Jefar el din. Saida had a ready tongue, a sturdy vanity and no loyalties; if she were not kept close in the tent, she might well gossip in the camp.

By now Saida was cooing lascivious suggestions that would make a ribald blush. At close range, she smelled faintly of goat. Liliane placed a boot firmly between Saida's breasts and gently propelled her to a less pungent distance. "I do not require your services, girl. As a Christian, I am infidel as much as any European in Palestine." She smiled faintly at Saida's flushed panic. "Do not fear. The French lord is master here. He will make the ultimate decision as to your fate. Possibly, you may earn your freedom, but I warn you, learn to curb your tongue within and without this tent or your days of choosing your bedmates will be briefly numbered."

Saida somewhat sullenly backed away, the quicker when she spied Kiki sidling up to his mistress for a date. "Are you afraid of monkeys?" Liliane asked idly, as she gave the small creature a morsel.

"They are dirty and they bite." Saida stared with distaste at Kiki's delicate nibblings.

"This one is cleaner than you and she only bites when provoked." Liliane glanced lazily at Saida. "You would do well to smile at her often. Sour faces depress her; then her temper suffers." She stroked Kiki's head. "Would you like to pet her?"

Looking as if she would sooner stroke an adder, Saida cautiously extended her hand. Sensing dislike, Kiki bared her teeth with a hiss. Saida recoiled. "What a pity you cannot be friends," Liliane murmured. She must keep a sharp eye on Saida. Kiki, as a veteran criminal, was an excellent judge of character. She knew immediately who would be kind to her and who to avoid. "Ibrahim was not your first master," Liliane said suddenly, not making it a question. "Who were the others?"

When Saida named several amirs with pride, Liliane became more dubious about her. Saida was lying; she was too young to have had so many masters, even if she were troublesome. And certainly they would not all have been rich and illustrious, for pretty as she was, she was a common village girl. Her early life would have been hard and brutal, and if she had spent only a year in a wealthy harem, she would have learned intrigue and deceit well beyond her years. Competition within harems was obsessive, not infrequently leading to discreet murder. Even if Saida were not ruthless, she could not be the trapped gazelle she seemed.

"You must be an extraordinary young woman to have had so many men in love with you," Liliane observed when Saida had finished her recital. When Saida smirked, Liliane added mildly, "One assumes you are also clever enough to be modest within a camp filled with womanless men. Milord Alexandre is beyond your reach; do not impose upon his patience . . . and mine." She gave Saida a cool smile. "Also, do not conceive the idea of poisoning my monkey. I am far fonder of Kiki than a lying slave."

Saida flattened in obsequious obeisance, her face dusting the carpet to hide her resentful glare. "Go," Liliane told her briefly. "You will sleep in my tent, but not in my bed. Tell the cook you have my leave to take a bath. If you venture beyond the tent, you will be sold to the dirtiest cameldriver in Acre."

After the girl was gone, Liliane sighed. Alexandre was right; Saida was going to be a damned nuisance.

Saida started being a damned nuisance immediately. Predictably, the Saracens, hot for revenge, attacked just after dawn. While Liliane, hot, dirty and aching for sleep, wearily assumed her place in the defense line, she thought enviously of Saida taking a cool bath in the tent. She took small comfort in knowing that Saida probably enjoyed that bath as little as she enjoyed fending off angry Saracens. Probably the girl was squealing herself blue at every scrub of the soap and every clash of the battle. All that long, horrid morning Liliane saw no sign of Alexandre. Finally, when the Saracens had been beaten back, she ventured to Richard's tent, where an archer had claimed he had last seen Alexandre. In a little less than an hour, Alexandre and Philip appeared from Richard's end of the line. Philip greeted her cordially. "I confess I was surprised to see you with Alexandre this morning. I hope you had good hunting again today."

Hunting. In that sense, Liliane thought grimly, Philip and Richard were alike; they thought of war as sport. "Aye, sire. Good hunting." She wiped heavy dust from her cheek, leaving a sweaty blotch.

"You will soon have more. Alexandre says he owes his skin

again to you.'' Philip looked at her sharply. ''What do think happened to his girth?''

''It could have snapped accidently, but given the hostler's experience and my lord Alexandre's attention to his equipment, I should imagine it was cut.''

''By whom?''

''That is for Count Alexandre to guess. I saw no stranger near the tack.''

''Do you suppose Louis de Signe could have ventured among the horses during the raid and tampered with my lord Alexandre's girth?''

''I might suppose it. I did not see it.''

''Your Moor is an oyster, Alex,'' the king said dryly.

''An honest oyster, sire.'' Alexandre smiled crookedly at Liliane. ''Sometimes more honest than I would like.''

Philip squinted at the sun-beaten tent tops. ''Now that you mention honesty, what have you done with that infidel trollop you caught, my lord Jefar? That one has the eyes of a true Jezebel.''

''Dropped her into a bath, sire.'' Liliane grinned. ''I doubt to find her cleaner than I left her. She will take a deal of perfume to be bearable.''

Philip laughed. ''In such conditions as this, even kings must be grateful for small favors. When you tire of her, send her to me. I shall have my servants drop her in sheep dip before I peck her.''

''I daresay the young lady will be flattered, sire,'' answered Liliane dryly. ''I doubt even she has thought of collecting a king for her lengthy memoirs.''

Philip looked taken aback for a split second before his green eyes took on an expectant gleam. ''Then you would give her up?''

''Oh, readily, sire, if you will yield me a little time with her. Her past master, one Ibrahim, was old and a vile profligate. She is likely diseased. If so, I have among my medicines some possible remedies that would assure you pleasure without vile consequences.''

Philip's gaze turned sleepy. ''Oh, by all means, test her. A week or so should reveal the method of your medicine.'' He clapped Alexandre on the shoulder. ''I will take my leave of you. Tomorrow, then?''

"Tomorrow, sire."

"What is happening tomorrow?" Liliane asked as soon as Philip had disappeared among the tents.

"The usual. We eat dust and slay Saracens. Philip just wants to make sure we are not going to miss another wonderful, fly-bitten day." He sounded more cheerful than bitter, a little pre-occupied; his mood made her wonder.

"Philip will not give up on the wench," he said as they started for the tent. "You had best pack her off east."

"Yes, I think you are right. The sooner she is gone the better."

"That is a come about. What happened? Did she kick Kiki?"

"Nothing so blatant, but I am wary of her mouth. I can just imagine her cooing confidences into Philip's ear."

"A flirt, is she?"

"Let us say she has a certain understandable enthusiasm for single encounters in hope of evading numerous ones."

He stopped dead in his tracks. "You do not mean she tried to seduce you?"

"Ardently. It was very reassuring to be advised my pecker could be persuaded to stand up like a wooden stick." At Alexandre's stifled groan, Liliane cut him a sly glance. "She is bound to have a go at being equally grateful to you, even if you are a loathsome infidel. Just how do you plan to 'handle' her?"

"Oh, I would not touch her without sheep dip," he drawled, then sauntered off in the direction of the armorers, leaving her to stare after him.

Let Liliane wonder, Alexandre thought wickedly. She had been playing a man too long; she needed competition as a woman to remind her who wore the real *cojones* in the family. She also needed distraction; he had dangerous plans a few nights hence that did not include her. That fetching slavegirl might prove a convenient catch after all.

That night, Alexandre was forced to admit that Saida was not altogether a windfall. Neither he nor Liliane was much pleased at the new sleeping arrangements. To be fair, he found that Saida was not at all the bold baggage Liliane had described, but rather shy and demurely grateful to him. He also found her exceedingly pretty with tolerable manners. Once he drew her out, she bloomed, only to grow uneasy again under Liliane's critical gaze.

Her curious peeps at him, alternating with nervous glances at Liliane, became amusingly appealing. That appeal wore off by dinner's end. Having another woman in the tent made him want Liliane more, and to have her made unavailable to him by acquisition of a tent mate was frustrating.

He tried to get around the problem by sending Saida early to bed. With growing impatience, he and Liliane lingered over their Turkish coffee. "Do you suppose she is asleep yet?" he wondered for the tenth time.

Liliane sighed. "If you were her, would you be?" She flopped against the pillows. "She probably has her ear to the canvas, wishing she knew at least three words of French."

"Are you sure she does not?"

"She knows one Saracen dialect besides Rifi and is illiterate in both." She grimaced. "The color of her language, however, is admirable. The wench has a rare turn with pornography."

"What exactly did she say to you?" he asked curiously.

With a sly smile, she whispered an embellished version in his ear, then delicately licked that orifice as a finale.

As if magnetized, his head followed hers as she moved slightly away. "I do not believe it," he breathed. "She *is* debauched for sixteen."

"Not nearly as debauched as I am," Liliane said huskily. She whispered a few words in his other ear that made his eyes widen, then take on a seductive gleam.

"I also have a suggestion, my love." He whispered something in her ear.

Liliane stared at him, then laughed merrily. "You are not serious!"

"Quite."

They both left the tent, while Alexandre waited outside with the guards by the fire, Liliane fetched the sleeping Saida's scattered clothes from the rug in her darkened tent, and returned to Alexandre's tent where she changed into them. After heavily kohling her eyes and rouging her lips, she wrapped a hooded aba about herself. A brass filet dripping with tiny topaz and jade beads, crescent moons and stars concealed the blond hair about her face, yellow harem veils the rest of her hair and lower features so that only her sultry, mysterious eyes showed. Upon seeing her with head meekly bowed as she emerged from the tent, the guards took her for Saida.

Alexandre closed his arm about her and glanced at the guards. "We shall return before dawn. No one else may either leave or enter here."

The guards averted their eyes discreetly. Alexandre had been faithful to his wife since leaving France; that he now wearied of celibacy was not their affair.

As the couple stole through the camp with its drifting soldiers and beggars, Liliane tugged somewhat nervously at Alexandre's sleeve. "How far is this place? I am attracting stares."

Not answering, Alexandre relished Liliane's discomfiture. Her uneasiness made her seem more feminine, their adventure more daring. He enjoyed having other men see her as a woman and envy him. They must be wondering, Where are these two going tonight? What will the count do to this beauty? How will he pleasure her? He smiled to himself. Tonight, I shall make love to Liliane for each of you. For all those wives and sweethearts you left at home, or long ago when you were still young enough to dream of rare and impossibly beautiful maidens. Such a woman walks among you now, here among the ravages of war, and makes you dream again. This, not kings, is what we die for: our sweet mirages that make tomorrow an elusive, fickle enchantress.

In time they arrived at a heavy wooden door in the harbor quarter; above the door hung a crudely carved sign in the shape of a leopardess, emblazoned with the words THE GILDED LEOPARD. "Here?" Liliane whispered in some horror. "Alexandre, this is the busiest brothel in camp!"

"Can you think of a better place to find privacy?"

"Alexandre, I cannot . . . surely, we can find another place!"

"Such as the beach, where we might have our throats slit by roaming Saracens?"

Unhappily, Liliane subsided. At Alexandre's knock, the door was opened by a monstrous black with a poised scimitar. Liliane edged behind Alexandre.

"We want a room." Alexandre jangled a few coins a discreet distance from the scimitar. "No wine, no food, no interruptions."

The black grinned mirthlessly. "You don't get monkey dung with that little silver. Try the alley."

"Try staying in business if this cesspit is declared a public nuisance," replied Alexandre coolly. "I can transfer your whole stinking trade to the alley."

The black's eyes narrowed. "And just who the hell are you?"

"*Le Comte de Brueil,* and he does not make idle threats, Ajax," murmured a husky female voice from the darkness of the arched hallway. "Get back to the public room. A fight's stewing over that new mulatto." After the black attended to that business, an impossibly fat, ugly woman lumbered with effort into the torchlight. "Do come in, *Monsieur le Comte.* I apologize for Ajax's rudeness, but you see, prices have gone up since you were last in Palestine." The woman's yellow-tinged eyes appraised them shrewdly. "I regard your patronage as an honor, milord. You shall have our best room and whatever luxuries you desire. If you are pleased, perhaps you will be kind enough to recommend us to your friends."

"I prefer to pay the going rate, Madame," Alexandre replied flatly. "Privacy and courtesy are the only luxuries I require, and as for recommendations, I do not pimp."

The woman shrugged, her purple silks heaving. "No matter. If our reputation was not already excellent, milord, you would not be here. Please"—she extended her mottled arm to the stairs down the hallway—"you will go up to the room at the far end of the first landing. No clients are now in that wing. You will not be seen." She cocked her head. "May I ask how long you will need the room?"

"The night."

She held out her hand. "Ten dirhams should be sufficient."

With reluctance, Alexandre counted out the money.

She bit the coins, then nodded, satisfied. "For another two dirhams, you may have the mulatto for an hour. She's almost virgin, still wild—"

"Thank you, no," Alexandre replied firmly. "I already have an almost virgin, still wild." Ignoring Liliane's stifled gasp of indignation, he pulled her up the stairs.

Once inside the seedy little bedroom, Liliane exploded. The only "luxury" the room offered was reasonable cleanliness. "I am no prude, but this is too much, Alexandre! I will not be treated like a whore. That horrible woman thinks I am—"

"The most profitable piece of female she has seen in years." He grinned. "She would probably like to buy you."

With unexpected abruptness, her anger deflated. "That would solve a good many of your problems, would it not?"

He sighed. "I thought we satisfactorily ended that subject at the oasis."

"By making love?" She sat gingerly on the bed as if expecting it to leap with vermin. "That settled nothing. You do not want me here, and I doubt if you will ever completely forgive me for coming."

"You have presumed a good deal so far," he said quietly, taking her hands, "but do not presume to do my thinking for me. You chose to come here, Liliane, and must deal with that decision without expecting continual reassurance from me." He stroked her face. "This is the second time before our lovemaking that you have used this uncertainty as a shield, as if you fear that I want you more from lust than love. Do you believe I brought you here because I want to demean you, to force you to my uses because you have defied me?"

"No . . . I am just tired, I think. In Spain, I heard the men talk of war. Diego hated war as much as you . . . but I never understood that hate until I came here and endured combat. I have seen men dead long before any arrow found them. Seen their eyes, pale and empty from numbing horror. Known that my own eyes were changing. Making love with you has become my most precious tie to life; so much hangs from that thread now that peril follows me even into your arms." She was silent a moment. "I am sorry. If I cannot be strong for you, my presence here becomes a burden that endangers us both. You're right; I must deal with my uncertainty alone."

Alexandre enfolded her in his arms. "Not alone, my love. Loneliness kills the spirit as much as fear. Because of you, for the first time in my life I have not been lonely, and I will not see you so. What we endure here, we endure together."

"How did I find you?" she whispered. "What deity smiled that day I rode into your castle? 'Twas a callow, vain girl you wedded. I have come so slow to wisdom, 'tis a wonder your patience has not long worn away."

He laughed softly. "I was no less a child than you when first we met. Perhaps we have taught each other maturity." He thoughtfully played with her hair veil across his fingers. "Speaking of being laggardly, have I told you tonight that you are particularly lovely in your Eastern folderols?"

"In a fashion," she murmured. "You intimated that I might fetch a pretty price.'

"Ah, yes." He kissed her lingeringly. "A very pretty price." The veil sifted to the floor. "Shall I pay a coin for each garment you yield me? A dirham of silver for this wisp"—another veil wafted down—"for that?"

"Not enough," she whispered. "I want your heart, as well, you miser."

Alexandre kissed her throat and the cleft of her breasts above the bangled yellow bodice. " 'Tis yours, with my soul for a trinket." With gentle teasing, he looked down at her. "If your heart be not of gold, as tradition would fondly have, I perceive I shall soon be in great difficulty."

Liliane wrapped her arms about his neck. "Monsieur, you shall be in a great deal more than difficulty. If you would keep me, be fierce. I am accustomed to a virile and violent lover. All the silver in the world will avail you nothing if you prove tepid."

"Tepid?" He cocked an eyebrow. "I shall give you tepid. Madame, when you leave this room, you shall walk with difficulty. Your loins will be as melted butter, your breasts as burst pomegranates." He frowned with mock fierceness. "Prepare. Your match is met."

Bit by diaphanous bit, he removed Liliane's veils to reveal a brief bodice that bared her slim midriff, and below that, a spangled kirtle with silk pantaloons. He grinned suddenly. "I have just realized Saida is a short baggage, insignificantly endowed. That you have not burst that bodice is no less than miraculous."

"I confess I am sorely confined," she murmured huskily, then deliberately arched her back. "If you were a gentleman, sir, you would help me breathe more freely."

"Madame, with my teeth." One by one, he worked at her buttons with his mouth, his awkwardness outweighed by his eagerness. Shortly, he peered with boyish satisfaction at her half-covered breasts. "I have always wanted to do that"—he sighed—"and *Jesu*, what reward!"

She giggled. "I shall afford you all the practice you require, sir. Only allow me to breathe a little better and I shall thank you properly for your determination."

He luxuriously bared her breasts and nibbled them until Liliane squirmed in eager anticipation. "Oh, what heaven lies in a bit of air! May I inquire as to your talent with kirtles? This one is so dreadfully tight!''

Directly, the kirtle went and even more directly Alexandre buried his face in the golden fluff between her thighs. Liliane let out a joyous sigh. Her sighs became ecstatic moans that carried beyond the room. Alexandre laughed. ''Temperance, Madame; I have scarce begun.''

When his head lowered again, she grabbed him by the hair. ''I am impatient, as well, sir. Have on, I beg you, before I go mad!''

He grinned. ''Have on, is it? Am I not too tepid, too tame for your fierce appetite?''

''You roused that appetite,'' she growled. ''Do you now satisfy it or I shall leap upon you and rouse the house!''

''How now, you surly wench,'' he retorted. ''What if I am not in the mood?''

Liliane flung herself at him, tumbling him to the floor. They rolled, wrestling and panting, her bareness exciting him wildly. With a flailing tug, she unfastened his braies and closed on him. ''There, I'll put you in the mood! Liar! You are not wilted!''

''Impudent wench!'' Risking a wrenching, he wrestled her onto her back. With a thrust of his hips, he buried deep, eliciting the surprised, elated cry he craved. ''Here, have that for your greediness! That, and that!''

''And that!''

He laughed in elation as she answered him with equal fervor, stirring him to more heated passion. As her long, beautiful legs flew wide and high, he caught and clamped them over his shoulders. His head lowering like a fired stallion, he thrust until perspiration soaked him and Liliane was fairly screaming with unbridled pleasure. Then his barely controlled passion surged, spilling and leaping like a current of fire over them both. Spent, he clasped her close. ''There,'' he whispered when he could finally catch his breath. ''So much for lust. The next time will be for love.''

A few hours later, Xenobia, the brothel madam, waddled along the lower hall. The floor above thumped. She eyed Ajax. ''Still at it, is he?''

The black nodded impassively.

I want a look at that Saracen girl, Xenobia decided. Either the Frenchie's been saving himself for six months or she's the finest

piece in Acre. Silently, Xenobia made her way to the top of the
stairs, then into the room next to the preoccupied couple. With
a fat finger, she flicked a cheap tapestry back and peered through
the small hole bored behind it. After a moment, she drew away.
A blonde, she reflected, and no Circassian.

Saida was still sound asleep when they got back to the tent.
After changing in Alexandre's tent, Liliane gave him a lingering
kiss. "Good morning, darling," she whispered. "We must be
depraved again sometime."

"Wait," he murmured, catching her hand. Cool silver dropped
into her palm. "You earned it. You could wilt a coconut tree."
His kiss was both hard and soft. "I love you. Do not forget
again."

"Perhaps I enjoy being a slow learner," she whispered against
his lips. "May I have another lesson again at midnight?"

For a split second, she heard him hesitate. "Tomorrow night
might be better." He nuzzled her ear. "A little sleep prevents
cracked coconuts."

"I am sorry, darling; of course, you are right. But this time I
shall use my earnings"—the silver jingled—"to buy my own
veils."

After her tent flap closed, Liliane dropped wearily on her pallet. She might have known. He was up to something again.

That day, the siege upon Acre was more or less uneventful.
The days of the city were numbered. The walls of the Accursed
Tower were becoming a mammoth pile of rubble; elsewhere
Christian sappers and catapults had dropped walls into huge
heaps, now tensely guarded by Saracen bowmen. If Acre was to
survive, Saladin must make a decisive attack. Richard's eyes were
merry and relentless; this game of waiting was about to end with
all the pieces his.

That night, Saida was a trifle less demure with Alexandre at
dinner. Although careful not to annoy Liliane too greatly, she
fixed her admiring eyes on Alexandre as if he were both Adonis
and Hercules together. For courtesy's sake, Liliane and Alexandre spoke mostly in Arabic, but Saida did not intrude herself
upon the conversation. At each of Alexandre's occasional witticisms, she giggled delightedly, her dark eyes flashing over her
rose veil. She refused to eat until the "men" were done, then

picked daintily at her food a little apart from them while Yves served coffee. When she was offered coffee, Saida took a sip, then made a face. "I am so sorry, but may I have a little honey?" Nearly a half cupful of honey later, she pronounced herself satisfied. As she drank her coffee, Alexandre tried to draw her out a little, but, casting a wary glance at Liliane as if afraid of her, Saida murmured only that she was an innocent girl of good family who had been stolen by desert raiders. She had been sold to one of Saladin's minor amirs who had been offered so generous a price by Idi ben Ibrahim that the amir had reluctantly sacrificed her.

Several holes yawned in *that* account, Liliane thought skeptically. Saida was most certainly a peasant, and raiders were more likely to prey upon the shores of Africa than their own lands. Saida's good family had likely been beggars, forced to sell an extra girl child. From what she had observed of Saida so far, she thought there might also have been trouble of some kind.

Alexandre seemed to entertain no such suspicions. With the easy charm that could prove so irresistible to females of any age, he was gentle with the girl. His appreciative gaze revealed that he was well aware that Saida was no child. Under the circumstances, Liliane felt uneasy.

The hour was growing late when Alexandre casually announced that he had an appointment with Phillip and that Jefar and Saida might as well go to bed. A quarter hour after he left, Liliane left Saida brushing her black hair and headed for Philip's tent. The royal pavilion was already dark. If Philip had not gone to bed, he was out. Alexandre was either meeting Philip elsewhere or diverting her on a goosechase long enough to be off on some errand of his own.

Running now, Liliane skirted the outer defense trench toward Richard's pavilion. The pavilion was still brightly lit with a small stir of activity. Several soldiers lingered by the surrounding campfires under the standards of six of the most important allied lords. A murmur of voices sounded from within the pavilion. She let out a sigh of relief. So there *was* a council; Alexandre and Philip were no doubt attending it.

Staying in the shadows, Liliane lingered about the outskirts of the fire, hoping to hear something about the council. She was shortly rewarded, but not in the manner she expected. "Well, they have gone again with cockleshells for helmets and willow

wands for smacking those damned mosquito heathen away," a
routier rasped to another man over one of the fires. "Flanchard
may be a devil, but he's right. That Frenchie's a raving idiot;
may the blackies take his skin tonight."

Liliane's heart went cold and numb. Alexandre had gone out
upon a second raid with Louis at his back.

Nearly killing her horse, Liliane managed to catch up with
Alexandre's rear guard two miles past the oasis and halfway to
the Saracen camp. Slowing to keep her distance, she kept well
behind until the camp was sighted. The raiders split in two wings
in preparation for an attack. Not knowing which wing was led
by Alexandre, she followed the right flank. The Saracens had
scattered guards along the outstretched arms of the camp, but
the center, where they thought no sane attack could occur, was
left open. Most of the fires were merely coals, the tents dark.
Saladin's pavilion was a distant glow of gold and blue at the
center of the camp, its pennants drooping in the still night air.
The moon was fuller tonight, the sky cloudless as usual, so the
raiders dismounted at a distance, leaving the hostlers to lead in
their mounts to mass inconspicuously with the Saracen strings.
If Alexandre gets out of this one, it will be a miracle, Liliane
thought miserably.

All she could do was wait well beyond the hostlers as Alexandre's men streamed silently into the camp. If she joined the
attackers, she would probably be mistaken for a Saracen in the
dark and get herself skewered. Too many minutes passed. She
saw the hostlers grow restless in the bright silver light; they also
sensed that something was wrong. Liliane slipped from her horse
and slithered along the dunes out of the hostlers' sight. She
threaded into the silent camp, then abruptly crouched as she
spotted a raider leaving a tent, then three more coming from
another tent to investigate a scarlet pavilion near the camp fringe.
They made no sound, nor was there any sound from any tent
they had entered. Moments later, they hurried from the scarlet
pavilion; from their erratic movements, Liliane sensed their bewilderment. She eased back the flap of the tent nearest her. The
tent was empty.

Then, as if from a ring of hideous hyenas, a howl arose about
her, curdling her blood. From the moonlight danced a thousand
Saracens, their scimitars brandished furiously high and trium-

phant. Her heart in her throat, Liliane pulled out her own blade. The trap was closed; there would be no escape. She longed to see Alexandre one last time, but time was already gone. With any mercy, he would die thinking her safe.

The howl rose higher and sheer terror swept over her, but Liliane stood her ground along with the other raiders caught near her in the trap. The Saracens swept forward, and she braced herself, her face white. Just as the first Saracen came down on his opponent, a cymbal crashed and an abrupt hush fell upon the Saracen host. Heads turned, then the mass parted. A tall, turbaned Saracen dressed from head to foot in white walked calmly through the gap. "Do you surrender, Christians, or resign yourselves to massacre?" he called in cool, clipped French.

"Death before your heathen mercies!" shouted a raider. "We shall die on our feet, not flayed out for the ants!" His sentiments were shared by all the crusaders. Saladin had once personally beheaded a captured crusader knight and given the knight's men to his headsmen.

"If you surrender, you will be taken as hostages. Then your fate is up to your master, *Melek Richard.*" The tall man smiled faintly. "If he proves indifferent, you will be subjected to no indignities and will be cleanly beheaded. Does that suit you?"

"Why should we believe you?" called a knight. To Liliane, he sounded like Derek Flanchard. "The Saracens we left dead on our last raid could not have inspired you to generosity."

The Saracen's smile flattened to a humorless line in his bearded face. "You are not forgiven; you are merely more useful alive than as hyena fodder."

"King Richard will not bow to you to save us," retorted the first knight. "You are wasting your time."

"I hope not"—the smile flickered again, grim this time—"and so should you."

There was silence, then Derek Flanchard spoke. "On whose authority do you make this offer?"

The Saracen glanced at him. "On that of Saladin; more exactly, my own."

"In that case, agreed."

Quick protest arose among the Christians. "What the devil? Never!"

"I order you to surrender and you will obey," Flanchard cut back. "I am the commanding officer present, as the Count de

Brueil seems to have most fortunately made his escape.'' The last was sardonically contemptuous, but Liliane was too relieved to feel angry. ''Throw down your swords,'' ordered Flanchard. ''If worse comes to worst, what are a few ants, after all?''

Surmising that Flanchard had never been to a Saracen picnic, Liliane reluctantly tossed down her scimitar.

With the twenty captured raiders, she was taken to a tent and bound to the poles. She had been virtually unnoticed until now; Saracens and raiders alike stared at her with hostility. Nearly an hour passed in glum silence, then six Saracen guards came for the raiders. Roped together, they were led to Saladin's tent.

Despite the tent's fabulous silks and tapestries, the great Saracen leader was seated on a simple prayer rug with several of his pashas similarly placed on either side of him. A brass hookah wafted a faint, exotic scent through the censer-lit gloom.

''Greetings. I regret the necessity of disturbing you at so late an hour,'' Saladin said politely. ''Will you have coffee?'' In some bemusement, the knights accepted tiny cups of rich coffee. Hesitating at first, they finally began to sip the sweet stuff as they tensely awaited the explanation for their summons; it was soon in coming. ''I regret''—Saladin spread his hands apologetically—''that our original arrangement has altered somewhat.''

''I knew it! You treacherous devils cannot be trusted!'' An English knight sprang angrily to his feet. Coffee splattered over the gorgeous carpet. Two guards sprang forward.

Saladin raised a hand and calmly waved away the guards. ''Your distress is understandable, but only Allah knows what breezes of fortune may blow from moment to moment. In this instance, the greater fortune falls to your enemies, yet take heart, for you are not altogether neglected. Your numbers have been increased by a most precious prize that adds to your worth both to me and to *Melek Richard*.'' He nodded to a eunuch. ''Bring in the Count de Brueil.''

Liliane's heart sank to her toes.

A moment later, Alexandre entered the tent and, ignoring his suspicious men, made a faint bow to Saladin. ''Great lord.''

Saladin nodded. For a moment, he studied Alexandre's cool face, then those of his rebellious men. ''Please be seated, *Monsieur le Comte*. Will you take coffee?''

''Thank you.'' As if taking his ease with Philip, Alexandre settled on the rug.

"You are an extraordinary man, milord," observed Saladin. "It is a rare commander who sacrifices himself for his men."

The knights looked aback, and Flanchard cast his gaze at the tent swag overhead.

"I led these knights here, Lord Saladin. Why should I not lead them back?"

"Why not, indeed?" Saladin smiled faintly as he stirred his coffee. "Still, you might have made your escape with thirty men. Your losses could have been far worse."

How does he know how many men Alexandre led here? wondered Liliane. Unless . . . Her musings were abruptly cut off as she glanced up and saw that Alexandre had noticed her. His eyes had gone almost black, his face rigid. She fixedly began to study the carpet.

"I have lost no one yet," replied Alexandre as mildly as if she had disappeared.

"That is true," conceded Saladin. Then he added a trifle ominously, "It is also true that your head is worth more than all the others put together."

"Then why not take my head and return my knights to King Richard intact? He will gladly pay their ransom."

"Why should I not take all your heads and skim Lionheart of the cream of his knights?"

"Because your honor would then be as dry and cheaply bartered as goat curds. I came to you freely, unarmed. Will you discredit yourself when your reliability may soon frame your bargaining position with *Melek Richard* concerning the surrender of Acre?"

"Acre still stands."

"Another day, perhaps," Alexandre returned carelessly. "The day after that, the hyenas may scour the place."

"Take this mad dog's head, *effendi*," spat the amir on Saladin's left. "He barks when his tail should be between his legs."

"Mad he may be, but cur he is not," Saladin replied mildly. "Have you no tolerance for courage?"

"This Brueil caused the deaths of eighty Saracens by stealth and butchery! Most were killed in their beds!" the amir protested furiously. "What valor is this! Having given the wolf the sheep's hide, shall we give him the sheep as well?"

"If we profit by preserving the flock to a safe haven, why not?" With a gentle gesture, Saladin silenced the amir's next outburst and turned his attention once more upon Alexandre. "My lord, for one hundred dinars each, you shall have the freedom of yourself and your men and safe conduct to Acre." Then his gaze flicked to Liliane and chilled. "One, however, I must retain. An enemy may be forgiven; a traitor, never. Jefar el din will remain for suitable punishment."

Like a spring uncoiled, Alexandre leaped to his feet. "I thank you for your great generosity, Lord Saladin, but Jefar el din is an honorable Christian and my friend. I will not abandon him to unjust treatment."

"No honorable man rejects Allah having known His light, and then turns against his kindred," replied Saladin flatly. "Be happy you leave with your Christian lives. Jefar el din must answer to our justice; your interpretation of Koran law is irrelevant."

Alexandre stepped forward in desperation. "You do not understand . . ."

Saladin waved the guards to flank Liliane. "Shall I take your friend's head before your eyes?"

The game was up. Liliane, starkly aware of the executioners breathing down her neck, wasted no time in conceding it before Alexandre did anything rash. With alacrity, she hauled off the haik. As her pale hair spilled to her waist, the men stared, openmouthed.

"What means this!" demanded Saladin. "Who is this woman?"

"My wife," Alexandre croaked dully. "As the keeping of a castle seemed to her too tedious, she would follow me to war."

A dazed grunt came from somewhere in the group, then a trickle of mutters and laughter. The laughter grew, particularly among the Christians who had observed Alexandre's "friend" in many an unladylike situation during the Acre campaign. The tension of the meeting found exaggerated relief. The tent fairly ballooned with laughter.

"God's blood, Brueil," Derek Flanchard cried at length, his eyes streaming with tears of hilarity, "do you know how many of us vowed you had gone over the gate to find a boy for a bedmate!"

The roar of laughter that met that statement made Alexandre turn so angrily scarlet that even the Saracens caught its drift; knight and enemy alike made him their butt of amusement. For long minutes, he stood frozen, enduring their careless mockery, then his eyes sought out Liliane.

As pale as Alexandre, Liliane knew that he would never forgive her. This time she had gone too far. "My lord had naught to do with my coming to Acre!" she cried in Alexandre's defense. "He bade me stay in France!" As soon as the words were out of her mouth, she knew dismally she had made another mistake.

Flanchard was deliberately audible over the racket. *'Le bon Dieu,* the man seeks to command a troop when he cannot govern his own wife!''

Saladin, noticing that Alexandre's severly tried temper was reaching the snapping point, decided matters were getting out of hand. If the hostages were returned wounded to Acre, Richard would never believe his knights accountable for their own injuries in a roaring fight. "Hold, Messieurs! Count de Brueil and I have made a bargain. You would be wise to take advantage of it before I have cause to reconsider." He clapped his hands, summoning his guards. "You will be escorted as far as *Wadi Mas,* and there given your weapons. Each of you is pledged to return me a head price of one hundred gold dinars by tomorrow's dawn." He glanced at Alexandre. "I presume the ransom is reasonable?"

Alexandre bowed stiffly. "You are generous, Great Lord Saladin."

"Also, you will make no further raids upon my encampment."

"Agreed."

"By all?" Saladin's dark eyes intently scanned the knights, who were relieved to be let off so lightly and squirming to be gone.

As one, the crusaders nodded.

Saladin smiled faintly. "May your honor prove your bond. Today, *Comte de Brueil* thrust his head under my scimitar for you; tomorrow shall tell if you were worth his trouble." His head inclined slightly toward Liliane. "*Madame la Comtesse,* my commendations; not only have you extraordinary courage, you have afforded us all a welcome and charming diversion."

Unsure whether to bow or curtsy before the Saracen lords, whose amusement had settled into disapproval of an unveiled woman in their midst, Liliane awkwardly ventured a salaam. *"Insh'allah, Saladin Effendi."*

"You speak Arabic, *Comtesse?"* Saladin was now watching her a little too alertly. He might think twice about letting her go if he thought she might have overheard information in his camp that would interest Richard and Philip.

"Only a few words, *effendi,"* she replied with careful shyness. "What I do not know, I invent. So far, none of these European gentlemen has noticed the confusion of the natives."

This time, Saladin and his amirs were the only ones who laughed. "Fare you well, then, *Comtesse.* Keep from battle hereafter, lest the natives more unhappily confuse you with these European gentlemen."

With little more ado, the Europeans were sent upon their way to Acre. There was little conversation until after their Saracen escort left them at the oasis. After the dust of their escort sifted down upon the eastern dunes, the raiders stirred uncomfortably in their saddles, pondering the evening's embarrassments.

"Well," a Breton said at last, "what are we going to tell their majesties about our ignominious capture?"

"The truth," Alexandre said flatly. "I led you all into a trap."

"Good for you," Flanchard said with a malicious grin. "Own up."

The Breton gave him a cool look. "There might be more to profit if the traitor owned up. Our councils were closed; there were no servants, no guards present. Just us."

Flanchard's face blackened. "If you are suggesting that I sold out, I shall cut out your lying tongue!"

"I am not naming names," the Breton returned calmly, "merely facts. Saladin, on the other hand, knew Jefar's name without asking." He paused to allow the significance to sink in. "Count de Brueil managed this affair well enough. He also could have left us to rot, but he did not, so we have no quarrel with him. We *do* have a bone to pick with a ratter."

Flanchard started to argue, but, noticing the unsympathetic looks on the raiders' faces, thought better of drawing attention to himself. He lifted a skeptical brow. "What about the *comtesse?"*

"I say we hold our tongues," said an English knight. "Milady fought bravely last night as she has done on many another occasion. More than one of us owes his life to her, and"—he nodded to Alexandre—"as our good Breton has pointed out, Count Alexandre has freed us all. Why thank our mentors with embarrassment?" He leaned upon his pommel. "I move we keep the countess's identity to ourselves. And as for the traitor, he *is* likely one of our troop. Perhaps the guilty one is an out and out traitor; perhaps he simply has a loose tongue. We must search him out, and not cause more confusion by starting gossip around the camp."

Flanchard scoffed. "How long do you really think a woman disguised as a Saracen warrior can be kept secret? Women of birth are rarely permitted to accompany the army for good reason. *Comte de Brueil* should have made his lady's masquerade known at once and sent her back to France. Also, while he may have negotiated our release, he made a nasty mistake tonight that caused our capture. We left five dead men back in Saladin's camp. Their majesties must be informed and a new commander appointed."

"And everyone knows who wants that position, eh, Flanchard?" drawled the Breton. "Maybe you have got traitors and 'mistakes' mixed."

"Did not Queen Eleanor of Aquitaine follow King Louis on crusade?" put in Poitevin. "No one insisted *she* go home!"

As they debated, Liliane held her tongue. Every time she had opened her mouth in the last several hours, she had brought nothing but trouble to Alexandre. Now both of them were on trial, a presently friendly trial, but one that would dictate their immediate and perhaps long-term future. She was also silent for another reason; she felt defeated. Louis de Signe was probably the traitor; while he had not managed to have Alexandre killed, he had damaged his reputation and military career. Alexandre was listening to his men argue as if only vaguely interested. He, too, must feel defeated, as much by her as by Louis.

The disagreement went on for some time; Derek and two English knights were the main dissidents. Finally, the question was settled in Alexandre's favor. While their majesties would be told of the trap, no accusations were to be made, particularly against Alexandre. Also, Liliane's identity was to be kept secret. To those effects, an oath was sworn, Flanchard being the last to grudgingly agree.

After Alexandre had politely thanked them and headed his destrier into the western desert, he said not another word all the way to Acre. The Saracens stationed on their route had been sent word by Saladin to allow the troop to pass. Amid hoots and catcalls of flanking Saracens, the raiders rode through their own defense works. Alexandre's face beneath his helm was pale with humiliation and anger.

Upon arrival in the camp, Alexandre went immediately to make his report to Richard and Philip. Liliane returned to his tent to glumly await him. She was fairly certain that Richard would make a rousing fuss, but hoped that at the end of the roaring, Alexandre would not be blamed for the raid's failure. Alexandre's tactics had been shrewdly planned and she suspected that Philip would have his own suspicions about Louis's part in the trap. Despite these glimmers of encouragement, Liliane had time to think hard and long about what bitter things her husband might have to say upon his return.

However, Alexandre did not return; he briefly paused by the tent at sunset to leave his mail and accoutrements with his armorer, then disappeared again into the camp. A little while before dawn, he returned, very much drunk and disinclined to discuss anything.

Three days passed much in this fashion, until Liliane became greatly depressed. When Alexandre did not return one night, she could bear the confinement no longer. After thrusting a scimitar through her sash, and sweeping the striped mantle over her aba, she fought the temptation to go looking for Alexandre and went for a ride on the beach. The full moon was low over the dunes and the beach nearly white with its rising glow. No enemy could approach her unnoticed for a mile.

Enemy. Who in Acre was her friend? To Alexandre's raiders, she was a freak; to his friends and compatriots, a turncoat; and to Alexandre, a source of shame. As the mare wandered down the beach, Liliane began to cry. She slid off the mare and stood weeping at the surf's edge. So sunk in misery was she that at first she did not see the rider coming quickly toward her. Upon hearing the hoofbeats' dull thud in the sand, Liliane whirled to remount, then saw the rider was a crusader knight. He called and waved to her. " 'Tis Derek Flanchard, Countess. You have no need for alarm."

Liliane was not alarmed, but she was certain Flanchard was up to no good. No oath would bind him to secrecy about her identity; he probably wanted payment for his silence. He dismounted and, leaving his destrier, came to meet her. "I hope I do not intrude, my lady, but when I called at your tent and one of your castellans ventured that you had come this way, I was concerned for your safety." His voice was solicitious. " 'Tis a lovely place but some distance from protection."

"As you may have observed these last months, sir," Liliane replied quietly, "I have little need of protection."

He laughed. "Aye, that is true enough. I have never encountered a woman like you, and have thought much of your beauty and daring these past days. Such a woman must have a brain, as well. A pity your husband does not fully appreciate you; he seemed much angered by your presence in Saladin's camp."

"Do you seek milord to reprimand him?" Liliane countered dryly.

"No, I came to offer him a proposition, but now I am much more pleased that he is not by your side. No man likes to have another man about when he encounters a beautiful lady."

When he moved to kiss her hand, Liliane firmly withdrew it. "You must seek my husband in camp, Sir Knight. I have no wish to hold conference with you alone. Please do me the courtesy of leaving me."

He made no move toward his destrier. "Come now, why so cold? Are you afraid I shall reveal your secret? I promise you, I have given my oath, and if you are kind—"

"Kind, sir?" Liliane's voice acquired an edge. "You have never been a friend to my husband, yet I have been courteous to you; for more than that, you must not look."

"But I do," he replied softly. "I look for much more than that. I have a fair influence with King Richard, and you are a rich and beautiful woman. Surely you would wish me to give a good account of your husband lest he lose his good name."

"Alexandre does not owe his good name to you," Liliane said curtly, "and he has friends. You would do well to be truthful and leave the rest to God."

"If I am truthful, I must not lie about your identity, my lady. A dishonorable oath has no validity before God. You must have grave reason to keep your sex a secret. What is a stray wife to Richard, after all? To Philip?" He watched her. "Shall I unburden myself of my sinful oath to Philip?"

She sighed in defeat and exasperation. "Why be coy, Flanchard? What do you want?"

"Gold. Six hundred dinars, to be exact. The extra hundred is for the head price I was dunned." He smiled in the darkness, his teeth moonlit-white against his dark beard. "Mostly, I want you."

"Settle for the gold," Liliane said coldly. " 'Tis all you will ever get, whatever you bray to Philip."

"I think not." His arm shot out and he pulled her roughly to him, his hand spilling the haik to hook in her hair. Struggling, she kicked him, but her pointed boots were too soft to do damage. She tried to scream and he yanked her hair so hard she thought her neck must snap. "Go ahead, scream," he urged breathlessly. "You will be ignored as some whore fighting with a customer." He jerked at the aba. "You will say nothing, and you will pay me in the morning!"

"Let her go, Flanchard," came a deadly voice behind them, "or I will stab you in the back!"

Flanchard spun, his arm locked about Liliane as he drew his sword from across her back. A dark familiar figure was silhouetted against the pale sand and shimmering stars. "Brueil! How now, I did not hear you come up." He sounded almost gleeful.

"You were preoccupied with trying to rape my wife." Alexandre was standing tensely, his sword drawn. His destrier wandered toward the surf. "Take your hands off her."

Liliane saw that he was stone sober. Everything was drained from him but an urge to kill.

Being dangerous himself, Flanchard knew the signs, if not the emotion, that now made Alexandre more lethal than any man in Acre. Love was alien to Flanchard; although greed was not, and he knew when to loosen his grip on a woman lest the cost of keeping her prove more than he wished to pay. In this case, he also thought wise to free his sword arm. He eased Liliane away.

" 'Twas not rape, Brueil," he said easily. "Your countess invited me here out of some notion that I might break my oath and reveal her charade. You have neglected your lady of late for the taverns, and she was more than willing to bargain her favors to keep her secret. When she saw you coming, she made a show of protest."

Liliane wanted to claw his eyes out. "You miserable liar! Alexandre has but to question our castellans to learn that you followed me here unasked!"

"But when you invited me to your tent, Countess, I did not

suspect you had a more private rendezvous in mind," Flanchard countered lightly. "Naturally, I was forced to inquire of the castellans where you had gone."

Liliane jerked her aba up over her shoulder. "Alexandre knows I would sooner embrace a pig than you, Flanchard! You waste your breath."

Flanchard eyed Alexandre. "I think not. A jealous man has a ready ear, does he not, milord?"

"As a guilty man often has a ready tongue," retorted Alexandre. "Quick to accuse all but himself. You have not only laid hands upon my wife, but slandered her. Defend yourself."

"Readily, milord." Flanchard leaped forward, his broadsword swinging at Alexandre's neck.

Fast as he was, Alexandre was faster. The swords met with a nerve-jarring clang over the subtle song of the peaceful surf. The men became a swirl of light and shadow, their weapons flashing sparks as they clashed. Whereas Flanchard was deadly cold, Alexandre was hot, and the fight became savage.

Gone was Alexandre's usual patience in battle; he was vicious and unpredictable, a hurtling, relentless comet to Flanchard's falling star. Flanchard was bigger, more broad and powerfully expert with a blade, but without armor, Alexandre was faster than Flanchard, and he lacked Flanchard's confidence in armored protection. Alexandre had to be fast and accurate or die. Hacking mightily, Flanchard edged him into the surf, bent on slowing his footwork. At length, his strategy worked.

Liliane muffled a cry as her husband went down in the wet sand. Flanchard lunged in for the kill—meeting Alexandre's blade point in his gullet as Alexandre hooked his foot wide about his foe's ankle to pitch him forward. Splurting blood, Flanchard toppled across Alexandre's chest, his eyes staring startled into the count's. His mouth gaped in an effort to protest, but his coughing gasp was choked off by the gurgle of blood in his throat. He died even as Alexandre thrust him away, leaving him twitching in a receding wave.

When Liliane ran forward, Alexandre rose and caught her arm. "Leave him to the tide. 'Twill save explanations to Richard and feed the crabs."

"I am not concerned for Flanchard, but for you," she said anxiously. "Are you hurt?"

"Nay," he said caustically. "I am a man of iron. Only the

sea's rust can make me falter; that, and a wife who weaves destruction about her like a winding sheet.''

"You know that I did not encourage Flanchard!" she protested.

"Aye, but you would bargain with him if needful. You would coax Satan to have your way.'' He caught up her haik and thrust it at her.

"That is unfair!''

"Fair or not, a man lies dead in a salt bath tonight because of your lack of discretion, not to mention your perpetual meddling. I had to kill him like a cur fighting another over a wandering bitch! I would to God—'' His face twisted as he bit off the next furious words.

"You wish you had never met me?'' Liliane finished softly, her throat aching from the hard lump in it.

"Do not . . .'' His face came close to hers. "Do not presume to decide what I think. Do not play upon my weakness for you. I will not have you probing inside my skull as you have so cruelly in my heart.'' He thrust her toward her mare. "Return to the tent and this time stay there.''

"Are you not coming?'' she asked quietly as she mounted.

"I will stay with Flanchard and converse with his ghost. I have an idea we shall have much to say to each other. 'Tis irony that a man wise enough not to love women should lose his life over one.''

Liliane looked down at him with stark pain in her eyes. "Alexandre, I meant no harm to anyone in riding alone tonight, but I could not bear your staying away any longer. In time of unhappiness, I have always turned to the sea.''

For a moment he was silent, then slowly, wearily, he touched her hand on the reins. "For all our differences, we are much alike, milady. This is a time when I would be alone with the sea.'' His hand tightened on hers. "I would speak no more harsh words to you when I am yet distraught. Tomorrow, perhaps, I will be less embittered. Please''—his hand dropped—"go now.''

Tomorrow, Liliane thought bleakly as she rode away from him, Flanchard will be no less dead, and kindness cannot replace love.

Alexandre was kind the next day, though it clearly cost him effort. He was moody and very quiet, and he made no effort to touch her again. The sharp-eyed Saida had guessed something was amiss between her rescuers and that Liliane no longer had her former authority; with alacrity, Saida set out to further undermine that authority. Any time Liliane might have persuaded Alexandre to discuss their differences, Saida hovered about him, drawing his attention to herself. Liliane was unable to assail the wall that had risen between her and Alexandre, and equally unable to deal summarily with Saida. Uncertain of herself now, she found that she was testing Alexandre's love and loyalty by allowing Saida free rein; and that rein grew long.

Alexandre became accustomed to Liliane's bleak silence and Saida's cheerful conversation, her small flirtations grown bold. Preoccupied with guilt for the raid's failure and his efforts to prove Louis's guilt, Alexandre paid little attention to Saida. As for Liliane, he was still so furious with her over the raid and Flanchard, he dared not give voice to his resentment lest he say too much and forever forge a barrier between them. Saida took his abstracted civility for encouragement.

Since Saida owned only the clothes on her back upon fleeing Saladin's camp, Alexandre had directed one of the servants to buy her a small wardrobe in the camp bazaar. The servant, Alphonse, who was hardly more than a boy, became carried away with dressing pretty Saida and bought some ornate and revealing costumes that had been created for the camp prostitutes. Three nights after the raid, Saida put on a green outfit that suited her purposes perfectly.

Alexandre arrived late for dinner. A summons from Richard had subjected him to yet another hour of tirades and reprimands, and his frustration of the last several days was on the verge of explosion. As he entered the tent, he gave Liliane's male dress a quick, impatient look. "Why not send the servants away tonight and dress as a woman for once? Oaths or not, the news of your charade will probably leak out soon enough."

"The longer it does not, the better," she replied quietly. "My relatives will have no great fondness for me, should they discover I have betrayed them."

Alexandre pulled off his mail shirt and tossed it into the corner. "I daresay they will be miffed. Reliability is not one of your merits."

"I was always there when you needed me."

"Oh, yes"—he grimaced—"even when I did not need you, even when you were a damned liability."

Liliane took a deep breath. "Do you want to quarrel, Alexandre? If you do, we may as well have it out now."

"Why, my love, we shall do as you like . . . as always." He threw himself down beside the small spread of linen that served as their table. "When have my wishes ever hindered your plans? We shall dine or pelt each other with fruit: all, all as you like."

She sat down opposite him and leaned forward earnestly. "Alexandre, I know you must be angry and rightfully so, but surely you realize I never meant to hurt you."

"Perhaps not," he replied flatly, "but that does not change the fact that I can now scarce handle my men. I am the monkey's tail these days. They are still gibbering with laughter behind my back, and Flanchard had the largest guffaw of all. His mirth at my expense still haunts me."

"Flanchard laughed at everyone, even himself. Your men are still loyal to you."

"They also pity me. Flanchard was right. A man who cannot command his own wife, cannot presume to command men." He stared unseeingly at the linen. "I have given my command to Lisle."

She was stunned. "Alexandre, you had no need to surrender command . . ."

"No?" His eyes looked bleak. "When I returned, Richard made it quite clear to Philip that he no longer had faith in me. That is known as an invitation to resignation."

"Why did you not tell me?"

"Because, my dear, I assumed you would know. You have known every other move I have made. And if I do not make it quickly enough, you make it for me."

She felt hideously guilty; he was right. "Alexandre, I am sorry—" The rest of her apology was cut off by Saida's sudden appearance. The girl wore a green costume so outrageously provocative that for a moment both Alexandre and Liliane were taken aback. Liliane was the first to find her tongue. "Saida, leave us! How dare you contrive so shameless a display?"

The girl's painted smile crumpled. "Oh, I feared you would not approve!" She threw herself at Alexandre's feet. "My other clothes are soiled and these are the last I have to wear! I had not the heart to send the servant boy back, for he had no more money and he wanted so to please me!'' Curling to her knees, she grasped her bodice. ''I shall tear this defilement from my body, my lord, if it displeases you! You have been so kind to me, and I have thanked you ill . . . ah, woe, I will tear my very flesh!'' She wrenched at the bodice and, with a piteous wail, raked her nails across her generously revealed breasts.

Hastily, Alexandre caught her hand. ''Saida, do no more damage! Your mistake is easily remedied. Do but put on more suitable garmets: the yellow costume is fetching.''

Saida clasped his hand to a rounded breast. ''Ah, my lord, feel my beating heart and know I would do naught to willingly displease you!'' Her sloe-shaped eyes became pools of inviting darkness. ''Do what you will with me. I am yours.''

Any man would have been understandably intrigued. When Alexandre's hand did not immediately move away, Liliane said sharply, ''Enough repentance, Saida. Change.''

Saida's eyes slanted toward Alexandre. ''Do you truly find my attire offensive, my lord? Am I so frightfully ugly?''

Alexandre carefully removed his hand. ''Few men would reprove such . . . feminine garments. Certainly, you are a pretty girl.''

A fat tear seeped down Saida's cheek. ''I am not pretty enough for so handsome a lord. I am most unworthy.''

''Shall we find you a lord more appreciative?'' Liliane suggested.

Saida's eyes went wide with apprehension, and Alexandre turned sharply to Liliane. ''Do not threaten the girl. She is harmless enough.''

''Particularly with her bodice fair dropped to her waist,'' Liliane retorted in French. ''She is so distraught that she may trip on her nipples trying to dive into your braies.''

He looked at her for a long moment. ''You have plagued me by playing a man; will you burden me with a shrew, as well?''

Flinching with hurt, Liliane rose swiftly. ''I shall burden you not at all. Do you wish me to leave you all together?''

''Nay,'' he said quietly. ''Stay. The girl holds no interest for me, but perhaps you will be reminded of a woman's ways.''

''Was I not woman enough when you took me to that place of whores?'' she reponded evenly.

''Satisfying a man's lust has little to do with being a woman. Hardened whores are scarcely women; they might as well be mules inured to burdens and indifference, so long as they claim their carrot: money.'' He looked at her levelly. "You, on the other hand, expect another carrot: revenge for Diego. I am your bait; so long as your uncle and cousin go for me, you have a chance to prove they killed Diego and go for their throats. I am in too many ways incidental."

Liliane had gone pale. "I once meant to use you as much as guard you, but no longer, and you know it. Do you *want* to hate me?"

"Perhaps I do," he murmured. "I do not know any-more . . . and I wonder if you know what you want." He waved to a cushion next to Saida, who was desperately trying to decipher what they were saying. "Please, sit. We both are tired. Have some brandywine." He took up the pitcher and poured as Liliane sagged numbly down on the cushion. In the face of his bitterness and disillusionment as well as her own pain, she did not know how to deal with his changes in mood. Logic told her she ought to fight them, but the rapidly growing fear that she had irretrievably lost him in Saladin's camp made her defensive. Kiki, sensing her unhappiness, crept to her side.

Spotting the monkey, Saida made a face and edged closer to Alexandre. "My lord, I am afraid of that creature. When you are not about to reprimand it, it tries to bite me. The nasty beast has even made its foul turds in my bed." She clung to his arm. "Please, my lord, I beg you, send it away."

Alexandre glanced questioningly at Liliane. "Do not look at me," she muttered in French. "Kiki recognizes a sow and her wallow readily enough."

"She also knows you dislike the girl," he replied evenly. "Send the monkey away. For one night at least, we shall do without fleas in our food."

"The fleas are more likely Saida's—" Liliane's defiant defense of her pet was cut off by the entrance of Alphonse with a platter of savory lamb, okra and fruit. As he settled the platter on the linen, he smiled and tried to catch Saida's eye. She ignored him. Liliane eased Kiki behind her and when serving herself, slipped the monkey a ripe pomegranate to keep it occupied and out of sight. She was sure Alexandre knew of Kiki's presence, but probably being no more anxious for another quarrel than she, he seemed willing to accept a compromise.

After the deflated Alphonse left, she and Alexandre began to eat, while Saida, in Saracen fashion, waited for them to be done before she took her share. In the silence, small, sticky smacks sounded behind Liliane. Saida's eyes narrowed. To cover Kiki's noise, Liliane began to chew with unnecessary relish.

A glimmer of a smile quirked Alexandre's lips. With slow deliberation, he selected a pear and bit it with dramatic salaciousness. Their meal soon sounded as if its every morsel were drowned in soup. Kiki pinched Liliane for another piece of fruit.

"Are you uncomfortable, my lord?" Saida queried sweetly at Liliane's start. "Shall I fetch you a less verminous pillow?"

"As the rest of our pillows are piled upon your bedding, I think not" was the equally sugary reply. "So many lively specks have collected there, you might consider training the rascals to perform." Liliane smiled wolfishly as she palmed Kiki a plum. "Your chaste nights may also prove less dull when devoted to innocent industry. Why chafe for lovers when a multitude of entertaining companions gambol through your sheets?"

Saida's eyes lowered demurely. "Perhaps I shall take your advice, my lord. It must be wise, as you seem to speak from bitter experience. How sad to have no companion for your bed"—her eyes cut coquettishly to Alexandre—"no soft flesh to comfort you, no red lips and round breasts to make your manhood fierce and proud." She cut a harder glance at Liliane. "If I do not wash, it is to preserve the alluring perfume of my woman's parts. Any man not dead knows that scent and its promise of rich fulfillment." She wrinkled her nose in delicate distaste. "Soap smells of pig grease and lye. What enticement lies in that?"

"I have never noted that rancid musk holds any particular enticement," drawled Liliane. "Rather, it ranks offensively with the effluvium of goats and mildewed cheese. Add a strong whiff of acrid mule sweat and one has an urge more to puke than to pursue."

Alexandre, who had been bemusedly gnawing a tough chunk of mutton while the women bickered, now hastily intervened as Saida acquired a warlike glint in her eye. "Enough, friend Jefar. We shall all have our stomachs turned at this rate. Besides, Saida is unused to having a supply of water sufficient for bathing in the desert." He gave Saida a polite but pointed smile. "As we are not currently lacking in water, an occasional bath will not much diminish your attractions. I must admit that, like Jefar, I prefer less heady scents from the women about me when I am on military campaign." With disarming Gallic charm, he kissed Saida's hand. "Surely, you would not wish me to be so distracted that I may lose my head?"

You have already lost it! thought Liliane, seeing red as he grinned at the giggling Saida. Jealousy and frustration wracked her. "Alexandre," she said sharply in French, "you forget yourself!"

His head turned slowly, his blue eyes icy. "Perhaps I am remembering. There was a time when there were no kings and wives in my life. Why begrudge me a little nostalgia?"

Liliane went white and Saida gave her a triumphant smile. In taut, miserable silence, Liliane watched Saida grow more open in her advances to Alexandre, his gallantries and flattery to her more lavish. He is teaching his headstrong wife a lesson, Liliane told herself bleakly. A hard lesson she would never forget; one her pride and heart found unendurable.

Something was dying in her as she watched them. In these last two years, her love for Alexandre had become the center of her life. Now her splendid, comforting dream was twisting into a nightmare. For many long months, she had lived beyond her strength as a soldier. For three nights now, she had not slept. The last, fragile barrier that had kept her sane in the midst of lonely, hideous destruction crumbled away. Her mind filled with ghosts of the children she and Diego had never had, Diego's death, Alexandre's desertion . . . losses. She had failed everyone!

Saida's coy laughter knelled the end of her marriage; there would be other Saidas. Hereafter, Alexandre's happiness could only be bought at the price of her obedience, and obedience belied her nature. For love of him, she might lie and feign docility . . . but she'd inevitably end by hating him as much as herself. She had no desire to return to France; nothing at Castle de Brueil would be the same again, except that it would be more of a prison than before.

Liliane watched Alexandre, wondering how she could ever bear to live apart from him. His every gesture, every word, felt its hook within her heart. Upon their first meeting, she had been drawn to his lively, wild air, to his mischief and vulnerability, to his strength and poetry. Aye, thief he had been, despite his lands and title; he had stolen her heart easily and she would never have it back again, nor would his heart ever be wholly hers again. Since Acre, he had subtly changed. His face, drawn beneath its tan, had lost its boyish look. His wit was undiminished but had grown acerbic beneath its charm. He seemed withdrawn, unaware of her, even of Saida. Since her coming to Palestine, she knew he had tried to stifle his building resentment with smooth detachment until he could ignore her interference no longer. Neither of them would ever forget the moment when he had been ridiculed by friend and enemy alike; that ridicule had hurt him far more than Richard's chastisement.

Yes, Liliane thought with tears welling in her eyes, he could easily learn to hate me, too. That is one failure I could not survive.

Kiki clambered up Liliane's back and caressed her face. At her lack of response, the little creature peered into her eyes, then scrambled about to follow her blind, wretched gaze at Alexandre. Saida was kissing him. For a moment, Alexandre did not move, then just as his hand lifted, either to press her away or embrace her, Kiki uttered a furious, whistling shriek. She leaped upon the girl's shoulders, catching her by the hair and slamming an overripe peach against her back. With a scream of rage, Saida flailed out at the monkey. When Kiki scampered out of reach, chittering with fury, Saida jumped to her feet to grab a censer. Whirling it by the chain, she took aim at her tormentor. Before the flaming censer loosed, Alexandre swiftly rose and caught her wrist. "Will you burn the very tent with your rash temper?"

"*He* set the vicious creature on me!" Saida snarled, her pretty face twisted with rage as her finger jabbed past his arm. "Reprove your precious Jefar!"

Alexandre turned abruptly, a curt reprimand on his lips, but saw only Kiki hurling imprecations from an empty pillow. His precious Jefar had gone.

12

The Fall of Souls

Alexandre searched for Liliane for many days—so many that they ran together. Even the news that Acre was about to surrender gave him no joy. He combed the camp and searched the brothels without luck. He saw no sign of her on the beach by day, and if she were there by night, he began to think she must have buried herself in sand. If Liliane *had* taken to the beach, he worried that she might have fallen prey to Saracen night marauders. She might now be lying in the stinking, common grave at the edge of the marsh.

Gradually, as his hope of finding Liliane faded, Alexandre came to believe that if she were not dead, she might have joined a northbound caravan or taken passage with one of the lateeners for southern Europe. Indeed, Alexandre hoped Liliane had gone, for the only plea she had ever made of him haunted his mind like a plaintive, never-ending whisper: "Do not cast me away in this wilderness. I fear I should never find my way back to you."

He had not only abandoned her, he had driven her away as surely as if he had struck her. He scarcely knew what had possessed him. Granted, he had been coldly angry and determined to show her that she might not tamper with his life as she pleased. As past slaps on the wrist had not daunted her, the demonstration had to be harsh, but he had not meant to go so far. He could happily strangle Saida, but the fault was his own. An explosion would inevitably have occurred between him and Liliane; Saida's flirtations had merely hastened it.

244

The days grew hotter, the mosquitoes unbearable, and still the city walls stood. The fighting became concentrated in pockets. Sappers fought toe to toe in the torchlight of their mole tunnels and in the great red sun; the crusaders fried in their armor as they held off Saracen attacks from the desert. Disease and fever swept the camp; one in five died. Hatred for those who kept resisting festered among the besiegers.

We are like a putrid boil on the land, Alexandre thought wearily. Like a sickness, we do not belong here. By all that is holy, I want to go back to the green fields and forests of home!

But it was less home he missed than Liliane. What if he never saw her again? Certainly, she would not return to Provence. What could she think it held for her now besides suspicious peasants, a seneschal who thought her a traitor and, when this infernal war was done, a husband who had no love for her?

He would probably never see Liliane again. That idea became a conviction, fixed in his brain like a dark obsession. He imagined her in a thousand places; in none of them was he at her side; in none of them, did she look at him with the trust and longing he needed from her. Her face was distant now, remote as one of the cold Alpine peaks that hid in the mists north of Castle de Brueil. He was alone again, more fearfully than he had ever dreamed. Without Liliane, he would be alone until he died. All Saida's allurements and contrivances for sympathy left him as untouched as trackless tundra. In the midst of this heat, he was encased in ice, preserved for . . . what?

Philip sought Alexandre's company often now that he drifted like an indifferent ghost about the camp. "Your friend Jefar has probably grown weary of this tedious business and deserted," Philip commented lightly. "He may even have been the spy, *your* spy, who contrived to have you all captured." He put an arm about Alexandre's shoulders. "Come, do not be glum. I have missed you at my table. We must be more together."

"I am in disgrace," Alexandre replied tonelessly.

"Fa! Do you suppose I hold you responsible for that raid fiasco? Leave scapegoats to Richard. He likes things neatly tied; you were the knot, that is all. Acre will be sewn up in a day or two; then his pique will be forgotten. You will ride beside me as you have always done."

As I have always done, Alexandre thought dully. Forever and

forever. "Thank you, sire. I want nothing else but to die in your service."

Philip eyed him sharply. "That is a two-edged remark. You are no use to me with your tail between your legs. What *was* this scurvy Jefar to you?

"A friend; perhaps better than I deserved."

"Leave what you deserve to me from now on." Philip's voice was flat. "You could do much worse than have a king for a friend."

"I am grateful for Your Majesty's interest."

"You had better be." Philip's light tone had returned. "Richard always goes for an enemy's throat. I can wait until the back is turned."

And so Alexandre returned to the royal table, but Philip's last words haunted him. What if Liliane had not gone? What if she had been stabbed in the back by her uncle and cousin? What if one of the raiders sworn to silence had revealed her identity and so sealed her death warrant with the Signes? He went looking for Louis.

Ten feet from the Signes' tent, Alexandre met an impressive guard in the darkness of the hovel alley. He closed his hand unobtrusively about his dirk haft, ready to prick the man's kidneys should he prove difficult.

"Do not be hasty, my lord," murmured the big man. "I serve not the Baron de Signe. I am King Philip's man. His majesty doesn't think you ought to settle accounts owing for that raid just yet . . . or anything else. He wants his nobles quiet and agreeable during the peace settlement. Diplomacy." His hand settled on his sword. "You know how it is."

Alexandre's lips tightened. Diplomacy might be diplomacy, but he suspected also that Philip, possessive as usual, did not want him to find Jefar. Philip knew something, but what?

Alexandre turned back to the royal tent. Philip was alone, ready for bed. He flopped back against his silken pillows with a careless air, but his eyes were wary. "So, *ami*, you are still wandering about tonight. Why so restless?"

"I am troubled by a question, sire," Alexandre said quietly. "I believe you have the answer."

Philip shrugged. "Possibly, but then I have never taken the divinity of kings seriously. Perhaps you should apply to the all-seeing Richard."

"Richard is not my friend."

"Ah." Philip smiled. "You are in a pickle. Friendship is blind."

"I hope not, in this case. Jefar has left, taking something I cannot do without. Do you know where I may find him?"

"He is a thief?"

"No, he had more right than any to the thing he took. Mine is an errand of . . . persuasion."

"Did you also seek out Louis de Signe tonight on an errand of persuasion?"

"I sought Jefar."

Philip casually lifted a goblet of ambrosia. "Jefar is beyond your reach."

Alexandre stiffened. "Where?"

"Saladin's camp." Philip's green eyes were gently mocking over the cup rim. "Why so shocked? Is it not natural for a Saracen to return to his own?"

"Did he go voluntarily?" Alexandre asked in a low voice.

"Oh, yes. He could scarcely wait to be gone. The pickets sighted him a fortnight ago heading into the eastern dunes." Philip's brows slanted wickedly. "Dare we hope we've found our traitor?"

"No," replied Alexandre, remembering the medallion of Almansor that Liliane had given him; she would be wearing it now. "Jefar would not have gone to Saladin for that."

Philip laughed sardonically. "Do you know him that well?"

"Admittedly, not so well as I thought." Alexandre bowed quickly. "I thank you, my sovereign lord. I am in your debt."

"Thank me by not going off on some harebrained ride to Saladin. He will not likely grant you amnesty a second time. If Richard has his way when Acre falls, any Christian in Saladin's hands will be flayed alive. Be resigned that Jefar el din has wearied of your company. Also be grateful that you are *outside* the walls of this wretched infidel city."

Alexandre did not answer and, as soon as he took his leave of Philip, he went to find his destrier.

Saladin watched Liliane as she stared across the sands in the direction of Acre. "Why return to Spain when your heart still lies in the desert, *Comtesse?* You have done little but gaze toward the city. Surely, if armies may contrive peace, a man and woman may not lose hope.''

She looked at him gravely. ''You have been most kind to receive me, Great Lord. When I return to the protection of Almansor, I shall tell him of your great generosity.''

''Will you send no message to the *comte?*''

Liliane shook her head. ''He might feel obligated to recover me. Far better that I simply disappear.''

Saladin eyed her quizzically. ''No price is too great for pride; so saying, men have warred since the beginning of time, and for that price shall Acre die.''

''You are sure?''

''Tomorrow the crusaders will walk Acre's streets with blood beneath their feet.''

''But you say the city is prepared to surrender, that the terms are agreed,'' she protested. ''Why would Richard butcher what will be freely given him?''

''You who are so proud ask this?'' Saladin reproved gently. ''There is a roaring in your royal lion's heart. If he drowns Acre in horror, other Palestinian cities will quail before him. His task as conqueror will be simplified.''

Liliane's lovely face went pale. ''Surely he will release the women and children.''

''Richard's men have been kept too long from their kill. They will not now dine with chivalry. He will give them their fill, so that they will follow him when he turns from Acre.''

Wearily, Liliane closed her eyes. ''I helped Richard to this. Fought for him without faith, conviction . . . heedless for the morrow. I did it all for love, and for justice of old crimes, but love does not sanction all, and justice cannot make right new crimes.'' She was silent for a long time, then murmured, ''I shall not return to Spain for a time, *effendi.*''

Saladin lifted a dark brow. ''Then you have decided to return to the *comte.*''

''No, I wish to go into the city . . . with your help. I lost my honor there, confused it. I wanted children badly once, and I owe the children that now play upon this earth some protection, at the very least. I have sinned; both Allah and God are owed recompense.''

''If you enter Acre as a Moor, you will pay with your life. You will either be regarded as one of us or as a traitor. If you survive our judgment, you will not survive Richard's forces. Are you prepared to pay so great a price for your confusion?"

"Shall I spend a lifetime in Spain remembering Acre?" Liliane smiled faintly. "I take the coward's way, *effendi*. Short memories, long sleep."

"Does one sleep in the lap of Allah?" he mused. "I wonder. Somehow, I think that cowards do not rest easily, that crime without conscience merits a more merciful end." His gaze followed hers toward the doomed city beyond dunes already somnolent under the setting sun. "I will see you enter Acre, if that is your wish, but once the sun rises, not even I can help you leave again."

"I understand."

"Can you swim?"

"Yes."

"Then you will enter the city with tonight's swimmers through the drainage ducts. You will be taken to a house where you will be safe. Do not speak outside that house or you will be killed as a spy."

Liliane laughed softly. "I thought my Arabic accent had improved."

His laughter matched hers. "Pride deludes us all."

"Who are the swimmers?"

"Because I must know what passes behind Acre's walls, messengers swim to and fro like fish each night." He sobered. "Tonight, they carry only news of approaching death."

"I am sorry, *effendi*," she said quietly. "I have helped to cause so much pointless waste."

"War is always waste," he said briefly, with the first touch of bitterness she had seen in him. "We who rule Allah's creatures are the greatest of His fools. How blithely we assume that His patience is eternal."

The desert was silent, the stars high and still. On just such a night, the Christ child was born, mused Alexandre as his horse labored through the high dunes. God's peace was as distant, Liliane as distant, as if they dwelt upon one of those glimmering mysterious stars. He must get her away from Saladin before dawn, when Acre's gates would open to rape, massacre and pillage, and when Liliane would be left to Saracen retribution. There were four hours now to sunrise. So much damage had been done—how could he persuade her to leave with him in time?

Suddenly the dune was mounted by ten riders descending from both sides of him. Urging his horse to gallop, the destrier slid in the sand, losing its footing as if scrambling through deep butter.

The Saracens closed swiftly in on him. Rising in the saddle to steady himself against the destrier's stumbling, Alexandre drew his sword. "I wish to see Saladin!" he shouted. He might be a dead man, but he was not yet cold.

Just as he braced himself for their attack, a shout reached him. *"Le Comte de Brueil?"* At his muffled, startled affirmation, a Saracen cried, "Follow us!"

Across the desert they led him, not toward the camp of Saladin but to the oasis. Puzzled, he dismounted to greet the tall Saracen waiting for him. "I am Sheik Faroud," the Saracen informed him. "You have come seeking your *comtesse?*"

"I have," Alexandre answered slowly, eyeing the grim, surrounding faces of his escort.

"Look for her in Acre," replied the sheik, "but come no nearer to our camp. Saladin himself can take no responsibility for your safety this night."

"In Acre?" Alexandre's spirits soared. "The countess has returned to the camp?"

The sheik gave him a pitying look. "She is within the city."

Alexandre went white. "That is suicide!"

The sheik shrugged. "As Allah wills. Who can explain the workings of women's minds."

"But where is she in the city?" Alexandre asked, desperate.

"Where no one will find her until dawn." The sheik's flat stare told Alexandre that he would get no more elaboration. The Saracen bowed. "You would be wise to make haste, milord. My men are in short temper."

Being in a less suicidal frame of mind than his wife, Alexandre speedily took his leave.

What now? Liliane was as far beyond his reach as if she had gone to the moon. As he rode, black images of what the morrow would bring loomed in his mind. He *had* to find her! He had to retrieve that mischievous, beautiful girl who had bewitched him in the forest of his demesne. He could see Liliane now, lightly poised with her fishing spear over the trout stream. She had been

playing then, had gone on playing until the games had turned
deadly and even she had been appalled by them. And when she
had tried to escape those terrible games, he had turned his back
on her. In bleak desperation, he had been forced to turn to an
enemy. Had Saladin sheltered her out of regard for his old friend,
Almansor, or had he seen a way to avenge himself upon a pair
of Christians who had helped bring about the fall of Acre? Whatever Saladin's reasoning, Liliane was in deadly peril.

As soon as he reached camp, Alexandre went to his tent. He
roughly shook Saida awake. Her arms went predictably around
his neck, and he firmly pried her loose. "Tonight, little desert
cat, I have better prey for you than a common knight." He lifted
her chin. "How would you like a powerful king to adorn your
pillow?"

Saida looked startled, then delighted, but within seconds her
smile became a frown. "Richard? But he is—"

"Richard is not the lover for you. What think you of Philip?"

She smiled slowly. "He is very handsome." Her forefinger
began to twirl a dark curl at her shoulder. "Is he generous?"

"If he does not pay you, I will." Alexandre gave her a feral
smile. "What say you?"

"Let me but comb my hair."

He pulled her to her feet. "Leave it. The king is hot."

On the contrary, Saida found the king cold. Not only limp,
but asleep and totally unaware of her coming. For a quarter of
an hour, she and Alexandre waited outside the royal tent while
Philip's chamberlain drowsily informed him that Alexandre had
brought him a fire-eyed wench in a nightshift.

"That little Saracen bitch?" mumbled Philip. At the chamberlain's dull nod, Philip crooked a lax finger. "It is about time.
He has probably worn her to a nub."

Moments later, Philip felt his bed give. He opened an eye.
Saida, distinctly unworn, smiled wickedly at him.

"How would you like her?" Alexandre murmured from the
shadows.

Philip stroked Saida's hip appreciatively. "Ripe as a peach.
Can she speak French?"

"Will you miss conversation?"

Philip laughed. "Not much. Besides, she looks noisy enough,
given encouragement. I love to hear a wench squeal." He

pinched. Saida squealed. "Ah, so you do speak the universal language, my piglet."

"She is a gift. I thought you might like a little something on the eve of victory," drawled Alexandre. "By the way, do you mind if I review the maps of the city while I am here? If I lead a battle group into Acre tomorrow, 'twould be well to know where the hell I am going."

"Good boy. Do your homework and make no more mistakes." Philip tumbled Saida under him. "Run along, and thank you for the present."

"Think nothing of it."

Leaving the king to his pleasure, Alexandre went into the rear of the tent, which had been partitioned for strategy councils. Scrolled maps were neatly stored in a tooled leather cylinder beneath a folding wooden table. He quickly reviewed the maps of Acre. The general outlay of the city streets was already familiar to him and the illuminated maps showed little more than the quarters of the city. He was more interested in the fresh water cistern system that eventually linked with huge cesspits and tunnels under the city walls on the ocean side. He found a large parchment covered with sketches and notes of the area, each carefully inked as spies reported their reconnaissance.

Among the camp's beggars and native innkeepers, rumors ran that Saladin moved messengers in and out of Acre by way of the cisterns. If Liliane had entered the city, this was the way she had done it, but which cistern was set close enough to the low tide to allow a swimmer to pass through it without drowning?

Alexandre headed for the quays. In a shack by the farthest quay an ancient native fisherman lived. Alexandre mercilessly roused the old man. "What is the shallowest part of the wall?" he barked.

The old man shook his head in confusion. "Fishing's better where it's deep. Why do you want fish tonight? I don't have any tonight."

"Look, I want to go fishing tonight and I wish to use your boat. I do not like deep water because I cannot swim." Alexandre dumped coins in the old man's hand. "I shall pay for everything."

"Tonight? You want to fish tonight?" The old man began to shake his head again. Finally he shrugged. "I don't rent my boat to a crazy man. Pay me another ten dirhams and the boat is yours. You drown, so . . .''

I drown, so . . . The man's last words haunted Alexandre a short time later as he sat in the ramshackle boat and stared uneasily at the black water lapping at the wall of Acre. The wall was many feet thick. If the cistern tunnel was built on an incline, it might run submerged for a long way, longer than his lungs would hold air. In the pitch dark, he stripped and dumped his clothes in the boat bottom. He tied a small bundle of clothes he had bought from the fisherman around his waist, then looped his sword and dirk to his boot thongs and tied it around his neck. He eased over the side and took a deep, prayerful breath.

In the water's lap, not twenty feet from Alexandre's rising air bubbles off the old boat's stern, a light Saracen skiff rocked to and fro. Alexandre had not noticed the boat, much less whether it was empty or not. The boat was empty—the tunnel was not.

In rising panic, Liliane pressed high and hard against slimy stone. Saladin had merely asked whether she could swim; he had not described the cistern tunnel. The two Saracens with her had dived from the skiff, leaving her to follow as best she could. An infidel female was of no account to them; if she drowned before reaching her destination, no one would be alive tomorrow to complain of their neglect to Saladin. Fearful of losing them in the darkness, she leaped into the water almost upon their very heels and followed so closely that she was once struck in the face by a kicking foot. Second followed inky second until her lungs threatened to burst. Finally, frantically, she thrust upward to butt her head painfully against rough stone. She clawed at the stone, tried to breathe. She was rewarded by a tiny whiff of air, then a ripple of water up her nose that choked her. Wildly, she tried again; this time she found more air, enough to calm her a little. Lying still against the water surface, she took short, tentative breaths until her lungs ceased to burn. With a fatalistic gulp, she submerged again and flailed after her callous escorts. The tunnel went on and on, allowing only inadequate snatches of air until her lungs scalded and her mind blurred. If she had not known the Saracen couriers had previously made the trip through this tunnel with success, she would have panicked entirely.

Finally, a disk of steel-gray light, so faint it faded almost instantly, glimmered overhead. Liliane swam furiously for the spot where she had seen the light, clawed higher and found hot August night. The couriers looked down at her strained, glistening face in the well.

One of them grunted. "Your Christian God must think well of you. In three months, we lost twenty men down there." He dragged her limp, exhausted body up.

Alexandre was lost. He knew in all sanity that he could not be lost so long as he kept moving forward, but the cistern was wider than his body, and in those horrid, strangling moments of fear when he could find no air at the top of the cistern, he became disoriented. He was no longer sure whether he was advancing in the tunnel or going back the way he had come. He was not even sure if he had the right tunnel. He had never liked closed places; they made him feel like a trapped animal. Now he was drowning in a black, watery cage that pressed in on him under tons of stone. For the third time, he went up for air that was not there.

Although she had a good sense of direction, Liliane was completely confused by the time the Saracens hastily deposited her in a tiny house near the harbor. The dark streets, filled with stealthy rustlings and the grieving wails of the doomed behind barricaded doors, wound mysteriously throughout the city. Sorrow seemed to echo, to be imbedded in the very stones of the streets and the blank, crumbling plaster of the walls. Acre had known many revolts, many wars throughout the centuries; and by tomorrow's sunset, the city's cries and murmurings would be ominously silent. They would wait, brooding, for that next dreadful moment in time when disaster would summon them to howl again. Was it only the battering of war machines and armies that eventually brought cities to dust, Liliane wondered. Or was it disintegration from within, an exhausted shudder that shook a city to bits upon the heads of its makers and destroyers alike?

After exchanging a few words with a slight man who bitterly protested Liliane's presence, the two Saracens shoved her through the door of the house and hurried off down the street. The resentful householder slammed the door shut behind her and thrust a heavy beam through the latch. For a long moment, he stared at Liliane with pure hatred, then with a muffled mutter, he turned to his family. A woman and two children huddled by the empty grate, their faces lit only by a fragment of candle stuck to the floor. The woman was probably thirty, the boy seven, the girl eight; because of starvation, they all looked older. Their food was long gone, and their few sticks of furniture had been burned as firewood. Their eyes had a despairing, bestial gleam. Hate sang about the room, adding its relentless note to the discordant chorus reverberating from Acre's ancient, shrunken gut.

"I have come to help, if I can," Liliane murmured in Arabic. Tiredly, she pulled off her wet haik. The Saracens gaped at her long, pale hair.

"Help?" the man spat. "You, a woman? And worse, a fool? Tomorrow you will die—we will *all* die. This once, Allah's will is no mystery." He shook his head in exasperation. "Not only must we suffer a foul end, we must also endure an infidel mad-woman."

"Does not Allah bid us all to bear madness patiently?" Liliane gave him a faint smile. "May I sit? Even the crazed grow weary."

"Sit. What does it matter?"

Liliane sat and unwound a knotted sleeve of her aba to take out an oiled parchment packet. She held it up to the Saracen. "I brought food."

He snatched the bundle, his family rushing toward him like a hyena pack. His face white, he ripped into the parchment. "It's wet," he observed in flat disappointment, then without another breath, he tore into a chunk of dripping mutton. The boy grabbed a handful of shapeless fruit. Their faces strained, the two females watched the food disappear. Finally noticing them, the man pushed the remains at them. With terrible sounds, they wolfed the scraps.

Perhaps I am a fool, decided Liliane as she watched them, but I do not wish to live in a world where starving women are allowed only scraps left by men. I was wrong to take part in a pointless war, but I was right to claim a freedom denied to me only because of my sex. War is not the only stupidity in the world.

Crouching now in the darkness, she realized that, given her nature and training by Diego, she could hardly have acted differently after marrying Alexandre. She was only sorry, bitterly sorry, that he had ceased to care for her.

Why did I think that in his heart Alexandre would not mind anything I did? she wondered. Saladin was right; like so many common humans, my sin was pride. In claiming my own rights, I denied Alexandre's. I wish I might let him know that I learned something—her gaze went out to the guttering candle—and that I will always love him.

The candle went out.

Dawn rose in eerie silence. The mammoth rampart of Acre flushed an ominous red in the first subtle rays of the rising sun. A fever seemed to have set upon the city and reached its crisis. Outside, the crusader armies gathered to await the official surrender before the gate; above them, no guards stood on the battlements, and all minds in Acre were wrapped in cold, mounting terror, were drawn inward to private thoughts.

A clarion cry of trumpets shivered through the hot air. Liliane rose slowly to her feet. The trumpets signaled the opening of the gates. Acre's commanders would meet with the crusader kings, prelates and high officials, then the city populace would be ordered to leave. To go where? To what? Miles of desert surrounded Acre. Down the coast were strung poor villages that would be unable to sustain a flood of population. Even if the refugees from Acre were not massacred outright by the conquering armies, they had no food left; anything of value would be taken from them. They would be preyed upon as they fled.

The little Saracen and his family were dolefully gathering their pitifully few bundles. Their hands trembling, they were scarcely aware of her now. She quietly intervened. "Those bundles would be best secured beneath your women's skirts and your own clothing. Do not put too much on the women or they will be searched." She did not add that they might also be raped if they could not run.

The Saracen seemed to ignore her, but then he abruptly waved for his family to redistribute their possessions. They had plenty of time; the ceremonies outside the gates would drag on for a while. Liliane sharply watched the Saracen's face. Not only was he afraid, but he had the look of a guilty man. No doubt he was wondering if his traffic with Saladin would cost him his neck. His dealings had no doubt kept his family alive during the siege, securing them a little food and money. He must have not dared to appear too prosperous and well fed lest he draw robbers and scavengers. Whether he was a patriot or simply supplying necessities to his family, she did not know, but now they risked being suspected of spying by the invaders.

Around forenoon, a messenger ran through the street outside, leaving a tiny cloud of dust on the cobbles. "All Saracens must now evacuate the city! Anyone found in Acre by noon will be considered a resister and slain. Everyone out! Everyone out by noon!"

The Saracen's wife let out a wail of fear and despair. "Silence!" her husband shouted nervously. "Have we not enough trouble without your screeching?"

The little girl huddled by the empty grate, her brother clutching at one of her braids. "Papa, I do not want to leave! Please, Papa, can we not stay?"

Their father's nerves snapped. "No! Shut up! I told you what would happen this morning. Now we must go! That's all there is to it! Move!" He grabbed his wife's arm and gave her a shove toward the door.

Liliane adjusted her haik higher about her face. "If you will trust me, I may be able to help you."

This time, the Saracen was less inclined to be negative about offers of assistance. He paused with his hand on the latch. "What can you do?"

"I hold high rank among the Europeans. I may be able to intercede for you and others among you."

The Saracen flatly shook his head. "You lost your influence once you set foot in Acre. You will be executed as a traitor and draw attention to us." His face went cold. "Once we reach the city gates, I do not want to see your face. Stay away from us."

"What you say may be true; then again, you may be wrong. Do you believe your children will survive the desert?"

"They are Saracen, not weak Europeans," he spat. "We will live to see you infidels driven into the sea."

"Your faith is strong," Liliane said softly. "May it sustain you in the days to come."

Moments later, they crowded through the street with the other evacuees. Liliane brought up the rear of the Saracen's little group, just behind the children. The streets were a cacophony of cries and curses, the rumbling of lumbering cart wheels and the clatter of light carriages. Litter bearers pressed forward through the throngs as their owners shouted imprecations at being delayed.

After some minutes, Liliane noticed a man watching them. He clutched a large bundle of possessions to his chest, a kohl-eyed slave girl scurrying at his heel. Beside them careened a cart full of carpets and rich household goods. The Saracen's wife noticed the man, too. Her face paled and she tugged at her husband's aba. "Hassim is watching us! He will point you out to the infidels to save himself and his goods. We will all be put to the sword!" When her husband took a quick look, then quickly averted his eyes, she tugged harder. "Ali, what will we do?"

"Stay away from him, that's all," he muttered, hurrying down a side street. "We look like everybody else. How can he point us out if he cannot find us?"

Liliane's eyes met his wife's. Both of them had guessed that Acre's residents would not be passed through the crusader ranks without some form of inspection. All Hassim had to do was wait with the inspectors. He would not be the only turncoat. Many would sell their neighbors to save themselves. Lies would be spent as liberally as truth. One look of recognition at Ali's face would sentence him.

As they rejoined the main throng and neared the press at the huge city gates, Ali's wife whispered something to her children. They stared at her in panic and she shook them. "You will do as I say!" With tears welling in their eyes, they ducked their heads, then nodded, darting peeks at Liliane. Their mother moved back to her. "Take them!" she muttered. "When you can, send them to my sister in Sidon." Without touching the children, she pushed away after her husband in the crowd. With the crowd buffeting them, the children watched their parents disappear.

Wondering how many children would be orphaned before the end of this day, Liliane put her arms about their shoulders. "Do not worry. We shall try to pass through the gate after we see your parents pass. With Allah's help, your separation may be brief."

But luck was not with Ali and his wife. Twenty yards outside the gate, Hassim waited like a large, threatening slug. His fat forefinger singled out Ali in moments. Liliane was tall enough to see over the the crowd where the children could not. Soldiers swept forward and dragged Ali and his wife into a miserable cluster of Saracens huddled together in a ditch ringed with guards. There were already almost two hundred people in the ditch; some

bewailing their fate, most numb with terror. Although the group
was mostly made up of adults, children howled and whimpered
among them. Hassim's sharp, darting eyes were searching
through the crowd again. Ali's wife had been right; Hassim was
looking for any prey to divert the guards from himself.

Liliane grabbed the children's hands and dragged them back
inside the gate. Swiftly, she pulled them against the wall into a
niche to escape the stream of people who were in a panic to flee
the city before noon. The shadows were already shortening. "Do
you know where the cesspits are in the old quarter of the city?"
she demanded of the girl, whose name was Yasmin.

Yasmin shook her head fearfully. Both of the children were
aware of the probable reason for retreating into the city. "I-I was
not allowed there," stammered the child. "The brothels—"

The boy, Habib, cut in. "I know where the cesspits are. I
often play in them," he said importantly. "I know what you
want, too. You want to hide in them, but they smell horrible
when the tide does not flush them."

"Any better ideas?"

"The minarets," he replied excitedly. "We could see everything. . . ."

Probably too much, Liliane imagined, remembering the
wretched people being herded into the ditch. "We would also
be trapped. The crusaders will search the towers, do you not
think?"

As Habib considered, his face fell. Liliane patted his shoulder.
"I suppose we will just have to hold our noses in the cesspits
while you scout for us. Will you do that?" She thought it best
to cater to his vanity. Saracen males could turn stubborn in a
second if they suspected that a female was trying to manage
them. It was a pity that when dealing with Alexandre she had
not remembered that European males were much the same.

When Habib finally nodded, Liliane added, "You will also
agree 'tis best to keep secret that I am no man?"

He reflected a moment. "Yes, so long as you do not try to
order me about."

At a brisk trot, the boy led Liliane and his sister through the
rapidly emptying streets toward the old quarter. The sun was
nearly overhead. A few highborn crusaders were already moving
their destriers and households into the city. Behind them, the
foot soldiers were barely held in check. Both casually ignored

the terrible screams that rose near the main gate. Sickened, Liliane could guess what was happening to the prisoners trapped in the ditch. At any moment the main army would be let go. "Habib, how far is it to the cesspits?"

"Not far now," he said over his shoulder. "The biggest one is near the old bazaar. Nobody will find us there."

He was wrong. To her horror, Liliane saw that the dark, foul cesspit was full of old people and beggars too feeble to attempt the desert exodus. A few women, mostly widows by their garb, cowered against the curving walls. The pit was perhaps thirty feet across, although so many pillars held up the roof that it was difficult to be sure. A broad, sloped walkway crowded with people encircled the pit, which angled steeply to the center filled with sand, grit and an occasional body. The tunnel by which they had entered was one of the head-high openings in the walls. Numerous smaller tunnels also emptied into the pit, which was drained by two low, broad tunnels sloping sharply down to the smell of rank sea water. A small iron grate high overhead let in vague, diffused light as if it were the drain of some interior courtyard.

Among the cesspit refugees were children, either orphaned street urchins who would have no source of sustenance outside the city walls, or children too young to travel who had been reluctantly abandoned by their parents. Babies lay fretting and wailing on the damp stones. Oh, my God, wondered Liliane desperately, what chance have these poor creatures? If they are not killed like vermin, they will starve! Beside her, Yasmin dropped down on the stones and began to weep bitterly. "I want my mother!"

"Shut up or I'll box your ears!" threatened her brother, near to tears himself. His bravado was completely shaken at the sight of such a crowd; he was beginning to realize the near impossibility of successfully hiding within Acre's walls. When the screaming had begun outside the city gates, he had tried to get beyond the sound as quickly as possible, as if running from the certainty that he would never see his parents again.

Liliane knew the panic would rise and spread any moment. An old woman near them was beginning to keen more loudly. These marooned people had to be silenced that they might not draw attention, then calmed so they would behave rationally. She pulled Yasmin to her feet and set the children to work. "Collect the babies and give them to the widows." Quickly, she strode along the walkway surrounding the pit and shouted, "Be quiet and listen to me, all of you. Your lives depend on it."

The miserable group stared at her apathetically; a few quieted, but most did not. She raised her voice until it echoed about their ears. "We must move well back into the small tunnels and take the children with us. Everyone is making too much noise here; if we go to the depths of the tunnels, the infidels will not be eager to come rooting after us, and the noise of the babies will be muffled."

"Why not strangle the little beasts?" snarled one of the urchins.

"You were not strangled at birth, were you?" retorted Liliane. "Use your wits. We are all stuck in the last rat hole in Acre. If you look out for just yourself, you are doomed. Come on, take up a baby . . . you, you and you . . . come on, get up!"

The urchins knew authority when they heard it; the women were used to obeying a man. One by one, most of them got to their feet and shuffled back into the tunnels; the ancient and the hysterics merely stared at her with apathy and loathing. Assuming a grim expression, she drew her scimitar. "No one will be left behind to reveal our presence."

In due order, the whole pack retired to the depths of the tunnels. Liliane heaved a sigh of relief. She was not up to slitting defenseless throats; to have her bluff called this early in the game would cost all of them their lives.

The black, slimy bowels of the pit and tunnels bore a reeking resemblance to the gut of a subterranean giant with lanky limbs and disgusting habits. Complaints arose instantly. "The nastier this place, the better," Liliane returned tersely. "If you were an infidel, what would you do for the next few days—pillage this city or stroll through its sewer?"

"They will come down here sooner or later," replied an old man.

"By then, we will be gone: a few at a time over a span of several nights." Liliane held up her large signet ring. "With this seal, I can obtain European clothes to smuggle you through the gates and arrange passage for most of you on lateens and in caravans to the nearest ports. You must have courage and patience."

"What about food? And water?" the old man queried. "We're all starved and the babes won't last another day."

"Food is the charge of you children of the streets." Liliane swept a hand to the urchins squatting against the wall. "Pickings should be fine in the midst of their ransacking homes and shops, as well as the bazaar business picked up by crusader camp followers and merchants."

An urchin with narrow black eyes and a shock of dusty hair grinned cynically. "Aye, the cannibals will be having a prime time." The grin went flat. "Why should we risk our skins to feed this lot? We can lay low and grab our own pickings. When everything settles, we fade back into the city."

"If these people become hungry enough, they are going to go out looking for food. They do not have your expertise, so they are likely to be caught and questioned before being dispatched. They will talk about the tunnels and they will talk about you." She gave the scrawny ten-year-old a cool smile. "Understand?"

He grunted in philosophical agreement. "The menu tonight is scraps. What about the babies? These manless dams are dry as an old oasis, and you'll find no infidel wenches to suckle the brats."

The boy had a point. What *was* she to do about the babies? For a long moment Liliane was silent. "What know you of the Gilded Leopard?" she asked him thoughtfully, remembering the brothel to which Alexandre had brought her.

He smirked. "Not as much as I would like." The other boys laughed, and he acquired a glint in his eye. "You think old Xenobia, the madam, employs a few wet nurses, maybe has a girl or two caught out and just delivered?"

"Perhaps."

"She will want money and will betray us for an extra dirham."

Liliane smiled inwardly. At least, one among them was beginning to think in terms of the group. "I shall take care of the money. Blackmail can work both ways. The question is, can you or one of your cronies get past the gate tonight?"

He eyed her lazily. "Leave it to me."

That night, the urchins took to the high walls and rooftops like a troop of silent monkeys. Any food left unguarded in the courtyards was fair game; olive and fruit trees were stripped of their last, topmost offerings; bundles lingering on pack animals were stolen.

Liliane had been right; the pickings were good since the Christians were in a mood to celebrate, and their own wine and supplies were readily distributed. While many of the victors were drunk and oblivious, there were many more who were often irritably belligerent. Any imagined slight, far less the impertinence of a thief, was enough to incite them to mayhem, so the children had to be particularly careful in their pilfering.

Three of them slunk through the rubble of the walls of the Accursed Tower into the Christian camp, only to find that the Gilded Leopard had been transferred to a more prosperous lodging inside Acre. After renegotiating the rubble, they invaded the windows of the upper floor of the new brothel, where they wheedled the prostitute sister of their leader, Raschid, into arranging a conference with Xenobia. A bit of parchment with the imprint of the Brueil signet, along with six silver dirhams, brought a cynical gleam to Xenobia's eye. "Mother's milk to feed a half-dozen babies, with payment to come, is it? The count's wench must have dropped a litter!" She grabbed Raschid by the scruff. "Who wants this? Where'd you steal this ring?"

Raschid glared back at her. "The gentleman that gave me this says you are to fill the tab with no delay or *Melek Richard* will have your fat ass with the gentleman's sword run up it."

She held him at slightly greater length with a wrinkled nose and a suspicious glare. "What does this gentleman look like?"

As certain as she that Liliane had stolen the ring, Raschid retorted, "Milord's got a cold eye and a quick sword, and he looks like a gentleman who would hang you up for hog bait." Why add that the man was also a Moor whose neck wasn't worth a clay pot?

Panting a little with the exertion of controlling the boy's squirming, Xenobia peered at him. Finally she nodded. "All right. You get what you need this time, but next time bring more money. We've just had a rise in expenses." By next time, she judged, I'll know what's what with Brueil.

Two hours before dawn, the urchins crept at intervals back into the cistern. They had brought back more than enough food to last for two days. Even the most apathetic of the group in the tunnels cheered a bit, and they all gave them a heroes' welcome. The boys who had made the expedition to the Gilded Leopard were last to return. Proudly they displayed a goatbladder full of mothers' milk to Liliane. Habib, earlier relieved to have been spared their dangerous mission, was now miffed that he had not been asked to accompany the scavengers.

Delaying only to praise them roundly, Liliane immediately set to feeding the babies. Their own stomachs growling with hunger, the urchins were obliged to assist with the feedings. "Come on, we're not *amahs!*" protested Raschid, as he grudgingly fed one of the wailing babies. Liliane could have relieved them of the chore, tired as they were, but she instinctively knew that they would now act with greater responsibility to the helpless members of the group. To save a life when one has previously acted selfishly marks a great shift in sensibility, particularly when that life is soft and defenseless. She fed Raschid herself when he had misgivings about putting his sleeping baby down. "The stone's too cold and dirty for it," he protested.

"You are quite right," she agreed. "Why not sleep with the little beggar? You can keep each other warm and, besides, he will want feeding again in a few hours."

"That's all right," the boy said stoutly. "I'm an owl, up all night usually." In moments, he and the baby were asleep.

And so it went for the next two days. On the third night, Liliane slipped four adults, Yasmin, and two infants across the wall with ship passage money. She also sent Habib, who was unpredictable and eager to go pilfering with the urchins. The infants had been given a little wine to keep them quiet.

The first expedition and the next the following night were successful. Then she ran into trouble. Not only did she not have enough money to secure all the passages, some of the old people and one of the women were too panicky to attempt escape. The worst blow was the most unexpected. The urchins sent to the Gilded Leopard returned with no milk and ominous news.

"You had best not use the signet ring again," Raschid told her. "Its owner, the *Comte de Brueil,* has not been seen since the night before Acre fell. He is thought to be dead, and the French king is hot to find out how he met his end. Anybody flashing that ring is likely to be hanged. We would have been snagged, only my sister warned us off. A nobleman by name of Signe has been to the Leopard in the name of the king. He set men about the place to trail us back here in case we showed up again."

At the boy's last words, Liliane's terrible fear lifted a little. If Alexandre had been killed by the Signes, Louis would not be searching for the killer. He was trying to make sure that Alexandre *was* indeed dead, as well as clear himself of suspicion.

What could have happened to Alexandre? Had he somehow discovered that she had sought sanctuary with Saladin? Merciful God, what if he had gone to the Saracen camp? Her spirits plummeted again, but she was not given the luxury to worry about Alexandre. She had before her two babies past feeding time, eight intractable adults and seven children to get out of Acre. Xenobia must know the urchins were hiding somewhere, and she knew Acre well enough to make a sharp guess at their location if Louis were to press her.

They must leave the tunnels immediately, she thought. The sun would now be setting and dusk was brief. She could do little for the adults who refused to attempt escape, but she could persuade them to continue hiding in the tunnels until she and the others were sufficiently scattered to stand a chance of getting away. She rigged backslings for the babies and gave the two oldest children the last of her money and orders to board a coastal trading ship for Nahariya; hungry or not, the babies would survive a day's journey. She could only pray that the two wily urchins could be trusted to find them food and homes instead of ditching them.

The remaining five children solved their own housing problem. "The infidels are already becoming careless," Raschid told her. "We can stroll practically under their noses. We'll hang around another week or two and go back to business as usual."

Satisfied that everyone was organized, she sent them to gather up their small bundles of food and clothing. Predictably, when the older people saw that their mainstay was about to disappear, several of them changed their minds and decided to leave with the children headed for the ships. Liliane bit her lip as she waited for the laggards; thanks to Xenobia, time was running out. Finally, impatient with their arguing, she waved the children to divide and start down three different tunnels. "Your guides are leaving," she told the bickerers flatly and strode off after the first group. Hastily, dropping odds and ends, the dalliers shuffled after her.

A few minutes later, their small, unlikely parade came to a panicky halt. From up ahead came the occasional, dull knelling of armor and weaponry, a stealthy scrape of feet. The flicker of distant torches off the walls far ahead looked bright to their fearful eyes. Armed men were entering the mouth of their tunnel. Louis must have discovered them; ironically, he had no ill will for a harmless lot of refugees, but would kill them all like errant field mice for the sake of discovering the one employing the Breuil signet ring. "Back!" hissed Liliane, then waved urgently to Raschid. "Take them through the small tunnel—the one you say leads to the back of the old mosque." She swatted him on the shoulder. "Quick! Be quick!"

He scampered off, the rest hurrying after him. Liliane followed, retreating as far as the big pit where the three tunnels met. Driven back from the other large tunnels as well, the other terrified groups were hovering there, uncertain of which way to go. She drew her scimitar, flicked it into the darkness. "The mosque, you! The bazaar, you!"

"But they're almost upon us!" a woman wailed.

"Hold your tongue and go!" Liliane snapped, her own nerves raw. She gave the woman's backside a whack with the flat of her blade that sent her full tilt down the small tunnel. The way would be longer and more treacherous than their original course. The old people would be slow; she must cover them for at least ten minutes to help them elude pursuit.

Although she had never pondered the precise moment of her death, she considered it now. With any luck, she might live another ten minutes; then she was going to be eradicated like a cockroach and left in this dark hole to rot . . . unless Louis found her body. She only wished she could see his face when he discovered how she had fooled him and Jacques for so long. Unfortunately, he was going to have the last laugh. Her heart pounding in her ears, her hands slippery on the scimitar, Liliane turned to wait for the first attack.

The first unwary fellow rounded the corner to catch the length of her blade across his throat; before he saw her lethal shadow, the next stumbled across the body of the first and raised his broadsword across his face almost as a reflex. His counterstroke numbed her hand, but then she was alone as her opponent prudently retreated from the gloom. His torch had fallen into the mire and darkness had closed again like a blanket. A sound to her right from the second tunnel made her whirl. A pike slammed down toward her collarbone. Desperately, she countered and went to her knee with the force of her assailant's blow. Rolling, she spun and jabbed for his crotch. Not sporting, she reflected grimly, but then she was not built for fending off broadswords. Another hiss sounded in the dark by her ear. As she chopped wildly, she heard a shriek.

This was not going to last ten minutes, Liliane thought dismally, and she was not going to be the winner. Her only advantage was in being more accustomed to the dark than Louis's men. Nearly a week spent feeling her way about the pitchy cesspits had given her the sensitivity of a bat. What she did not see, she heard. A slight reverberation from a distant wall told her as much as if it were daylight in there. What matter? Once Louis knew his men were discovered, more torches would arrive. Once the third tunnel was penetrated, she could not possibly hold them all off. Should she retreat to a point where the interstice narrowed?

Liliane's deserate effort to think clearly was abruptly cut off by the clash of swords in the third tunnel which led from the central pit she defended. What the devil was going on? Wild ideas flew across her mind. Had the Saracens rejected the peace treaty and invaded the city? Did she have allies? But who would help her? Certainly not the Saracens. A sword sheared at her from the darkness and she leaped back. The dull glow of torchlights advanced. She scrambled back to evade another swipe that drew sparks from the stone. She caught a flare of torches down the second tunnel, a glimmer around thrashing silhouettes in the third. Her allies, whoever they were, would be quickly cut off and surrounded if she could not provide them room to retreat.

Bracing herself to block the men moving down the first two tunnels, she moved forward again, but slipped on crumbling rock and fell against the side of the pit. Hot steel entered her side. All her muscles burning in her arm and chest, she lifted her scimitar to ward off the next blow, but her wrist seemed to melt against it. The blackness became horribly complete.

13

The Single Thread

If Alexandre had not fallen at that moment, Liliane would have
vanished into memory. He came to this realization almost as he
tripped backward over her inert body and deflected the sword
blow that would have decapitated her. As it was, the descending
blade nearly severed his ear. Only his unkicking boot and his
bouncing off the stone wall kept him temporarily in one piece.
He slammed upward with his sword, heard a gurgling grunt and,
with an effort, fended off the heavy falling body of Louis's man,
who had struck down Liliane.

He might never have known that his convenient cushion was
Liliane, but for the smoothness of her face against the back of
his neck and a long strand of hair that had escaped her haik.
Even then, she might only have been some strange female corpse.
Jerking himself up, he looked down and caught a glimmer of
red-gold reflected in the advancing light of the glittering torches.
His heart seemed to stop suddenly. To have searched for her so
long and fruitlessly, then find her so unexpectedly, so horribly
in this clammy hole, stunned him into shock.

Was she dead? he wondered in swift panic at her stillness. No!
He had not known who defended the other tunnels, only that the
defense had broken and that he must fall back. Figures loomed
above him and he slashed mindlessly, as viciously as a cornered
animal. For blind moments, he could think of nothing but driving them away from her, hacking at them, destroying them. The
attackers faltered as if confronted by a demon, the torch-bearing

rear guard scattered by thrashing elbows and crushed feet. Yelps sounded as clothing and hair were singed.

Then a howl, hideous, hollow and terrifying, filled the cisterns as Alexandre sounded his fury. Those accustomed to sapper fights might not have hesitated, but these men were not used to fighting underground. Dark, dank tunnels filled with hellish din and fire were most intimidating. They fell back to regroup.

In that brief moment, Alexandre swept up Liliane and ran blindly, with no idea of where he was going in the strange black place. The cistern maps he had examined in Philip's tent had not included this ancient system. Over and over, he slammed into walls and columns, and painfully scraped his head and shoulders on corners. He heard the pound of pursuing feet, the pulse of blood running from his ear down his neck, echoes everywhere. His heart was straining, bursting.

Then abruptly, he slammed into hard, rubble-scattered dirt and fell with Liliane to the ground. He had taken a wrong turn, come up against a cave-in. He forced himself to lie still, fight off the panic that shrieked in him, brought back the mind-melting horror of being strangled in black water with his face shoved bloodily against a mammoth mountain of stone, its grave slab inexorably crushing down on him. At this moment he was barely aware that he was lying against Liliane; he could only recall the terror he had known when trying to swim under the Acre wall in search of her. He must have gone mad for a time in that water-filled tunnel, for there had come a time when he remembered only black ghouls plucking at him; huge, black worms coiled about him, trying to cover his face, trying to drag him down into their watery hell. When he'd come to sanity again, starlight was dim on his face from a cistern opening. He was clutching a narrow ridge of stone in the crumbling mortar, and his lungs were choked with water. Nearly a half hour passed before he could clear his lungs and summon the strength to drag himself up to the surface.

The cistern well had opened into the bazaar, deserted after midnight except for a few prostitutes and ribalds. He'd crawled into the shelter of the shadows from the abandoned stalls, and huddled shivering and choking on blood and water. When he'd held his shaking hands a few inches from his eyes, he'd seen that most of his fingernails were either split to the base or torn away completely. His face was puffed raw from grinding against stone.

His cut, swollen lips tasted of blood. He felt like butcher's meat, a naked, vulnerable child. If someone had touched him, he was sure he would have flown into fragments like a shattered crock.

With the gratitude of a blind man restored to sight, he'd gaped fixedly at the stars' pinpricks of light. He could breathe boundless air, smell the stench of refuse and fellow humans. A wildly affectionate sense of brotherhood enveloped him like a warm cloak. After a time, he'd realized that he was perspiring from shock. The image of Liliane danced elusively before his eyes, then faded. He'd fallen asleep.

He'd awakened to find a bony dog sniffing and licking the raw flesh of his face. Dazedly, he shoved away the dog, who snarled then slunk away. He had not thought any dogs would be left in Acre; this one must have been tough, ready to make breakfast of his corpse. He grimaced at the thought of his wrecked face, then winced. It was the morning of the surrender, a few refugees, wanting to stay ahead of the crowds and see the ceremonies at the gate, were beginning to filter through the bazaar.

He painfully got to his feet, every muscle screaming. His brain beginning to function again, he felt for his sword; it was still strapped across his back. He was faintly surprised it had not been filched by a ribald; but since his body had hidden the weapon, the bazaar riffraff must have thought he was a beggar. Strings of passersby were staring at him. If he'd had a shred of humor left, he would have given them a ghastly, mocking smirk. Stiffly, he fell in with the group, which edged away. He ignored them. Sooner or later, Liliane must appear at the gate if she placed any value on her life. Bleakly, he wondered if she *did* care what happened to her.

For hours, Alexandre had lurked by the gates, but saw no sign of Liliane in the heavy crowds. The crowds thinned and, under the high sun, the gates closed ominously. Sick with dread, he retreated into the city where he mounted an abandoned dwelling overlooking the wall adjoining the right side of the gate. The ditch where a band of Acre's wailing inhabitants had been massed was beginning to fill with bodies as Richard's executioners slit throats, turning the living into sprawled dead, fodder for flies. Desperately, he sought a glimpse of Liliane, but at this height, could recognize no one with certainty. His raw fingers locked in the geometric screen, Alexandre watched the chivalry of England, France and Jerusalem butcher nearly two thousand men, women and children.

Screams and dull red blood trickling in the dusty streets told the fate of hundreds more who had not wanted to leave their homes for the scorching desert. Bitter tears of hatred seared his face. Let Liliane be mercifully dead, he thought fiercely, that she may not see what she fought for. . . . His head slammed against the screen. No . . . God be merciful and keep her alive! Let not her beauty be sunk in this obscenity!

Finally, the mass in the ditch was still. Alexandre was not quite sure how long he'd clung to the screen; perhaps his mind had retreated into blackness again, this time as a refuge. His private, lonely hell was better than the one that multiplied like the facets of a fly's eye. In his hell he heard a hollow, primal wail as if the very desert beneath the city screamed in horrid, anguished warning. The building beneath his feet heaved and trembled, as did the screening beneath his fingers; but perhaps the shaking was only his mind, for when he braced to be swallowed by some cataclysmic upheaval, he found all was still. The air was still. His mind was still. Nothing was going to happen.

Perfumed death rose through the sunlight with a nauseous pervasiveness, like a slow caress across his face. Once, not far from here, he thought bitterly, men like this had raised a stench like this in Jerusalem. Part of the guilt is mine, his mind added miserably, for I helped make possible the destruction of these helpless wretches of Acre.

Alexandre's black despair was broken by the sound of feet moving quickly. The gates had opened to the victors, who were now taking possession of their spoils. He unlatched the screen; being found now would require him to answer too many difficult questions. Besides, he might kill the first European he met.

He left the tower and went far enough into the city to elude the first invaders. Upon reaching the Street of Clouds, a narrow byway of rich villas rising high above the wall that blocked out the sea, he took up a position in a house on one corner of the street's entrance. There, he awaited his steward, Yves.

Before attempting the city walls, he had given Yves instructions to take a house for him on this street. Yves and his retainers were not long in coming, for the best houses would fall to the first arrivals. When Alexandre stepped into the street, Yves

blanched. "Mother of God!" he exclaimed, raising his spear.
"What foul spirit are you!"

As the rest of the retainers took aggressive stances, Alexandre
gave a hollow laugh. "Have I so changed in a space of hours
that you do not scent one of your own wolf pack?"

"My God!" Yves gasped in mingled relief and horror. Behind
the steward, bows were hastily scraped, but the retainer's eyes,
round and uncertain, never left Alexandre. "My lord, we feared
you dead."

"And why not?" Alexandre's voice was cold and light. "Make
ready the small villa at the street's end. Steal whatever is lacking
from the other houses. Take any weapons." His orders were
given tonelessly, absently. Almost as an afterthought, he added,
"Go look in the ditch of Acre dead for Jefar el din. If you find
him, bring his body here." Then he walked up the street toward
the house he had chosen.

The steward and retainers stared at one another, still not completely convinced that they had found their master. This stranger
spoke good French, but his face was bloody clay; it might have
belonged to anyone, and yet . . . who but Alexandre de Brueil
would have wanted the heathen remains of Jefar el din? Upon
this evidence, they finally managed to accept the ravaged figure
as their own.

For the rest of the afternoon, Alexandre sat upon the awning-
covered roof of his new villa, looking out to sea. Occasionally,
he answered a query from Yves, but never did he look at anyone.
He waited for a scrape of the villa gates, the return of a litter
bearing what remained of Liliane. He had not the courage to
confirm her death himself. He knew with great certainty that if
he descended into that carrion, his wits would desert him forever. To find her there would be an end as final as an arrow
through his skull. At sunset, he sensed Yves behind him.
"Well?" he murmured.

"My lord, all is ready. Will you dine now?"

"Dine?" He had not eaten since noon of the previous day, yet
not even a murmur of hunger disturbed his stomach. "No. Celebrate among yourselves." He paused. "What word of Jefar el
din?"

"Naught, my lord. I sent two men who found no sign of him
there or upon the field. That is not to say he is not dead. Before

the men began to search, the guards had already thrown many corpses into the marsh."

Alexandre watched the flickering of the last red light on the water. It had long ago occurred to him that he might never know what had happened to Liliane; might never know whether she was dead or alive. That terrible uncertainty would be his punishment for the rash episode with Saida that had driven Liliane from him. Already the uncertainty was unbearable. "Leave me, Yves. I will see no one else tonight."

After Yves had gone, Alexandre waited until the last glimmers died from the sea and dusk was murky, then he rose in a single motion. In a few minutes, the rooftop was empty. Alexandre crept catlike over the tiled parapet of the neighboring house and vanished into Acre's labyrinth. He searched for Liliane but found only soldiers bent on making revelry, pillaging and finding whores. Drunken quarrels were rampant; street fights erupted, the sergeants blind to the disorder. In a few days, Richard would hang a few troublemakers to restore order, but that night the men were given no restraint. A few inhabitants who had escaped the afternoon slaughter were dragged from their hiding places and put to the sword. Women were raped and likewise dispatched.

Alexandre's absence from the villa did not go unnoticed. Yves, uneasy about his strange, depressed mood, crept to the rooftop an hour or so after darkness had fallen. After worriedly checking the cobbles on the street below, Yves searched the master bedchamber, then the rest of the villa. The guards confirmed that Alexandre had not left by the gate. Alexandre's peculiar behavior coupled with his disgrace in Richard's court might bring the whole household into difficulty. Yves called the servants together. "In the next day or so, admit no one to the villa and say the master is out, whether or not it is true."

"What if a summons comes from their majesties?" a hostler inquired.

"Say the count is ill with a shaking fever. No prudent soul who cares for his own health will demand proof."

Alexandre returned by dawn, but during the next few days, he pursued the habits of a vampire, spending his days hidden from the sight of man, his nights prowling the city and eating almost nothing. Yves and the household became convinced he was losing his mind.

During that time, they had a few callers, who left swiftly upon being told of Alexandre's ailment. A page sent from Philip inquired every morning after Alexandre's health. On Thursday, they received a caller less diplomatic: Louis de Signe. Signe refused to be turned away without seeing Alexandre.

"I come upon a private matter," he insisted. "It is most important."

Signe was the last person Yves wanted to admit to the house. Courteously, but firmly, he refused. "If you like, milord, I shall relay your message to the count when he is improved."

Louis scowled. "You would do well to grant me audience now, you presumptuous peasant. Delay upon this matter will cost your master ill, and you worse."

Yves spread his hands in Gallic helplessness. "What can I do, milord? I have my orders."

Louis grunted, looking thoughtful. "A few persons are beginning to suggest in Richard's court that your master may be dead"—he stared appraisingly at Yves—"and that his household wishes to keep its creditors away by pretending he is ill. Could that be so?"

Yves fidgeted. He knew perfectly well those "few persons" at court would be the Signes, eager to clutch at any straw in their hopes of finding Alexandre dead. "Milord, these rumors are unfounded," he protested. "I went over the household accounts myself this morning. We owe no one and have no reason to fabricate such a tale."

"You," Louis said grimly, "are a liar and a villain. The Brueil signet has been used twice already this week to establish credit at the brothel of the Gilded Leopard. The count was nowhere near the place and the accounting has not been paid."

"What!" stammered Yves, confused and horrified. Alexandre was not rich; in no way could he afford for some villain to run up bills in his name. "Milord's ring must have been stolen!"

"Stolen, bah! Who is to say you yourself are not responsible?"

"Me?" Yves was no longer able to hide his anger. "Me!"

"You are in charge of feeding Brueil's household, are you not? What do you suppose was purchased at the Leopard?"

Yves flushed red with irritated impatience. "We are both men, milord! What else would one want at the Leopard besides—"

"Milk!" Louis crowed triumphantly. "Milk, you thieving wretch!"

Yves turned utterly blank. "Milk? At the Leopard?" From an abyss of confusion, he found a feeble rebuttal. "Milord, we are men-at-arms. We do not drink milk."

"Ah-ha!" Louis marched off with his guardsmen.

Milk. Ah-ha. Louis de Signe. At length, Yves decided that matters had reached such a dire point that he must speak with his master. Gently. And hope that Alexandre had enough wits left to put the situation right.

"Milk," said Alexandre, after Yves had rather vaguely explained everything.

"Milk, milord." Yves's face took on a wistful air. "Can you make anything of it?"

Alexandre stared at his forefinger and meditatively twisted the signet that matched Liliane's ring. Then a slow smile began to creep over his face. "Children," he said softly. "Babies."

Yves's hopes sank. "Milord?"

Alexandre ignored him. His dark face had taken on the light of a sunrise. He leaped to his feet. "Babies! I might have known!" Firmly, he seized Yves and kissed him on both cheeks. "You splendid old fart! By heaven, I could almost kiss Louis today!"

You might better nest with the barn owls, Yves decided hopelessly. The featherdown of your poor brain wouldn't weight a moth.

Contrary to Yves's morose judgment, the moth had wisdom enough not to venture out until dark. Alexandre knew enough to remain bait. Louis had a whiff of something and it smelled of milk. Babies had to be fed frequently. If Liliane were aiding abandoned babies and had found a supply of milk at the Gilded Leopard, she would return there. Louis would lie in wait to capture the bearer of the signet for evidence; he would not carelessly carry a tale of Alexandre's death to Philip.

By nightfall, Alexandre had taken up a position at the open-air tavern across from the Gilded Leopard. He was scarcely settled when he spied a small, furtive shape scampering across the brothel roof. It disappeared into an upper-floor window. Another few minutes passed, then several of Louis's men filtered into the tavern and took places by its windows. They paid no attention to his scabbed, eye-patched face among the other battered ones gathered there. More of Louis's crew drifted to inconspicuous locations across the street. The small shadow emerged from the brothel window and, more swiftly than before, slunk across the tiles to jump to an adjoining rooftop.

"There's the little fox," hissed a man near Alexandre. "Let's go!"

Alexandre, who by this time knew the city by night better than Louis's men, led the chase. He followed at a discreet distance until the chase grew hot, always keeping himself between the fox and the hounds. With Alexandre close at his heels, the fox was joined by the rest of his litter; they conferred for a few moments under a wizened acacia, then raced off in a pack. Alexandre started after them, then heard a yell from across the tiny square.

"There they are!"

Thinking quickly, he yelled back, "You'll never catch me, you clumsy lummoxes!" And darted down the near alley.

"Who's that?" snapped a voice.

"Don't know," returned another. "Must be one of them. Let's split. You take that one, I'll take the kids."

"Oh, that's nice," the first retorted ironically. "I draw the only one big enough to use a sword!" He sped off after Alexandre, which was foolish, for he died two minutes later.

Alexandre returned to the square to recover the scent, but the children were taking sharp evasive action. They had lost their pursuit a few streets away. One pursuer was ferreting about the alleys when Alexandre strolled up to him. "Any signs of them?"

The guard took him for one of his companions. "No, but it may not signify much. Xenobia has a fair idea of where they'll go to ground. Come with me."

The guard led him to the cesspit on the far fringe of the bazaar. "We'll wait here for the others. They'll be along quick enough."

Alexandre looked at the black mouth of the cesspit. "The brats have been hiding in here, eh?"

"Here and a dozen other rat holes around here, likely. Thieving little bastards. It is time the city was cleaned of them."

But not by you, thought Alexandre, slipping out his dirk. One quick slit and he would be down the tunnel before the exterminators.

He was not quick enough; the pursuit arrived, first a few men, then small groups until they numbered above twenty. Louis was among them. He scanned the faces, probably to make sure he was getting his money's worth. His glance flickered over Alexandre, flickered back, then moved on. "Move quickly now," he instructed the men. "I do not wish to warn them." He divided the men into three bands. Alexandre and a few other men were to take the entrance near the bazaar, the others winging out a few squares beyond it.

Alexandre made sure he was in the lead, a small torch in his left hand, his neck prickling as he entered the monstrous blackness. He would have preferred to take on Saladin's whole army than enter the tunnels. His skin was as clammy as the stinking walls. He forced himself to move quickly ahead, blinking for his eyes to adjust. He had to reach the children before the other men located them.

Then he heard noises and high-pitched, furtive whispers ahead. The children! His throat tightened. He made an unnecessary splash, stepping into a puddle of muck, and scraped his sword along the wall, hoping to frighten the children away. The men behind him were too close. Hearing running footsteps ahead, he flung himself to the ground as if he had fallen accidently and blocked the tunnel. His torch went out, plunging them into blackness. "Hey, look out!" he called to avoid being trampled from behind. "I stumbled. Give me a minute."

Two men tumbled over him, barely catching themselves by grabbing at the walls. "Get up, you damned idiot," hissed one. "The brats are just ahead; you can hear them."

Alexandre fumbled at their knees. "Where?"

"Ahead you fool! Get up or I'll slit your gizzard where you are."

Alexandre sliced the thug's femoral artery. As the doomed man grabbed his leg and howled in terror, the men behind him hesitated. The sound echoed in the tunnel like the shriek of some vile monster.

Distracted by the racket, the other thug swung wildly with his sword at the murky darkness ahead of him. Alexandre's counterstroke took him off at the knees. Another guard came just behind him, then another, their torches silhouetting the man before them and leaving Alexandre to strike from the shadows. Alexandre backed up, taking them one at a time. His arms grew weary, his heart swollen, his hands bloody and treacherously slippery on his sword hilt. As he retreated inch by inch, he heard sounds of fighting behind him. Steel sang. Someone's sword was defending

the other end of the tunnel against Louis's mob, a Saracen sword
by the high music of it.

Alexandre redoubled his efforts, but knew that he could not
last more than a few minutes. He was too tired, and there were
too many of them. Then the sword behind him had ceased to
sing, and hideous silence reigned. He'd retreated quickly to over-
take the defender's vantage point before it swarmed with the
enemy and cut him off. In his urgency, he'd stumbled, fell backward upon a soft body. A lock of hair was silky beneath his
neck. A woman, he'd thought distractedly as he warded off a
blow that came down unexpectedly from his left. His arms heavy,
he'd dispatched his attacker, then shoved himself up. His whole
body tingled with the sensation of having touched someone familiar. He smelled a faint, elusive scent that inexplicably made
him long not to die alone—to see Liliane just once again. And
then a flicker of torchlight had distantly glimmered in the tunnel,
and beneath his bloody hands he saw the golden silk of her hair:
Liliane's hair. In the next heartbeat, he'd caught her to him and
fled with her.

Now . . . now he was staring at the debris blocking the tunnel,
and he was brought back to the present. Hope seeped out of him
like Liliane's blood over his fingers. He backed away from the
cave-in, stumbling down another tunnel. He heard the sounds of
Louis's men closing behind him. He came to a halt, knowing he
must turn now and face the baying pack if he were not to let
them take him and Liliane like cornered, toothless cats. In the
darkness, he imagined her hair in the sun as she worked on the
unicorn and golden leopard tapestry at Castle de Brueil. He
rubbed his cheek against the silky curls spilling across her shoulder. "We were fitter mates than I knew, my fair love," he whispered. "If there be a God, let Him have more mercy than justice,
and not keep me from you. . . ."

"Dither on," a youthful voice mocked nearly at his ear, "and
Allah will display his mercy quick enough."

At Alexandre's violent start, the voice crackled, and above a
small candle, the face was a disembodied mask of Pan. "Come
on, do you think we have all night to wait for those clods? Follow
and be quick!"

Alexandre, who had never in his life taken an order except
from father and king, did not pause to quibble. He followed with
desperate haste. His guide followed one tunnel after another with

the certainty of a ferret. Shielded by his leader, the candle glow was hard to follow, and he knew his and Liliane's own bulk would block it entirely from their pursuers. At length, they emerged behind the ruined mosque in the old quarter. In the faint moonlight, Alexandre was unsurprised to see a child before him. The boy looked as if he were about eleven, scruffy and hard-eyed.

"I am the oldest, so I stayed," the boy announced as if someone had accused him of some crime. He stepped closer, then swore. "So Jefar's a woman! I should have guessed. No man would have bothered with all those babies!" His voice held a sharp note of disillusionment, then turned husky. "That's a mess. She alive?"

Unoffended by the boy's bluntness, Alexandre shook his head tiredly. "I think so. I have not had time to find out how much damage has been done."

"Haven't got the time now, either. Come on. I know a place." The urchin headed into the ruined portion of the mosque, then down a steep, narrow flight of steps that crumbled away into a tiny room with a partly collapsed ceiling. One wall was a hill of rubble. "You were on the other side of this in the cesspit," the boy commented. Near the wall was inlaid a geometric design in colored stone. He pressed a triangle below the center, and without a sound even after centuries of neglect, the wall swung back a span. "In here."

In the light of the boy's candle, the dilated eyes of several children squatting on the floor looked enormous. Each of the children bore a baby on his back. One baby was awake, glassy-eyed and apathetic as if it had been given a narcotic. The children scrambled back in terror at the sight of Alexandre's clothes, crying in Arabic that he was an infidel. As he closed the stone, Alexandre's guide swore at them. "Shut up! Shut up, you gibbering monkeys. He's all right." Faint disgust edged his voice as he jerked his head at Alexandre's burden. "He came after *her.*"

"Her? Jefar el Din?!" Shocked curiosity got the better of fear as they stared.

Ignoring them, Alexandre laid Liliane on the floor and pressed his fingers to her temple. Their eyes on his pale, tense face, the children waited. "Well," the eldest finally demanded, "is she dead?"

"No," Alexandre replied softly. "Thanks to you, she is not."

"That ought to be worth a few dinars to you." The boy shrugged at Alexandre's hardening expression. "No need to be offended. She would pay me if she had any money left. Paid passage up the coast for most of the old wrecks and kids down there. Paid for them, too." The boy nodded at the other children. "Only they will not likely leave tonight." He gazed at Alexandre with complacent familiarity. "Where have you been, anyway? Chasing shadows?"

"All my life, I think." Alexandre tore cloth from Liliane's aba and began to pack it against the seeping wound in her side. Suddenly his head lifted. "Shh. I hear something."

The boy nodded and whispered, "Our friends from the tunnels. Do not worry; they cannot hear us if we keep our voices down."

"Are you certain?"

The boy nodded. "I found this place three years ago. Think I would not check it out?"

"Why did you not hide here instead of the cesspits?"

"If we are stuck here long enough, you will find out." He briefly held his nose. "No air after a few hours. Less with so many people. The air shafts must have stopped up with debris after a few centuries." He jerked his head toward a pile of crumbling bones in a dark corner. "When I found him, I knew something was wrong with the place. The problem wasn't the sealing block, so . . ." He sidled over to peer at Liliane's wound with the practicality of one accustomed to death. "Nasty." Liliane's hair fascinated him. "She is as much Turk as you. Why would she dress like a man to live in a sewer and look after a raggedy bunch like us?"

"She was weary of war and did not want anyone else to die."

"She is a little crazy, isn't she? In war, it is a lot easier to kill than save lives. Wars are for killing." He sat back on his heels. "She could fight, though. I never thought a woman could really fight." His head jerked around as one of the babies whimpered. "Shut that brat up! Give it some more wine."

They waited two hours; the air was becoming unbearably close. At length, Alexandre stood up. "I must go outside to see if our friends have left."

His savior, who called himself Raschid, jumped up. "No,

that's my job. I know the mosque and all the streets around here. I'll be less easy to spot than you."

Alexandre smiled. "Perhaps I should come along to guard your back."

"No, you should stay here and look after the children. If I do not come back, it will be up to you to get them out." He issued orders with the superior authority of one confidently aware he has saved another's life. His head lifted. "And do not worry. If they catch me, I shall not tell them anything."

Alexandre's smile softened. "I know." He tossed Raschid his dirk. "You may need this."

Raschid thumbed the jewel-studded hilt, then ran his thumb critically along the fine blade. "Not bad. We Saracens make better, of course, but this will do." He thrust the dirk in his sash. "Douse the light." When the candle went out, he opened the door, letting in a breath of fresh air, then the block closed behind him with a whisper.

Alexandre sat with Liliane and the children in the silent, stifling dark. A half hour passed; the air grew unbreathable again. He opened the block and peered into the darkness. Only rats rustled across the old mosque floors. Cautiously, he ventured out and checked the rubble at the rear of the building. Moonlight shone on the mounds as if they were dunes in the midst of the city. A scratch of stone sounded behind him. He whirled, his sword half drawn. "Hey!" came a rough, familiar whisper. "It's me. I've snitched a wagon. Bring your lady and the kids."

Alexandre wasted no time. No doubt about it, Raschid was a marvel. Commandeering a wagon must have been as easy as conjuring up a flying carpet.

"Got any place to take this bunch?" the boy queried when everyone was aboard his conveyance, a canopied contraption mounted on a ramshackle wagon pulled by a donkey.

"My villa. I will drive."

A few streets from the Street of Clouds, Alexandre jumped down from the driver's seat. "Take over, *mon brave*. I had better make sure we do not have company." He trotted toward the villa. Sure enough, at the villa gates Louis blustered with the remains of his cesspit crew. Yves was pale but determined. Atop the villa walls poised Brueil men-at-arms with crossbows.

Using his rooftop route, Alexandre slipped into his bedroom, rapidly stripped and pulled on a loose robe. As an afterthought, he hastily dunked his dirty face in the washbowl and wiped it on his sleeve. Then he adopted a sickly appearance and wandered out upon the villa roof to peer down at the crowd in the street. Startled, they stared up at him, Louis's black eyes filling with confusion, then anger.

"You are making a damned pest of yourself with your concern for my health, Louis," Alexandre called down querulously. "Enough racket is coming up to raise Lazarus. As you can see, I am up and about, so have the civility to be off."

His face nearly black, Louis started to say something, then thought better of it. "My apologies, my lord," he gritted. "Perhaps you had best have a talk with your steward about using your signet ring to run up his dairy accounts. 'Tis likely to cause peculiar rumors."

Alexandre casually held up his ring. "Never listen to gossip, Louis." He strolled from the rampart, leaving the muttering crew below to disperse. Looking down into his own courtyard, he summoned up three bowmen and a pikeman. He had redressed by the time they reached him. "Come with me."

He led them over the roofs to where the cart waited on the street. "Escort this cart to the harbor at cost of your life. The occupants will embark to Nahariya. Draw no attention to yourselves and their boarding. You, pikeman, climb in; that pike is conspicuous."

The pikeman pulled back the canopy, then started. Dark eyes stared at him in fear and hostility. "Milord," he stammered, "these are beggar brats!"

"Each worth his weight in gold." Alexandre ruffled a child's hair. "The little ones will be wanting their milk before they leave. See to it." Then, with the children's help, he carefully eased out the limp form of Jefar el din, whose telltale fair hair had been discreetly retucked into the stained haik. Her white face fell toward his chest, and the children eyed her with sad resignation.

"Hey!" Raschid called as Alexandre started to turn away. "You forgot your dirk!" Reluctantly, he thrust it forth.

"Keep it, but pry out the jewels, else they tempt unsavory characters."

"Huh, these baubles will be better than an invitation to a party." Raschid grunted in derision. "I am as unsavory as they come." He grinned and flicked the dirk tip. "Point taken, though. A jewel or two ought to set me up with my sister and a few likely wenches. Pity that blonde of yours is not in business; she would be a plum draw.'' He sobered. "A man with any stomach to him would not mind wedding a woman like her''—his eyes narrowed sternly—''and if you have not, you ought. I shall be back in a week to see if she is all right.''

"Point taken," Alexandre replied softly. He waited, watching until the cart rattled to the end of the street and rounded the corner. A few small, tentative hands waved from the canopy's back slit. His throat tightened as his eyes dropped to Liliane. If you must die, my love, you could have chosen no better cause, no better inheritors of all you valued in life. For these, Christ went to the cross with love and self-sacrifice. Who am I to judge, where He and you did not?

He carried Liliane to the main gate of the villa, and with a terrible sense of loneliness, waited for the servants to admit them. She was so quiet—Liliane, who had rarely been quiet. She had been filled with energy, never waiting for events to shape her, but rather shaping them. Had she never seen a sword, she would have been a fighter. She had gone on fighting until she had been beaten down more by him than by any enemy. She had lived for justice, and he, whom she loved most, had given her little, for pride had been his icy, faithless paramour. Now, for the rest of his life, he might lie with pride and find it bloated, mocking company.

The retainers were much startled and dismayed to see Jefar el din again. Having never trusted the Saracen, they also feared that Richard's favor would only decline further if Alexandre's harboring of Jefar were known. Yves fretted all the way up the stairs to the bedchamber. "If the Signes find out about this, they will squeal like pigs to Richard. They are just looking for something . . .''

Alexandre ignored him. He laid his burden down on the bedchamber pallet. "Close the door and curtains,'' he ordered.

With a sigh, Yves swept them closed and turned back to the bed to see Alexandre remove Jefar el din's haik. He gasped. "Mother of God! My lady! No, it's not possible! What demon has done this?''

"Demon, Yves? You have scant knowledge of women if you underestimate their capacity to change themselves from one form to another. They will do it on a whim, for revenge, for love''—

he stroked Liliane's cheek—"and this one has proven particularly willful."

"Milady followed you from France." Yves sat weakly upon the end of the pallet. "When I think . . ."

"Do not think. And do not talk—to anyone. Liliane has saved my skin from the Signes more than once in Palestine; they would kill her if they realized it."

Yves's homely little face became long. "In a whistle, they would." He flicked a glance at the blood staining Liliane's aba; from the expanse of the blotch, he feared that the Signes might be spared any future effort in dispatching their disloyal cousin. "Shall I send for a Hospitaler?"

"No, he would report to Richard and the news would leak; even Philip must not know that Liliane is here. Send me Vincent; he's done enough patching and stitching in his time."

Not enough for this, predicted Yves, but went along as he was bid.

Vincent was equally unoptimistic. "I've done my best," he said quietly when he was finished tending to Liliane's wound, "but, my lord, the cut is deep. I doubt your lady will live. Even a Hospitaler could not save her now, after such loss of blood."

"She will live," Alexandre said flatly. "Providence would not let me find her, only to have her die."

Providence is mysterious, thought Yves, particularly when one presumes to know its course. He and Vincent discreetly took their leave.

Alexandre tried to make Liliane more comfortable. She was beginning to stir restlessly as the pain of her wound penetrated her deep sleep. Though nearly as tall as he, she looked small now, as if shrunken in upon herself. Nights without sleep in the tunnels had told upon her; anyone who saw her beauty now must do so through the eyes of love. She was pale with the sickly cast of ivory; her eyes were stained beneath with shadow.

Alexandre was deeply troubled for want of a trained physician, but he knew that Louis would have the villa watched and be suspicious about the visit of a Hospitaler knight; also, Hospitalers commonly bled their patients, which from Alexandre's observation, commonly led to the patient's direct demise. Practical Vincent had better sense than the Hospitalers, but little knowledge of fine surgery. Liliane was still bleeding and in need of internal stitching beyond Vincent's skill. Also, in this climate, wounds festered quickly; a mere blister could turn deadly. With haunting doubts he would not voice aloud, Alexandre lay down beside Liliane and, for the first time since childhood, prayed.

Exhausted, Alexandre fell asleep, only to awaken perhaps an hour later to feel blood seeping between his fingers. Liliane was so terribly still that he feared she was dead. She must have stirred violently for the bandage was partly dislodged.

Fighting panic, he applied a new bandage; in less than ten minutes, it was nearly as sodden as the first. The wolfish phantoms in his mind now snarled like fiends. She *was* going to die! His prayers were as ashes, and no sun would rise for Liliane to end this dark night.

Her last memory of him for eternity would be his desertion. . . . He sank to his knees, feeling nothing, her lax wrist caught in his hand as he slumped against the bed. His mind blackened as the stain upon the bed linen widened. Her pulse was fading. She was going . . . where?

Shall I go before thee to that unknown? He wondered in despair. Shall I await thee with some candle burning to light thy way? He groped for the oil light upon the stone, then for the dirk, only to remember it was gone. Where was his sword? His fingers white on the clay lamp handle, he rifled the room for his sword with increasing impatience. I must find it, he thought tensely. She is leaving so quickly . . . where is the damned thing? It has always been ready enough to snatch a life! Yves . . . blast him, Yves must have taken it!

With a raging cry on his lips, he jerked open the door curtain . . . to see Raschid and a wizened Saracen. Raschid held up the dirk to show a gap in the jewels of its handle. "Old Ahmed does not work cheap on an infidel, but he is worth a small ruby. I thought you might be needing a physician, so I brought him in the cart."

Alexandre stared at them for a moment, then stepped back into the bedchamber. "Liliane is bleeding to death," he muttered vaguely, "and I have need of my sword. Yves has it. If you will excuse me, I must find him."

Raschid and the old man exchanged looks, then the physician went directly to the bed. "Never mind, I'll fetch your sword," Raschid soothed Alexandre, catching his arm as he started to leave. "You stay here. Ahmed may need your assistance." He propelled Alexandre toward the bed, then scurried out of the room to find Yves.

Yves was sitting morosely in the kitchen, applying himself to a large wine flacon. "Have you got your master's sword?" Raschid demanded in gutter French.

"Who the hell are you, you dirty twerp?" slurred Yves over the flacon.

"I'm not a drooling drunk neglecting his duties," Raschid cut back.

"Who's neglecting his duties?" Yves unsteadily waved Alexandre's sword with a regal air. "Everything is in control."

"Good lad," Raschid approved archly. "I suppose you can even boil water."

"Naturally."

"Then apply yourself to a pot, man! Your lady is in need of it." He strode off.

When he reached the master bedchamber, Raschid cast a sharp look at Alexandre, who hovered at Ahmed's elbow while he plied his needle. Alexandre had a curious air of calmness now, which Raschid was not sure he liked. He smiled at Alexandre reassuringly. "Yves is cleaning your sword. When you want it, just sing out and I'll bring it up to you."

Alexandre's patient eyes seemed to reply: You lie, but I can wait.

Raschid moved to the bed. Standing at Alexandre's side, he divined the cause of his uneasiness. Alexandre's body held the tension of an arrow ready to be loosed from a bow. "How does it go?" Raschid murmured to the physician.

Ahmed fixed a grim red-rimmed eye on him. "Would you care to put a dirty finger or perhaps milord's toe on my suture knots? I have so much assistance I cannot concentrate. Please take this edgy young gentleman for a walk."

"We must humor the old man," Raschid gently advised Alexandre, taking his arm. Alexandre did not resist and followed him quietly out onto the upper patio overlooking the sea. "Have you slept? Eaten anything?" Raschid inquired of him. Alexandre merely looked at the water. "I see." Raschid waved down at the gate guard. "Tell your Yves to send up wine by way of our good doctor. Hear that, Ahmed? We shall have wine with the special spices I brought." The only reply from the bedchamber was a grunt.

Raschid heaved himself up on the wall to smile reassuringly at Alexandre. "Your lady may get well, yet. Old Ahmed's stubborn as a goat. I learned long ago to pay him in advance; then he will lie on nails rather than lose his patient. A matter of professional pride. . . ." He went on chatting until the wine arrived. He poured a gobletful from the pitcher and handed it to Alexandre. "Come on, it will do you good. You may have a very sick patient to look after during the next week or so, you know. You cannot help her if you are laid out flat."

Indifferently, Alexandre drank. Less than a quarter hour later, he was flat on his back. Fleetingly, before he passed out on the rooftop, he remembered that Mohammedans did not touch liquor. Old Ahmed the goat and Raschid the liar had drugged him. Not only that, they kept him drugged until Liliane took a turn for the better.

Three days is a long time for a man to stay drunk; even Yves lacked that much ambition. Though he fussed and fumed about the presumptuous usurpers in his household, he delivered soup with the regularity of an hourglass and went back to brazenly bullying Philip's page, whose inquiries had grown tiresomely pressing.

On the fourth morning, Alexandre awoke with the sun in his eyes and his own stench in his nostrils. When he groggily thrust himself up on his elbows, his head screamed like a stabbed gull. With a moan, he fell back down. The padding of sandaled feet sounded by his head. He shuddered and grabbed at an ankle. Raschid danced neatly out of reach. "Good, you're up and about. You look fit enough to be hanged."

"If I ever get my hands on your miserable throat," Alexandre whispered hoarsely, "I am going to throttle you more surely than any rope." He rolled over and vomited, scarcely able to lift his head high enough to keep from choking himself. When he was done, he took a deep, unsteady breath, then abruptly, harshly remembered. "Is Liliane . . . ?"

"See for yourself."

Alexandre dragged himself to his feet and wove to the curtain which was half open to admit a breath of sea air to the sickroom. Liliane lay quietly, her chest gently rising and falling. "She's asleep," Alexandre muttered unevenly. He absently rubbed the stubble at his jaw; from his beard length, he guessed that three, perhaps four days had passed.

He stumbled forward to take Liliane's hand as if it might break in his fingers; her hand was warm. She stirred, her stupor beginning to lift. Very soon now she would awaken. "Sweet God," he whispered. "Sweet God, bless that toad, Ahmed, for eternity."

"What about me?" prodded Raschid, lounging in the doorway.

"You, I am going to strangle with silver gloves and send to pimp for houris who will make you the richest guttersnipe in heaven."

Raschid laughed. "I want a melon-titted fat one for myself."

Alexandre started to laugh, too, then his expression abruptly altered. He retched again, in dry heaves. "Why," he muttered at last, "when there are a dozen more gentle drugs he might have used, did Ahmed have to poison me?"

"He made the selection at my request. A man whose gut is miserable cannot concentrate upon losing his mind."

"You damned, diabolical . . ." Alexandre held his aching head. "I owe you more than my life, Raschid. I am not rich, but I shall try to give you whatever your greedy, magnificent heart desires. Name your reward."

Raschid grinned as he watched Liliane stir again. "Oh, do not worry. You can afford it." Without more ado, he sauntered to the bed, leaned over it, and placed a leisurely, precociously expert kiss on Liliane's lips.

For several moments, Liliane did not move, then her eyelids flickered and slowly opened. Dazedly, she stared up at the boy. "What . . . was that for?" she queried with a faint smile.

Raschid winked. "To demonstrate the advantages of embracing a man rather than a sword, Madame. I hope you have learned your first lesson." Giving an elaborate sigh, he inclined his head toward Alexandre. "With my deepest regrets, this retching, unwashed lout of a Frenchman must conduct the bulk of your studies." He lifted her hand and kissed it. *"Au revoir, Madame la Comtesse.* A pity we did not meet in your youth." With a flamboyant bow and superior smile for Alexandre, he departed.

"In your youth," Alexandre murmured dryly, "he was dragging his diapers and teething on whores' ankles."

He had meant to make Liliane laugh, but she did not. She had not even looked at him. Then slowly her head turned and her lovely eyes met his. "It was you . . . in the tunnel."

"Like your laggard but faithful wolfhound." He took her hand. "Saida is gone. I gave her to Philip. She was quite willing to go to his bed, having never known mine. She is with him yet, if he has not tired of her."

"As you have tired of me," Liliane whispered. "Duty is dry fare when one has known feasts." Her hand lay lax in his.

"Do you think I searched all Acre, from the minarets to the very sewers, for you out of duty?" Alexandre kissed her fingers. "Can you imagine how delighted I was to hear that the prestigious Brueil signet was being used to buy milk at a whorehouse?"

"Are the children safe?"

"They are now in Nahariya." His voice lost its forced levity. "You saved many innocent lives, Liliane. Even Raschid is grateful, for once in his cynical life."

"You saved us. I owe you thanks," she replied faintly.

"Give your thanks to Raschid." He told her of being lost in the cisterns, of the cart and old Ahmed. "Never was there a kiss more unselfishly earned than the one Raschid claimed, and little enough reward for all his brave service."

"Then he has served us more wisely than we serve Philip," she murmured obliquely, "and evaded the chains of gratitude."

Hearing the note of strain and fatigue in her voice, Alexandre stroked her brow. "Sleep now. Forget the war and Philip. Forget everything but that you must rest and heal, and that I love you." He kissed her softly, then began to hum an old French lullaby; whether from the lullaby or her exhaustion, he did not know, but in moments she was asleep.

14

Golden Earrings

During the next few weeks of convalescence, Liliane could not forget the war. Through her restless dreams swarmed armed men, terrified women and homeless children, as well as her own phantoms of her beloved parents and Diego. Mockingly, Saida danced before her and multiplied into a thousand laughing, triumphant images. Then she saw hard blue sky and the rising sand of a desert storm. The storm spiraled down into a quicksand that was sucking her into its suffocating maw, and Jacques and Louis, Philip and Richard watched her as if she were an unnatural insect being dispatched. About her in the pit, those who had been massacred outside the Acre gates were feebly struggling. She was enveloped in choking blackness that became a cistern tunnel where she fought deadly, hideous shadows that advanced as crawling serpents. No matter how many she vanquished, more appeared until their segments upon the stones were multiplying like maggots. Alexandre fought beside her, but when she gratefully turned to him, she saw that his arms rose and fell as if weighted with lead. His eyes were cold and distant, yet he defended her mechanically. "No, no!" she cried. "Alexandre, it must not be like this!" Then a sword flashed in the darkness, and just before it struck her down, she saw that it was his.

"Liliane!" Alexandre's voice was near her ear, his arms were about her. She struggled, trying to fend him off, but his arms tightened. "Liliane, it is me. You are safe, my darling. You are having a nightmare."

290

Liliane's head jerked, then she let out a distracted sigh and opened her eyes. Alexandre was cradling her, trying to soothe her. "You see, I am here. I shall always be here for you. . . ."

Even if part of you has learned to hate me, she thought dazedly.

At the end of the second week, Liliane's pallet was moved to the awning-covered roof, where she was able to sit propped up on pillows and find relief from the heat that built by noon in the bedchamber. Gratefully, she let the sea breeze wash over her face and throat and arms, bare for once of Jefar's aba in the light of the sun. Bathed and oiled, her body was loosely clad in a sleeveless, white cotton chemise Raschid had brought as a gift from his sister.

With her golden hair hanging in a straight fall down the back of the pillow stack, she felt warm, disembodied, sexless, as if she had ceased to exist; both Liliane and Jefar were gone. They had died in the darkness somewhere beneath Acre. And now, who was this lost and aimless spirit that remained? This walker of gray, drifting clouds that dimmed the sun and shadowed the earth? This shell that belonged to neither earth nor hell nor heaven? Love's loss had emptied her and set her free . . . now she was without purpose, without anchor.

Where hast thou gone, my heart, that you no longer beat within me? she wondered sadly. My eyes see the sun, yet merely frame its shape. My hands may touch another's flesh, yet feel nothing. Like Diego, I dwell in some other place beyond mourning. My own Alexandre has become a shadow filled with echoes. I would summon him close but cannot, so uncrossable is our distance. I would call to him, yet hear in return only my own despairing voice. I have become like the Greek nymph Echo, whose endless cry must fade unheeded.

Liliane heard Alexandre's familiar footsteps on the narrow stair that mounted the courtyard wall of the villa. Quietly, he walked to the pallet and, seeing she was awake, sat cross-legged beside her. "I have brought you something from the bazaar. A few Saracen vendors are back; it is beginning to look normal again."

"Normal." She spoke the work with quiet puzzlement.

"I know." He stared long into her eyes, then out to the sea. "Storms pass quickly and leave little behind of their passing. The new scars are already fading on the city stones and in the streets; missing faces will soon be forgotten. A mother, a lover, a friend will remember the dead for too short a lifetime."

"History will remember what lies in that ditch beyond the wall," she observed tonelessly. "When lions become jackals, all nature is offended."

"I watched the kill," Alexandre said softly. "Never before have I wished I were of another species." His blue eyes darkened. "For a time, I feared you were among those massacred." For a moment, he appeared to be about to continue, then he held out a small silk-wrapped parcel. "For you. I hope you like them."

With slow fingers, Liliane undid the wrapping. A pair of golden earrings of fine, gold wire with tiny, ingeniously wrought birds and inlaid flowers of lapis lazuli lay upon the silk. "They are beautiful." She looked at him directly. "Are they to turn me into a woman again?"

His eyes held hers, then he picked up one of the earrings and traced the clever shape of the bird. "Art cannot improve upon nature . . . yet artistry has its own rare voice, its strength to outlast wars, religions and epochs. These bits of gold were wrought for an exquisitely feminine woman, that all who see her may remember that great beauty and compassion sometimes grace our grotesque humanity." He lay the earring in her open hand resting upon the pallet. "A thousand years from now, another dusty, disenchanted warrior may so hope to adorn his love with these pretty birds and flowers. In their night, the warrior and his lady will wonderingly muse upon the ancient lovers who first delighted in so fanciful a gift. I have asked much of you; will you yield me yet another boon and wear my tokens?"

"Was ever a gift so beautifully given?" she murmured. "And yet, I fear I may not in honor accept it. In these last months I have done murder in the name of love and loyalty. From this life I sent many a soul with whom I had no grievance. My hour of the sword is done; my penance now begun. 'Twill not be long before Richard will carry this crusade from Acre and spend it upon the length and breadth of Palestine, but I shall not see it." Her lovely eyes darkened. "You shall have your wish at last, Alexandre. When I am healed, I shall leave the Holy Land."

A mixture of stunned relief and dismay filled Alexandre's eyes. "I know not what to say. I have dreamed of you safe in Provence . . ."

"I shall not return to Provence, but to my own country."

He caught his breath as if it pained him. "To Spain? But why? There is no need . . ."

"I have a need to see my home again."

"Provence is your home."

"No. I wanted to make it so, but that was the sweet delusion of a young bride. I am not wanted at Castle de Brueil and I do not feel young anymore, Alexandre, but very old; as old as Diego when he died. Not only my body but my spirit must heal; for that, I must go back to the land and people that offer me honest welcome."

"Am I no part of you?" he asked hoarsely. "Can you not look to me for sustenance?"

Liliane's heart felt as if it were cracking. The part of her that was Alexandre was the only part of her that was cruelly alive, burning as if scourged. The pain would burn with increasing harshness as long as she lived with him and let the remains of their love be stripped away. "No. We must go our different paths, Alexandre; I to Spain and you after Philip. I think destiny laughed the day we met."

Alexandre argued against her going to Spain as Liliane knew he would; he left no tack untried. She was grateful for his determination but remained resolute. Finally, he resorted to her sense of duty. "What of Diego? What of your cousins whom you have resolved to punish? With you in Spain, they will continue their crimes."

"I have learned many hard lessons in Palestine, Alexandre: one is that murder cannot punish murder; another is that you are quite competent to deal with my cousins. For all good intentions, my interference in that area has never been welcome, and in sum, I have proven more troublesome to you than the Signes themselves. If Philip discovers you have hidden me all this time, your difficulties may become permanent."

"Aye, he might banish me back to France." Alexandre earnestly caught up her hand. "If you were there, I should reckon myself well out of favor and thank him in my heart."

"Philip knows your heart well enough, Alexandre, and he knows best how to keep it. He will have you, willing or not, at his side. He is France, whose lilies frame your soul. True, I might wait at Castle de Brueil while Philip witches you away, for years . . . withering years of loneliness and loss. But I am not so strong as you may think. For all my parading in a man's guise, I am a woman with a woman's needs. I have found I cannot bear . . . loneliness.'' She paused, fighting for a steady tone, though her mind was blurring with pain. ''I want an annulment, Alexandre. Philip will be only too glad to arrange it with his bishops, as he did his own annulment from Queen Ingebörg to marry Lady Agnes.''

Alexandre's face went dead white, but he said nothing. His silence grew frighteningly long.

''Alexandre,'' she asked at last, ''do you agree?''

''Why not?'' he replied tonelessly. ''I have given you little enough in land and titles, less of happiness, and nothing of security. I can offer no future but my wandering and desertion. One of us must be wise.'' He glanced down at the earrings. ''If you will not wear my gifts for honor, then one day wear them for love remembered.'' His eyes were inky now as if a dark storm were rising in them. ''Upon that day, I will love you as I did the first moment I saw your hair in firelight, heard your first trill of laughter. The night will forever blind me, for in its stars, I shall ever see your eyes when they were full of love for me. This was mine . . .'' His voice shaking, he abruptly drew away. A moment later, his boots sounded on the stone steps. She heard him call a curt order to the gatekeeper; the bar scraped up to let the gate creak open, then he was gone.

Liliane turned into the pillows and sobbed.

Sometime later, she heard a muted sound. Thinking it was Alexandre, she lifted her head. Raschid's dark eyes studied her with more shewdness than she liked. Kiki, who rode on his shoulder, took dates from him but kept her soulful eyes on Liliane. ''I saw the *comte* in the street. He had all the cheer of gallows bait. Methinks you are well enough to quarrel.''

Her face stiffened at the unaccustomed sternness in Raschid's tone; she had become used to his spoiling her. ''Alexandre and I owe you much, Raschid, but not explanations for our private life.'' She gingerly eased herself up on the pillows. ''Will you take tea with me?''

''Tea.'' The word sounded like a click. ''A tepid brew, served in your European fashion.''

''Shall I stiffen it to rigor mort with honey, as you Saracens like it?''

He caught up a loose pillow, then dropped cross-legged on it.

"A taste of honey might not be amiss around here. And as for rigor mort, why not drop your Alexandre in the cup?"

"Raschid . . ."

He held up a hand. "No lectures, please. If I could bear instruction, I would be in school. Call Yves and order up your vile tea; I have at least learned by now I shall get no wine."

She lifted a tolerant brow. "You have no more religion than learning. Do you never fear for your impious soul?"

"Shall I look to you for catechism?" His eyes were ironic.

She laughed faintly. "No, I suppose not. Still, you may look to me for any help you ever need." She paused and her mood turned a shade shy. "Would you ever consider coming with me to Spain?"

"To flirt with bulls? Why should I?"

"I have no child, Raschid," she replied slowly. "If I were to choose a son, I would choose you."

He gauged her seriousness, then replied quietly, "I am greatly honored, but my home is in the Crescent. One day the death-worshiping Spaniards will force the Moors from Spain and turn the whole country into a bloated corpse; even lice do not love to dwell upon corpses. Besides," he added lightly, "if I were to choose a mother, I would not choose you. My intentions would not be properly filial." He watched her smile sadly, then went on. "Also, a woman unfit to be a wife is unfit to be a mother. A certain generosity is wanting."

Her head turned sharply. "What do you mean by that?"

"What I said. Your husband is not a happy man. I should think that has something to do with you. Don't you love him?"

Abruptly, she rang the brass servants' bell. "Shall we change the subject, Raschid?"

"No, I like it well enough," he replied equably, "and if you are beginning to debate whether to have Yves serve tea or throw me out, be assured I shall raise an embarrassing uproar."

Liliane sighed. "I do not wish to throw you out, Raschid, but you are infernally impertinent."

He grinned. "It's part of my charm. Would you want a sheep for a son? I am fond of you in my fashion, though I lust for you more than is strictly polite. That Frenchman you married has his faults, but he is not a clod to be trodden underfoot. He is flat this day, I tell you, quite flat. I ask again, with the greatest of delicacy, is your dainty foot to blame?"

She sighed with depressed resignation. "I am returning to Spain, Raschid. Alexandre and I shall live apart until he is able to procure an annulment."

He wrinkled his nose. "Nasty word, annulment. So final."

"Yes," she replied bleakly, "it is that."

"Ah, I understand now"—he nodded sagely, watching her face—"the two of you are going to get an annulment neither of you wants; that sounds quite sensible."

Yves appeared at the head of the stair. "You rang, Countess?"

"We would like tea, please, Yves, with plenty of honey."

Yves closed his eyes in disgust. "As you like, Countess." He trotted down the stairs.

Raschid resumed the attack. "Why an annulment? Surely a skewer to the offending giblets is much quicker."

She ignored his sarcasm. "Alexandre does not love me. At least, not as much as he thinks he does . . . as much as he did. . . ."

"Better and better. I ask for sense and you give me the maundering of a butterfly." He handed Kiki a date.

Liliane glared at him. "*Will* you let me talk, you infernal little tyrant?" And so she did, in a way she could not to Alexandre or any other living person. All her shredded hopes, and battered illusions came pouring out. She and Raschid had walked the edge of death together. He was her celibate lover, her child and caustic friend. By ingenuity, he had saved her life, and some lost part of her prayed that he might save her love.

Raschid listened in silence while their tea arrived and, untouched, turned stone-cold. "Give heed to me now," he said quietly at last. He told her of a man gone nearly mad for love of her, of his rigid fear at her bleeding, of his stark, stumbling terror that he would lose her. "If you would be done with your Frenchman, let him follow Philip on his next campaign for he will not return." He stood and patted her hand. "Think on it. Nothing is so hopeless as the first handful of dirt cast on the dead."

After he left her, Liliane *did* think—hard and long. Then she fastened Alexandre's earrings in her ears.

Alexandre was late in returning. When he did not find Liliane in the bedchamber, he went quickly out to the rooftop, only to find her pallet vacant as well. He looked around the roof, anxiety edging his voice. "Liliane?"

"Here, on the parapet," she called softly. "When the clouds uncover the moon again, you shall see me perched here like an owl waiting for mice."

"Ever the huntress," he murmured as he noted her dim silhouette against the night sky. He went to the parapet and sat down a little distance from her.

"Come closer," she whispered. "Louis is having the villa watched. See, a beggar with little possiblity of clients is a little way down the street. For a blind man, he stares this way a great deal."

Alexandre took a place beside her. Her nearness made him sick with a loss that no wine in the Acre inns had been able to assuage. He had not the heart for getting drunk, so he had sat quietly on a street corner, much as yonder false beggar, and watched the flow of crowds, the stream of resurgent life through the city. He felt apart from humanity these days; even Liliane's return had not altered his detachment. Today, he had wanted to reach out to someone—some stranger filled with vitality, some brightly dressed child, and talk of inconsequential things, complain of the price of mutton, admire a toy. He wanted to snatch at the normal life he had rarely known, win back Liliane and go home. Instead, Liliane would return to Spain and he would go on marching across Palestine. I am never going to see her again, he thought, the knowledge hanging upon his heart with dull, murderous weight.

"Alexandre," Liliane said quietly, "I had a talk with Raschid. Even as a child, he seems to be wiser than either of us. Certainly, he sees life more simply than we do, perhaps because he is not in love." She touched his hand. "Quite simply, I love you. If you still want me, I will wait for you in France."

He stared at her, thinking that he must have heard her amiss out of wishful dreaming. "You do not want an annulment?"

"I never did. I only wanted you . . . and one other thing, perhaps."

"My love," he said huskily, "for you I will pluck down the moon for your mirror, bring back the jewels of Babylon to light your hair, tell another thousand impossible lies . . . for grace of heaven, do you mean it?"

"With all my heart."

The look in her eyes made him tremble. As if she were a mirage that might disappear, he touched her cheek, traced a smile that in the darkness was shy, mysterious. "What would you have of me, my love? You need but name your desire, with my heart for a plate."

"Your confidence is reassuring, milord," she teased gently. "What say you to getting your wife with child?"

"You want a baby?" He was startled but delighted.

"Or five."

His hand covered hers. "I never knew you wanted children. You have never spoken of them, and I assumed that your mind was too full of Diego and your cousins to entertain a family."

"To some extent, that is true. I dared not dream of complete happiness when so much remained undone. Any heirs of yours would be a threat to Jacques's ambitions to acquire your fief, and yet I cannot know when that threat may be ended. Years may pass, until hope for children passes with them. Diego and I could have none; it was my one great disappointment in our marriage." She laid her head on Alexandre's shoulder. "I desperately want a child of yours, Alexandre. So much has been lost in Acre; we might have lost each other, as well. If I must share you with Philip, I will have your children to love, that our love may not be too far separated." Then, as if uncertain of where she had lighted, her head lifted, her eyes anxious. "Do you want babies, Alexandre?"

He smoothed her hair. "I have always wanted them; I only thought that you might not. Today, when I watched children in the street, they seemed a promise of hope, each new life a chance of making the world fresh and good-hearted, with no kindness and gallantry wanting." He paused before continuing. "Despite all our love, we have never committed to each other, rarely talked of our deepest needs; that we finally confide our want of children is the proof. Love came so easily to us that we have not seen the need of endeavoring to sustain it. We have taken love's flower and let its seeds scatter where they might in heedless trust that new blooms will ever spring forth." He touched her flat belly. "Here I will plant my seed of love with care and devotion, then watch over you tenderly. Be sweet earth to my rain and sun, and within a single span of seasons, our miracle may unfurl with all the joy of new and remembered paradise."

"Hold me close, my darling," Liliane whispered, "for I would dream of that joy and have long missed your arms about me."

Enfolding her in his arms, Alexandre cradled her. "You will stay with me, then? These little birds of gold that sing in your ears do not lead me to false hope?"

"Nay, I shall not run away again," she whispered. "Coward that I was, I am done with running. Whatever the future holds, I shall meet it, so long as it holds you."

His lips lowered upon hers and the old moon shone full upon them. A quick pulse beat between them, the rhythm of desire and impatience. Their kiss grew as hot as the moon was cool, their limbs heavy with passion, yet never did they move. The silk of Liliane's hair was crushed gold in Alexandre's dark fingers. Then, heart to heart, he swept her up with gentle yet fired intent. From moonlight to darkness, he carried her swiftly.

White linen spilled, then Liliane's ivory skin bared to Alexandre's tawny embrace. Long was their kiss, sleek and slow was their bodies' intertwining, the play of his dark fur upon her golden pelt. Secret places were caressed, tasted. All languor vanished as they conducted a trembling, delicate invasion. Passion's tender spies gained eager welcome, lured sweet treacheries that persuaded surrender. Tiny sprites of the moon danced in soft celebration upon pillow and wall, an ancient dance of lovers' joining, of conquest and glad defeat when two become one upon the field of delight.

Ghosts of lovers past seemed to hover near in the streams of moonlight, their smiles at once sad and pleased. Wraiths of myth these lovers parted in life to wander lost, only to find remembrance through living lovers' lips. Their murmurings echoed the sea waves with silken, somnolent sighs. Sweet, sweet, ah, sweet, return.

Upon this sea-sounded desert night, Liliane and Alexandre were aware only of each other. Their well-known bodies were newly formed, the pungent earth of their desire new-loamed and forgetful of past strife. Alexandre's ripened hardness found warm haven. Liliane threw her head back, her body arched and eager to receive his gentle, ever deepening thrusts. Their rhythm became a surging, a slipping of earth into sea. Wave upon wave of exquisite sensation washed over them, scattering their realities, renewing their need. Foam laced their bodies, spun them into one glittering rise of spume. The pinnacle was a wet, white light that hovered unbearably, only to spill at last against a beckoning shore. For a long while, they lay in each other's arms, listening, for in the sea they heard a singing harp, high and unbearably sweet.

" 'Tis Orpheus seeking his Eurydice,'' Alexandre murmured, burying his face between Liliane's breasts. "Poor fool. I think I should have followed thee as far as he his lost love.''

"Fie on Eurydice that she lured her lover to such endless sorrow,'' Liliane returned softly. "Fie on me who brought you to such a despair.''

"Could I choose, I would not love you less, my darling.'' He chuckled wryly as he turned upon his back. "Was youthful passion ever prudent?''

Liliane rose on her elbow to look down at him and affected a solemn tone. "Why, my good fellow, we have been two years married. Is not prudence merely a matter of time? Piffle to enduring passion, I say.''

"What do you say?'' He rose up and pressed her onto her back with a wickedly intent stare.

"Piffle,'' she replied in a stifled tone, "piffle, piffle . . . piffle . . .'' He kissed her. When his head lifted, she dragged him down again. "Prudence can stay in its own mud puddle.''

The next days were halcyon, for Alexandre and Liliane were alone together beneath a silent sun in a serene cerulean sky. Only for meals did they summon a servant to the roof. Melons, lemons, grapes and olives mounded a brass tray beneath the canopy. The juice was cool and untouched. Their hours of lovemaking were spangled with poetry read from Alexandre's battered book; their lazy naps were interrupted by massaging each other with scented oils. They sang, they laughed, but most vitally, they talked. Childhood secrets were told, disappointments and joys recounted. For the first time in their marriage, they were free of intruding responsibilities, free to love without hindrance.

"What goats we are,'' Liliane teased one afternoon as they lazed together on the pallet just beyond the canopy.

Alexandre's grin flashed white in his darkly tanned face, then he stretched in unrepentant satisfaction. "I must concede some merit to pagan bacchanalia.'' He popped a grape in his mouth. "Ah, gluttony and sloth.'' He swatted her lightly on her bare bottom. "All hail, sweet lechery.''

"Hail, hail." She laughed, turning over to face him nose to nose. "How many times have we made love in the last four days?"

"I have not counted." He kissed her lingeringly. "Why do we not start again, so I can bite tiny notches on your earlobes . . . and shoulders . . . and throat and—"

Liliane's giggle was cut off by the sound of voices at the foot of the steps. A clipped, imperious tone subdued Yves's oddly querulous one. She sat bolt upright in dismay. "Philip!"

As she grabbed for her shift, Alexandre snatched up his loincloth. Hearing footsteps start up the stairs, they both looked desperately about for a place to conceal Liliane, but Philip was already in view—followed by Saida. Saida's jaw dropped; Philip, more accustomed to hiding his reactions, stared at Liliane briefly, then his lips curved in a thin smile.

"I should have known that you had more diversion than a fever, milord, but then perhaps your fever has broken, only to be replaced by another." He strolled forward and kissed Liliane's hand. "My compliments, Countess. The southern sun agrees with you . . . much better than a Turkish stain."

"Thank you, Your Majesty." Liliane forced her hand to remain steady in his grasp, for like a cat playing with a mouse, Philip showed no inclination to let her go. Now he was eyeing Alexandre with a thoughtful air that prickled her neck.

"May I ask how long your countess has been with us, milord?"

"She accompanied me from France, sire," Alexandre replied evenly.

Not about to let him shoulder responsibility for her, Liliane added quickly, "I came to Palestine against my husband's wishes and knowledge, sire."

"But not without his most grateful welcome," Alexandre finished unperturbedly. Ignoring the fact that Philip was still holding Liliane's hand, Alexandre warmly clasped the other.

Philip languidly released Liliane's fingers. "Any man would be gratified by such lovely company. What a pity to dress this beauty as a Turk." He dropped cross-legged onto their abandoned pallet and waved to Saida, whose surprise had given way to sullenness. She settled next to Philip and glared at Liliane with open loathing. "You have kept your pretty secret well, Alexandre, *mon ami*. Am I the only fortunate who is party to it?"

"Other than Derek Flanchard, yes, sire," Alexandre lied. If Philip decided to make trouble, Alexandre would keep the men of his raiding party clear of it.

"Ah, yes, Derek the Deceased; at least, I assume he is deceased; he never struck me as the sort to miss the kill, far less the profit. Did you, by any chance, dispatch him?" Philip's green eyes held a dangerous gleam.

"He attempted to force himself on my wife," Alexandre answered flatly. "I merely relieved her of the necessity of sticking him."

"Tsk. I would not have thought Flanchard such a lecher. His brain always seemed cast in steel. Ah, well, my mistake. I am too often misled in gauging men." After that pointed remark, Philip slid a glance at Saida, who now was draped over his shoulder. "I came, venturing to return a certain loan to you. I see I may now consider the obligation unnecessary."

"Indeed, sire," replied Alexandre. "The loan was more in the nature of a gift."

Saida, unable to comprehend a word, watched them with suspicion. Philip patted her knee. "I thank you, but I would be gratified if you would accept full repayment. The debt is more than I can endure; restitution alone will let me rest. My nights grow wearisome, my mind dulled for daily duties, et cetera, et cetera, et cetera." His set smile stated clearly: Take the bitch.

"If you insist, sire," Alexandre replied grimly. Saida's return could only cause trouble . . . and delight Philip. The trouble was already beginning, for Liliane had disengaged his hand.

"Do you like Acre, Countess?" Philip inquired sweetly as he observed Liliane's sudden coolness.

"Very much, sire, now that the siege is over."

"I confess that I find the city dull these days, but then I lack a woman's liking for peace." He rose and kissed her hand again, then purred over her signet. "Enjoy your stay, Countess, but mind you stay out of the sun; it ages European ladies." With a touch of his forehead to Alexandre, he trotted down the stairs.

That she had been abandoned quickly dawned on Saida. She ran to the wall to glare down into the street as Philip joined his retainers. A string of Saracen oaths were cast upon their heads, drawing a peal of laughter from Philip. With a kiss of his fingers, he turned his back on her. Saida rounded on Alexandre with an explosion of Arabic.

Sighing, he summoned Yves. "Fetch Raschid. Tell him I have a young lady here who is ripe for a business proposition."

In less than two hours, Saida was out of Brueil hands and into Raschid's. Neither Raschid nor his new acquisition was eager to long remain partners in trade. She was miffed that having been a king's concubine had not sufficiently impressed Raschid, and he knew a virago when he saw one. "I'll rent her out," he confided. "I know a rich merchant who loves to be browbeaten. He misses his dead mother."

That night, as Liliane dined with Alexandre on the rooftop, she toyed uneasily with her food. "What do you think Philip will do about my deceiving him?"

"*Our* deceiving him." Alexandre grimly plunged a knife into a pear. "I do not know. Something. He has got a long, vindictive memory." The pear split. Alexandre gazed thoughtfully at the two halves. "Just now, I think he has other things on his mind. He is bored and he did not come to Palestine just to tag after Richard. If Richard is getting all of the glory from this campaign, what does Philip want, besides distracting Richard from carving up France?" He pronged a pear half and offered it to Liliane. "We had best make the most of our holiday, darling. I have a feeling Philip is about to drop a little rain on Richard's head that may wet us all."

Alexandre soon proved correct in his prediction. A few days later, a summons came from Philip. "You are wanted, milord," a stubby page informed Alexandre. "The king is ill."

In that moment, Liliane saw in Alexandre's concerned face his affection for Philip. Despite their differences, they had traveled many long roads together. Alexandre is stronger than his father, she reflected. He is loyal to those he loves, and so wins their loyalty. He treats weak and strong alike, and is fair when he need not be. Ah, Diego, I have been blessed in being wed to two such men. I wish you could have known Alexandre; he would have been both friend and son to you. Keep him from Philip's webs; let not his faith in Philip's friendship return a fatal reward.

Alexandre found Philip wan and listless upon his royal couch. His pallor smacked of fever—the kind that came and went, draining a man until he died of it or was weakened until any passing illness could kill him. "My liege, I am grieved to find you so," Alexandre told him huskily. "I am at your service."

At Alexandre's taut, worried face, Philip smiled affectionately. "I rely upon you, *mon ami,* as ever. In a sea of false friends, you have been my secure harbor." He patted the coverlet. "Come close to me and listen." When Alexandre had done so, Philip murmured, "Go to Richard and tell him that I am ill. So far, I have kept my condition close secret lest rumor run amok. My physicians tell me I have the shaking sickness, which will prove fatal if I remain in Palestine; therefore, I must return to France." Alexandre's expression turned a trifle wooden, and Philip added reassuringly, "I am aware this is a mission no man could relish, but Richard, for all that he may rail and be suspicious, will believe you. He is a good judge of men and has marked you well. He knows you would not lie to him, even for me." He paused, his eyes closing for a moment. When he looked up at Alexandre again, he said quietly, "I shall not force you to this; I but ask you as a friend."

"Sire, when you might ask my life and be willingly granted it, I would not refuse you." Alexandre's eyes were level. "I have but one request, in hope that your condition may possibly be cured. A certain Saracen physician, in my experience, is greatly skilled. If I might have your leave to summon him . . ."

"A Saracen?" Philip laughed faintly. "Even if I were to approve him, my nobles and subjects would not. Had he the best intentions in the world, if I died under his care, his life and that of a great many Saracens would be exacted in retribution. The political atmosphere of this entire area would change, all future treaties by compromise rather than slaughter made nearly impossible. No, *mon ami,* your Saracen is out of the question." He extended his ring for Alexandre to kiss. "Go now, with my apologies to King Richard."

Alexandre kissed the ring.

Richard was furious at the news of Philip's intention to abandon the crusade. Not only was he losing his strongest ally, he would be releasing him to scheme and consolidate his dynastic power in France. Richard had won the first stage of his campaign in Palestine; both his prestige and ambition were committed to winning the rest of it. He could not leave now to watchdog Philip in Europe.

"Philip is sick? God's blood, I smell a jackal at work," Richard snarled. "Philip is likely as weedy as I am, with a wench under his bed! Sick, my arse!"

"He seemed so to me, sire," Alexandre replied quietly. "His majesty shows all the symptoms of the shaking sickness."

"Bah! Any quack physician can make a man ill; the cure is the catch." Richard impatiently paced his pavilion while his chancellor stood out of his way. No man who valued his position would want a share of the decision Richard contemplated. Finally, Richard's red head swiveled. "I shall see your royal patient myself, milord. Out of my way!"

Richard stormed to Philip's tent, Alexandre following closely. When the English king emerged sometime later, his face was black with anger. "Go, damn your eyes!" he stormed at Alexandre and the waiting courtiers. "Begone and bad cess to your lily-livered hides!"

Liliane was reading the poetry book by a nearly guttering candle when Alexandre entered their bedchamber at the villa. "What has happened?" she asked, seeing his closed face.

"We are going home," he replied simply.

15

Home

Castle de Brueil
October 2, 1191

After less than two months' of Philip's illness, Liliane and Alexandre rode through the portal of Castle de Brueil. Cheers rose
from the battlements; serfs and children ran shouting behind
them. Everywhere, varicolored bits of cloth waved in glad greeting, and Kiki, perched on Liliane's pommel, chittered with nervous excitement and waved her little cap.

Charles, with Father Anselm in tow, strode out into the courtyard to meet them. His face filled with gladness, Charles caught
Alexandre's bridle, then his hand. "Welcome, milord! Provence
has been a weary place without you!"

" 'Tis good to see you, my friend, and you, Father Anselm,"
Alexandre replied warmly. "During these past months, I have
greatly felt your loss. Lady Liliane and I rejoice to be home."

While Father Anselm burbled his welcome, Charles's gaze
flicked to Liliane in her Eastern samites and Massilia velvets,
then grew chilled. "My lady." He bowed with elaborate politeness. "We feared you dead."

"Your concern is heartening, sir," Liliane returned lightly,
"but I am doughtier than I look."

Alexandre chuckled, then slid off his destrier. "Milady has
been adventuring in Palestine," he murmured to the two men,
"and grown cocky. You must be patient with her airs; few women
have endured such dangers and lived to prate of them."

Charles eyed her warily as Father Anselm asked, astonished,
"Milady followed the crusade?"

"Indeed she did, and saved my life more than once, but that, you will keep to yourself for sake of her safety, as will the men who accompanied us." Alexandre held out his wrist to Kiki, who scampered up his arm to perch on his shoulder. "For all you know, *mes amis,* Liliane was homesick for Spain and these past many months enjoyed the Malaga sun." Alexandre swept Liliane down from her saddle and thoroughly kissed her. "My wife is a ravishing Tartar and I am a lucky man."

Over Alexandre's shoulder, Liliane's amused eyes met Charles's and Anselm's. "You must be patient with my lord's airs, Messieurs. We are expecting a baby."

Anselm's eyes widened. "My lord, an heir?"

"Perhaps an heiress," teased Liliane.

Alexandre whirled, still clasping Liliane to his side. "Perhaps twins—triplets! I vow we shall have a baker's dozen before we are done!"

Looking up at him with love shining in her eyes, Liliane laughed. "Darling, I am not that much of a Tartar!"

Father Anselm beamed. "I cannot tell you how delighted I am that you are presenting milord with even one child. He has always wanted a family!"

Alexandre caught Charles and Anselm by the shoulders. "Come into the hall and we shall tell you of our travels. You will be far from bored, I promise."

As they passed into the castle, Liliane looked up at its mossy ramparts with a fondness she had not expected. Having been relegated to the occupation and maintenance of men, the great, cool rooms were as Spartan as ever, but spotless. Charles had evidently run the castle as a military garrison.

Within these walls Liliane had known hard times and good. That which she had once fled, she now welcomed, and dreaded only Alexandre's absence. How long would they have before Philip summoned him again? Wise enough not to press Alexandre's defiance, Philip had let him return for leave to Provence instead of commanding his company north to Paris. Aboard the royal ship, Philip had been charming to them both, but he spent most of his time in his cabin conferring with his ministers. Every day, he seemed less ill, and his color improved although he scarcely saw the sun. Once in France, Philip's energy and ambition were fairly tangible. In Richard's absence, he had plans to expand his power, and Liliane had no doubt that Alexandre was part of them. When the royal retinue left Massilia the morning after their arrival, Liliane began to count the days until Philip's summons came.

Once the servants were greeted, the retinue dismissed, and Alexandre and Liliane were alone with Charles and Father Anselm in the hall, Alexandre left out no detail of Liliane's courage and loyalty in recounting her determination to guard him from both enemy and assassins. When the account was over, Charles sat quietly for a considerable time, seeming to daydream while Father Anselm pounded Alexandre and Liliane with questions about holy places and relics. The priest was particularly fascinated with Kiki, who flirted with him outrageously. Liliane was surprised at the priest's innocent envy of their vivid adventures, for she had thought his interests lay mostly in full porringers. She was far more surprised at Charles when he stood finally and bowed again to her, this time without mockery.

"My lady, I welcome you back to Provence with all my heart," he said simply. "I will guard you and your children with my life."

Startled, Liliane sat quite still, then slowly, as she realized that he was deeply earnest, a quiet delight filled her face. She rose and softly kissed Charles on both cheeks. "My lord and I count ourselves greatly fortunate to have such a friend, sir. From this moment, you shall be as my brother."

A flicker of shyness in Charles's eye suggested to Alexandre that his friend might be hard put to sustain a brotherly detachment, and why not? In the sunlight slanting from the southern windows, Liliane looked like a vision woven in gold. Her shimmering blond hair, caught in its gilt and emerald filet, hung in a heavy braid that tempted a man's fingers. Her lovely face, which had been tranquil, was now flushed, her amber eyes bright with emotion as she faced Charles. This was a woman to love. He wanted Charles to love Liliane, but he envisioned that love as the chivalrous adoration one might pay to an untouchable goddess, not the need and desire of another man's wife. For all his cool calculation, Charles was impressionable; once his loyalty was given, it was wholehearted and passionate. Charles was lonely, his only prospects in the world linked to the Brueil demesne. He must take care that Charles was not led into unhappiness through his new devotion to Liliane.

Firmly casting aside his jealousy, Alexandre grasped Charles's shoulder. "Guard my family with my full trust and gratitude, *mon ami*. With God's good grace, our children will prosper here and endure for many generations to come." He turned. "May we ask your blessing, Father, upon our venture?"

"You have it most heartily, milord." The chubby priest beamed. "I look forward to baptizing a great many babies for you and milady. Bless you, I say; bless you all!"

For Alexandre and Liliane, the next weeks were spent in inspecting their fief. Charles had done his duty well. The crops had been good this year; the larders and storage sheds were full, and the hay was already stacked in the fields. The stock appeared to be sturdy and well able to endure the mild Mediterranean winter. The serfs were healthy and, while satisfied with Charles's rule over their affairs, happy to have their kindly master home.

In view of her pregnancy, Liliane was greeted with subdued courtesy rather than the silent hostility she had once suffered. Now, at least, she had the devoted loyalty of Alexandre's men-at-arms, who curtly reprimanded any imagined slight, to the bewilderment of the peasantry. As Alexandre had been in Palestine and Liliane supposedly in Spain, gossipers had begun to murmur that her child might not be his. Thanks to her new allies, those rumors were swiftly doused and, as she was so recently pregnant, the gossip could claim no foundation.

Each day, when their duties were done, Alexandre and Liliane took long rides upon the beach. Despite its rocky irregularity, the coast reminded them of sunny Acre as it might once have been in time of peace. "I often expect to see Acre's walls looming over my shoulder when we turn homeward again," Liliane told Alexandre one evening. "Castle de Brueil seems so small, so soft with age and ivy. Here, hounds instead of jackals clarion after rabbits, and the forests, lush even in their autumn cloak, make the pale, eternal desert seem a dream from another world." She looked into his eyes. "Now I know why home has meant so much to you. After I first went to Diego at Malaga, I was rarely more than a few days' ride away from my childhood home. I took being there for granted. Now I see Castle de Brueil as one of my children: precious, a little fragile, and in need of my love and protection."

Alexandre laughed softly. "So this crumbling old wreck is your child. How maternal you have become." He reined in his destrier, and, puzzled, she halted her own mare to watch him dismount. He lifted her down from the saddle. "Come, mother of the world, and walk with me. We had little enough chance for strolling the beach in Acre."

He led her for some distance in companionable conversation, then wandered to the water's edge. The lap and curl of the waves was gentle, its sigh soft. "Like a baby's gurgle," Alexandre murmured, his hand tightening on Liliane's. "Have I thanked you today for giving me a child?"

Liliane laughed, then laid her head on his shoulder. "You have, sir, just this morning, as you do each and every morning when you make love to me. 'Thank you, darling, for our child,' you say solemnly, as if you had nothing to do with the gift. Then you make such loveliness for me while the sun warms our bed. . . ."

"Say you so solemnly, as if you had nothing to do with our lovemaking." He turned to wrap his arms about her. "I adore you." He kissed her softly, then with rising need. "Shall we make our loveliness here under the sky, with the sea to sing to us and lullaby the babe?"

"Aye, my lord," she whispered. "Love us both. We welcome thee with all our hearts and rejoice in thy affection."

She tugged his head down and kissed him with such longing and fervor that his body fired as if he had touched a flame. Sweeping his cloak about them, he drew her to the sand. Their lips met again, gently, then fiercely, their bodies growing impatient, their wills pressing back the impulse to thrust away their clothing and join with the urgency that would make their lovemaking too brief a blaze.

They had learned to savor each other, to let each caress build the coals of their passions slowly to a white heat. Alexandre parted Liliane's clothing and his own as if baring the secrets of the magic between them. She was warm silk against him, her breasts as round beneath his lips as the glorious fruit of Persia. Honey was in her mouth, between her thighs; in his manhood was a leaping fire, eager to set the sweetness of her aflame. His mouth covered the sensitive peak of her breast, sucking it to a taut, bursting point against his tongue. Liliane moaned softly, her fingers sliding along the length of his hardened shaft, tightening rhythmically with his quickened breathing.

Their caresses became a pulse, swelling to an almost unbearable ache. His lips trailed her armpits, beneath her breasts to her belly, his fingertips teasing the secret heart of her, probing gently, exquisitely to trace the path of their desire. When at last, she trembled and cried out softly her need of him, he let her guide his hardness into her soft depths, find her arching passion, her welling response to his slowly deepening thrusts. Their bodies moved as one, melted together. She wrapped herself about him, her lips brushing his chest until he was driving without restraint, with shivering sensation, with ecstasy that seared them both. Her breath, warm and damp, came quickly against his neck, her cry of rising excitement peaking, matching his own. He gasped, shuddering as his body spent itself in falling flame and left him supine in her close embrace.

"I could not hear the sea's lullaby," Liliane confessed with a smile to her lover a little time later. "Our bodies were singing too loudly."

"Good sea, we beg your pardon," Alexandre called to the surf. "Do give us leave to try again." With a wicked grin, he began to softly whistle in Liliane's ear. Giggling, she feigned an effort to push him away, but as his lips covered hers, she gave a happy little sigh and tugged his cloak over their heads.

Despite the gladness of the Brueils' homecoming, the renewed prospect of trouble with the Signes soon threaded its familiar way through everyone's minds. Charles broached the subject one golden afternoon while he and Alexandre rode across the stubbled fields. "I suppose we will be shortly hearing from our jackal neighbors to the north now that King Philip is on his way to Paris."

Alexandre grinned. "No so soon as you might think. Philip loaned Jacques and Louis to Richard for the remainder of the campaign. He was not inclined to tolerate petty spats at his back while his intentions are set on regaining the Aquitaine. He will make the most of Richard's absence and pray he ends with an arrow in his gizzard, so that wizened John rules in his place. Prince John is no match for Philip."

Charles looked vastly relieved, then suddenly squinted puckishly. "Tell me, was Philip really sick? He seems to have recovered quickly enough upon setting foot upon French soil."

Alexandre's grin faded. "As King Richard observed, any doctor can make a man sick. My own honor was compromised by

Philip's deception, for though I had doubts, he banished them. I truly thought him ill."

"You love him. He would have played upon your concern."

"Do I detect a note of dislike?"

"One cannot dislike a man for being a king. Deception and play of power are the nature of the beast"—a dry smile flitted across Charles's features—"so to speak." He eased back in his saddle. "Surely, we must thank Philip for relieving us of the Signes. He is still your friend?"

"Mine perhaps. Not Liliane's. He finds her unwelcome competition for my attention."

Charles stared across the fields. "Then milady has acquired three dangerous enemies in defending you. 'Tis well her cousins are yet in Palestine; they would not like her bearing you an heir. Were they here in France, her life and the child's would be at grave risk."

"The child's perhaps. If Jacques killed Liliane, he would lose all legal claim to this fief. And yet"—Alexandre's gaze followed Charles's—"her new popularity with my men-at-arms may raise his suspicions. If he troubles to find out why she is so beloved, he will soon learn what she was about in Palestine. Then, *mon ami*, I would not give a copper for her life."

"Sooner or later, you must fight him. Best sooner. Go for his throat the moment he sets foot on French soil."

"And start trouble where Philip sought to avoid it? I might destroy Jacques and Louis, but Philip would show his thanks by making all our lives hell. He might reclaim this demesne." Alexandre's eyes narrowed as he scanned the northern horizon where the Signe fief lay. "I must either produce proof of Jacques's attempts at murder and treason, or provoke him into some new nastiness and catch him at it. The trouble is, provocation could lead to a war between us. My serfs are the ones who would suffer most."

"As the old south wall has been repaired, the serfs can take sanctuary in Castle de Brueil if war breaks out. They might risk their villages being burned if it meant being rid of the Signe threat for good. We can beat Jacques now. We can shelter the serfs and rebuild the villages. We have enough provisions to take care of everyone *and* resist a siege. I almost wish that he would come back and try something."

"You crave the smell of war?" Alexandre asked quietly.

Charles smiled crookedly. "I know you're sick of fighting. I suppose I would be, too, if I had seen as much as you have. Truly, I look upon a fight with Jacques less as amusement than necessity."

"You may be right, *ami*, but I will not be the one to start it, even for Liliane. She would be the last one to wish to be the cause of a bloody conflict. I have kept her foiling her cousins secret to hold her safe, but she has suffered enough for her connection with them. She is the lady of my demesne and my heart; I would not have her reviled for God knows how long by those who owe her faith and fealty. She is due all their affection and honor." Alexandre's mouth narrowed into a hard line. "I must catch the Signes in one of their own traps."

The autumn days passed slowly in a hazy blaze of russet, orange and gold that made the blue of sea and sky so vivid they seemed to have a life of their own. To enjoy utter peace was an invaluable treasure, and everyone took advantage of it, particularly Alexandre, whose delight at being home was infectious. By the end of October, he had covered every inch of his demesne, and at the end of every day he scribbled lists of projects and improvements. He set workmen to implement his ideas; only in the worst weather were they idle.

One night, Liliane wrapped her arms about his neck and peered over his shoulder as he made ink sketches on parchment. "New catapults? Are you expecting trouble with the Lombards?"

"Trouble is inevitable, but not with the Lombards." He turned his head slightly to kiss her cheek, then pulled her into his lap. "I have had word from Massilia. The Signes have left Palestine. They landed in Massilia yesterday at dawn."

She went white. "So soon? But they were promised to Richard!"

"Richard distrusted them. He thought they might try to assassinate him on behalf of Philip, so he sent them home."

"What shall we do?"

"Charles is convinced that we are strong enough to beat Jacques. He wants a fight."

"But an outright confrontation would be fatal. Even with the mercenaries Charles hired, we are not strong enough to best my uncle after losing twenty men in Palestine; he outarms us and outnumbers us three to one.''

"Yes," Alexandre replied quietly. "I fear Charles is weary of minding home fires and would see them turn into a bonfire. He is rarely rash, except on my behalf. Perhaps I should have taken him to Palestine and let him be rid of his restlessness.''

"What do you think we ought to do?''

He stroked her cheek. "I think you ought to keep close to the castle, and I ought to wander abroad.''

Her eyes widened in horror. "As bait?''

"It is me they want.''

"Alexandre, that is insane!''

"Not if I am exceedingly sane about where I go and when. Not if I have a ten-man escort, plus a secret second escort to follow me within hailing distance. Not''—he smiled faintly—"if I make no secret of my movements.''

Liliane was silent for a long moment. "You mean to provoke Jacques into making the first move so you can report it to Philip.'' She caught his hand. "Alexandre, that is too dangerous. You could easily be killed! If you are, Jacques will see that our child does not survive you. We must think of some other way. When I first came here, I thought of a diversion that I had no chance to use because of Philip's summons to the crusade. It might be a possibility now.''

She told him of her plan to propose to Jacques that he dress his troops as Italian mercenaries, so that blame for an attack might not be laid at his door. "The difficulty is that he may not confide to me when he will attack. I must try to name an expedient time to him so you can arrange an ambush. Signe bodies in Italian garb should smell fishy enough to Philip.''

Alexandre smiled at her quizzically. "I am glad you are on my side, my love. You are a very clever woman.''

"Will you consider it?''

"I cannot permit your being the liaison, Liliane. Jacques will not ride in the attack. Like a spider, he will wait in his lair and later try to figure out what went wrong with his plans. Then, coming to the logical conclusion, he will try for you.'' He cut off her protest with an adroit kiss. "I shall consider your plan, darling, but I will not risk your beautiful neck.'' He nipped her lightly. " 'Tis much too delicious.''

Catching Liliane up and carrying her to the bed, he missed the troubled distraction in her eyes.

That night after she and Alexandre had made love, Liliane lay long awake. She was deeply distraught, for the Signes' return presented her with an old dilemma. She had vowed to cease interfering with Alexandre's affairs, as her last efforts had proven both dangerous to their marriage and his life . . . but now she had to do something.

Alexandre knew as well as she did that his plan to bait Jacques was precarious. At best, he might get Louis, but not Jacques, which would provoke an attack. If they did attack, Philip could not be counted upon to intervene. Alexandre was endangering himself to keep from endangering her. He must also know she was the logical liaison with Jacques; within reason, Jacques would trust her if he had not learned of her thwarting him in Palestine. He would contact her, either to use her or destroy her. To draw enough of Jacques's forces into play to severely damage him, she, not Alexandre, must be the bait.

The next morning, Liliane rode alone to the message oak and sent Kiki up to fetch the tube; it was still there, empty. She left a brief note. A week later, her note was untouched, so she left it there. A second week passed and the note was still in the tube. Was Jacques merely occupied with the general business of homecoming, or had he found out about her? Was he planning something? Uneasily, Liliane rode home, and day by day, her tension grew. Alexandre was venturing near the Signe border with his men; soon she knew he might risk outright provocation.

In her anxiety, she began to notice previously inconsequential developments: for one, she was thickening in the waist and having to let out her laces. Soon she would have to give up riding and find some other way to reach Jacques. She also began to puzzle over Fremier the cleric, to whom no one ordinarily gave much attention. He had not been at Castle de Brueil upon his lord's homecoming, but upon leave of absence in Arles to care for a sick relative; the relative had recovered within a few weeks of Alexandre's return.

She would have been pleased if Fremier had stayed in Arles. She had developed a vague dislike for the man; he was too subservient, too silent. He had a way of drifting through a room without attracting notice . . . and without interrupting conversation. Often she had looked up to find him watching her placidly. He seemed strangely patient, as if waiting for something. If he were a spy, he would know she had betrayed her cousins. He could have informed Jacques of her deceit soon after her marriage; yet apparently he had not. Having no evidence of his guilt, Liliane forced away her suspicions; Fremier was probably no more than he seemed: a harmless cleric.

Her greatest uneasiness lay in deceiving Alexandre, when she had sworn she would never do so again. He would never believe that she could lie to him and utterly disregard his efforts to protect her. At long last, he trusted her completely. How ill she was repaying him!

She had hoped to withdraw from all her intrigues with Jacques upon returning to France. Palestine had cured her of wanting to deal with violence. She wanted only to be Alexandre's wife, the mother of his child, the chatelaine of lovely Castle de Brueil. She wanted peace. Why was it ever so impossible?

When, upon the next afternoon, a page wearing the Signe colors presented himself at the castle, Liliane knew that peace was about to end. "Your cousins are declaring a tourney," Alexandre dryly informed her when the page had departed. "We are graciously invited as a gesture of future goodwill."

"You must not go, Alexandre! Jacques means some wickedness; that tourney will be a deathtrap!"

"It will also be Mahomet's mountain. I have no great wish to waste my time playing the fox for Jacques in the forest." He touched her cheek. "Have no fear. You are thinking of Diego, I know, but he was not looking for an arrow in the back; I am." When her face showed no sign of reassurance, he drew her into his arms. "Come, where is your prodigious sense of adventure? You have wanted proof that Diego was murdered; at the tourney, you are likely to get it."

"I do not want it this way, Alexandre," Liliane said desperately. "When I came here I was reckless and selfish. Is there no way I can show you how precious you have become to me?"

"Aye," he replied softly, "there is a way." His lips lowered upon hers, gently yet with the certainty of possession. He lifted her into his arms and carried her to the bed.

Aye, there is a way, Liliane thought dazedly as her senses awakened to him. I can love you with all my body, heart and mind . . . yet naught I can do will matter against an assassin's cold intent.

* * *

The tourney was held on the field skirting ponderous Castle de Signe, with lords from eight surrounding fiefs invited. Usually tourneys were clumsy affairs with a few knights slogging around in the mud before an indifferent audience of peasantry, but Jacques had set up a private pavilion, placed chairs about the field and marked it off with great pennants in his colors; smaller pennants backed the chairs of his fellow landowners. "Nothing like declaring his ambitions in Provence," Alexandre murmured to Liliane as she bound her colors to his arm.

Glancing at Jacques, crammed toadlike in his chair at the center of the line of nobles, Liliane was inclined to agree. "The nobles hate him, yet they do not dare publicly insult him. He is too dangerous."

"That is why I do not want you going near him without your escort. Extend your courtesies, then keep to the area of our tent." When she said nothing, he caught her hand. "You promised that if I brought you, you would take all precautions. Remember?"

"I remember." They had gotten into a roaring argument when she refused to be left at home. Only her apparent surrender had won Alexandre's acquiescence.

To assure her safety, he had brought a forty-man escort and planted them about her so thickly that she could scarcely see the tourney field. She suspected such protection was as much to deter *her* as Jacques from any pranks.

"Who are you matched against?" she asked as Alexandre's attention returned to the squire fastening his armor.

"Cortillon, Gribes, and Louis the Malevolent, *naturellement.*"

"Do not tease. Louis is not the laughing sort."

"Neither is his pretty cousin. Do smile, or he and Uncle Malevolent may believe you are worried about me."

She smiled, then through set teeth, whispered, "I am stiff with worry. Be careful!"

Alexandre grinned. "I am determined to be a grandfather, darling." Tucking his helmet under his arm, he cuffed his squire lightly. "Pick up anything left on the field after I match Louis de Signe. No one else must get to it first, understand?"

The boy nodded. "I'll be quick enough."

As Alexandre led Liliane away toward the Signe party, she

muttered, "Are you not being too prophetic about your last remains?"

"I hope not." He waved to four guardsmen to accompany them. "Just now, I am more interested in surviving our courtesies to your uncle."

As they approached him, Jacques's toadlike head swiveled to follow their progress. His smile was broad, but his eyes were flat and ruthless. Louis stood behind him, his armor encasing his short, brutal body like an indestructible block. Jacques seemed more interested in Liliane than Alexandre, his head cocked as he studied her with sharp curiosity.

Despite her green samite bliaud and gold-set ruby filet, Liliane suddenly felt very obviously pregnant, and very vulnerable. Alexandre sensed her increased tension, and his arm tightened about her shoulders in firm reassurance. She felt a strong wave of love for him, for so often he knew her feelings; his sensitivity made her current intentions seem all the blacker.

"Welcome to our tourney, Milord de Brueil," Jacques said jovially as Alexandre bowed briefly to him. He smiled at Liliane's perfunctory curtsy. "Liliane, we have missed your pretty presence for too long. You must visit us at Castle de Signe during the Christmas festivities. I hope you will be well entertained this day; we are expecting yet another seven knights to enter the lists."

"You are gracious, milord," replied Alexandre. "One may always rely on your family to provide lively entertainment." He smiled faintly at Louis. "I am impatient for our contest to banish the rust of inactivity, but then you have never played the country squire, have you, sir?"

Louis's black eyes stared back. "I play at nothing. War is but duty for a practical man."

"No one has ever accused you of being amusing, Louis," Liliane observed lightly. "Why not run along with Alexandre to your brawling while I relieve Uncle with the latest gossip from Spain?"

Now all three men were looking at her: Louis, with sullen resentment; Alexandre, with startled wariness; and Jacques, with speculation. She forced herself to drop casually into the chair beside her uncle and look up at Alexandre. "Did you not say something about impatience for the fray, darling? After all, I have not seen Uncle Jacques since our wedding."

Her tactic dawning on him, Alexandre swiftly reached for her wrist. Just as quickly, she evaded him. Jacques smoothly intervened. "You must let Liliane stay, milord; she will be our Queen of Love and Beauty and reign over the tournament. Her place of honor should be next to me. You are entered early in the lists, I believe, and should finish with Louis just before luncheon. You and Liliane must dine with us."

Alexandre's expression clearly said that he would sooner risk a meal with Caligula. His eyes narrowed as he towered over Liliane. "The choice is up to you, my love."

"I should like to stay." With an effort, Liliane looked away.

Alexandre turned on his heel and strode toward the field. "Accompany the count, Louis," murmured Jacques, "and remember your manners." With a short snort of impatience, Louis stalked after Alexandre.

Jacques benevolently urged his companions and servants away. "Now, my dear," he purred, settling in his chair, "what is your news from Spain?"

"The cork trees are quite a change from the oaks of Provence. They are productive but neglected. They might produce an extraordinary yield with some attention."

"You inspected them?"

"More than once. I ventured to offer a little advice to a caretaker, but it was ignored."

"Perhaps the caretaker thought you might be preoccupied with womanly matters. One gathers you are to be a mother soon?"

"Accidents happen . . . particularly at tourneys." Her hand caressed his arm. "Darling Uncle, are you going to make me a widow today?"

"Would you like that?"

"I have ever preferred freedom to obligation, particularly to you. I should like to be done with this business. You may have observed that my husband and I are not fond."

"On the contrary, compared to most noble couples, you are turtledoves. Your husband seems intrigued with you."

"Alexandre's infatuation suits my purpose; certainly it has made my living at Castle de Brueil more comfortable, if tedious." Her beautiful face adopted an arctic expression. "If anything should happen to him, I should like to return to Spain. Do what you like with Alexandre, but have the kindness not to bother me with details. I never want to see rustic France again."

"That might be arranged," Jacques said obliquely.

"Good. Then I might arrange for you to get into the castle. Would you like that?"

He was silent for a moment. "I am such a methodical man, my dear. Rarely does anything hurried appeal to me."

"Something hurried might occur to Philip." She played with the emerald on her finger. "Alexandre tells me that Philip knows Louis betrayed his raiders to the Saracens."

A tiny tick twitched at Jacques's mouth. "How could the king possibly believe that?"

"A certain turncoat named Jefar el din spied among the Saracens and heard talk among Saladin's lieutenants. Philip is also a patient man, but Louis's days are numbered . . . and when Louis goes, you will follow, for all the world knows he is your left arm."

Jacques was pale now. "And who is my right?"

"Why not a woman?"

"That depends. Does this woman know why Philip is biding his time?"

"His illness in Palestine was feigned. Do you understand now?"

"Consolidation." Jacques's fat fingers tightened on his chair. "He means to summon us to Paris. Why make an example of us in Palestine when he can do it before all France and exhibit his control over the south, from the Rhône to the Italian provinces." He looked up at his flamboyant pennants. "Up until now, Alexandre's and my adversity has suited him well. Our quarrels have helped to keep a balance of power in Provence. If that balance fails in my favor, Philip fears he may have to contend with me one day over this region."

"Exactly."

"So if Alexandre de Brueil were dead and Jefar el din unavailable, Philip would lack his chief witnesses and be obliged to reconsider his strategy." He stared at her. "What is your price for this discouragement?"

Be careful, her logic warned. You must seem real to him; he will not believe you have blossomed into his sort of monster overnight. "I want my child. If the child remains in France, you will kill it and possibly me in time, just to keep your affairs neat. I have no intention of rotting away at Castle de Brueil to hold it for you. Once the child and I are safe in Spain, I shall sign

Alexandre's lands over to you . . . but do not rely on paying any friendly visits to Malaga as you did last time. I shall have you shot on sight."

He laughed dryly. "You need not worry. I am growing too old and fat for such gallivanting. Besides, I have no desire to worry about my right hand shooting me when my left hand is already eager for the opportunity."

Her attention turned to the field where a fallen knight was being helped from the field. His opponent was trotting off the far end of the field to his squire, while Louis and Alexandre were mounting their destriers. Both were dressed in the new style of hauberk: a coat of chain mail over a heavy leather shirt. Over a closely fitted hood covered with chain mail, Alexandre wore a bucketlike iron helm with a slit over the eyes, while Louis wore an older conical helm with a nose guard. Alexandre's hauberk was polished to near white; Louis's was painted black. Their hands were covered with mitts made of mail.

Louis was not impressive aboard a horse, but Liliane knew from Palestine that he was extremely hard to dislodge from his saddle. He was strong and sturdy like a battering ram. In contrast, Alexandre resembled a slim steel reed. He was deft, quick and lethal, but he also followed the code of chivalry, while Louis had no such handicap.

Her stomach was knotting. To distract Jacques, who could spot an opponent's fear with a ferret's accuracy, she affected a casual drawl. "So you think Louis might betray you?"

"He was suckled on treachery. Nothing else has any taste for him. As I have shaped him, so will he grow." Jacques stretched his plump legs. "I must say that, for a spider, he is fit enough; so is your husband. Quite a splendid-looking young man, Alexandre de Brueil. Many a woman would rejoice to find him in her bed. He is virile, handsome, intelligent . . . even decent." He eyed her slyly. "Tell me, dear, is that last quality his flaw?"

"Quite right, Uncle," Liliane answered coolly as she watched Alexandre and Louis trot to opposing ends of the list corridor. "Diego was an old man; Alexandre a decent man. Next I want an exciting man."

"Have you ever considered Philip?"

Her eyes widened slightly, then she smiled. "Philip would hardly be likely to welcome a Signe into his bed just now."

"Oh, I think you might be beautiful enough—and clever

enough—to tempt him. After Palestine, he could use a little distraction.''

''Particularly from you and Louis.'' Her hands tightened on her chair as the two men on the field exploded into a charge at each other. They smashed together with a brutal crash that staggered their destriers. Desperately, Liliane waited as they reeled . . . then righted, trotting back to their starting points. She saw Jacques looking at her white knuckles. ''Anticipation, Uncle. Merely anticipation.''

''Will you consider Philip, then, my dear?''

''Not so long as I have a husband, Uncle.''

She heard him laugh over the crash of the lances.

Alexandre and Louis charged again and again. Their mutual hatred was evident, their urge to kill hanging like a bloody pall over the field. With equal skill, they took the bobbing, weaving points on their shields, cushioning the massive blows with a twist or lean of the torso. If that tactic failed, they leaned into the blow and, with sheer muscle power, tried to shatter the opposing lance; anything to keep the lance head from slipping past the heavy shield and striking the body, perhaps breaking bone even through the chain mail.

Muttering rose from the crowd; everyone present was aware of the years of bad blood between the Brueils and Signes. Neither man, although taking terrible blows, would go down. Liliane sensed that Alexandre's past animosity was doubly fired by his anger at her familiarity with Jacques. Again, the destriers' muscles coiled and the two knights bore down on each other. The collision was a horror of splintering lance. Louis's lance skipped off the top of Alexandre's shield and struck him high in the shoulder, easily spreading the chain link. Alexandre's lance missed Louis altogether and Alexandre went down.

Liliane was transfixed with fear. Like a squat vulture, Louis waited on his mount as Alexandre lay still. Liliane came to her feet so abruptly her chair toppled. Stumbling over her skirts, she raced out onto the field with her husband's squire just behind her. She dropped on her knees by Alexandre's side to see the long, deadly splinters of Louis's lance head protruding from between the steel rings of the hauberk. Her heart racing as if it would burst her chest, she worked frantically at the armor lacing. Distractedly aware of the squire's seemingly aimless scrabbling

over the turf surrounding Alexandre, she shrieked, *"Par Dieu,
leave off! Aidez moi!"*

Alexandre's head moved slightly as the squire worked at his
helm; when it came off, Alexandre's face was gray with pain,
his eyes open and unnaturally dark. "The splinters," he whispered. "Gather the splinters . . ."

Thinking he meant the splinters in his wound, Liliane began
to try to remove them with trembling fingers while the squire cut
the lacing. "No," Alexandre gasped, "the ones on the ground.
Hurry!" The squire shoved his knife into its sheath and, under
Louis's black gaze, quickly gathered up bits of lance head about
the wounded man.

Louis swiftly waved over some of his yeomen. "Help him."

Ten of Alexandre's men had raced ahead of Louis's men to
form a ring about their fallen lord. The squire drew his knife
and glared up at Louis. "Back, milord! You intrude!"

After scanning the hostile faces about him, Louis let sanity
overrule social status and he withdrew.

Alexandre's wound was deep but high, the deepest of the
splinters forming a narrow slit. When Liliane withdrew it, the
blood flowed freely. When she ripped off her cap and packed it
against the wound, the blood soon stopped. She sighed with
relief. "If the wound does not fester, you will live, milord."

His lips white, Alexandre made no reply as the squire helped
him to a sitting position so that his padded gambeson might be
stripped off. Liliane temporarily bound his wound with light
bandaging so that he could be carried to their pavilion. Once
inside the tent, she carefully removed the rest of the splinters.
The process was painful, but Alexandre made no sound, nor did
he look at her until his final bandage was tightly in place. "Oh,
my love," she whispered against his cheek, "I thought Louis
had killed you."

Alexandre eyed her sardonically. "I am a lucky man. Lucky
in war and love. I have a wife who plays in my enemy's lap while
I snap at his heels like a terrier after an elephant." His head
turned from her stung face toward the hovering squire. "Let's
have a look at your field scavengings."

When Liliane anxiously touched his face, Alexandre pushed
himself up and held out his hand to the squire. Into his master's
palm, the boy dropped several large fragments of wood backed
with crumbling clay. Atop it, the boy placed a snapped-off steel-

capped lance point, about two inches long. "Louis's lance cap was clay," Liliane breathed in fury. "It had to break and uncover the steel head!"

One by one, Alexandre laid the fragments in her palm. "Enough evidence to suit Philip . . . and all the proof you are ever likely to have that they killed Diego."

As the fragments piled, so did realization gather in her mind. "You *let* Louis have a solid blow at you!" Fury and concern welled in her. "Mother of God, are you mad to bait him so? You may be killed next time!" Her voice lowered urgently. "Louis saw what the squire collected. He and Jacques do not dare let you live long enough to show it to Philip."

"So they will try again soon. Good." Alexandre settled back on his pallet. "If they are in a hurry, they will risk mistakes." With a strength surprising in a wounded man, he caught her wrist. "You made one today by putting yourself on public display with Jacques. If I should meet with a nasty end, you will be suspected of helping him arrange my death."

"I already have a black reputation. . . ."

"Enough to be caught in the middle of your own schemes. If I die, Philip will demand your head along with those of your relatives." His grip tightened painfully. *"Stay away from them!"*

"Is that a command?"

"Yes, the one I said I would never give you."

"I am not your vassal, Alexandre, but your wife," she reminded him quietly. "A free soul."

"I could lock you up again," he breathed huskily.

"You will not. Now please let me go; you are hurting me."

Alexandre released her. His squire invited Lords de Cortillon and de Gribes in as witnesses to view the evidence of the clay lance cap. And Liliane went out to Jacques.

Jacques and his party were waiting outside their pavilion as she approached them. "May we hope that Milord de Brueil's injuries are not serious?" Jacques said solicitously.

Liliane studied Louis. "Milord de Brueil will live to grow old. You were overeager, Cousin."

As Louis started forward, Jacques rose quickly from his chair. "No, Louis! Milady is overwrought. Any assistance we may give . . ."

"None is presently required, thank you, Uncle." Her eyes locked with his. "Another time, perhaps."

"Yes, of course," he murmured. "I shall inquire again within the week."

"For a patient man, you were never given to delay, Uncle. *Au revoir*. Louis . . ." Liliane dropped a deep, mocking curtsy and left them staring at her back.

She had no choice now. She had to deal with Jacques, just as he had to chance her willingness to betray Alexandre. Alexandre had forced both their hands.

The morning after their party returned from the tourney, Liliane met early with Charles for a ride. "I have to move now," she told him. "We have talked privately in these past weeks of this possibility. Do I have your support?"

"The tourney does speed things," he agreed grimly. "Aye, I will help and so will my guardsmen. I just wish we had a way to snare Jacques, as well."

"If we yank enough fangs from his jaw, he will have to back off, at least long enough for Philip to finish the kill. Jacques will probably make a run for Italy. He should be satisfied with poaching upon the pope. Clement cannot abide Philip, as he thinks a united France cannot but feed upon Italy."

She led Charles directly to the blasted oak and let Kiki fetch the tube. This time her note was gone and in its place was a scrap of parchment which said simply, "Name the time and place."

She wrote a note and showed it to Charles. "This Sabbath dawn. The postern passage under the south wall. Dress as Italian mercenaries." Below the writing, she added a tiny map.

Charles studied it with a small smile. "You did more than go over the wall last year. That postern gate and tunnel system must have taken you some time to explore."

She laughed dryly. "I did not find the entrance from the old tower passage for a whole year. I seem to have a certain affinity for tunnels, perhaps due to a legacy from my scuttling relatives. Blood tells, they say."

Charles studied her speculatively. "I hope not; otherwise, I am betraying the best man I have ever known."

"You will not be sorry, Charles."

He said nothing, but when they passed the castle on the way to the shore and saw Alexandre watching them from the tower window, she knew that Charles was already sorry.

* * *

The cleric, Antoine Fremier, swore moodily as he peered up into sunlight rising through the branches of the oak. He was becoming too plump to climb trees at his age. He scrambled up to the hole where the message cylinder was hidden and pried it open. As he surveyed the parchment inside, his sulky frown became a calculating smile. Finally he had the weapon for which he had been waiting so long and patiently.

Baron de Signe had nearly had him killed when his niece had informed him of the altered notes. Fremier had narrowly escaped with the desperate rebuttal that Liliane was lying to see if Jacques had set a spy on her. Despite Louis's prods with a heated iron to his ribs, Fremier doggedly kept to his story. At length, either believing him or not wanting to risk suspicion at having a new face in Alexandre's household, Jacques had sent him back to Castle de Brueil. Every time Fremier salved his burns, he anticipated the day he would be recompensed for them.

He tugged out a new bit of parchment from his waist pouch and rewrote the note. He carefully folded the original and tucked it into his pocket.

Alexandre suspected that Liliane was contriving some plan when she was so long gone riding with Charles. He could question them until kingdom come without their telling him what they meant to do. He could imprison them in the dungeon, but Liliane had been right; he would not go so far. He could either have them spied upon, which turned his stomach, or he could beat them at their game by moving first. Whatever her intentions, Liliane had turned them all into antagonists, and he was odd man out while she allied with Charles.

Charles had fallen in love with her; could she not see it? Or did she not care? Alexandre rubbed his brow. His head was beginning to ache as it had when she had been ill in Acre. They had so nearly lost each other. . . .

His hand stopped. Perhaps they *had* lost each other. Perhaps something subtly vital to their love had died, only he had been too relieved and happy to be aware of it.

Once the phantoms of doubt began, they multiplied, although he tried to banish them. Liliane was not the daring, reckless young bride he had first known; she was quieter now, older. If she had been calculating before, she was better at it now, with implacable determination. War had changed her; he had changed her. He had deserted her once; had she ever really forgiven him at heart? In his arms, she was more passionate than ever, but was she lying to herself, lying to him? Was she turning to Charles for that something that he could not give her? After all, she had not wanted to marry him in the first place; duty had bound her to him and might be keeping her with him now. She carried his child; that would be enough to chain her to him.

Alexandre turned his mind to the nagging ache of his wounded shoulder to distract himself from his mounting doubts, but they danced about him like relentless imps. She loves me! he wanted to shout. She is only concerned for my safety and the preservation of our people! She cares nothing for Charles but as a friend. But Alexandre was no longer sure. If she wishes to be free of me, he vowed grimly, I will neither hold her nor let her risk her future by meddling with her uncle to protect me.

He called the head guard to the tower chamber. "What do you know of your captain's plotting with milady against Baron de Signe?" he asked bluntly. "Is anyone else involved?"

The man gave him a blank look. "I know nothing of any plot, milord."

Although he was certain the man was lying, Alexandre let him go without reprimand. Liliane had made his men-at-arms her partisans. He wished he had his hands about her adorable neck.

He rose from his chair, donned his riding clothes and strung his crossbow over his good shoulder. He went down to the guard-room and summoned twenty men to arm themselves. The lieutenant hurried after him as he went to have his own destrier saddled. "My lord, where shall I tell Captain Charles you have gone?"

"Hunting." He left the lieutenant staring after him.

Alexandre and his men were gone by the time Liliane and Charles returned from their ride. "Milord knows we're up to something behind his back," the head guard quietly informed Charles and Liliane as they dismounted. "He took out a third of the men, armed like boars and not hunting as he said. He is not likely to use a crossbow on deer."

"He is trying to draw Louis out before we do," Liliane said worriedly. "Do you think Louis will be on the prowl in the forest if he believes he has certain access to the castle?"

"I do not know," replied Charles, "but if he does not see

milord out baiting him as usual, he will suspect a trick. We will just have to sit tight until Sunday dawn.''

And so they did, but without Alexandre's company. When two days passed without his return, Liliane frantically sent out his squire to look for him. ''Milord is well enough,'' the boy reported upon his return, ''and sends his greetings. The hunt occupies him very well, but he has seen no game, I think.''

''No sign of Louis, eh?'' mused Charles.

Liliane was not listening. ''Greetings! Is that all he sends?'' she railed. ''Not a single word of affection? Does he not know that what I do, I do for him?''

Charles sent the squire away, then turned to Liliane. ''Can you really blame Alexandre for resenting your interference?'' he asked quietly.

Her hands knotted together as she paced the hall. ''No . . . no, I cannot blame him. He is right to be furious. . . .''

Charles followed her. ''Do not blame yourself. You can follow no other course than you have done, if your uncle's power is to be destroyed. He must commit a large force to our trap on our terms, at our time. You were the only one who could have achieved that. Alexandre is concerned for your safety, yes, but I think he is also concerned that you and I grow too close in this endeavor.''

''But he knows I love him! Why should he be jealous?''

Charles gazed at her spill of shimmering hair, her flushed cheeks, her eyes bright and wide with surprised indignation. ''Because he has reason to be jealous, milady. If you were not married and I were landed, I would pay you suit.'' He laughed briefly at her dumbfounded look. ''Of course, you would pay me no attention, as you have paid my mooning no heed these last weeks, for I doubt if Dame Fortune would be so generous as to erase Alexandre's claim to your heart.'' His amused look turned wistful. ''Alas, he has it all and I am too late. He knows me better than you do and sees my disappointment.''

''Charles,'' she whispered, ''I am sorry. I never meant . . .''

He shook his head. ''You never knew, but do not fear; I love Alexandre, too. When this business is done with your uncle, I shall leave Provence.''

Liliane went to him. ''Charles, do not. It is not necessary now. This is your home.''

''Nay, that it has never been, for all your husband's kindness.

'Tis time I sought my own way, my own place. I am no farmer, milady . . . and less a poacher.''

A mischievous glint had entered Charles's eyes, and Liliane suddenly wondered how much he had guessed of her and Alexandre's meeting prior to their wedding. She had no time to pick his brains for he kissed her hand and headed from the hall. "Forgive me, milady, but I must see to the postern gate lest your cousin find it plugged. A pity that we cannot allow him to drown in Brueil muck.''

Why do I have the horrible feeling that we are all drowning? she wondered.

Two hours before the dawn of the Signes' expected attack, Charles led his men down into the tunnel to wait. When they were stationed on both sides of the corridor where it divided, he led another group out to wait in the copse of trees a few hundred yards from the nearly hidden gate. Once Louis's force entered the tunnel, Charles's men would close it behind them so they could not retreat.

As Charles entered the trees, he could see Liliane on the south tower, her silhouette faintly outlined in the fading moonlight. She was taking a great risk in pulling the border sentries back and luring Louis to Castle de Brueil—if she had miscalculated, they could all die for it, and she would die the most horribly. Louis had a vengeful nature.

When he was well within the trees, he motioned his men to lie low among the leaves and brush in case Louis used the copse for concealment. Burrowing down, they waited.

In less than a half hour, a few wraithlike horsemen threaded through the copse. Pikemen darted behind them. Bringing up the rear were men with drawn swords. Flattened in the leaves, Charles recognized Louis as he passed, advancing through the darkness toward the postern. Charles held his breath, waiting for one of the enemy to stumble over a hidden man, but no cry of either warning or struggle stirred the misty silence. Perhaps fifty yards from the postern, Louis halted, waiting for his men to regroup behind him. They moved forward, then at the last moment half of them veered away to continue toward the east side of the castle. "Where the hell are they going?" whispered a yeoman a few feet from Charles's elbow.

Feeling sweat break out on his spine, Charles peered tensely

at the waning shadows of Louis's troop. The rest of his men
waited outside the postern. "The old tunnel . . . Good God,
they're going for the wrong one!"

"They seem to know what they're about," the yeoman hissed.
"No shuffling there. Looks like somebody directed them to the
old tunnel."

"Well, that someone was *not* the Lady Liliane, if that is what
you're hinting," snapped Charles. He jumped to his feet and
softly blew the reed whistle that hung about his neck. The quail
call trilled through the copse. In moments, twelve men were
about him. "Come on, lads. We must warn those poor devils in
the tunnel that the quarry's gone down the wrong hole!"

Within the cistern, the men lying in wait to ambush Louis
were growing impatient and wondering how long he was going
to wait. The night was nearly gone, the dawn's first dull light
penetrating the tunnel opening. In a quarter of an hour, Louis
would be unable to approach the castle without being seen.

Suddenly they saw him behind them, a mass of men bristling
with pikes at his back, blocking their way back into the castle.
In front of them, the tunnel opening's first dim light blacked out.
Night had again come upon them.

A moment later, Charles and his men surged upon the enemy
at the tunnel mouth; all silence ended and the slaughter began.

From the rampart, Liliane saw the flash of blades pick up the
faint light in the mist and realized what had happened. Having
ducked down behind the wall to keep from alerting Louis's
stealthy band, she had not seen them split until too late. Now
the mass of the castle defenders were trapped as she had meant
to trap Louis. White-faced, she motioned swiftly to the guards
on the wall. "Quickly, go down and get behind Louis in the old
tunnel to relieve our men!"

To her dismay, they backed away. "You betrayed us, you Judas
witch!" They broke and ran down the stone stairs to crank open
the drawbridge and escape. The guards on the other walls joined
them within minutes.

"Come back!" Liliane cried desperately. "You are wrong!
Come back!"

Her pleas were useless, barely audible over the rising noise.
She turned to grip the rampart wall. Below, five men were running hard from the castle: the last of her reserve men and Charles

were being chased by Signe bowmen. A rain of arrows pursued their retreat, and before the men reached the copse of trees that had once been their haven, three of them were dead. The bowman entered the copse, and scant minutes later, a lone horseman burst from the far trees and galloped for the north.

Charles, Liliane realized with a wild surge of hope. Charles has gotten away to warn Alexandre! And to tell him I have given his castle and retainers into the hands of his enemies . . . to tell him that I have betrayed him. . . .

16

Cat and Mouse

Her face composed, Liliane was waiting alone in the great hall when Louis and his guards burst through its doors. Her hands locked on her chair arms, but she did not rise. As he advanced with sword drawn, her heart pounded in her breast. He wanted to kill her, and if Jacques had given him orders to do so, she had only seconds left to live. "Well," she said coolly, "we have been successful. I shall be leaving for Spain today."

His eyes mocking, Louis bowed. "Our uncle requests that you wait until Count Alexandre has been captured. He also wishes you to be present for the ceremonies that transfer the Brueil demesne to his possession. He has pressing affairs at the moment, but he should arrive in a few days. Surely you can use that time to pack your belongings."

Liliane rose. If Louis could pretend to be uncaring, she would assume the same tone. As she was obviously his prisoner, pressing to leave would be pointless and only arouse suspicion. "Why not? A few days will not matter." She started to descend the dais, expecting at each step to be run through.

Louis waved her to halt. "Please, resume your place; it suits you so. Why, every time I think of you, Cousin, it is upon a fine chair above my head . . . just as you were in Spain. You were so remote and detached, you seemed untouchable, just as you do now."

"Louis," she replied flatly, "I do not like you and I have more profitable things to do than bandy conversation."

332

"Then you will agree that it will be profitable to us both to see that our victory is accepted quietly by your husband's castellans." He waved to a guard, and the man went to open the hall's great wooden doors. With a rank of Signe guards on either side of them, a line of battered prisoners filed into the room.

Liliane was vastly relieved to see so many of her people alive. She had so long thought of them as hers, but now they stared at her with disillusionment and hatred. These men had believed in her, fought for her and Alexandre; now they despised her as a traitor just as Alexandre would do. She forced her expression to remain impassive as she resumed her chair.

The prisoners shuffled to a halt before the dais, and Louis smiled at her as he spoke to them. "This is your lady, in whom my uncle is well pleased. She had given you unto us, as she was meant to do from the beginning."

A burly yeoman hurled himself at Louis. "Smug, blaspheming, unnatural monster!" The chain about his neck abruptly tightened and, choking, he was dragged to the stone floor. His hands, bound behind his back, twitched as his breath was cut off. Louis placed his booted foot on the man's neck. "And this is the end that will befall those discontented with our succession." Abruptly, he shifted his weight and the neck beneath it snapped. Liliane could not hide her horror, which Louis instantly noticed. "Weak-stomached, milady, or entertaining second thoughts? Our uncle relies on you, after all."

"Have your fun, Louis," she said coldly. "Your amusements were ever cheap."

"Certainly, *your* favors have never been to my taste," he retorted. "I have merely bedded you to please my uncle."

As a choked gasp went up from the retainers, Liliane came to her feet, her face white with fury. "Liar! I would sooner befoul myself with some loathsome toad!"

"Fie, Cousin," purred Louis, "to pretend virtue when all present know you have it not." He mounted the dais and stuck his face out to nearly touch hers. "Love me, Cousin, or"—he turned to gesture flippantly at the dead body on the floor—"leave me."

"I will leave you, Louis," she hissed. "Take my chair; you will be a dwarf in it!" With calculated daring, she thrust him aside and left the dais.

His hand went to his sword and trembled there; then it slowly relaxed as she passed between the ranks of guards. She was his prisoner; when Jacques arrived, Louis had no doubt of her fate. She would be his, like a butterfly given to a spider.

Alexandre sensed that something was wrong. He had made an open show on Jacques's border now for four days and nothing had happened. He had left the castle to Liliane as proof to her of his faith and trust. If Jacques intended to strike at him, he would have done so by now. He might instead strike at the castle; better to return there to protect it than parade aimlessly in the north. Before he left, he took the precaution of leaving more lookouts along his border. Trouble had to come; he smelled it with all the sensitivity of a wolf trained to cheat death.

But he did not smell it at Castle de Brueil until too late. The castle looked the same as always, its peaceful gray walls russet-capped in the late afternoon sun. Autumn leaves swept across the meadows like dancing minstrels; the bare trees were gray spikes against the blue-green pines. He loved no other sight on earth as he did that of his lands . . . with Liliane's hair floating on its sea winds.

The helmed castellans greeted him as usual with a brief lift of their weapons as he rode across the lowered drawbridge. Dismounting in the courtyard, he gave his reins to his squire and headed for the hall. Except for the men on the wall, the castle was nearly deserted; everyone would be at dinner.

Just past the great doors, he halted, peering through the ruddy, slanting light with startled apprehension. The hall was empty except for a lone figure sitting in his chair at the far end. Even at a distance, he knew that figure was not Liliane. In another few steps, he saw that it was Louis. He whirled to guard his back, only to feel a smashing blow against his head. Blackness dropped about him like a cloak; the last thing he heard was Louis's grunt of laughter.

Alexandre awoke to the sting of smoke in his nostrils and a sawing ache at his wrists. Sensing that he might be wise not to awaken too quickly, he peered dazedly through his eyelashes. The dungeon torture chamber, unused since his father's death, came slowly into focus. The hideous torments he had seen there as a child had made the sealing of the room the first command of his regency as count. He might have guessed Louis's first act would be to reinstate torture.

A chill of apprehension trembled along his spine. Louis would pick him apart like a fly on a needle. What had he done to Liliane? He hated her and enjoyed only whores, but to rape her out of sheer spite would be well within his ken. She might be already dead. Alexandre knew that a quick death would be her more merciful fate.

Dread settled upon him. He had heard tales of Louis among the serfs of the countryside; those near Castle de Signe lived in constant panic. Louis was a killer as cold as a shark. No conscience troubled him, no enjoyment of sadism for its own sake. Louis killed and maimed for one reason: to create terror and thereby increase the family power. For all purposes, Jacques ruled the family, but Louis was his shadow, and even Jacques knew that shadow would one day attempt to overwhelm him.

Such a lethal danger could intimidate men much more clever and often more powerful. Linked with Jacques, Louis was dangerous. Alexandre had no doubt that Louis would one day bring Jacques down if Jacques did not destroy him first. Without Jacques, Louis's day of absolute power would be short, but the dead he left behind would not be upon the earth to celebrate his fall.

Abruptly, a vicious jab at his sore shoulder caused his eyes to snap open. Louis's dark, stubbled face was two inches away. "Couldn't let you nap the day away, milord, and delay the entertainment." He smiled without humor. "Which would you first prefer: the heated pincers at your genitals or at your tongue? Shall I have an ear, an eye? Tell me, milord. Now that I am your host and you my guest, I would render you all hospitality."

"Where is Liliane?" demanded Alexandre. "What have you done with her?"

Louis's heavy brows lifted. "Why, nothing. I confess to being preoccupied with you. Shall I call her?"

"Let her go, Louis. She will do you no harm in Spain. Take this demesne, but set her and the retainers free." He knew his pleas were pointless, but he had to try. "Philip will demand an accounting if you kill both of us and seize the retainers, as well. Use a little discretion."

Louis pretended to mull the suggestion over. "So you think I should kill you and call your death an accident . . . taking care, of course, to reduce you to such screaming, tiny pieces that even the fish could not recognize you as human, far less Count Alexandre de Brueil. With you having 'drowned at sea,' I might send your lady to Spain, after having her deliver her child at Castle de Signe. Brought up by Signes, your heir might prove excellent assurance of her silence.'' He watched Alexandre's face tighten in cold rage. "Then again, cutting the child from her now would be so much simpler; two at one blow, so to speak. Witnesses and stray claimants are such a nuisance. With all of you silenced, my uncle might tell King Philip anything he liked.''

Alexandre surged against the chains, his face filled with murder. Involuntarily, Louis backed away, then caught himself. He waved sharply to the guard. "Bring the Lady Liliane.'' When Alexandre swore at him, Louis kicked him in the stomach.

"You are wanted in the torture room, milady,'' the guard said shortly. Liliane knew from his face that Louis had either captured Charles or Alexandre. With her hands stiff at her sides, she left the tower chamber and followed the guard. Her only chance now, Alexandre's only chance, was for her to make Louis believe she had collaborated with Jacques . . . only she was afraid he did not much care. He wanted her and Alexandre dead, and tonight nothing would stop him from having his wish.

The small torture chamber held none of the elaborate contrivances Liliane had seen in Spain, so successful at converting the unwilling to Christianity by bringing them to the point of last rites. This chamber had the basic brazier, whips, pincers and rack, any one of them capable of reducing a human being to a mess of flesh, mangled and inhuman.

Through the glow from the brazier's scarlet coals wavered the silhouette of a prisoner on the far side of the chamber. Liliane's heart lurched painfully as she recognized Alexandre hanging from iron rings imbedded in the stone pillars. A trickle of blood had seeped from his hairline and dried on his face, and he was breathing raggedly, but his eyes were alert and he seemed unhurt.

At the look in his eyes when he saw her, she almost started forward, but she caught herself. Louis was watching her; any sign of sympathy would immediately seal Alexandre's fate. She nodded casually to Louis, then to Alexandre. "Good evening, gentlemen. Goodness, Louis, you *are* conscientious. How did you catch him?''

"He walked unsuspectingly into my net,'' drawled Louis.

"Apparently the possibility of your betrayal never occurred to him."

"Why should it?" She strolled over to Alexandre and peered at him with cold, clinical detachment. "For nearly two years I played the adoring wife." She trailed a finger down Alexandre's chest. "I was rather good, was I not, darling? You believed my every lying word."

She had hoped that Alexandre would take the cue and play her game, but his reaction was more extreme than she had hoped. His blue eyes narrowed. "You gulled me all along . . . for this! Just so you could sell me out to Jacques de Signe? I do not believe it!"

"Believe it, darling," she replied sardonically. "Did you suppose that I could live here in a provincial backwater"—her hand contemptuously swept upward—"with the amenities of a privy? Did you think I would let you run through my fortune to build this rockpile to a mean semblance of respectability?"

"I . . . *we* thought to make Castle de Brueil a home! You carry my child . . ."

"Most inconveniently," she snapped, as if her patience had run out. She turned to her cousin. "Louis, I *am* growing tired of slack-witted men. Kill my husband and you destroy our only protection from Philip's revenge. A live hostage is better than a dead provocation. Alexandre will last longer in the larder if he is undamaged."

"So you think I ought to treat your erstwhile lover with kid gloves." Louis slowly shook his head. "Naturally, you expect to be better treated yet." He shook his head again. "My apologies, Cousin. Suppose, while you watch me pry a bit of the truth from your lord, you add details to his account. So much better to answer freely than take your turn with me after he is dead."

"Do not be a fool, Louis!" she said with harsh desperation. "Jacques will not want this!"

"My uncle is regrettably absent," purred Louis. He picked up the pincers. "I think I'll have an eye first: one of those fine blue eyes the court bitches so admire."

The pincers moved toward Alexandre's face and Liliane tensed to launch herself at Louis's arm. The guard would be at her instantly, but if she could force Louis to wheel off balance, she might use him and the pincers as weapons against the guard.

Then, just as she started to uncoil, a voice drawled from the shadows near the door, "Wait a little, Nephew. Your lovely cousin has a point. Why throw away a bargaining tool?"

Louis whirled. "Uncle! When did you arrive?"

"A little while ago," Jacques said vaguely. He moved forward, his vast bulk as awkward as a sea cow on land. He peered up at Alexandre's taut face. "Dear me, so resentful." Then he glanced at Liliane. "Good evening, my dear. Louis giving you trouble?"

She forced an indifferent smile. "My cousin is, as always, overeager."

"Yes . . ." he sighed, "but then you must realize that your husband has long been Louis's particular irritation. One cannot blame him for his urge to scratch."

"Uncle, listen," Louis urged. "This bitch has been lying to you all along. Fremier was right about her laying a trap. The first tunnel was filled with waiting yeomen armed to the teeth. The seneschal came to relieve them from the copse."

Jacques looked about for a chair. "Is this true, my dear?"

So Fremier *was* a spy, Liliane reflected bitterly. Just how long had the cleric been at his dirty business? "Charles, the seneschal, discovered my plans," Liliane lied coolly, then upon inspiration she added, "I sent Fremier with a coded change. Did he not give it to you?"

"You found out Fremier?" snapped Louis. "I would sooner believe a swan kissing crocodiles."

"Or a greedy tallymonger," murmured Jacques. "My, my, to think that Fremier claimed all the credit for our ease of entry into Castle de Brueil." He winked at Louis. "You must be stern with him. Perhaps his punishment may divert you from damaging our prisoner too greatly."

"Uncle," Liliane intervened, "if I might make a request. I should like custody of my husband." She ignored Louis's derisive snort. "I have a bone to pick with Alexandre: a private matter. You may be better aware than my cousin, Uncle, that a woman is best able to torment a man. We need Brueil's living body to bargain with Philip"—she smiled evilly at Alexandre—"but we do not need his living mind. Let him be chained in my chamber for a time; you will never need fear him again."

Louis started to protest vehemently, but Jacques cut him off. "Humor the girl, Nephew. She has done us a great service. By the time Philip discovers what has happened, the tale will be thick with rumor. We have time enough to suit Milord Alexandre's account to our needs. We shall call a council of lords in Arles, where he shall testify that the maintenance of this demesne was beyond even his wife's dowry, which he had overestimated upon their marriage.'' He stroked his jaw as he gazed at Alexandre's defiant face. ''At that time, milord will affirm the peaceful transfer of his fief to us and propose an annulment. If he is clever and holds his tongue thereafter, he will stay alive long enough for Philip to possibly grant him a more hospitable fief in the north.'' He peaked his hands over his porcine belly and sighed; Alexandre's hot blue eyes said that the moment of his acquiescence would be long in coming.

''Run along, Liliane. Take your hothead and do what you like with him. If you cannot persuade him to be sensible, Louis most assuredly can.'' He signaled the guard to bring leg irons. ''You are likely to have your turn, Nephew; be patient.''

''Thank you, Uncle,'' Liliane said quickly as Alexandre was reshackled. ''You will not regret your confidence in me.''

''Ah, the eagerness of women to turn men into blithering idiots,'' Jacques murmured as she left, leading the guard with Alexandre. At his signal, two pikemen fell in behind them at the door.

As soon as the door closed, Louis gave vent to his anger. ''What the hell are you doing? She is obviously as two-faced as Janus! She tried to ambush us, and now she's out to save Brueil's skin, just as she did in Palestine.''

''Dear me, really?'' Jacques drawled. ''I do not recall seeing Liliane in Palestine and she is a difficult woman to hide.''

''I had several conversations with fat Xenobia, the owner of the Gilded Leopard. Brueil once had occasion to visit the place in the company of a stunning blonde, whom no one saw before or after that night. I think Flanchard found out that something odd was going on, and Brueil killed him for it. That something probably had to do with either the blonde or that Arab friend of his who kept getting in our way. Why would Alexandre, of all men, choose an Arab for a friend?''

''Alexandre has never been predictable; that is why he has remained alive.''

''Well, the Arab had a generous hand in keeping him alive in Acre. You admitted that Liliane forced you into moving on Castle de Brueil by telling you Philip knew of my betraying the raiders to Saladin. How did she know? Alexandre might have guessed, but he couldn't be sure without learning it from the Saracens. Who would be better able to go among them than one of their own—that damned Jefar el din? Jefar el din, who slept in the tent next to Brueil's and seemed to guess our every move. Do you know what I'm beginning to think?''

"That Jefar and Liliane are one and the same," Jacques replied dryly. "A bit far-fetched, don't you think?"

"Perhaps, but you have to agree it's possible. How can you trust her with him?"

"I trust her with him because he will keep her occupied. I want to keep her happy, Louis. I have a use for Liliane; when she has filled that use, you may have her. You may also kill Alexandre.''

Louis's face cleared. "You never believed her; you just want to dangle her in front of Philip as a sop and distraction." His lips curved in a rare, genuine smile. "I grant you, Uncle, I underestimated you."

Jacques eyed him smugly. "You always do."

"That wall." Liliane indicated the wall opposite the bed in the bedchamber, and the guard obligingly pinned Alexandre up. After the guard had been dismissed, Alexandre tested the strength of the hook above his head where his shackles had been fastened; the hook was secure.

"Release me, Liliane," he demanded curtly. When she did not move, his voice grew even harder. "It seems that Fremier had a hand in this, too. I would like to strangle him now, but I will not strangle you . . . just yet."

"That leaves numerous other ways of dispatching me," she observed quietly. "Just now, you appear to be contemplating them in turn."

"You are carrying my child; until he is born, you are safe . . . from me, at least. Jacques and Louis are going to dine on you."

Liliane watched him. His eyes were emotionless, his body very still, as if he had encased himself in armor to separate himself from her. She chose her next words just as carefully. "Do you believe that I betrayed you?"

"Do you deny that you planned the seizure of Castle de Brueil with Jacques at the tourney?"

"If you put it like that, no." The hideous suspicion that Alexandre had not pretended to think her a traitor simply for Jacques's and Louis's benefit was quickly growing in Liliane's mind. He had every right to be furious that her failed venture had lost him everything, but how could he believe that she meant it to happen? Had he so quickly forgotten her loyalty in Palestine? Pride and resentment swept her. "You *do* think I am a traitor!"

"I think I am hanging in chains in my own bedchamber while my worst enemies have the run of my people and my inheritance. My wife admits turning everything over to them on a platter." Alexandre's voice was growing angrier with every word. "You conspired with my best friend, with those toads—you confided in everyone but me! I would have died for you, Liliane, but I did not have quite this manner in mind!"

Liliane was immensely relieved. He was furious about her intrigues, but he did not seem to think that she had been after his head. The question was, would he ever forgive her for ruining him?

As she moved penitently toward him, Louis opened the door and thrust in his head. "Enjoy her well, milord; I have!" With a mocking smile at Liliane's horrified face, he withdrew.

For a stunned moment, Liliane stared at the door, then she caught sight of Alexandre's face . . . and realized that if he were free, he *would* have strangled her. "He is lying!" she cried. "You must know he is lying!"

"Just as Derek Flanchard was lying? I wonder if you even know truth from lies any longer! Our marriage has been filled with deception from the beginning! I can believe nothing you say! Louis, at least, is consistent!"

"Louis is full of malice! He would like to see both of us miserable."

"Well, he is certainly getting half his wish. You used Charles; why should you not try to use Louis?"

"I did not use Charles and certainly not in the way you imply! He wanted only to help you—"

"No," Alexandre said harshly, "that is not all he wanted, and you know it. You are still lying, Liliane." He shook his head in disgust. "Why do you care what I think? I am carrying enough iron to weigh an elephant. I cannot interfere with you now. You have damned us all, and be damned to you."

Her eyes stinging with tears of indignation, Liliane started to

lash back at him, then she abruptly held her tongue. To try to
vindicate herself when he was so furious was pointless. She could
not reproach him for his anger, but his lack of faith in her hurt
her greatly. She had never thought that he could turn against her
after Acre; *par Dieu*, she was wrong!

She must give both of them time to calm down, to remember
that love, not lies, had been the foundation of their marriage.
The loss of Castle de Brueil, their responsibility for so many
innocent people whose lives would be ruined, weighed upon
them too heavily now to incite bitterness and frustration. "I will
not quarrel with you, Alexandre," she said unevenly. "I only
ask you to listen to your heart; that, at least, has never lied to
you. If we are to get out of this, we must work together."

"That request," he retorted, "is a bit belated. The men who
lie dead because they believed in you would offer you now a
round of hollow laughter. As for me, the greatest fool of them
all, say that I have learned prudence at last. Go to hell, milady,
or wherever you like, but get out of my sight!"

Liliane's nails dug hard into her palms. "I shall go, sir; but
anon, I shall return. Perhaps you will come to reason in the
interim!"

Alexandre heard the door slam behind her, and a profound
silence fell about the room. He could scarcely think for anger.
This was his home, where his mother and sister had lived their
short lives in simple decency. Liliane was as different from his
mother as the flaring, brilliant sun was the moon. She had never
seemed suited to this quiet place, and now she had ruined its
peace forever. The events of the past few days, Signe faces with
Liliane's among them, the bodies he knew had fallen in the castle's seizure—all whirled in his mind. Liliane scheming with
Jacques while she wore an innocent flower crown of Love and
Beauty, smiling up at Charles, rolling in bed with Louis. . . .

But Liliane had not betrayed him; she had not, had not . . .
his mind was screaming with torment. Why would she defend
him in Palestine, only to destroy him now? So you would trust
her, the demons of despair hissed. So that you would finally trust
her enough to let her take your fief from under your nose. Besotted fool!

Alexandre could feel his doubts subsiding even as he decried
Liliane. If she had lost Castle de Brueil, she lost it for love, for
me. She could be Hecuba herself and I would love her. He threw

his head back. Liliane, return! Tell me any lie save that you love me!

He waited for her until dusk, but Jacques was the first to come. Alone, the fat baron ambled laboriously into the room, closing the door and peering up at Alexandre benevolently. "Do not be concerned, my dear Alexandre, I have not come to gloat. If your confinement were left utterly to me, I would have those uncomfortable shackles unlocked, but Louis has a plebian nature. He refuses to give you run of the castle, and until you prove your trustworthiness, I must agree to his demand. Would you care for brandywine?"

"And miss the excitement of being drowned off a boat?" Alexandre retorted dryly.

Jacques swirled the contents of the wine pitcher. "Oh, I would not poison you at this early date. I do not wish to kill you at all. King Philip is much too fond of you. Louis, unfortunately, misses that point, but your wife is much more astute. As you may have heard, she has been a great help to me."

"So I gather," Alexandre replied tautly.

"But I wonder if you gather just how much?" Jacques mused as he poured wine for himself. He sniffed the wine, then drew a tame mouse from his sleeve and offered it a sip from the goblet. He smiled at Alexandre's sardonic expression. "You know Louis's impulsiveness." He watched the mouse run up and down his sleeve, then take another sip, its whiskers dripping. In a few moments, it settled unsteadily in the crook of Jacques's arm. He stroked it. "Asleep, the drunken mite. Not all mice have a taste for liquor, but this little fellow is quite a tippler." He sat upon the bed and casually quaffed the wine. "Your wife has been just as reliable in her way. We have been in regular communication since your marriage, and actually sometime before that, while she was married to Diego del Pinal. Thanks to Liliane's cooperation, his death was quite profitable to us."

Alexandre's head jerked up in disbelief. "She helped you kill Diego?"

"Old men should never marry young women; there, I have been sensible. Youth grows restless and, in Liliane's case, ambitious. You have noticed her love of freedom, her willfulness and strength? Not an obedient girl, that one. Mercifully, Diego never knew what happened that day she went riding with him. Mind you, I am not saying she killed him; no shred of proof

indicated that it was anything but an accident. But"—he smiled—
"it was convenient."

"For all of you," Alexandre rejoined curtly.

"Oh, yes," Jacques said softly. "As your death will be if you
do not cooperate with us. I want more than your signature on a
piece of parchment to confirm my succession to this fief; any
butcher could force that out of you. I want your public and verbal
agreement to my succession at Arles, and I would prefer that you
look hale and hearty for the ceremony."

Alexandre's eyes narrowed. "And you are leaving my persuasion to Liliane."

"Put gently, her life and your son's depend upon your persuasion. I need you; however, I do not need her . . . grateful though
I am." He sipped his wine. "Trade Liliane for your life, my
boy. She is a veritable scorpion. Whatever she breeds will live
to turn on you. If you really want the child, I shall see that you
get it, but I doubt if you will thank me in the end." He drained
the goblet and wiped his mouth with his sleeve. "For now, play
her game if you do not wish to end like Diego. But thwart my
niece and she just might love you to death." He rose, adjusting
his sleeve so the mouse would not fall out, and waddled to the
door.

Louis waited for Jacques at the foot of the tower stairs. "What
was that all about? Did Brueil agree?"

"No, of course he did not agree," Jacques replied calmly,
"but would it not be interesting if he killed his wife for con-
sorting with the king?"

Louis frowned in puzzlement as he absently swung a terrified
Kiki by the neck chain fastened to his belt. "So you've been
putting nasty ideas in his head. I thought you were saving Liliane
for Philip."

"I am, but if she proves unreliable and ready to carry tales to
his majesty, we might do well to turn her into a more flexible
chess piece. Philip would not likely come to the aid of a liege-
man who had publicly branded him an adulterer."

Louis let the choking monkey drop to the floor and speculatively watched her try to catch her breath. "Might not Brueil
murder Liliane prematurely? He has an unpredictable temper."

"Either way we are safe." Jacques patted Louis's shoulder.
"Goad Alexandre from time to time in your inimitable way,
Nephew; he will soon jump at anyone's throat."

* * *

That night, Liliane returned uneasily to the tower chamber. A shaft of moonlight slanted across Alexandre's face; he was looking at her as if she had transformed into a spider. With a slight shiver, she lit the candle on the table, then noticed the empty goblet and guessed who had encouraged Alexandre's loathing. "Louis has been back to taunt you again?"

"Jacques. He was most informative." Alexandre's teeth bared in a feral snarl. "You have been his spy from the first, have you not?"

"I worked with him. I had to—"

He cut her off. "You never seem to have choices, milady wife. Diego was your supposed reason for first 'working' with Jacques"—the shackles rattled as he jerked forward—"only *you* killed Diego."

Now she understood what vile accusations Jacques had made. She took a ragged breath. "In a way, I did kill Diego. Jacques threatened to assassinate him unless I—"

"I do not want to hear it," he hissed as if his head ached. "I have heard and seen too damned much of late. From now on, just stay away from me."

"You demand the truth of me," Liliane cried, "and when I give it, you will not listen! What right have you to assume my guilt when the proof is offered by such a perfidious monster as my uncle? You are even ready to believe that I would dishonor myself with Charles and, heaven forbid, with Louis! My real sin was that I gambled and lost Castle de Brueil! My sin is against the dead! If I must lose you for my sins, I will shoulder the punishment, but I will not survive your lack of faith in me. In Acre, I paid for your trust with my blood. If I have lied to you, those lies were bred of your prepetual suspicion. . . ."

"Why do you think I left the castle to you?" he cut in. "I left that you might know once and for all that I trusted you with my lands, my people, my life. What would you have me think when I returned to find my wife at the right hand of my mortal enemy? Even Jacques and Louis do not trust you!"

"I care nothing for serpents who would attack their own tails"—Liliane caught the chain at his wrist—"but to be struck repeatedly by my own husband is intolerable. You think me venomous? So be it." Her head lifted defiantly. "I will play the serpent for you. I will turn your blood into a burning river in your veins until you call me witch! As I beguiled Charles and Louis, so I will torment you. As they had me, so you shall have me.'' Slowly, she began to unfasten his shirt.

Realizing her intention, Alexandre stared at her with startled fascination and loathing. His jaw tightened as she tugged loose his chainse. "I can tell you now, Madame, I would rather be fondled by an asp than a Signe, be she sheathed in the Devil's own charms.''

"You need not fear your new Medusa,'' Liliane murmured. "She will not turn you into stone, but into another element entirely.'' Her flaring anger turned to resolution. She would make love to him tonight in the despairing knowledge that it must be for the last time. Knowing he would not take her, she would take him. Past memory of his flesh was upon her mouth, her fingertips, her body. She wanted him so fiercely that she would force him to want her in the same way. No other woman would touch him so. When he touched another woman, he would remember her, with hatred, perhaps, but also as the incarnation of passion . . . of love, even if twisted out of recognition. I want him to feel Jacques's and Louis's lie! she railed silently. How may I touch him so and not love him! She traced his ribs until his skin twitched slightly.

"Ah,'' she whispered, "the mockery of love. It will torment us both.'' She moved away and undid the lacings of her bliaud, then slipped the garment over her head. The fine silk of her chainse was nearly transparent by candlelight, its filmy weave lying smoothly over the high porcelain curve of her breasts, the long line of her hips and thighs. She eased loose the lacing between her breasts so that their voluptuous swell was partly revealed, the nipples a rosy shadow beneath the silk. As if Alexandre were not there, she slipped a cloak about her shoulders, then opened the door a crack and murmured something to the guard.

Alexandre strained to hear, but he caught nothing of the few phrases that passed between Liliane and the guard. He had been unprepared for the heady, immediate sensation he experienced as she disrobed. Her body was so familiar to him, yet now she was another woman, some wicked mistress that he longed to destroy, yet who still fascinated him. He willed his body to show no sign of his interest, but he could not help wondering how long he would be able to keep up his pretense.

Liliane was ravishing and clever, as well as furious. Caught between anticipation and revulsion, he wondered just how far she would go to crack his control. Had she ordered the guard to bring up a few nasty toys from the torture chamber to ensure his humiliation? Alexandre's mind hardened. He had never been able to look at her without desire, and well she knew it. However, tonight she would lose her little game.

Liliane wandered to the window as if thinking to herself. Concealing her body, the cloak's heavy scarlet wool served to make the purity of her profile, her paleness by moonlight an ethereal vision, yet the ripeness of her body sang of the earth.

How irresistible she looks, how easy she was to love, Alexandre thought in sudden anguish. She is the magic of dreams, yet my dreams of her have turned to nightmares. She had cause to hate me for my treatment of her in Acre; for that, I could grant her some desire for revenge, but no; she contrived my downfall long before she first saw me. Did she know me, that first day we met in the wood? Did she know me then and mark me for cold seduction, only to achieve my destruction? Bittersweet memories swept him with bleak force, and he cursed himself. She has touched me not and already I am tormented!

Then Liliane turned to him. In her face he saw a mixture of sadness and mockery, whether for him or herself, he could not tell. "Alas, my love, that we are brought to war, where peace was our craving," she said softly. "Cruelly, we wreak havoc with each other and curse our meeting; yet we are joined for good or ill, and only death shall part us."

She came to him and touched his shoulder as if greeting a friend or bidding him farewell. "I shall counter thee with a woman's weapons. If thou are the victor, I shall not rail against fate, for I will have been vanquished by a man, fully courageous and courteous. To die for such a love is no dishonor; perhaps it is an end to be sought." Her hand dropped lightly to his chest. "Into the fray, my love."

"Give this up, Liliane," he whispered. "We are finished."

"Nay." Her fingers trailed caressingly down his flesh. "We have but begun." She went away from him then and sat on the bed. He watched her, wondering what she was going to do. She did nothing except look at him with a brooding, almost detached expression.

In time, the guard returned. A cowed servant entered with the copper bath, three more with waterpails. One of the servants was Yves, who shot a quick look at his pinioned master, then lowered his head.

If only someone could get to me and shear these chains, thought Alexandre. Water splashed into the tub and the relief he had felt upon first seeing the tub came over him again; at least Liliane had not ordered up hot coals. The servants departed and they were alone again.

Then Liliane bathed, her body luminous in the moonlight. First she dropped the woolen cloak, then slipped off the chainse quite naturally, as if he were not there. With a tightening of his groin, he watched her step into the tub and shiver at the water's chill. Her hair was a pale red-gold stream down her back, curving to her buttocks; the vee between her thighs was a beckoning glow.

She was beautifully feminine, with all a woman's gentle curves. Within her was his child, his immortality, part of his soul. She had taken him inside her and he had loved her unbearably. Even now, he wanted to touch her so much that his fingertips spread beseechingly even as his mind recoiled. All satin sheen was she, ivory and gold . . . witchery, witchery. Pride and lust, thou art man's damnation, and I am the lowest of fools for wanting her yet.

Liliane looked up, saw his luminous eyes, and her own grew bright, as if candles had been lit within them. She leaned her head back against the curve of the tub and, with a trace of shyness, touched her breasts like a young girl first discovering her blossoming. The peaks glistened, her nipples hardening under her delicately exploring fingers. Alexandre felt a rising heat in his loins and the inevitable swelling of his manhood. His heart was beginning to beat too quickly, the braies that covered him concealing too little now. He tried to concentrate on the manacles chafing at his wrists, twisted his arms to make the irons cut, but with the pain came a heightened awareness of his senses, so quickly inflamed by the cool, naked vision who tempted him with such seeming innocence.

Under his hot eyes, Liliane rose from the water; it streamed down her skin in a diamond sheet as she stepped from the tub and walked slowly toward him. Her fingers were cold as she touched his bare skin, growing warmer as she slipped back his chainse. Her lips teased his flesh, his sides, his armpits, then trailed to his nipples. He gasped as her tongue, small and pink, tasted him with exquisite delicacy. His nipples hardened and his hands locked upon the chains. "Leave me!" he whispered harshly. "Cut my throat, if you must, but cease this shameless mockery!"

"I mock thee not," she answered quietly. "I do but love thee." She knelt, and her fingers found the fastening of his braies, loosened the lacing. "Believe, my love . . . believe . . ." she whispered as his maleness swelled free against her burning cheek. Then her soft velvet mouth found him, took him until he cried out in hatred and in love. His fountaining arched in the dim light even as his body arched like a whip. I am my own lash, he thought as the darkness closed about him. She rends me with my own heart's blood.

That night was like no other they had known. Alexandre wanted Liliane as a burning brand seeks the flesh, but she was elusive, ever beyond his grasp, even as she touched him intimately, so intimately and completely that no part of him could be kept from her. By dawn, he trembled when she pressed him against her, his exhausted body still like a wire, drawn taut with desire. Her breasts were soft against his loins, and when she kissed his lips, he bit her and drew blood, only to find that blood upon his aching manhood when she made love to him again. Craving burned him, and although the floor beneath them was slippery with his seed, he was unsatisfied. He wanted to bury himself in Liliane like a sword, destroy her as she had him. He wanted to feel her flesh yield in his quick hands, wanted to drive hard and hot within her treacherous, quivering body. Let me have her but for a little time, he screamed silently to whatever devils might listen. Give her to me!

At length, he had a more banal urgency than lust. "For pity's sake, Liliane, have Yves bring a chamber pot. I am fit to burst."

Liliane smiled slightly as she slipped on her robe and ordered up the pot. Yves placed it discreetly at Alexandre's feet, his eyebrows raising only slightly at his master's appearance. Alexandre cut a scathing look at the guard who watched them. "Must I not only take a public piss at a target, but pelt it with droppings, as well?"

The guard grunted, then grudgingly unshackled his wrists. "Three more guards are outside the door. Try anything and we'll have your gizzard for breakfast."

"Life among the cannibals," Alexandre observed to Liliane, "would suit you very well, my dear." He rubbed his wrists, picked up the pot and took it into the tiny, curtained alcove. The guard caught his shoulder, checked the pot, which was half full, then the alcove, which was empty. He shoved the curtain closed. A moment later, Alexandre emerged from the alcove and bowed. "Thank you for your patient attention." He thrust out his wrists for the shackles, a sardonic light in his eyes as he jerked his hands away defiantly.

For a moment, the guard looked tempted to strike him, but thought better of it; perhaps because he had orders to leave Alexandre to Liliane. Judging from the circles beneath Alexandre's eyes, she evidently had attended to her task. The guard shackled Alexandre and, to vent his irritation, shoved Yves out of the door and slammed it.

"Do not anger them too much, Alexandre," Liliane said quietly. "They are tired and on very short leash."

"I have not had so fatiguing a night since the age of thirteen when I discovered a randy boy and rabbits have much in common."

Liliane laughed. "Do not boast, darling. Pursuing the peasant girls at your first breath of puberty was not admirable."

"Amusement is rarely admirable. If I survive being married to you, I shall dissipate without an ounce of remorse." His fingers waved idly. "Ladies, come one, come all. I shall not love you, but by God, I shall make you sing contralto!" His eyes mocked her. "To sleep, my sweet, and dream of me among choirs of bawds resounding your requiem."

Her smile faded, and her eyes darkened with hurt and regret. "Wherever I shall be, rest assured that I dream of thee," she replied softly. With the cloak wrapped about her, she lay down on the bed and snuffed out the candle.

In the last moment before the candle went out, the image of her golden face was emblazoned on his mind. The curve of her cheek and lips, the slight shadow her lashes made beneath her eyes lingered when all was darkness. I might bray for bawds, he thought in desolation, but my whole soul covets angels, for my ruined love is the incarnation of their sweet beauty. All women, whether low or divine, shall bear her face for me. When I die, I shall see her yet as the last I shall know of loveliness. He closed

his eyes and the shining image of Liliane's face touched his; her
eyes became his, her lips curved against his breath.

How can I sever thee from myself? Alexandre railed in silent,
hopeless anguish. I must, yet death would be more welcome. It
is far easier to turn to cold arms of death than to the warmth of
Liliane; easier to embrace emptiness than memory. Jacques
planned this; by destroying my illusions, he means to make me
prefer death to life, to rack my mind and heart past caring for
anything but peace. He places my lost dreams before my eyes
and mocks me with them. Liliane will drive me to despair and
capitulation. She leads me to a glimmering hope with lies—false
hope in the shape of Louis's garrotte, his assassin's blades.

Alexandre's face slowly hardened. Nay, I will not take hope
from a woman. I will exorcise love and cleave to revenge. My
cold mind, my cold heart will stretch no more on a villain's rack,
but live for tomorrow's promise of vengeance.

He pressed his arms together and, from his sleeve, plucked a
lockpit; it stank from the chamber pot where Yves had hidden
it. He really must wash his hands before he throttled Liliane.

Liliane stirred restlessly. She had not been able to sleep deeply;
fatigue alone kept her in a fitful doze. She must get Alexandre
out of the castle before dawn. She knew Jacques too well; he
could easily be playing a double game, about to change his mind
and be rid of his opposition. As Alexandre had said, Jacques did
not trust her. He must have use for her; otherwise, she would be
dead. Alexandre was the greater threat to him and in the greater
danger. She must release him now—and never see him again.
The moments of passion had passed and still Alexandre hated
her. They would be torn apart, and for the rest of his life he
would go on hating her.

Once Alexandre was free to go to Philip, Jacques could not
let her live. He might keep her as a hostage for a time, but
eventually he would kill her; she knew enough now to bring him
to the execution block.

The child might die, too, but at least Alexandre would survive. One might live, where all three would have died. My child,
my husband! her mind screamed. All I love is to be wrenched
away!

Suddenly she sensed a presence, like a hostile shadow overwhelming her. At first, she thought she was assailed by a night-

mare, then dazedly she realized that the nightmare was terribly real as a hard hand came down upon her mouth.

"Scream and I will break your nose," hissed Alexandre. "Do not move a muscle." A manacle closed over one of her wrists, then the other; a piece of his chainse went forcibly to her mouth. In moments she was shackled to the bed. "You have had your little game; now I will have mine," he whispered harshly. He jerked aside the cloak that had twisted about her body, then his mouth was upon her like a fiery brand, making her thrash and fight the shackles. All her awareness was led by his mouth, his hands, hard and deliberate and exciting upon her. He was as merciless as she had been, giving pain with pleasure until she moaned against the gag. Finally, he thrust her legs apart and, holding her so she could not escape him, his tongue darted into her, sending needles of exquisite sensation stabbing into her. She shuddered and arched with age-old pleading. "So now you are the suppliant," he whispered. "Tell me. Tell me what you want of me. Show me . . ."

Her eyes dark with desire, Liliane strained against the manacles so that he caught her arms to prevent their bruising. "Nay, do not struggle," he said. "You shall have your craving, and more." With tantalizing slowness, he unfastened his braies, let his sex surge free to graze her fleece. Deliberately, he slid his manhood through the pale gold of her pelt, over the slight roundness of her belly, the rise of her breasts to their peaks, until her nipples swelled beneath the glide of his sex. He teased her lips, but would not let her have him. He traced her flesh until she lifted herself to him, opened to him with beckoning allure.

Soft, soft, she yielded, welcomed, closed about him until he was slipping into an enveloping heat that made him tense with the effort to hold himself back, to make Liliane beg for him as he had meant for her to do. Cupping her buttocks, he lifted her, moving her against him until she responded with a liquid submission. His thrusts deepened, and lifted her higher, thrusting deeper still until he was buried in her womb and she was pinioned by his powerful maleness, giving way to him, seeking him with blazing hunger.

Alexandre's own starvation took hold and he surged within Liliane. Her body shuddered and his own was slippery with perspiration, his hands sliding upon her bare skin as his sex quickened its burning drive within her. Molten, they were together, forged together, melted together, until Liliane cried out against her gag and Alexandre's hands bit into her flesh. She was unaware of the pain, felt only the pleasure of his hard-driving body. A deep scarlet decended upon them like a blinding cloak; a swirling shower of sparks seared their flesh to burst at their joining. Alexandre threw his head back, his muscles straining as his body trembled with hers. And then she was full of him, the seed of his passion alive within her, and her heart sang.

Alexandre lay still upon her, his breath coming hard and quick as he tugged the gag from her mouth to let her breathe. For a long moment, he did not speak. When he did, his voice was husky. "You are my destruction, Liliane. Long ago you set love's snare and I was trapped forever within it, doomed to pursue you unto death. For all your evil, you love me, too, in some strange way. Still, you will pay for betraying my people, for they never shared my madness for you. They shall have my heir to one day rule them, and you shall have Philip's justice."

"What will you have?" she whispered.

"Nothing," he murmured against her mouth. "Nothing but the memory of this." Then he kissed her as if his heart were breaking.

Liliane looked up at him, her eyes filled with misery. "Learn to hate me, Alexandre. Do what you will, if it wil! ease you a little; but leave me now. I would not see them kill you."

He laughed shortly. "And leave you here with my child as their pawn? Nay, lady wife." Before she could protest, he thrust the gag back into her mouth. "You will go with me, if I have to carry you." He swept the scarlet cloak over her nakedness, then swiftly fastened his clothing. Despite her struggles, he unmanacled her, then bound her hands behind her back with a strip of linen from the bedsheet.

Alexandre, Liliane wanted to scream, you know you can never escape with a pregnant woman! The dawn is too close and there is no sanctuary within miles!

As Alexandre dragged Liliane to her feet, he was well enough aware of the obstacles he faced. The murky darkness before the dawn was beginning to fade to steely gray. If he could get to Pierre le Blac and a horse, they might have a slender chance of escaping.

He looped the manacles over his shoulder, then threw her fur mantle around her and picked her up. He carried her to the secret door and, with a quick kick of his booted foot, released the mechanism. Once they were in the secret passage, the door closed behind them. Keeping to the wall, Alexandre moved quickly down the stairs to the second door that led to the tunnel beneath the castle. No one was in the tunnel, but the entrance that opened on the rocks beyond the outer wall had three guards, their presence revealed by their low, intermittent conversation.

Alexandre set Liliane down in the dark curve of the tunnel, then silently unlooped the manacle chain from his shoulder. In seconds, the chain dropped over a guard's head, jerked taut beneath his ear to snap his neck. As he dropped, the chain swung free to smash against another startled face. With his free hand, Alexandre caught the dead man's spear and thrust it into the whirling third man. The bloody-faced second guard dove in, meeting an upward swing of the chain that snarled his spear and jerked it wide of its target. Alexandre's spear dragged free of its prey, then buried in the second man's throat just as he was about to shriek for help. Alexandre then searched the bodies, finding a dirk and shortsword. He thrust both weapons into the waist of his braies, then darted back into the tunnel to retrieve Liliane. He found her nearly at the mouth of the great hall, for she had gotten to her feet and tried to scramble back into the castle. With a snarled oath, he caught her up and hauled her, struggling, down the black tunnel to the gray dawn beyond.

"Tell your master it is Sir Roge of Auguen, you miserable swine!" The small knight in full chain mail and helm at Castle de Breuil's drawbridge gate glared up at the unseen guard in the dark crenels above the gate. " 'Tis colder than St. Agnes's bed out here, and I demand entrance!"

"Your pardon, noble sir, but my lord count has given strict orders that the drawbridge shall on no account be lowered before cockcrow. The hour is early and I dare not wake him."

"I demand to talk to the sergeant of the guard, cretin!"

"I am the sergeant, Sir Roge. I beg your forgiveness, but the castle is recently in a state of distress, and I may not allow you entrance until cockcrow."

"Curse you with the pox! I will deal with you when Sir Rossignol sings! You will rue the day in your miserable life when you forced Sir Roge to idle among the frogs." The short, squat knight in green surcoat turned to his retainers. "Michel! Tether the horses over by that outcropping. Be sure to rub my destrier down well, you dolt, and cover him against this dreary damp. Raoul! Get a fire started!''

Not twenty feet from where a winded Alexandre emerged from the tunnel under the moat with Liliane in his arms, a stake was being driven into the rocky ground. His short, savage blows showed that Michel was in no better humor than his master. Although Alexandre pushed carefully through the bushes which screened the entrance of the tunnel, the thick branches snagged Liliane's hair and caused her tears of pain.

The alarm bell in the castle began to peal, warning Alexandre that he had no time to size up the situation as he would have wished. Seeing Michel turn to gape at the still-dark castle, Alexandre launched himself through the low brush and flung Liliane up onto a bay mare, then turned on Michel. No neophyte, Michel whirled with his dirk when Alexandre hit him across the side of the head with the flat of his short sword. A dull *bong* revealed that Michel thought enough of his brains to protect them with iron under his shapeless, wool cap. His keen dirk sliced through Alexandre's sleeve, but before a struggle could ensue, the hilt of Alexandre's short sword connected with Michel's chin. Michel went down heavily, sprawling over the picket rope as he did so. The destrier neighed shrilly at the jerk on his bridle.

As Sir Roge threw a withered branch on the fire, he called out sharply, ''Michel! What goes on there?''

At that moment, shouting men carrying torches appeared at the battlements, and the drawbridge began its noisy descent. The rising firelight illuminated the prostrate Michel and Alexandre as he mounted the nervously shifting destrier. With her hands tied, Liliane was desperately trying to balance herself as best as she could on the skittish bay mare.

''Halt! You miserable thieves!'' Having shed his harness, Sir Roge whipped out his dagger and ran to his horse, screaming, ''Raoul! The rest of you blind varlets! *Aux armes!*'' He reached the rearing bay just in time to stagger under Liliane's weight as she slid over the horse's rump. Only Alexandre's cry, ''Liliane!'' and the surprising sensation of a warm, womanly breast in his hand kept Sir Roge from immediately dispatching Liliane in the heat of battle. When he saw that she was bound and gagged, his chivalrous inclinations took over. ''Abductor of women! Cursed villain! Die, foul friend!'' He hurled himself at Alexandre, who was trying to control the rearing destrier and untie the picket line. As Liliane kicked at him, Sir Roge stumbled and went down underneath the sweeping blow of Alexandre's short sword, which instead of cleaving Sir Roge, sliced the picket line.

Wheeling the destrier as Raoul and another man-at-arms came pounding up with sword and bucklers to cover their master, Alexandre saw that the possibility of retrieving Liliane was hopeless. She had well timed her tumble from the mare. The drawbridge was down and Jacques's men-at-arms were streaming across it. Most were heading toward the firelight, and he knew the mounted constabulary would be right at their heels.

"I will be back, you witch!" he snarled. "You will not have my son to ruin!" He wheeled the destrier again and kicked him with all the anger and bitterness that had festered in his heart the last few days. The destrier sprang forward, tumbling Raoul into the brush and clearing Sir Roge by inches. An instant later, destrier and rider had vanished from the firelight as Louis and his men surrounded Liliane.

17

The Deadly Game

Like a clever fox who knows his terrain by scent even in darkness, Alexandre eluded pursuit. Dawn found him well away from
Castle de Brueil and headed for Paris. He steered clear of the
fief of Fichon; its old baron was a cautious ally of Jacques and
might try to cut him off. Near nightfall, he approached a forest
along the Rhône and tethered the destrier near a stream where
he could forage on the dry bracken clinging to the bank.

The spot was so like the one where Alexandre had first met
Liliane that, though he had not eaten for many hours, he had
little appetite for the rabbit he snared. He kept the fire low, his
senses alert. Tonight he would enjoy no sleep, for he planned to
linger only long enough to rest the destrier. The Signes would
know well enough where he was going; his pursuers would not
be far distant. The bit of rabbit he ate was nearly raw for he
doused the fire a short while after sunset lest its flicker be spotted. Out of sight of the smoldering embers, he sat against a tree
and stretched out his legs to rest a moment before the long,
harrowing journey ahead; the Signes would probably chase him
all the way to Paris.

Perhaps a quarter hour after he settled, Alexandre heard a twig
snap. As silently as the rising mist, he came to his feet and
moved behind the spot where he had heard the sound. As he
crept through the trees, he watched the faint, dusky patterns of
his surroundings for the slightest change. Nothing moved, but

he sensed something, almost a vibration, moving toward the smoking remains of his fire.

Then he spotted a faint shadow crouching in a cluster of trees on the fringe of the small clearing. Cloaked in darkness, a man was watching the browsing destrier. Alexandre circled stealthily behind him. His dirk slid out and poised an inch from the base of the intruder's skull. "Move a hair and you will never grow another," Alexandre murmured.

The man froze. "Alexandre de Brueil?"

The dirk touched his neck. "Who is wondering?"

The stranger took a deep breath. "Charles." A hard slap on the shoulder threw him off balance. He fell to one knee and twisted to look up, his face first relieved, then red with shame. "Milord, you have been to Castle de Brueil?" At Alexandre's curt nod, Charles's rugged face flushed even more. "I would not blame you if you used that dirk. Upon my escape I tried to find you and your hunting party, but you must have already left for the castle."

"Why the hell did you not go to Philip?"

"I tried." Charles grimaced with exasperation. "I was half-way to Paris when I learned that he was not thirty miles from Avignon. His majesty is making the rounds of Provence. My guess is that he's out to rally support for a move on the Angevin lands. I am headed to Avignon now. Your campfire was laid scarcely a quarter mile from mine; I hoped it might belong to someone from Castle de Brueil trying to reach Paris." He rubbed his knee. "I take it Louis is not far behind?"

"You may save your subtle hints," Alexandre returned dryly. "Louis is in full cry, and you may rise and relieve your knees. You were never suited to subservience; the grinding of your teeth could be heard for a mile." He gripped Charles's elbow and hauled him to his feet. "Now, tell me how you and my lady wife let Louis's wolf pack into the castle, then give me a reason why I should not split you on the spot."

Charles quickly told him of the oak tree and the tunnel. "They must have confused our message and taken the wrong tunnel," the seneschal finished glumly. "Milady directed the Signes to use the first tunnel, but they split forces and half of them went to the second one. I do not understand how they knew about it."

"Quite simply." Alexandre's tone was flat. "Liliane went back alone to the tree and changed the message."

The confusion abruptly left Charles's eyes. "That I do not believe. She would never betray you."

Alexandre laughed harshly. "Why not?"

"She loves you," Charles replied simply.

"While she dallies with you." Alexandre grimaced. "She has made dolts of us all. If she manages as well with her uncle and cousin, she may yet survive to gull Philip and rule France."

Charles went pale. "Milady is still within the castle?"

"Like a maggot burrowed into a dead dog."

"Milord, they will kill her!"

Pain lanced through Alexandre's grim expression. "Aye, 'tis likely. For once, she has bitten off more than she can chew. Traitors have a fatal talent for venturing too far."

Charles's face hardened. "I tell you she is no traitor, milord. She did leave the castle after we visited the tree." Seeing Alexandre's sardonic expression, he added, "And being pregnant, she could not have taken her old route by the tower passage and moat. I tell you, if she is no traitor, the real one will make his claim for reward from Count Jacques. Her life will not be worth a fig—"

"But for barter," Alexandre finished quietly. Thoughtfully, he looked back in the direction of Castle de Brueil.

Charles watched him for a long moment. "You mean to have her back even if it costs you your life. You mean to punish her."

Alexandre slowly turned with cold menace. "You agree she *is* mine to punish, my hot-eyed Lochinvar?"

Chilled, Charles chose his next words with care. "I confess I love your wife, milord. Had she returned that love, I could not in honor have remained at Castle de Brueil. As it was, milady had no thought for me. Her eyes were full of you—her heart full of you. All her strivings were for you. Kill me now, milord, if you crave revenge, but I beg you, take great care in judging your lady, lest you destroy the last thing that you hold dear. Retrieve her only to vent your hatred, and you will commit a heinous crime against one who meant you well."

So this is the test, Alexandre thought; Liliane's last demand upon my trust. Do I still love her enough to risk the last shreds of my honor and pride for her, knowing that she will doubtless trample them? And yet, Charles is right; however evil Liliane may be, she deserves to be judged by a dispassionate law rather than the vengeance of a thwarted lover. He moved toward the destrier.

Charles followed him quickly. "You will try to save milady, then?"

"I will not see her die by Louis's garrotte," retorted Alexandre. "I will not promise her the same protection from the king's justice." He swung himself up on the destrier. "Follow me to Avignon, and hold your tongue before the king, or he will demand Liliane's head on a pike!"

Alone in the tower room, Liliane shivered in her cloak. When the smirking guards had escorted her to Jacques to explain how Alexandre had contrived his escape, she had pretended dumbfounded ignorance. She had been asleep, only to find Alexandre free and threatening to strangle her with his chains. After he had forced her through the tower passage, she had flung herself off the stolen mare in order to escape. She had to convince Jacques that she wanted only to get away from Alexandre. The real truth, which grated her fine horsewoman's soul, was that she had fallen off the rearing nag.

With apparent calmness, Jacques had listened to her story, then had her taken to her room. How much her uncle had believed of her tale, Liliane did not know, although the manacles and gag must have helped. She greatly disliked the way Louis stared at her while she was being questioned. Like the guards, he knew that she was naked beneath her cloak. Dirt from her fall had streaked her face, and her hair was tangled about her shoulders. Although she coolly kept her dignity, she sensed that Louis was no longer put off by her rank and manner. Louis now had something in his head that gave her chills—a growing malevolent lust.

The door burst open. With two guards at his back, Louis filled the opening. "You are wanted, milady," he purred, "in the dungeon."

Outside her door waited the traitor, Fremier, with an apologetic smile. Fremier was now as safe as if he had settled on the moon, and she was as doomed as if she had fallen off it.

Alexandre found Philip a half day's ride from Avignon. The royal retinue had raised tents in a sprawling meadow beneath a monastery-topped crag. A holiday air hung over the camp; the fighting was over for at least a month or two, and jongleurs, entertainers and peddlers had come out from Avignon to draw the men to the fringes of the camp where gambols and wares had been set up. As he and Charles pushed through the crowd, Alexandre spotted Philip's green-capped head tall among the spectators of a tightrope walker who had strung his rope high between two pines. He put out a hand to bar Charles's way. "Stay out of sight. I had best handle Philip alone. He is likely to ask many an awkward question about Liliane's part in this mess."

"What are you going to tell him?"

"For now?" Alexandre smiled grimly. "That I think her as innocent as the driven snow. I can always change my mind once we have gotten her back."

Philip hailed Alexandre heartily when he noticed him coming through the guards, who touched their helmets offhandedly and turned back to watch the tightrope walker. "So, *mon ami*, you are scarce two months at home and already restless for the court. May we hope that your lovely lady wife has accompanied you?"

Alexandre bowed deeply, then kissed Philip's hand. "Milady has not come to Avignon, sire," he said quietly. "May I beg a moment of privacy?"

Philip's green eyes glinted with alert interest. "Of course. Only haste from Castle de Brueil could make you so dusty." He immediately headed for his pavilion, his reluctant guards in tow. Once inside the royal tent, he pulled the flap closed. When he and Alexandre were alone, Philip took up a flagon. "Brandywine? You look parched."

"Thank you, sire, but my business presses."

Philip studied him. "What's the matter, Alex? Has your lady taken to a troubadour?"

"Her uncle has taken Castle de Brueil. Liliane is a prisoner within the castle."

Philip's brows rose with surprise. "Really? A prisoner? I heard that Lady Liliane was on the best of terms with the baron . . . particularly at his tourney."

"Gossip is fond of painting Liliane black. I am convinced she is loyal, sire."

"You would be—you are daft about her."

"Does that displease you, sire?" Alexandre returned swiftly.

"If it softens your head," retorted Philip with equal quickness. "Just what do you expect me to do about your mussed nest?"

"Nothing, my liege, that you feel is not due me by my past service to the crown. In that time, I have never asked anything of you."

"Ah, sly, sly, but blunt. You demand six years' payment at a moment's notice."

"Eight years, Your Majesty," Alexandre mildly corrected. "I was seventeen when I entered your service."

"Ah, yes. Now here we are less than a decade later. I may shortly rival Charlemagne, while you have lost your single, puny fief to a woman's smile."

Alexandre's blue eyes became icy. "If Your Majesty counts my worth in insults, I will trouble you no more. With your leave . . ."

As Alexandre turned swiftly to go, Philip caught his shoulder. "Come, come, do not be peevish with the man who can make or break you. Go off in a tiff and you may find the way back to me a rocky one." His tone softened, became caressing. "Tell me, what do you want of me?"

"I want Liliane—more, I want Liliane *and* Castle de Brueil."

Philip cocked his head as if considering. "That's a pickle. I want the Aquitaine. I am going to need all my army and more to take it, and the time is now ripe. If I go cavorting off to play games at Castle de Brueil, the time for taking the Aquitaine may turn rotten. Mind you, I would like to help . . .

"But prefer Liliane dead."

"Come now, personal preferences do not enter into it. If I take Castle de Brueil for you and get your lady back, you will never be happy going on the road again with me, will you? And if I find that she has had more than a finger in her family's plots to take the castle in the first place, I am bound to try her. I really doubt if you will forgive me for hanging her, even if she is guilty. If I temporarily solve your problem, I make a permanent one for myself. Frankly, *ami,* I believe that you are better off unattached."

"Is that your final word?"

"Oh, it is most assuredly, if regrettably, final."

"Then the next time you go 'on the road,' do not expect to see my dust trailing you. I will not fight you, sire, but in future, I will also not fight your wars."

"The end of our friendship, eh?"

"I would have died for you once," Alexandre replied quietly. "Is it more foolish to die for a woman's empty smile than a king's?"

Philip's eyes narrowed. "A woman will rarely kill you for insulting her; a king may be less tolerant."

"Do what you like with me, my liege. I expected your answer before I came. To lose one's dearest friend, love and home in the space of a few days is hard. To lose one's life . . ." Alexandre shrugged and tossed Philip his dirk. "Do it now. Finish the job."

Philip tested the blade thoughtfully, then tossed the dirk back. "As I have lost only a friend, I can afford to be generous. In eight years, I have learned that I will never find your blade in my back, Alex. You really have no skill for disloyalty and deceit; so it is time that you left politics. *Au revoir.* If I would wish you ill, I might wish that you retrieve your love."

Alexandre slid the blade back into his belt. "As we will not meet again, sire, I will say *adieu*. If I were to wish you ill, I would wish that you obtain your love and have all France to rule. 'Tis a load to humble any man."

Philip smiled faintly. "There is the difference between us—I am not a man, but a king. You must be the man for both of us."

For a long moment, they looked at each other with sharp regret and remembered affection. Then Philip clasped Alexandre's shoulder. "Win your headstrong Amazon back. As you are of no use to me, she may as well have you. Live in peace with her if you can; that is my gift to you, whether it prove paltry or splendid. If fortune smiles, you will regain your castle and grow old among your children and green fields. I shall not call you to war again."

A crooked grin crossed Alexandre's lips. "May I have that in writing?"

Philip laughed. "Begone with you or I shall carve the vow on your backside."

When Alexandre started to unfasten his braies, Philip shook his head. "Well enough, you shall have your petty bit of parchment with my fattest seal. Satisfied?"

"If your Royal Justice will leave Liliane to me."

"Reluctantly. A good beating now and again would do wonders for her temperament."

* * *

Charles was waiting on the edge of the camp, his eyes alight with admiration of Philip's finely equipped military escort. Catching sight of Alexandre coming toward him, his interest in the escort abruptly waned. "The king refused?"

"Predictably." Alexandre's air was tense, his hands quick as he untethered the destrier.

Charles scowled. "The gratitude of kings is notorious, but I had thought him your true friend." With mounting anger, Charles caught the reins of his own destrier. "What does the damned bastard expect us to do? Ram down the doors of Castle de Brueil with our bare heads?"

"Do not curse Philip, Charles; he had his reasons." Alexandre mounted. "And *we* are not going to do anything. You are headed to Jacques's demesne."

"Where are you headed?" Charles inquired suspiciously.

"To Castle de Brueil to parley with Jacques."

"Parley? Alone? He will have your head off and mounted over the gate by cockcrow!"

"I hope not. I need to keep my head at least until tomorrow."

Charles climbed into the saddle and gave his master a weary look. "Pray, tell me, does God arrive at high noon to bury Jacques and his vermin under a tidal wave?"

"Quite the opposite. By noon, I want you, His humble servant, to start a small fire." Briefly, he told Charles his plan.

Charles let out a long and expressive sigh. "That's ripe. We are to retake Castle de Brueil with naught but mad, unmitigated gall." He touched his cap. "Milord, we who are about to die, salute you."

Curled up in the driest corner of the dungeon, Liliane waited. After solicitously sending her a shift, Jacques had gone to bed and calmly left her to suffer all the torments of anticipation. She wished she had a rope or a weapon to commit suicide. A quick death was much preferable to what Louis must be plannning.

Scuffles of rats in the murky darkness echoed the stealthy panic that prowled the edges of her mind. She was utterly alone, except for the child within her; the child that must cruelly die without once glimpsing the faces that would have loved him, without experiencing the world that awaited him with its sometime sweetness. My little one, she cried silently, is there no way to tell you how much you were wanted? With what hope your father and I waited for your first cry?

Your father . . . my husband . . . my love. How alone must he be this night? If God be merciful, let Alexandre love again and someday put the terrible memories of loss behind him. Let him hate me if he must, but remember our child with kindness. . . .

Dawn could not be far away now, although she had no way of reckoning time in this windowless pit. Bordered by the moat, the dungeon seeped and stank. All sound was magnified, all life banished, but for the miserable prisoners snoring and coughing in the dark.

When she had first been shoved into her cell, the trapped castellans had mocked her, eventually becoming too steeped in their own misery to pay her further attention. She was fortunate to be in a separate cell; had Louis put her in with the captured castellans, her end would have been shortly and brutally met. She could only think that Louis must have something nastier in mind.

Liliane had little longer to wait in suspense. Minutes later, the key to her cell scraped in the rusty lock. With a chilling soul, she heard Louis swear under his breath, then smash off the lock with the hilt of his sword. The surrounding snores stopped as if with a single, intaken breath. "Where are you, dammit?" hissed Louis. "Answer me, bitch!"

She shrank against the wall, then heard a scratch of flint. A tiny light flared and lit Louis's heavy face. To her surprise, he looked uneasy. "Come here," he growled. When she did not move, he caught her wrist. "Don't play your games with me, bitch. I'm not the fool you think. You cheated me of your pretty lord's hide in Acre, then let him escape from us last dawn, but you'll pay for your little schemes. I warned Jacques that he was an ass to give you so free a hand."

"Oh?" Liliane tossed back. "Did you call him ass just so? Or were you afraid of him and sniveling as usual?" Let him kill me quickly, she thought desperately. Let me make him mad enough to strike me down without thinking.

He slapped her sharply, stinging her cheek. When his hand descended again, she instinctively shielded her face. His hand stopped an inch away from her mouth and shifted to her throat. He jerked her forward and shook her sharply. "Games again, wench? Oh, no, you won't get out of what I'm going to do to you. 'Twas not your lying note in the oak, but Fremier's. Fremier's!'' he shouted and rattled her again. "You cheated us all along by protecting your damned Alexandre and thought you were clever. I tell you that you're stupid, stupid!''

"If I am so stupid, why is Alexandre free to go to Philip?'' she spat. "Philip will have your heads for attacking him!''

A look of fear seized Louis's blunt features, but his eyes still simmered with hatred. "Philip's in Paris. Much can happen on the road between Paris and Provence. Whatever comes, you will not live to see it!''

"You are no match for Philip, Louis. He expects an ambush. He has run better than you out of the best part of France." She watched his eyes. "You cannot hold both Castle de Brueil and Castle de Signe, Louis. You have not enough men to stand off Philip. You have diverted his ambitions in the Aquitaine, and he will pry you out of both castles and flay you for treason.''

"Why should he leave the Aquitaine at all?'' snapped Louis. "Why should he bloody well bother with this puny fief? If he's off on one of his forays, he won't give Alexandre the time of day.''

"Keep telling yourself that, Louis, until the time the royal executioner splits your smelly skin.''

"Still sure of yourself, aren't you?'' he hissed. "Still too good for a man with the same blood as you. Don't like the way I smell?'' He caught her by the hair and ground his mouth over her. When she tried to jerk away, disgusted, he dragged her close again. "You will be well used to the smell of me by the time I'm finished with you.''

When he started to push her down, a crash of chains rattled the cell grate. Another jangling smash sounded farther away, then another and another as the listening prisoners, realizing now that Liliane was no traitor, vented their contempt of her abuser. The crash of chains became deafening.

"Keep it up,'' Louis shouted fiercely, "and I'll rape your lady bitch and cut out her brat to throw to the dogs!''

Silence fell. "Now,'' breathed Louis, jerking Liliane's averted face toward him again, "let's waste no more time . . .'' When she clawed him, he hit her again, this time so brutally that she felt herself about to lose consciousness, felt him tearing at her cloak. . . .

Abruptly a rectangle of light sheared across Louis's back, illuminating his startled, angry face. "What the hell?"

"Milord," said Antoine Fremier, holding aloft a torch, "you are wanted upon the west battlement."

"I'll be along. Get out!"

"Lady de Brueil is wanted, as well," the cleric continued implacably. "The *Comte de Brueil* has returned."

"Alone?"

"Apparently."

Liliane's heart sank.

The west battlement was murky with a pre-dawn mist, the far towers barely visible. Dragged hurriedly along by Louis, Liliane stumbled on the damp stone rampart lining the thick, creneled wall. Beyond the wall, the meadow lay in the darkness, fading slightly at the horizon to dimly silhouette the copse.

On the rampart near the drawbridge clustered a mass of bowmen; in their midst, his fat bulk protected by the wall, Jacques peered through the crenelation down into the mist. Clutching his fur cloak close against the morning chill, he turned at Louis's footsteps, then squinted at Liliane. "You are wanted, my dear." He waved at an indeterminate point across the moat. "Toss an endearment to your husband, so he will know you are intact."

Louis shoved Liliane forward. Her hands icy on the stone wall, she called out in a strong voice, "Alexandre, begone! You have naught to gain here but our jeers . . . and an arrow in the back!"

"Rest easy, my loving wife," a cool voice returned mockingly from the mist. "I did not come for you."

Instantly, Louis directed the bowmen to pinpoint Alexandre's voice. Five arrows were fired into the darkness. A moment later and many yards distant, Alexandre laughed. "Ah, Louis, you were ever sporting."

With an angry flick of his finger, Louis redirected the archers and another volley of arrows were loosed. Having again relocated, Alexandre teased, "Good fellow! At this rate, I shall soon collect a dozen full quivers."

Jacques sharply slapped down Louis's hand as it raised. "Have done, you fool! The light will come soon enough!"

Liliane felt Louis tense, not only with the urge to snap back at his uncle, but because he had heard what she did—an unmistakable note of tension in Jacques's tone. The only reason that a man with a garrisoned castle at his back had to fear a man alone would be the anticipation of reinforcements arriving for his adversary.

Alexandre sniffed Jacques's unease, as well, for he grimly concentrated upon rousing it as his only weapon. "Come now, milords, 'twould be best to bargain while you still have tongues left in your heads. King Philip was in a nasty mood when I left him arming this side of Avignon."

Louis stared at Jacques. "That's why you're a'quiver!" he hissed. "You learned that Philip was a day's ride away! Both of us will be bound for the block!"

"Be silent, damn you," spat Jacques, "and let me find out what the varlet wants!" He peered gingerly around the abutment. "What exactly have you in mind, Milord de Brueil? Not that it matters, for Philip is arming to take Aquitaine, not this paltry place."

"His majesty has altered plans," retorted Alexandre. "He dislikes ambitious traitors at his back." His voice seemed to drift about, for wary of the archers, he stayed on the move. "I want you out of Castle de Brueil, you old vulture, and I want my heir. If I do not get them, you are going to be sitting atop a pile of rubble come Sunday, with your guts in your laps."

"That is uncivil of you," purred Jacques, "and most premature."

"Come first light," Louis snarled over his uncle's shoulder, "You will be the one knitting with his entrails."

"I am not so easy to snag as all that, toad, as you have learned by chasing me this past many days. Besides, if you do anything rash to me, Philip's irritation is bound to be unleashed on you. Difficult to be diplomatic with your peckers stuffed in your teeth, hey?" Alexandre's tone lost its forced gaiety. "Now trot down my wife and pack yourselves back home."

Louis turned furiously upon his uncle. "You've done it this time! You must have turned senile not to make sure that Philip was in the north!"

"There was not time!" Jacques snapped. "How was I to know that he would leave Paris so soon after returning from Palestine? I had to strike while the moment was right."

"A moment *she* set!" Louis whirled on Liliane. "You arranged this mess, you bitch!"

"I had no idea that Philip was in the neighborhood," retorted Liliane. "Answer for your own messes."

Just as Louis started to strike her, Jacques jerked her to the open crenelation, then with startling strength, lifted her to stand up on the wall. A lone, slender figure in the flaring torchlight, she shook, almost losing her balance as Jacques clutched her skirts. "Brueil, if Philip attacks, Liliane dies. I shall throw her off this battlement onto the rocks. You had better call off your royal greyhound."

Alexandre held a tense silence, although he had known that Jacques must resort to just such a course. With her hands tied behind her back, Liliane might fall accidentally. He had damned well better speed the negotiations.

"A traitress is nothing to me," he bluffed. "Do as you please with her." He saw Liliane's face twist in pain at his words, and for a moment, he feared she might throw herself from the wall.

"You want the brat she'll drop, don't you?" snarled Louis. "What if she's breeding the next Count de Brueil?"

Alexandre forced his voice to stay steady. "I can sire more heirs. Shall we end this farce and get on with your evacuation?"

Jacques was sweating now. Liliane saw it, as did Louis and Fremier behind him. The cleric murmured something to Louis, and she saw a calculating gleam appear in Louis's eyes.

"Yes, Fremier," he murmured thoughtfully, "I think now would be a good time to reconsider many things."

"Be silent! We reconsider nothing! Keep your incessant whining to yourselves!" Jacques ordered sharply. He turned back to Alexandre. "I do not buy your tale, Brueil. Either give yourself up, or your wife and child come down."

As Jacques restated his position to Alexandre, Fremier fretted nervously, trying to speak. Louis tugged Fremier aside and whispered to him. Fremier's face twitched, then he shook his head. Louis bent his head to the little man's ear and whispered something else. Finally, tremulously, the cleric ventured to Jacques's elbow.

"Milord, you have taken no account of my contribution"—as Jacques turned on him with incredulous anger, Fremier's voice rose higher—"my claim in this. Your niece did nothing but foil you at every turn with lies and treachery. 'Twas *my* doing that spoiled her plots. I want the gold you promised now. I wish to leave Castle de Brueil at once."

"Leave then, you insignificant flea, and be damned to you," wheezed Jacques, impatiently brushing the cleric aside.

Fear and horror settled on the little man's face. Suddenly realizing that Jacques had never intended to reward him, Fremier's voice became strident. "My money, my lord. I have been loyal these many years. You must pay me—"

"By God, you sniveling, little swine," roared Jacques, at last losing control of his goaded temper, "I have you to thank for lying reports that lined your own pockets! Be off and be grateful that I don't hang you!"

The cleric's face went white, then turned red with rage. "Call me swine, you great pig! Trample upon me as if I were nothing! Give my my due, I say!"

With a great thrust of his massive hand, Jacques sent the cleric crashing onto his backside. "Throw this trash over the rampart," he ordered the guards curtly. "I have had enough of him!"

But before the guards could move, Fremier lunged at Jacques's throat, his poignard swinging high. Jacques tried to fling him off, but the poignard plunged into his chest even as a tall Norseman shoved through the guards and snatched up Fremier. He lifted the small kicking man and hurled him, still squealing in rage, over the rampart. His shrieks were abruptly silenced by the black rocks below.

Jacques had fallen back upon the wall, his chest painted with scarlet. A fastidious man, he was both disgusted and horrified by his own blood. For a long moment, he stared at Louis, who met his eyes with a brutal lack of emotion. Then his head came about like a striking snake. "Brueil!" he screamed. "Surrender now or Liliane follows that pig!"

Alexandre knew better than to hesitate—the game was up. Jacques was panicking and behind his gloating expression, Louis must be as well. If they were pushed any further, Liliane would die—Liliane, who was obviously no traitor. Liliane, who had taken the blame for what the broken man on the rocks had done. To save her now, he had one last chance that he must play within the enemy grasp, even as it tightened into a death grip.

"Lower the drawbridge," Alexandre called, as if defeated. "I am coming in."

"No!" shrieked Liliane. "Go! For God's sake, go!"

"Sorry, darling." *For everything,* he added under his breath, and mostly for what must happen next.

The drawbridge creaked down, and as the first light softened the sky, Alexandre entered Castle de Brueil.

By the winch, the gate guards disarmed him as Jacques was laboriously helped down from the battlement. Although Jacques was breathing heavily, his panic seemed to have gone and he had allowed the Viking to put a temporary bandage on his wound. Alexandre saw the pink froth at Jacques's lips and wondered if he realized that the wound was mortal; Louis certainly did, although his fleshy face showed only concern.

By the pearl-gray light, Liliane's paleness made her seem ethereal. She had regained her composure, but fatigue and fear had taken their toll. She looked at him only once as they bound his hands behind him, and then turned away as if the sight of him were somehow unbearable. By the faint light, Alexandre saw Louis's marks on her face. I shall kill him, Alexandre thought with deadly calm. Whatever else happens, Louis dies.

Supported by Louis and the Viking, Jacques greeted Alexandre with a detached friendliness that suggested his pain, but was also the demeanor he adopted when he was about to dispatch someone. Once his decision was made, Jacques often behaved as if the doomed party had already ceased to exist. "Come, come, Alexandre," he murmured with an effort, "do not look so grim. I have merely claimed two hostages instead of one; that is all. Who knows, by the end of the week you and your Liliane might be free as birds. Isn't that right, Louis?" His vague smile turned on his nephew. "We must go into the hall, break our fast . . . have a little entertainment. All this dickering has left me with a sharp appetite."

For what? wondered Alexandre as Louis patted his uncle reassuringly on the back. I would sooner walk into a cannibal feast.

After Jacques was carried into the hall and settled in the high chair, he heaved a sigh and peered nearsightedly at Alexandre. "I am just trying your chair, mind you. Power can be so fleeting"—he slid a rheumy glance at Louis—"but the young rarely anticipate defeat on the eve of the victory they have gained. That has been your flaw, Alexandre. Your father, brutal as he was, understood power, but you who have held little of it, rarely exercised what you possessed. Never waste whatever control you have of time, particularly when time is short—"

"Uncle," Louis interrupted solicitously, "you must have your wound tended. Will you retire to your chamber?"

"And leave this chair to your ambitious backside?" Jacques smiled at him fondly. "You have not the shanks for it, boy. Bring me a glass of wine and have patience. Grow a little round, instead of blunt." As Louis sidled off to order the wine, Jacques waved at Liliane. "Come here, my girl, and stanch this fountain in my breast. I would not grow faint too soon. After all"—he cast his idle stare upon Alexandre—"your husband would have us wait upon the king." As Liliane reluctantly inspected his wound, he continued, "When do you suppose that Philip will honor us, Count Alexandre?"

"By noon . . . if it does not rain."

"It might rain," observed Jacques. "Then again, the moon might stream sunbeams like a whey-pressed cheese and the sun might rise at night." He patted Liliane's hand as she bound his wound with the strips that one of the guards brought. "Mightn't it?"

"Where you are going, Uncle," she said mildly, "you might see anything."

"Sly boots. You know what I know, do you not? It would be a kindness to take you with me rather than leave you to Louis. He does not deserve you." His big hand tightened on her wrist. "You do not deserve to be meekly surrendered to Philip. You have been very naughty, my clever girl."

With the trembling Kiki aboard his shoulder, Louis returned with the wine, and Jacques languidly took the goblet from his hand. "Almost as naughty as Louis . . . on one of his more imaginative days. You really ought to be punished. . . . " He started to quaff the wine, then hesitated. "Ah me, I lack my mouse. Liliane, would you?" He saw her blanch and Alexandre start to move forward. "No, not good for the baby. Louis, dear boy, do the honors."

Louis looked startled. "I filled the goblet myself, Uncle; it's quite safe."

"Oh, I daresay, but I am much too old to give up my little habits. Indulge me."

After tossing Kiki to a nearby tabletop, Louis readily took the cup and downed a gulp. "There, you see." He held out his hands. "I am still upright. Would you like me to give some to Brueil and see if we both start to twitch?"

Jacques idly watched Kiki creep beneath the table. "Why not? You would like to go out together. You could claw at each other all the way down to hell . . . unless Alexandre is bound for the other place, which I very much doubt. You are not in a state of grace just now, are you, Milord de Brueil? The Lord bids you forgive your enemies, but you are itching to cut some throats." Jacques waved a careless hand. "Drink, Brueil. My mouse is not so neat, but much quicker."

Louis held the goblet to Alexandre's lips and Alexandre turned his head away. "Hold him," ordered Louis. Alexandre aimed a knee at Louis's groin that would have wrecked him had Louis not dodged it with his thigh. He put down the cup, took off his heavy buckler and wrapped it around his fist, slamming it into Alexandre's stomach. Alexandre doubled over, stunned with pain.

He heard Liliane cry out, barely saw the big Viking grab her before she could get to him. Mailed hands seized his arms and yanked him to his knees, then Louis forced wine down his throat. As Louis stepped away, Alexandre dully registered a glow of satisfaction in his enemy's eyes that exceeded mere brutality.

The wine *is* poisoned! Alexandre realized with sudden horror. The poison must work slowly, and only Louis has the antidote! He means to ensure Jacques's death, and he has achieved mine into the bargain! With widening eyes, Alexandre watched Louis offer the goblet to Jacques and the warning on his lips was stifled by bitter rejoicing. Die, you old scorpion! he thought as Jacques upended the goblet. Die, and be damned with us all! Now I have but to down Louis before I go. . . .

But Alexandre was mistaken—Jacques had decided how to use the time he had left. "I apologize for Louis," Jacques murmured as he weakly wiped his mouth with his sleeve, "but you have always been a difficult young man to deal with, Alexandre. Your father was stubborn, too. A pity you could not have been as stupid as he was; you have kept us at bay much longer than he ever could have done, for all his bloody efforts." His eyes turned cold. "To cap it all, we made the mistake of giving you Liliane. One might have supposed she'd be grateful to be relieved of that dotard Diego." For a few moments, his icy stare remained fixed upon Alexandre, then he settled deeper into his chair. "I think . . . I think at last that I shall discover just how clever you are, milord." He caught up the goblet again. "Someone fetch a chess board and pieces."

Louis's eyes narrowed. "You're going to play chess . . . now?"

"Oh, my wits are not dulling yet, Nephew. Shall we see how fast they go?" He motioned to the guards to bring Alexandre closer to the dais. "There, sit at my feet, young milord. We will have a game with stakes you can manage, despite your recent losses. You shall wager what remains to you." He waved to the Norseman. "String Lady Liliane up to the wall there. You, Louis, fetch a crossbowman."

Heartsick, Alexandre now saw how it all was to end. Liliane might have led her uncle to his ruin for murdering Diego, but the dying Jacques did not mean to go without gaining his revenge. "Ah," said Jacques, "I see by your eyes that you have guessed the game. I hope you have kept up your chess."

Alexandre had not. Over the past years, he and Liliane had occasionally played a game, which he won more often than not. However, since returning from the last crusade in Acre, he had given most of his time to his demesne. He and Liliane had spent their hours together playing a more entertaining game than chess. Alexandre knew that Jacques was a master chessplayer.

Alexandre's eyes met Liliane's with a gaze that held all the pain and love he was feeling. Forgive me! he wanted to cry to her. Forgive me for doubting you, for those last days we might have spent together in love, not recrimination. Forget my idiotic jealousy and remember only my need for you. Forget all the years we might have had, our child, the happiness. Ah, God, he wanted to scream, curse me to hell!

Liliane's face filled with compassion, and he knew that she sensed his utter despair. But he could not give way to it, he must keep his wits, fight for time. . . . How the hell was he supposed to best Jacques until noon, or more probably, until one of them succumbed to the poison? Jacques must be weak from blood loss, and he had taken the poison first. Louis was probably even now downing the antidote.

But when Louis returned, the gloating expression had left his face; he looked nervous. Was he afraid the antidote would not work?

Jacques caught Louis's expression as his nephew set up the chess board. "Afraid that Philip will interrupt our play, Nephew? Do not be. He will not be coming to Castle de Brueil today or any other before he has feathered the Aquitaine in his cap."

"On the rampart, you were less confident."

"Any man can be undone by the heat of the moment. I admit, for a time, I was worried, but now that I have had time to reflect, my mind is easy." He smiled faintly. "You see, I know Philip better than milord Alexandre, who has been his bosom friend. Philip, in many ways, could be my twin. Ambition and practicality are his guardian devils, as they have been mine. Richard's absence in Palestine is too rare a chance for Philip to miss retaking Plantagenet lands. He will not waste a moment of his opportunity on this tiny fief. Upon my death, my lad"—he patted Louis's shoulder—"you will have everything you deserve."

For a moment, Louis's suspicion overshadowed his greed. "Why suddenly so eager to see me your successor? A mere wound will not stop you; you will live another twenty years."

Jacques sighed. "Boy, I am in such pain that another twenty minutes seems a burden." He noted the bowman's entry. "You, young Alex, are you ready to begin our game?"

"May I speak first with my lady?" Alexandre requested tensely.

"Why not? But mind, do not dally. Invalids are notoriously short of patience."

Alexandre walked slowly toward Liliane until they were a handbreadth away from each other. "I love you," he whispered. "Can you forgive me?"

Her hand moved as if she would touch his face, then she smiled softly. "I knew that you loved me when you came back to Castle de Brueil. We are bound together, you and I. I have no more to regret than our ending."

His whisper became almost inaudible. "You may have a chance if I can delay the end of the game." Briefly, he told her of his order to Charles.

Her eyes widened. "Milord, you are a fox worthy of my uncle!"

"I fear not. The burden may fall to you." He pressed his lips to hers, then murmured against them, "Pray tell me you have not been letting me win at chess!"

"Nay," she breathed, "I am neither his match nor yours, but I have watched him favor certain gambits. His slyness may outdo him. Never will he take a direct path if a twisted one beckons."

"Milord, you have tarried long enough," Jacques called.

Alexandre kissed Liliane passionately and without words.

Louis strode up and jerked him away. "Enough of that," he hissed. "If my uncle's archer doesn't get her, she's mine!" He gave Alexandre a shove back to the chess board.

Jacques appraised the smoldering fire in his young opponent's eyes. "A show of temper will not do, Milord de Brueil. In chess, a cool head is all."

"Speaking of all," retorted Alexandre coldly, "just what do I get out of this game? Suppose you lose?"

"Dear me, let us see. What do you say to a clear shot at Louis with that crossbow?"

"The hell you say . . ." snarled Louis.

"Just teasing," purred his uncle. "Suppose I let you live until I die, Alex."

"What of Liliane?"

Jacques shrugged. "As she is relatively inconsequential to me but vital to you, you may keep each other company until Louis takes charge of her."

"Louis is not to have her."

Jacques stirred restlessly. "You must take that up with Louis. I have finished bargaining. Begin the game." His voice held an edge that had not been there before, and Alexandre wondered just how much endurance the old man had. The bandage upon his chest was already brightly stained and Jacques's movements were becoming fitful. Was his wound affecting him or had the poison begun to take its insidious toll?

What horror was happening inside his own body? He felt nothing yet except desperation and the beginning of a headache. He stared blindly at the board for a moment, then forced himself to concentrate. He must play very well, better than he had ever dreamed of playing. Sweat prickled his brow and dampened the first chess piece he touched. Taking as long as he dared, he finally made the move.

Jacques nodded approvingly. "Good. Good choice." He flicked forward a counter pawn.

Alexandre made sure that five moves took an hour. Each time he made a move, Jacques commented on his wisdom as if judging a novice. But at the end of another hour, Jacques had fallen silent. His moves were not so quick, his manner was subdued. He had taken two of Alexandre's pieces and Alexandre had taken one of his.

Both men were pale, Jacques clearly uncomfortable. Alexandre's headache was beginning to throb all the way down his spine. Once, when waiting for Jacques to make a move, Alexandre saw Louis rub his forehead, then surreptitiously go through the coin pouch at his waist. Looking for something? he wanted to taunt. Lost your way out of your own trap? Only when he looked at the fatigue on Liliane's drawn face, did he feel desperation. They were moving into the third hour. Every minute that he prolonged the game took its toll on her.

Jacques clipped a piece. Louis came over to the board and ran his hands through his wiry black hair. "How long are you going to take at this? It's a damned bore, if you ask me."

"No one asked you, Louis," his uncle replied. "Why not chat with the bowman about back-shooting? That should interest you."

Louis's hand halted abruptly in his hair. "Why the insinuating remarks? Haven't I looked after you?"

"After your fashion, I should say devotedly. Now be a good ogre and run along."

Louis ignored him. "Look here, I say we up the wager. For every piece you take, the bowman takes a shot."

"That is a thought."

Alexandre's hackles rose. "You agreed to a full game!"

"So I did," Jacques replied with an effort, "but then I have never been very reliable. You must admit that Louis has a point. We are progressing rather slowly. I should have thought you would be more impetuous."

"With my wife and child at stake?" Alexandre leaned forward. "Play a game fairly for once in your life, Jacques. Winning will offer twice the satisfaction."

Jacques's lips curved maliciously. "Seeing my treacherous niece with an arrow in her throat will give me sufficient satisfaction, milord. Watching your face when that arrow flies home will crown the pleasure. You play well, too well to fall back upon chivalry. You have discredited me and my family, turned all of France against us—"

"Your repeated treacheries and assassinations did that, Jacques. Do not pretend your lack of guilt so close to Judgment; 'tis another sin upon the many."

"Then what is one more sin? I like my comforts. Heaven offers only stiff saints and board beds. Satan will not keep me in hell, but send me again into the world to plague it in his name.''

''Is Louis so sanguine about answering for his evil?'' retorted Alexandre. ''His end may be at his heels, for all he knows.''

Jacques chortled at Louis's stiffening face, then went into a coughing fit. Limply, he raised a protesting hand. ''No more of that! I shall die early of amusement. Picture Louis . . . pricked on Satan's fork.'' He jabbed Louis in the ribs. ''Squirm, you puny malcreant!'' Then his mood abruptly altered as the agony in his chest reminded him of the passing time. ''Bowman, take heed. The next chesspiece I take will put an arrow . . . through my niece's hair. Should you miss, welladay.''

His teeth clenched, Alexandre applied himself to the board, but Jacques's deadly warping of the rules had its effect. He forfeited his next piece.

Alexandre held his breath as the blunt bow drew back; its arrow sped and shivered amid the shimmer of Liliane's hair, an inch from her ear. Alexandre let out his breath. Thank God, the bowman was a good shot! Liliane was white as a new linen chainse, but she had not batted an eye. He forced himself to empty his mind of all distractions as his gaze raked Jacques's field of pieces. In pouncing on one of Alexandre's bishops, Jacques had left one of his knights open: in another two moves, Alexandre had it.

Jacques blinked as if forcing his attention, then sighed. ''More wine, Louis. Our young stag waxes keen.''

Hastily, Louis brought the wine. ''May I be excused for a time, Uncle? 'Tis near noon and I really should check the guard.''

Jacques shot him a sidelong glance. ''And miss the moment you have been panting for? Or is it something else that makes you impatient?'' He nodded to the Norseman, leaning bored in the corner. ''Stop paring your fingernails with that ax, Olaf, and see to the guard. My nephew is keeping me company.'' His reptilian gaze slid again to Louis. ''I should not wish to die without my loving successor at hand, should I, Louis?''

With a cynical look at Louis, Olaf went to see about the guard. As the game dragged on, Louis began to sweat a little more than Alexandre. Jacques noted his discomfort. ''Fie, Louis. You wanted my power, did you not? Badly enough to set that wizened clerk on me . . . ah, yes, do not squirm; I noticed your little

. . . tête-à-tête with him on the battlement, despite my . . . pre-occupation with milord Alexandre here.'' Jacques smiled, a ghastly smile now, twisting his features with his fatal pain and ebbing strength. ''Now you will have to handle any future complications with Philip all by your slug-witted self. Uncle will be safely dead and free to haunt you.''

When Louis looked swiftly about to see if they were alone, snaking his hand to his dirk, Jacques croaked, ''No need, my newt, I shall be dead before the hourglass empties . . . and you will rule all you survey. I want only to see Liliane . . . precede me from this world. An angel to heaven, a devil to hell. All we waiting demons shall work for your ruin, Louis, and be assured, if we do not mangle you upon this earth, you will . . . be ours beyond it.''

Jacques moved his queen, and with a grim smile of triumph, Alexandre claimed it. Jacques's brow puckered. ''I must . . . be losing my touch. My mind wanders under a cloud . . . black and foul. I have you, though, Brueil. One last move . . . and your king . . . and lady are mine.'' He reached heavily for the piece, then his hand dropped helplessly. ''I . . . cannot. Louis, Louis . . . move my bishop to . . .'' His rheumy eyes began to drift. ''Kill her . . . now. Now . . . I cannot wait . . .''

The bowman nocked a new arrow and drew back. Louis abruptly waved him to lower the bow. ''Sorry, Uncle, but I have better use for the bitch in my bed . . . and you've lasted long enough.'' Slipping out his dirk, he lurged with brutal force at Jacques's paunch, sinking it deep. Jacques's mouth sagged open as his last breath left him even before the dirk touched him. Louis wrenched the weapon out. ''Damnation! The old dog was lucky to the end!''

''You're not,'' drawled the Norseman, leaning against the jamb of the hall's great doors. He strolled into the hall. ''A fire is roaring to the north. Castle de Signe appears to be going up like a dry tree.''

Louis whirled on Alexandre as he waved to the Norseman to bind his wrists. ''What are you up to?''

''Nothing, at the moment. As you can see, my hands are now tied,'' replied Alexandre. ''Philip's, on the other hand, are not.''

''He's attacking Castle de Signe?'' cried Louis. He pounded past Olaf to the battlement.

As soon as Louis was gone, Alexandre addressed the Norseman. "Free me and you will be richly rewarded."

"With chickens?" the Viking mocked, studying Alexandre's waxen face. "From what I've seen, that is all you have to spare."

"I have jewels hidden away," put in Liliane. "More than you will ever see tagging after Louis. King Philip is Count Alexandre's loyal friend and he outnumbers Louis; he will kill you all."

"I've seen no kings—just a fire," Olaf said lazily. "Anyone can start a fire." He grinned. "I haven't seen any jewels either. You will have to tell me where they are."

"Cut us loose," urged Liliane, "and I shall show you."

The Norseman shook his head. "That's asking me to put the cart before the horse. When I'm bought, I stay bought, unless somebody flashes a better price before my eyes." His teeth flashed again, his smile wide and friendly.

Liliane turned in desperation to Alexandre.

"Kiki," he said slowly, wearily. "Summon Kiki."

As she realized what he meant, Liliane's face brightened. She trilled a high whistle, then made a series of clicks with her tongue. When a few minutes passed and nothing happened, she repeated her call. A wary frown furrowed the Norseman's brow. "Who's Kiki?" he demanded, shifting his battle-ax from his shoulder to poise at the ready.

"Possibly the source of your better price," replied Alexandre. He stealthily tested his bonds; they were not only secure but cutting into his swollen wrists. Thanks to Louis's poison, the ache in his head had spread throughout his body. "At any rate," he advised the Viking, "Kiki scarcely reaches your knees, so you can relax your weapon."

The Norseman did not budge. A moment later, a small furtive creature edged into the room. After wringing its hands for an instant, it darted for Liliane and scurried to her shoulder, where it peered with worried eyes at the startled Norseman.

"This," Liliane told him, "is Kiki." She rubbed her cheek against the monkey's fur, then drew its attention to the brooch at her shoulder. "I want another jewel, Kiki," she murmured. "Another pretty, just like this one. Bring, Kiki. Fetch . . ." The monkey slithered to the floor and was off.

The Norseman lit out after her, but he was back almost immediately, shaking his head ruefully. "That's a quick beast. What in Wodin's name is it?"

"A monkey," Liliane told him. "A pet from the Crescent."

"Fancy that. I have heard of those things . . . monkeys." While the Viking mused, Louis returned.

He strode furiously up to Alexandre and slapped him. Alexandre's blue eyes flared wickedly. "Cut me loose and try that!" In answer, Louis slapped him again. Alexandre's foot hooked his ankle and dropped Louis onto his backside. Louis jumped up, his dirk snaking from its sheath. Olaf quickly stepped between them, his ax blade diverting Louis's lunge at Alexandre's throat. The ax blade gave a brief, sweet ring that ended in a grate of steel.

The Norseman grimaced but blocked the raging Louis's blade again. "A fit of spite won't do now," he told Louis flatly with a cooling look in his eye that caused the other man to hesitate. "If you have trouble with your king, keeping Brueil alive may be our only way out of it."

"You take orders from me!" spat Louis. "Not the other way around. I'll have you spitted—"

"Will you now?" Olaf's eyes narrowed. He moved ominously forward as Louis backed up. "You're making one mistake after another, aren't you?"

Louis seemed to reconsider his position. "I was angry," he said sullenly. "For two years now, Brueil has caused me nothing but difficulty."

"I can imagine," drawled Olaf. From the corner of his eye, he caught a glimpse of Kiki returning to Liliane. Emeralds and ice glittered about the monkey's neck. With a nod of her head, Liliane motioned the monkey to stay out of sight. Instantly, Kiki disappeared under the trencher table. Olaf appraised Louis's nervousness, Alexandre's now icy calm. "What do you make of the fire, Milord de Signe?"

"Castle de Signe appears to be burning," Louis answered reluctantly. "I've sent a man to be certain."

"Expecting a siege there?"

"Of course not! Philip was supposed to be in Paris!"

"How many men will he have?"

"Enough to take Castle de Signe," Alexandre answered for Louis. "He had forty knights and three hundred soldiers with him at Avignon. Your best chance is escape by sea."

"I'm not going to run!" snapped Louis. "Do you think I'm going to settle for nothing? My man will be back in less than two hours, and then I'll decide!"

"In that time, we could be well out at sea," observed the Viking, "or we could be caught here like rats in a trap."

"We wait," said Louis stubbornly.

Olaf shrugged.

They waited until Alexandre felt as if a knife was being driven into his skull and his bones were cracking. Liliane had been cut down, and she was sitting on the steps of the far side of the dais. She was beginning to watch him intently, and he knew she sensed that something was wrong with him. She was trying not to let Olaf and Louis guess her concern, for they would misinterpret it and doubt Philip's presence. Just now, Alexandre's pretense of calm was undermining Louis's resolve more than any verbal insistence would have done.

However, Alexandre was dying by fractions and keeping the pain from his face was becoming nearly impossible. And all for a futile purpose. The most his and Liliane's ruse could do was keep them alive until Louis's man arrived with the news that Castle de Signe was intact and not a royal pennant was in sight. At least, Alexandre reflected grimly, the pacing Louis was being distracted from Liliane. When that distraction vanished . . .

The time trickled slowly by. Louis's face grew pinched, his circuit about the room taking him with increasing frequency to the north windows. Sometimes, after staring at the spreading smoke over his fief, he pressed his forehead hard against the stone for minutes at a time. His jaw was rigid, a line of pain furrowing between his brows. At length, the Norseman glanced at him. "Not two hours, you said? By my reckoning, your man's had nearly three."

"More than enough time to be back," observed Liliane. "Your spy is either captured or dead, Louis."

Louis shot her a venomous look. "Perhaps he's just been delayed. His horse could have taken a spill, gone lame . . ."

"And, as Uncle Jacques said, the moon could stream curds and whey." Liliane turned her attention to Olaf. "Do we go on waiting?"

He leaned on his ax. "Ask Milord de Signe. He will be first to hang if he gives the wrong answer."

"Well, Louis?"

Louis stared at her blackly, then rubbed his forehead; it was the same pasty hue as Alexandre's, and his jaw was rigid with pain.

"Make the coast, Louis, and you have a chance," Alexandre baited hoarsely. "You can go to Italy. Stay here and you are as dead as Jacques and me."

For a moment, Louis looked taken aback, then his eyes narrowed as he realized that Alexandre must have guessed about the poison. He gnawed his lip as he fingered his dirk. "Very well," he said at last, "we go."

A quarter of an hour later, with Liliane mounted on the saddle before him, Louis abandoned Castle de Brueil. Behind him rode the bound Alexandre, and Olaf and the hired mercenaries, followed by ten of Louis's knights and a stream of hurrying foot soldiers. Across the dry fields, a trail of dust rose and filtered away to the north, where it mingled at last with a dirty cloud of smoke.

They arrived shortly at the sea where Cannes, a small fishing village that had remained almost unchanged since Phoenician times, clung to the rocks. Louis reined in before the wind-battered hut of the village elder. A middle-aged man hurried out and squinted up at him. "How may we serve you, great lord?"

"Boats," demanded Louis. "We must have all your fishing boats."

"What then will we use for our fishing?" protested the elder. "Our livelihood depends on our boats."

"Your lives depend on giving me what I want," Louis roared. "Where are the boats?"

The elder waved at the empty beach, then pointed at a single, ancient fishing craft beached below in the rocky village inlet. "Out. All the boats are out after the day's catch. That one is unreliable in heavy seas."

"I'll take it." Louis pounded off toward the boat, his band trailing after him. Women and children scattered from the stretched nets they were repairing on the rocks as the horsemen and scrambling foot soldiers threaded down the paths trickling to the inlet. Louis reached the boat first.

The Norseman remained upon the higher rocks with a bowman he had ordered to his side. "Milord de Signe," he called down when Louis had dismounted and dragged Liliane from the saddle. "That boat will hold only six people. Who will go with you?"

"The Lady Liliane," yelled Louis, dropping her in the boat, "you, and two men-at-arms."

"What of the rest?" Olaf waved at the descending men now hesitating uncertainly on the rocks.

"They can go where they like," replied Louis distractedly as he untethered the boat. "I'll see they're paid when I return to France." He turned on Alexandre and unsheathed his sword. "This one, I don't need anymore."

As the sword swung high, Olaf's ringing voice stopped it in mid swing. "Brueil is worth something to me, and you will pay us now!" The Viking cocked his crossbow.

"Be reasonable," shouted Louis. "I have no gold with me and without Brueil, Philip has no reason to think that any of you had anything to do with the seizure of his castle!"

"Just now you are a penniless, erratic man, Louis," said Liliane coolly. "They are learning they cannot rely on you or your good faith." Her voice lifted to the angry men on the rocks. "Forget Louis de Signe! You will never see your gold from him now. He is leaving you to be run down by King Philip. Your only hope lies in turning to Count Alexandre!"

"What of our necks?" shouted one. "Why shouldn't the count hand us over to King Philip for hanging?"

"You have my word that you will be safe from punishment," Alexandre said hoarsely. "The only man who must answer to the king is Louis de Signe."

His men's faces revealing their readiness to turn on him, Louis grabbed for the boat's bow.

"Halt or be drilled!" cried Olaf. Louis froze. "Treachery I can stomach, but I will not follow a gutless bully who will one day knife me on a whim," said Olaf. "There may not be a penny's difference between you and Brueil, but from what I've seen, you fight best when your opponent is tied, Signe. Suppose we see how you fare in the same predicament." He motioned to the bowman. "Drop the sword, Signe, or he'll drop you." When Louis hesitated, Olaf added grimly, "You thought him a fine enough shot to turn on a woman and her unborn babe, man. 'Twill settle my stomach to send you after your conniving uncle."

"I can take him!" blustered Louis, still clutching his sword.

"And I have wealth enough in Italy. I'm good for every livre my uncle promised. All you have to do is come with me to Rome, Olaf, and I will send you back with enough gold to twice reward the rest of you!"

"Gallows bait can't spend gold, Signe," yelled a soldier.

"That says it!" cried another. Shouts went up from more of them.

Olaf held out his hands. "Enough, lads. You'll see Count Louis prove his worth to us. Off with your weapons, Milord de Signe!"

His shout was taken up and the inlet rang with demands for Louis to obey without delay. Staring about at them with blood-shot eyes, Louis spat, then flung the sword up onto the rocks.

Olaf came down the rocks and ordered Alexandre pulled off his destrier. He sawed the bonds off Alexandre's wrists, then roughly chafed his numbed hands. "Stand with right ankles to-gether," he ordered the two men. Dazedly, Alexandre watched Olaf bind his ankle to Louis's. "Get in the boat with the count-ess," commanded Olaf. Awkwardly, Alexandre climbed into the boat with Louis. Olaf climbed in after them, then summoned another soldier to row them out into the inlet.

The water was still, bluer than the reflected sky, with inky depths near the jutting rocks. "Here," said Olaf when they had reached the middle of the inlet. He tossed two dirks over the side, then turned to Alexandre and Louis. "The rest is up to you. I deal with the survivor." Liliane gasped as Olaf powerfully shoved them overboard.

Alexandre instinctively kept from floundering as the water closed over his head. The impact of the cold water was agonizing to his throbbing skull, but it cleared his misted wits. He'd had all he could do to stay on his horse during the ride from Castle de Brueil; Louis must be in equally bad shape. He jackknifed down into the darkness, peering desperately for the dirks. Louis was nearly at the bottom, his hands spreading out as he probed through the underwater rocks.

Suddenly Louis came up with a weapon and whipped around to face Alexandre. Alexandre fell back as Louis snaked after him. The knife slashed out and Alexandre felt a stinging in his calf. He kicked Louis hard in the stomach with his free foot, propelling him back. Catching a glimmer of steel half buried in the pebbles, he kicked down for it. His straining fingers found the knife as Louis followed him down for another slash. Twin scorpions locked together, each with a silver stinger, they slashed wildly. The water began to show inky tendrils of blood.

Alexandre was incredibly tired. A kick to Louis's thigh pushed him toward the surface, as air suddenly seemed more important than life. Dragging Louis with him, Alexandre fought his way to the surface to relieve his burning lungs. His head broke water, and through a glaze of silver, he saw Liliane's frantic white face. Clutching the boat side, she was pleading with Olaf.

Alexandre took a quick lungful of air, then went down again to meet Louis within a breath of breaking the surface. Louis's dirk thrust for his belly, and Alexandre grabbed his sleeve to prevent himself from being skewered. They wrestled together, each trying desperately to bury his blade and end the fight. The fierce struggle without air was over quickly as their muscles were utterly exhausted. Thanks to his brief gasp of air, Alexandre had a few extra seconds. Louis grew bug-eyed and broke their clinch to claw toward the surface.

Alexandre reached up after him and buried the dirk to the hilt. Louis's face looked distorted, bubbling away in a filter of scarlet. His wild movements slowed, then went slack as his body hovered like a suspended spider. Then slowly, he began to sink. Alexandre did not wait to watch him settle among the crabs. With splitting lungs, he swam laboriously for the surface, trying to drag Louis behind him. His body and mind were leaden now, growing heavier with each weighted stroke.

Dimly, he could see the water paling, but rather than growing clearer, it was blurring, beginning to slowly whirl about him like a narrowing funnel whose conduit to the surface was now a single, dwindling light. He was not going to reach that light . . . was not going to see Liliane, their baby, anything ever again but the wet, encroaching darkness that was stifling the life from him.

Then, suddenly the point of light became a big hand that fiercely hooked under his armpit. Light and air broke around him, and he was scraped over the boat's blunt-edged gunnel. Someone was tugging at his leg still in the water, and suddenly he was free. Vaguely, he could feel Liliane's hair, hear her jubilant voice as he hung on the gunnel, its edge forcing the water out of him. He choked, moved his head weakly to plead for someone to haul him into the bottom of the boat before he vomited, to no avail. He vomited.

"Wodin's eye," he heard Olaf swear, "he must have swallowed half the sea."

"Help him into the boat," Liliane pleaded with Olaf. "Can you not see there is no more water in him?"

After momentary deliberation, Olaf heaved Alexandre over the gunnel and let him drop into the boat bottom.

A saw of oarlocks sounded as the boat headed for shore. The bow hull scraped on rock, then swung as someone caught the mooring line. The boat bounced as Liliane jumped onto the rocks. The oarsman and Olaf caught Alexandre by the feet and armpits and virtually pitched him to two waiting men. He groaned as they carried him roughly up a path winding to the bluff. Behind him, Liliane was urging the men to take greater care with him. When they huffed to a flat spot on the bluff, they obligingly dropped him. Instantly, Liliane was at his side, crooning to him as if he were a baby.

Alexandre tried to sit up, then settled for a weak pat on her cheek. "I am . . . all right, darling . . . just need to adjust . . . my gills."

"Oh," she said simply, gratefully, then hugged him until he thought she would break his neck. "I was so worried! You look dreadful."

That reminded him that he was on borrowed time. "Where's Olaf?" he muttered.

"Rest a little. You do not have to deal with him now." She stroked his hair. "Do you want me to talk to him?"

He shook his head. "Thinking Philip may be . . . on their trail, they will all be impatient. You talk to them; I shall talk to Olaf." He pushed himself up as she called to Olaf. After the Viking hunkered down by him and Liliane had gone down the bluff to work her charm on the other men, Alexandre briefly informed him about the poison.

The giant nodded. "Does your lady know?"

"No, and I do not want . . . her to know. She has had too much strain in the last few days. Much more . . . and she may lose the baby. I do not know how long I have, but . . . when I am gone, I want you to see her to Spain. If you guard her well, it will be worth your while."

Olaf grinned crookedly. "You would trust me with a beauty like that?"

"Perhaps I am a gambler."

"Guess you have to be," the Norseman observed dryly. He considered for a moment. "All right, done; but don't expect chivalry out of me. I'll get her there, but I won't coddle her." His grin flashed again. "Still, I might not be against a little nighttime sympathy for her widowhood."

"Lay a hand on her," Alexandre said flatly, " and I will roar up from hell to have your balls for stew meat."

Olaf threw back his head and laughed. "I like your spirit. I had a feeling you would chew up old Louis. By now, he's nose to nose with his uncle. There's a pair to plague each other till Armageddon!" He hoisted Alexandre to his feet. "See your lady back to Castle de Brueil. I'll see her to Spain and save my sympathy . . . unless she asks for it, mind you." He steered Alexandre toward his destrier with an ear-splitting bellow. "We're heading back to Castle de Brueil, lads! Help the lady into the saddle!"

Nineteen men obliged.

Castle de Brueil had never looked so wonderful to Liliane. The autumn color of its fields seemed to spread a brilliant carpet of welcome in the sinking sun. At its fringe rolled the indigo sea, and the sky overhead was a wash of coral and gold. Beyond a brush of pines and chestnuts hovered the castle itself, its graceful old turrets reflecting the sun as if inlaid with abalone.

Persia cannot rival this! Liliane rejoiced. She wondered how the castle could have seemed so unappealing when she'd first seen it upon the day of her wedding. She had made so many false assumptions then, and made many mistakes since; yet looking back, she might have done little differently. Now that she had gained Jacque's confession of guilt for Diego's murder, what was her future role to be? Being a wife and mother appealed to her greatly, and yet . . . to say farewell to the old days of freedom would be difficult. To always wear gowns, sit at her loom and dandle her children did not altogether appeal to her, but . . . if such domesticity pleased Alexandre, she would make the sacrifice.

Her eyes shining with love, Liliane looked at him riding beside her. He needed a woman's care and soothing. She had never seen him look so bedraggled and grave, save when she had nearly died in Acre. And perhaps when she had rescued him from the riverbank just after their marriage. That day, which had promised so little, had given her so much. Since then, Alexandre had given her love, their child, and a future that offered many riches of the heart. This generation of the Brueil line might not be powerful in France, but it would have honor.

Peasants began to trickle from the fields as they approached. Having hidden from Louis and his men before, the peasantry was afraid that the mercenaries were returning to wreak further havoc. Alexandre waved them forward. "You have no more to fear," he called. "These are now Brueil men and they will not harm you. The Count de Signe and his nephew are dead."

A cheer went up and the word passed ahead of them as fleet-footed serf boys sprinted toward village and castle. The draw-bridge crashed down and pennants ran up on the turrets of Castle de Brueil. From the parapets issued shouts and glad cries of those who had taken sanctuary within its stone walls after Louis's evacuation. *Vive le comte! Vive la comtesse! Vive l'armée!*

Glad not to be set upon with scythes, *l'armée* waved its caps. To everyone's surprise, Philip loped across the drawbridge with a grinning Charles behind him. Philip caught Alexandre's bridle. "Do not look so dumbfounded. I lent Charles here a dozen foot soldiers to make the wee spark he proposed at Castle de Signe look convincing." He slapped Alexandre's leg. "You really should not assault castles by yourself. My tax collectors would have difficulty convincing the populace that I need to support an army."

Alexandre slid off his horse, affectionately caught Philip's shoulder, then gave it a light punch. "I am grateful, sire, but not enough to take on any other castles for you."

Philip laughed. "I shall keep my word, but only because it is to you."

For a moment, the king gazed quizzically at Liliane. "The castellans tell me you are quite the heroine. It seems that I leave Alexandre in good hands."

Liliane, who had dismounted to gratefully embrace Charles, turned to the king. "Milord Alexandre has many faithful friends, sire. Castle de Brueil will always have a warm welcome for all of them. I hope you will not leave us long for the north."

Philip kissed her hand. "I will return to give your first-born a bounce on the royal knee"—his green eyes teased hers—"so long as you name it after me."

Alexandre grinned. "Why not? Philippa has a nice ring."

As the two men chatted with Charles, Olaf edged behind Liliane. "You know," he murmured, "this isn't a bad place. Are you certain you want to go back to Spain?"

"Why should I?"

When he took her aside and told her why, Liliane nearly fainted. He steadied her elbow. "Don't make faces and screech. You are not supposed to know. The count may have vomited up enough in that boat to last for some time, and I'm not wild to go to Spain with a lot of petty amirs trying to chew each other up. Business in Andalusia, you might say, is a little too good. Now, do you know anything we can pour down your husband's gullet that might turn things about?"

Liliane's mind raced frantically over the potions and herbs in her medicine bag; but nothing served. "I have no way of knowing what Louis gave him; antidotes must be very precise."

"We could split open old Jacques and take a look at his innards; he had more of the stuff than the other two."

The idea was revolting, but the moment Liliane dismounted in the courtyard, she and Olaf headed through the cheering crowd into the hall to find the remains of Jacques.

The spectacle of the glassy, bovine expression of surprise on Jacques's dead face was horrible. Unperturbed, Olaf drew his dirk. With a grimace, Liliane turned her back. Jacques had been bad enough in life; in death, he was rank indeed. She dreaded having to examine him and, closing her eyes, was quite sure she was going to shortly upheave as violently as Alexandre had done at the coast.

Just as Olaf started to carve, Kiki scampered out from under the table to greet her mistress. At the sight of the emerald and diamond necklace about the gay sprite's neck, Olaf and his intention to inspect Jacques's potbelly froze.

To hasten matters, Liliane tossed Olaf the necklace. "Please, admire the jewels later and get on with my uncle. Every moment counts!"

"All the way to thousands of livres," muttered Olaf, swiftly assessing the block-cut stones. He stuffed the necklace into his leather jerkin, then turned back to his task.

He was interrupted again when Alexandre entered the hall. He strode unevenly forward and saw what Olaf intended. "You told her!" he said curtly. Then he saw Kiki and his tone abruptly turned coaxing. "Kiki, come to me. Come, Kiki. I shall give you a pomegranate. . . ."

Whether due to the patent lie or the urgency underlying Alexandre's tone just after his display of anger, Kiki stared at him and clung more tightly to Liliane's shoulder. Liliane's gentle effort to dislodge her did not help.

"Kiki, you little witch," Alexandre pleaded with growing desperation, "come to me."

"Don't frighten her," Olaf boomed at him, "and she might."

Kiki, displaying a latent fondness for aggressive males, particularly one who was defending her, scurried to Olaf. She clambered up his brawny arm and hugged him. He beamed at her. "See, what did I tell you?" Adroitly, he felt in her little vest pocket to see if she had any more jewels about her. He came up with a tiny glass vial of Moorish design with faceted sides that did resemble a jewel. "Rubbish," he muttered and started to toss it aside.

"Stop!" Alexandre yelled with startling fervor. "That must be Louis's antidote!"

"Don't say," drawled Olaf, and handed it over. Alexandre feverishly uncorked the vial and downed its contents.

"Do you think it will help so long after you were poisoned?" Liliane asked worriedly.

"Can't hurt," said Olaf, preoccupied with Kiki. She gave him a broad, anthropoid smile and Olaf's big teeth bared in delight.

"Mon Dieu, you two were made for each other," muttered Alexandre. He sat abruptly on the floor and stared at the empty vial. "Louis," he prayed aloud as Liliane wrapped her arms about his neck, "for once in your life, I hope you did something right."

Epilogue

Liliane bore her child in May. "A girl!" shouted Olaf gleefully. "Alex, my rogue, you're in for it now. If the little wench looks anything like her mother, you will be fighting her suitors off with a club!"

"If she is anything like her mother"—Alexandre kissed Liliane's ear—"she will be a deal more trouble than that."

With Kiki staring balefully, Olaf carried young Philippa out to show her off to the castellans. "Kiki is jealous," observed Alexandre. "She has been too spoiled to take to a baby."

"Would you rather have had a son?" Liliane asked quietly as she rested upon the pillows.

Alexandre grinned and shook his head. "I never get enough of you, so another mischief-making female about the place is welcome." He squeezed her hand. "You have been sedate of late . . . and do not tell me you were too round to race about the countryside. I have been worried about you."

"I thought you wanted a ladylike wife." Liliane's voice held a note of uncustomary shyness.

"I thought so, too, once. Now that I have her . . . I want back my Liliane of the forest—the prankish Liliane who laughed and could not be managed." His voice softened. "I miss her badly."

She smiled crookedly at him. "My last prank nearly cost us our fief and lives to boot. Are you certain you want such a troublesome wife?"

"Quite certain." He kissed her fingertips. "I am also certain that Kiki is going to elope with Olaf the same way Charles took to destiny's road with Philip."

Liliane giggled. "You may be right. She will detest squalling and smelly diapers. Olaf is smitten with her."

392

"I am smitten with her former owner." He kissed her throat, then her soft mouth.

"Oh, you mean the hairy old thief I stole her from in Massilia?" she breathed against his lips.

"I mean my Liliane," Alexandre whispered. "Is she back?"

"She is back and she is going to give you a dozen girl babies just like her." She kissed him lingeringly.

"You miscounted, darling. The brother that can manage them all makes thirteen."

"Our lucky number." She drew him down again.

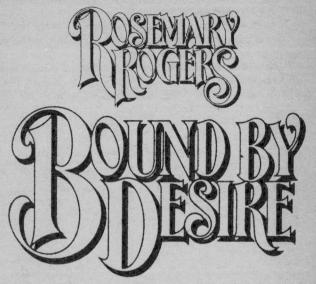